LAKE TAIMANA

AN OTAGO WATERS' NOVEL

STEPHANIE RUTH

Copyright © 2022 by Stephanie Ruth.

All rights reserved.

No part of this book may be reproduced in any form or by any electronic or mechanical means, including information storage and retrieval systems, without written permission from the author, except for the use of brief quotations in a book review.

This is a work of fiction. Names, characters, places and incidents either are the product of the author's imagination or are used fictitiously. Any resemblance to actual persons, places, organisations or events, live or dead, is purely coincidental.

ISBN 978-0-473-61715-8 (Paperback)

ISBN 978-0-473-61716-5 (Paperback, POD)

ISBN 978-0-473-61717-2 (Epub)

ISBN 978-0-473-61718-9 (Kindle)

ISBN 978-0-473-61719-6(Digital Audiobook)

Cover design by Tī Kōuka Publishing

 Created with Vellum

*For Lyssa and Mel, and the Cheesy Crafts crew,
who not only understand and believe in me,
but also make me laugh.*

I can't tell you which of those qualities I cherish more.

LAKE TAIMANA

What does it take to shift deep-seated betrayal?

Adele Fergus switched back to her maiden name with plans to never look back—never think about her naïve, short-lived marriage to James Montague. But that was before he turned up on her Wānaka doorstep with her missing diamonds, a crazy back-story, and persistent requests for visitation with his ex-stepdaughter.

Adele's hell-bent on keeping James at arms-length, but it's not easy with old attractions still running hot. What's more, she's beginning to suspect she may have left him on false information.

Divorce was never in James' game-plan, so when his ex-wife's jewellery unexpectedly comes to light, he's drawn back to her—welcome or not—and he isn't leaving until he has all the answers.

Is it worth risking everything to start again?

The more the exes re-learn to trust each other, the more they come to realise someone was intent on dragging them apart from the very beginning. Someone close.

Authors note: Although this story ends with an HEA, it also includes references to a historical miscarriage, depression, and suicide. Please read at your own discretion.

CONTENTS

Chapter 1 *TAIMANA - diamond*	1
Chapter 2 *PIHIKETE - cookie*	8
Chapter 3 *KARĀHE - mirror*	17
Chapter 4 *WĀ KĀINGA - true home*	26
Chapter 5 *PAPANGARUA - quilt*	37
Chapter 6 *TAHETOKA - amber*	43
Chapter 7 *WHAKATUMA - challenge*	51
Chapter 8 *WHANGAONO - dice*	60
Chapter 9 *PUTIPUTI - flower*	68
Chapter 10 *KŌRERO - narrative*	81
Chapter 11 *WAIATA AROHA - song of love*	92
Chapter 12 *WHARE - house*	100
Chapter 13 *HĀNEANEA - sofa*	110
Chapter 14 *RUA - two*	118
Chapter 15 *WHAKAOHOMAURI - surprise*	126
Chapter 16 *WHĀNAU - family*	138
Chapter 17 *KUIA - female elder*	149
Chapter 18 *TIKA - truth*	159
Chapter 19 *KANIKANI - dance*	169

Chapter 20 *TĀTORU - threefold*	181
Chapter 21 *PŌURI - regret*	193
Chapter 22 *TŌURANGI - rain*	208
Chapter 23 *KAHUKURA - rainbow*	218
Chapter 24 *PUKAPUKA - book*	233
Chapter 25 *TEINA - younger brother*	244
Chapter 26 *RETA - letter*	253
Chapter 27 *PIANA - piano*	264
Chapter 28 *AHI - fire*	277
Chapter 29 *POKOREHU - ashes*	286
Chapter 30 *RĒWERA - devil*	297
Chapter 31 *WĀ MUTUNGA - full time*	313

Want More?	329
Sneak Peak	331
Te Reo Māori - Māori Language	339
Nihongo - Japanese Language	343
Acknowledgments	345
About the Author	347
Also by Stephanie Ruth	349

*"I never hated a man
enough to give him diamonds back."*

- Zsa Zsa Gabor

1

TAIMANA - DIAMOND

The hardest naturally occurring substance on Earth.

James readjusted the package under his arm with great care, and considered the likelihood of detonation. The contents themselves weren't remotely explosive. Not in physical terms.

Could still blow up in his face, though.

Changing his mind, he backtracked to settle the well-wrapped box on the passenger seat of his rental car, and locked it. A hug wasn't the kind of reception he was expecting, but for some reason he needed his hands free and unencumbered when he finally saw Adele Montague again.

Fergus, not Montague, he had to keep reminding himself. Adele had taken her maiden name back after the divorce.

James shifted his shoulders in discomfort.

She might not be home. It wasn't like he was expected. He could well be interrupting, asked to come back another time or told to bugger off altogether.

Adele's place was a cottage-style bungalow, with a standard white rose guarding each side of the porch steps. Nothing grand or showy. A welcoming scent. A home.

Knocking firmly on the front door, James began to wish he had something tangible in his hands after all. He fisted them by his sides, then unfisted them—shoved them into his pockets, then yanked them out again. They were resting uneasily on his hips when the woman who still sizzled up every salient thought in his head opened the door a crack.

"James?" Adele eased the door wider to reveal her whole, unbearably tempting person. Her eyes were wide and startled, crystal-blue like the lake he'd just glimpsed on arrival into this poky New Zealand township.

"Dell." His stunning wife.

Ex-wife.

"You're in Australia." There was some confusion in Adele's statement—in the fingers fluttering at the base of her throat.

James offered her a half-smile. "Clearly, I'm not, though."

"What are you *doing* here?"

"I came to deliver your jewellery box."

"But, I sent a letter with instructions." Adele leaned a little further out onto the porch, her eyes shifting towards his rental car. Searching for what, exactly?

The scent of Adele's favourite hair product reached out to him, teasing. Tropical rainforest, with a hint of coconut. Light, fresh, and achingly familiar.

Unfamiliar was the flash of silver at the curved indent of her nostril, the tiny stud adorning her freckled nose, reaffirming the fact things had unquestionably changed.

Adele glanced back at him, then away, catching him staring. "I sent your lawyer my postal address."

"I decided to deliver it in person."

For a man who'd been unsure of a door slammed in his face, this wasn't such a bad reception. His ex-wife was fiddling with her hair, drawing attention to those strawberry corkscrews and making his own fingers itch to rummage and furl. She looked so damn pretty in her T-shirt and jeans, gnawing on her bottom lip.

"But, why?"

To see her. Just to bloody see her. Get her out of his system, once and for all.

Yeah, not likely.

James shrugged. "I had some business come up in Otago, and the diamond is five-carat."

"Right, the diamond." Adele looked down at her bare feet and wiggled her toes. There was silver there too, in the form of a toe-ring. It effectively hid the slim scar she'd been left with years ago, after a particularly nasty bluebottle sting. "I didn't think about that. But a secure courier—"

"It's great to see you, Dell," James interrupted.

"Is it?" Adele shook her head faintly. "I haven't—"

"I couldn't—" They both spoke at the same time, adding to the awkwardness.

He should've bought her flowers. Why didn't he think to do that? Bird of Paradise, her favourite. Big, bold and structured. Or lilies, the brighter the better.

Were her favourite. Once.

Things changed. People changed. It'd been five long years, after all.

"Go ahead," Adele offered, waving a hand in his direction.

"Ah, I was just going to say I couldn't get a park on the street, so I've pulled in behind your cleaner. I hope that's okay?"

"My cleaner?" Adele leaned forward, once again checking out the unevenly matched cars parked up the shingle driveway, nose to bumper.

There was a much older, heavily logoed cleaner's vehicle in front: Spic'n'Span home cleaning and property management services. Apparently 'elbow grease' was their middle name.

James wasn't sure it was advisable to use the word grease in a cleaning slogan, given the fact it evoked the image of, well… *grease*.

Adele began to laugh, a small chuckle that curled James' toes. Warm and mirthful. "Oh, James." She wound down to a tight little smile. "That's *my* car. I clean my own place." She waved a hand to incorporate the house behind her, and James belatedly recognised the Spic'n'Span logo on her T-shirt. "And a bunch more."

"Oh, right." When they'd first met, Adele had been working as a legal secretary for a high powered law firm. Admittedly part-time due to being a solo mum, but a million miles from domestic help. "You, ah… You enjoy that line of work?"

Adele's lips flatlined, and she stared James down for a moment before replying.

He quashed the urge to take a step backwards.

"Oh, absolutely. It's a joy getting down on my hands and knees and scrubbing other people's porcelain. Dream job." Adele's caustic tone was wince-inducing.

"Company car though. Bonus," James quipped, attempting to scramble to higher ground.

"Management perk." Adele's demeanour remained cool, as did her eyes. "It's an honest living, and it keeps mine and Saffy's heads above water."

His ex-wife hadn't invited him in, and didn't appear to be considering it.

James cleared his throat and tried a new tack. "I thought it might be less of an intrusion if I came when Saffy was still at school. She tells me she finishes at three?" He smiled, knowing full well it would take more than a stretch of his lips to win Adele's trust back.

They'd been through the mill and back during their short marriage, and with so much left unsaid, James wasn't expecting anything other than reservation from this woman.

Adele raised her eyebrows in lieu of answering.

"There's some paperwork that goes with it; a couple of things for you to sign. But we can do that out here, if you'd prefer?" He wouldn't ask for an invitation inside, but he wasn't above hinting.

Again with the cool stare. The sunny afternoon had begun to morph into a distinctly cold front.

Adele's visible shock on opening the door to him had been compounded by James' lack of finesse in handling their meeting, and he wasn't sure how to proceed from here.

He'd thought he was prepared to see her again—had talked himself into a reasonably calm state—but everything about Adele threw him off axis. Whenever he opened his mouth, she seemed to take another metaphorical step backward.

"Just give me a moment." Turning to stride back to the car, James unlocked it to remove his briefcase and the package he'd carried as hand-luggage from Sydney. Returning to Adele, who'd remained resolutely in the doorframe, he offered her the sizeable box.

One Meiji period lacquered jewellery box, with nine hand-painted interior drawers in excellent working condition. All of its owner's original contents present, and accounted for… Bar one.

Adele didn't advance to take the package as James had expected, and he hesitated. She too seemed undecided, blinking at him from her half-in, half-out position in the doorway.

"You don't want it?" He lowered the box slowly, nonplussed.

He'd gravely miscalculated. Through everything, he'd thought this would be the one item that still meant something to her.

Of course Adele wanted the jewellery box. It was the man holding it she could've done without ever laying eyes on again.

It was a little surreal seeing the great Aksel James Montague at a loss. In both business and personal life he always appeared to be in charge, in control, moving swiftly and confidently in whichever well-researched direction he chose. Adele had no idea what had possessed her ex-husband to hand deliver her personal belongings to the deep recesses of this Otago lakeside town, but for once, the C.E.O. looked well out of his depth in his expensive suit pants and business shirt.

"You could give it to Saffy," James ventured.

"I will *not* be giving it to Saffy." Presenting her nine-year-old daughter with an antique of this value? No way. It belonged to Adele, and her alone.

Still, she couldn't seem to bring herself to reach out and touch the package in her ex-husband's hands—her memories suddenly too real, and too raw.

"No. Right." James drew back slightly, and she could see she'd offended him by the upward thrust of his chin. He tucked the box awkwardly back under one arm. "Of course not." He cleared his throat. "I have the independent assessment; the credentials to authenticate…" he trailed off. "You could sell it, Dell. Buy yourself something nice."

No. Neither could Adele see herself ever selling this particular piece.

It was the only thing she could be certain James had personally chosen for her, because she'd been with him at the time. And it stood as a reminder her she hadn't been completely bonkers to believe marriage to a virtual stranger had held the potential to work. No matter what her family had thought of the idea, she hadn't been totally nuts to rip her small daughter from everything they'd called home, and relocate to Australia to be with James.

Not stark-raving mad in the beginning, anyway.

Adele had spotted the Japanese jewellery box at an antique market on her honeymoon in Venice, and was unable to walk past it.

God, what a romantic city. The pure ridiculousness of its existence, perched precariously on its sinking foundations, was enough to draw in the lovers, the writers, and the artistic dreamers. The staunch beauty of the old buildings, pride unmoved by flood and sunken wealth, still appealed to Adele like no other.

So paradoxical sitting amidst the battered old European treasures and junk, the Meiji box had been meticulously made, and carefully maintained. The time and workmanship given to the painting of the central pheasant alone would've sold Adele on it, but the tiny brass handles and hinges on the concealed compartments pulled at her inner child, too.

The price, once converted, was astronomical. Adele had bought used cars for less. She hadn't even bothered attempting to barter the seller down, and had walked on.

Unbeknownst to her, her brand new husband had crept back and arranged for both payment and delivery to their little boutique hotel. And she'd cried, because the action was so sweet; so thoughtful and attentive.

Adele sighed. She had no tears left for James. Not for the man standing before her offering this priceless box full of unwanted memories. No longer as a symbol of enduring love, with whispers of romance from faraway lands, but as some kind of olive branch.

"I guess you'd better come in, then," she conceded ungraciously, considering how far he'd travelled to hand-deliver her personal effects.

James could've sauntered off the set of a Yves Saint Laurent photoshoot, and it wasn't fair he presented so well, when Adele was currently sporting the dragged-through-a-hedge-backwards look. He caught her eye as he stepped over the threshold, close enough to brush against her arm and send a shockwave clear down to the soles of her feet, making her wish she'd done something with her hair this morning other than just running her fingers through it.

With James' heritage and colouring, the flaxen hair and quick-to-tan Nordic skin, you'd expect blue eyes. But her ex-husband's irises were a bright bottle-green, and the unusual combination had always hit like a hoof to the gut.

Adele huffed an irritated breath out from between her lips, not particularly appreciating the view, nor her body's ridiculous reaction to it.

Not even a little bit.

2

PIHIKETE - COOKIE

Full of things wanted, but not needed.

There was a printed list of contents, and Adele ran her eye over it warily as James stood next to her.

His open briefcase was a familiar sight, sitting next to the still-wrapped jewellery box on the kitchen bench.

Three strands of African glass beads, and one of polished, antique-set amber. A silver charm bracelet, with twenty-four original charms intact. Three pendants, semi-precious stones set in silver. One corresponding long linked chain.

One solitaire diamond, five-carat square cut, set in platinum. One eternity ring, also in platinum, with three rectangular cut diamonds—never worn.

Adele squeezed her eyes closed for a moment before reading the final line.

Missing: One platinum wedding band, diamond studded, with the inner inscription: Forever yours, A.J.

"Would you like to open it?" James inquired, sounding very much like a high-end sales assistant. "Check it's all there?"

"No, thank you. I'm sure it's fine." Adele lowered the list in her hand, placing it back on top of the insurance assessments. "You decided to keep the wedding band, but not the other diamonds?"

"No." James hesitated before continuing. "I'm afraid your wedding band wasn't recovered with the others."

Because the kitchen was what you'd call cosy, James was standing a little too close for comfort, and there was tension around his mouth that hadn't been there before.

"I would've given them back to you when I... When *we*... You know. But they were gone by then, so... " Adele frowned. "I don't understand how they were found together. Weren't they pawned? Sold off individually? It doesn't make any sense."

James shrugged, but didn't attempt to look Adele in the eye when he made the gesture, and something about that niggled at her.

"Sometimes that's just how it is," he murmured, almost to himself. "When one thing comes to light, they all do."

"Except my wedding band."

"Yes. Except that."

Fishy. Difficult to put her finger on why, exactly, but Adele mistrusted the way James said it. She tapped her fingertip to the list, coming to a solid conclusion.

"You can keep the diamonds."

James did look at her then. Swiftly. "Your rings?"

"*Your* rings," she corrected him. "The engagement, and the... The other one." She couldn't bring herself to say eternity when it came down to the crunch, because it made the gifting a joke, didn't it? They'd only managed three years together. She waved her hand in a flyaway gesture. "You could trade them in, and get your money back. Buy something new for your next wife."

James had a temper, but he did a fairly credible job of not letting it show. There were little telltale signs though, like the slight flare of his nostrils, and that tiny muscle tweaking in his jaw.

Adele could beat him blind at poker, she knew his mannerisms too well.

"I realise the solitaire wasn't the most practical design for a woman who—"

"Cleans toilets for a living?" she slid in on a tart note.

James' frown deepened, and his nostrils flared a little wider. "I was going to say a woman who's so active."

"*Right.*"

"Believe me, or don't. But if I could do it over, I'd choose differently."

Do it *over*?

Surely James, like herself, was thankful it was finished; relieved it was all but tied in a bloody Hermès bow? Maybe he was meaning he'd be inclined to pick out his own engagement ring next time he asked someone to marry him, rather than sending his P.A. to select the best in store.

"Something less ostentatious," James added, and the way he curled his lips around the words made them sound like a direct quote.

It did sound like something Adele would say, in the heat of the moment.

Trust James to remember all the unflattering details.

He had the memory of an elephant, encased in the body of an agile leopard. All lithe, muscular, and intent.

A coolness had edged into his eyes—changeable and dangerous. Adele knew that look just as intimately, and was perversely pleased to have evoked a smidgen of emotion.

"Did I use that word?" she asked, falsely nonchalant.

"I believe so." James turned away, presenting Adele with his aristocratic profile as he eyed the shabby wooden love-seat in the garden through the lounge slider. "Among a few other choice ones. Though I'm assuming they were directed at my person, rather than my choice of jewellery?"

Adele had really let rip over her stolen belongings—used words that hadn't crossed her lips before or since. She'd flown into a rage when the beautifully lacquered box had gone missing, heightening the stress of a truly awful year.

And James had been less than helpful with the police report, having been under the impression Adele had pawned the lot and faked the break-in. Taking the lead from his mother, he'd all but accused Adele of amassing escape money and plotting to leave.

She *hadn't* been. Not then.

Adele had only been gone from James' swanky house in Balmain for twenty minutes, just long enough to pick Saffy up from her Sydney preschool, and had arrived back to find the front door swinging open.

James' laptop, the TVs, and high-end accessories were all conspicuously untouched. It was Adele's personal effects that'd been rummaged through.

Her *very* personal effects.

"I was upset."

"Indeed." James turned back to her, and Adele was unnerved to find his demeanour had softened. "So was I."

He was joking, right? Adele laughed, a little uncertain of his angle, but James' expression didn't shift.

"You mean about the break in? Me 'leaving the door open?' " She bracketed the quote with tetchy forefingers.

"I never said you'd deliberately left the door open."

"You *implied* it; told the police officer I'd been 'distracted.' "

James drew a hand through his hair. "You *were* distracted. Things weren't going well."

That was putting it mildly.

By that stage, they were hardly speaking, and their marriage had become little more than a paper-thin façade. Dressing up for engagements they were expected to attend together, pasting on smiles and platitudes, then going home to separate beds.

A cold war. Without comfort. And ultimately, without trust.

"Yeah, well. You saw to that," Adele countered with some bitterness.

"It takes two, and you know it." The old James might've raised his voice—shown at least a touch of irritation. But this new version merely looked resigned to her snark. That's what came with distance and time; emotions got dulled, and feelings became muted.

Perhaps James could care less about what had gone down, but Adele's stomach still knotted at the thought of her husband's hands on another woman when he'd made vows to her.

The silence between them was broken by the oven timer beeping, and Adele was grateful for the interruption to her thoughts.

Flouncing away from her ex-husband, ex-lover, ex-everything, she used the oven mitt to slide out the tray of cookies and rest them on the stovetop, before shoving a second waiting tray into the heat.

James stepped a little closer and took a deep sniff—reminding

Adele of Winger, her daughter's border collie, and the fact she had to pick the one-year-old pup up from the vet soon.

"Chocolate-chip? Saffy's favourite."

"Yours too, I seem to remember."

"Yes. Mine too," James conceded softly.

He was standing too close again, his contours and atmosphere a lot more familiar than his aftershave. Unlike the crisp cool notes she used to associate with him, he was wearing something green and leafy—mossy wood tones that teased the senses.

James had a mischievous air; a twinkle in his eye, like he was about to lean in and...

"Hey!" Adele slapped the hand that snaked around to steal the nearest cookie. "I hope you burn yourself," she muttered.

It was the first time Adele had touched James in five years, but a slap was fitting, and more than earned. She'd been itching to slap him since she'd finally realised what was going on behind her back, but had never given herself the pleasure.

"That's never worried me."

"No." Getting burnt had never worried James, and that still hurt. It smarted that he could grin about it, juggling a hot cookie and licking melted chocolate off his fingers.

"Can I see her?" The smile was still on James' face, but ebbing.

"See who?" Adele frowned.

"Saffron."

No. Absolutely not. It wasn't okay for James to saunter in and shake things up out of the blue. Saffy was settled and content. They both were.

Adele opened her mouth to speak, then closed it again. There was an expression on James' face she hadn't been expecting.

Longing.

"You really miss her," she whispered, conflicted by her own corresponding surge of emotion.

"Of course I miss her." James eyes flashed, and she thought she caught a glimpse of barely controlled anger just below the surface. "Every bloody day."

Adele flinched back when his hand reached out as if he was going to touch her cheek, but it subsided before making contact.

"The place was so empty, Dell, with you both..."

"Gone?" she finished for him when his voice trailed off.

"Gone," James agreed with a disquieting seriousness.

Adele wished he wouldn't look at her like it was *her* he was regretting.

She went to take a step away, and panicked when she was brought up short by the oven door. James had seen the attempt though, and a shadow crossed his face as he backed up, giving her the breathing space she needed.

It wasn't like James *hadn't* seen Saffy. She'd travelled as an unaccompanied minor to Sydney to mark her fifth, and seventh birthdays—to Adele's extreme disquiet. But her daughter had been dutifully returned two weeks later, unharmed and full of 'fantastical' stories.

Adele had been forced to cancel the ninth birthday trip, through no fault of her own, and Saffy was still sore at her about it.

Saffy spoke to James online, too. But although Adele made a point of being privy to those short video conversations, she never showed herself. If she needed to speak with James, she left him a recorded message or placed a phone call to his solicitor. Saffy was under strict instructions to keep her mother's life out of discussion, and after initial childish rebuttals like: 'I'm not allowed to say,' and, 'Mummy says that's private,' James had gotten the drift, and stopped asking after his ex-wife.

There were packages too. They arrived periodically to Adele's P.O. box with treats for Saffy. Toys, clothes, art and school supplies that were no doubt chosen, wrapped, and sent by some leggy creature from James' office—just doing her job, and her utmost to impress the boss.

But the concept behind the gifts counted. Saffy felt special because James continued to spoil his stepdaughter long after Adele's short marriage to him had crashed and burned.

Honestly? Adele was kind of surprised James kept it up. He was a busy man, and it probably took some wrangling on his part to call at the same time every Monday afternoon and chat to his ex-stepdaughter, even if only for ten minutes. Adele owed James that. He'd been good to Saffy, and her daughter absolutely adored the lying, cheating bastard.

"I think Saffy would like to see you." Adele caught the flare of excitement in James' expression, and felt like a complete cow for having entertained the thought of keeping them apart. This wasn't about her own comfort-levels. "I mean, she'd love to," she amended. "You could pick her up from school today."

"Thank you. Really. I'd appreciate that." James' sincerity shone through when he grabbed Adele's hand and squeezed it, making her feel that much worse for snatching hers back so quickly.

"Does that mean you're sticking around for a bit? How long are you planning to be in Wānaka?" She manoeuvred herself slightly further away, incredibly uncomfortable with the casual touch that had once been so commonplace between them. "You've got business here, you said?"

"Ah, until the end of this week-ish. After the weekend."

If Adele hadn't known James well, he would've appeared to give those hazy plans in a relaxed manner. But known him she had, in every way, shape and form. His mouth had just taken on that shifty, evasive flatline that alluded to an untruth, and one index finger had reached up to touch his earlobe.

Liar, liar, pants on fire. What the hell was he up to?

"A few days?" She chewed on her lip. Better than chewing on her nails, which she was suddenly itching to do after months of abstinence.

"Yes, around that, if it's alright with you?"

"You're asking me if it's alright, when you're already here?" Adele wrinkled up her nose at him as if he smelled bad, which he most certainly did not. This whole conversation would've been a damn sight easier if he had.

"I am."

"Where are you staying?"

"Is this a cross examination?" James quirked a single eyebrow before making short work of his remaining cookie. Three bites in all, and the whole thing vanished. His eyes flicked towards the hot tray before meeting hers again, tongue swiping the single dot of melted chocolate from the corner of his mouth.

"Don't even *think* about it."

"What?" James raised his hands in mock innocence, waiting until she was distracted transferring them to the cooling rack before stealing a second one.

"Cut it *out*!" Adele wasn't fast enough to contain a quick hoot of laughter. The man had no self-control when it came to sugar. "They're for a bake sale at Saffy's school tomorrow," she explained, moving the cooling rack a little further down the bench and away from roving hands. But if she thought that would stop James pilfering, she was sadly mistaken, and a third cookie disappeared shortly afterward.

Where the hell did James put them? His physique hadn't changed much in the eight years since they'd first met, and though Adele watched what she put into her body and exercised daily, she couldn't say the same.

Blame it on almost hitting thirty, or a distinct lack of sex. Maybe Maddie's poppyseed and cream-cheese muffins had something to do with it?

Maddie—babysitting—*tonight*.

Damn. She'd forgotten to book Saffy's regular sitter and get cash out, and asking Maddie to come on such short notice wasn't fair. The incredibly social part-time barista would probably have made other plans, and might feel pressured to drop them.

Maybe Adele could wrangle this somewhat uneasy situation between her ex and herself into something mutually beneficial?

"I've got a date tonight," she began, nutting it out as she went. "So if you'd like to hang out with Saffy again this evening, you'll save me having to ring around for a sitter."

"You've got a *date*?" James spluttered, speaking with his mouth full. It was so unlike him Adele stared, fascinated by both his surprising lack of social grace, and the crumbs on his shirt.

His well-to-do mother would be most unimpressed.

"Yes, James. Even frumpy mums like me get asked out on occasion." Adele's ire rose with James' growing colour, and she realised she must've hit his insinuation squarely on the head. "It's unbelievable the lengths some people go to for a quick roll in the hay. I mean, if I play my cards right, they even buy me *dinner* first," she added facetiously.

"That's not what I meant," James muttered, fully red now.

"Oh, I know *exactly* what you meant."

"No." James grabbed her arm as she went to swing past. "You don't." His eyes sparked green.

"Hands *off*." Adele tried to play it cool, but having James in her direct vicinity was proving she was anything but.

"Of course. You're dating," James amended, removing his hand at the same time.

Lucky, because Adele had been about to remove it for him.

"Take a flying leap with your platitudes, James. If you want to have time with Saffy, make yourself useful and be at the school gates at three." She stomped over to switch off the oven and dump the final tray on the stovetop with a clatter, though the cookies were well underdone. "Drop her home by four, then babysit again at seven. Think you can handle that?"

"Of course."

"Good. Now, move your damn car. The cleaner's leaving."

3

KARĀHE - MIRROR

In which the reflected image is clear.

Adele was twofold nervous. Her ex-husband was due back at the house in less than fifteen minutes, and she was going on a blind date with a total stranger. Make that threefold nervous. She was fast running out of time, and still couldn't decide what to wear.

The house had been relatively tidy, right up to the what-to-wear fiasco. Now her room was an absolute bomb-site.

"The blue one," Saffy stated decisively, tugging the dress in question back out from under the pile of outfits accumulating on Adele's bed.

Having met Saffy at the school gate, James had taken the her out for a hot chocolate. Consequently, Adele had been fending off excited chatter about her ex ever since he'd dropped their daughter back home at precisely four o'clock.

The way Saffy went on about her dad, you'd think the man farted rainbows, and Adele was over smiling affably and pretending it didn't rankle. Discussing clothing was much less confronting.

"I think the blue one's a bit, um… short." Low cut. Sexy… Too young for her?

"I like it best." Saffy remained unmoved on her first choice.

Partially to keep Saffy happy, but mostly because she'd run out of options, Adele tried on the sleeveless V-neck again. It was a bit on the va-*voom* side for a first date, but she knew exactly what shoes and jewellery to accessorise with to make it less vampy and more fun.

Why *shouldn't* she look sexy? Blind date. Who knew what the fates might bring? It was just a case of swallowing her bloody nerves.

Saffy began hanging the remaining clothes back in Adele's closet.

"You don't have to do that, love."

"But, Dad—"

"I can shut this door. He won't see the mess, I promise," Adele placated as she scooted through to her closet-sized ensuite to try to tame her hair into something less bramble-bush-esque. Eventually opting for a handful of leave-in coconut conditioner to calm the frizz, she left it out around her shoulders.

Enough time for make-up? Yes. *Just*.

Colourful glass beads next. Reaching towards the precious jewellery box James had returned earlier in the day, Adele ran her fingers over the image of the pheasant, wondering again at the odds of it turning up with all her old treasures intact.

Well, *almost* all of them.

Alone this afternoon, after the vet-run, she'd torn the wrapping off and poured over the details.

Pulling out the largest drawer containing her African necklaces, Adele chose the chunkier of the two in primary colours and slipped it over her head twice. The first line as a choker, the second knotted below. Opening one of the smaller drawers that held her diamond rings, Adele stared at them for a long moment.

They didn't look entirely real, nestled there together on a cushion of velvet.

Ostentatious. Yes, they were that.

Beautiful. They were that, too.

About to close up the jewellery box, Adele's eyes caught and held on her charm bracelet. Was that a mermaid? She'd never added a mermaid, had she? Her hand reached out to take the weight of the silver chain and its multitude of familiar dangly bits. Twenty-four in all, one to signify every year of her life up until…

Wait. What?

Fingers automatically counting charms like a rosary, Adele found a sweet little unicorn she didn't recognise either. How could that be?

Twenty-*five*, twenty-*six*...

There were now twenty-*nine* charms attached. Not the age Adele was when the charm bracelet went missing in Australia, but the age she was now.

Added since she'd last seen the cluttered bracelet was a unicorn, a mermaid, a rainbow, a cloud, and a dragon. None of which belonged to her. Where the hell had they come from? The person who'd stolen the jewellery box?

The thief had good taste in trinkets, if that were the case. She snorted, then shook her head. The whole situation was weird. James owed her a much more coherent explanation.

Considering the fact the box could easily be stolen again, Adele wondered if she should lock it up somewhere. Looking around the poky little bathroom, she began to chuckle. It wasn't like she had a safe in this rented bungalow, and she sure as hell didn't have any spare cash to pay for separate insurance.

Up until she'd met James, Adele had never owned anything precious enough to consider security, and probably never would again.

When she emerged from the ensuite, her bedroom had been reordered, and tidied. It wasn't Saffy's natural state to pick up after herself, let alone others, making Adele realise she wasn't the only one feeling nervous.

"Come here, Saff." When her daughter stepped closer, Adele snagged her into a tight hug, heart contracting. "Thanks so much for helping with my room."

"I want to show Dad around."

"Of course you do." Of course she did. Dipstick.

"Do you think he'll like it?" Saffy scoped the double room—simply furnished, with a portrait of Adele in crazy coloured pastels above the bed.

"Absolutely." Adele stated with conviction, though she had nothing to back that up with. James came from money, and his Sydney home was architecturally designed—modern minimalist.

Everything the man owned was the best of the best; designer clothes, European car, Italian shoes. Looking at her run down two-bedroom rental through James' eyes didn't bear thinking about.

"He's here to see you though, Saff. Not the house."

Saffy smiled—a wide, happy grin that melted all worries away. She looked so like her birth-father when she did that, Adele suffered another thump to the sternum.

Adele could call James a lot of things, but tardy wasn't one of them. She had no inclination to see Saffy and James meet up again, so let her daughter get the door when the bell rang at exactly seven.

Slipping back into the ensuite and locking the door, she stared at herself in the bathroom mirror as she listened to the ruckus in the hall.

"Dad!"

Silence.

That would be the hug.

"Hi, darl." Drawled. Almost self-depreciatingly Aussie.

"You smell nice, did you have a shower? But you didn't shave! Has anyone ever told you your whiskers are *orange*? Is that present for me?" James' answers were too low to catch, but Saffy's voice rang out again, and she was laughing. "Get *down*, Winger!"

The border collie whined, feeding off Saffy's excitement, paws scrabbling to gain purchase on the wooden floor as she hurtled backwards and forwards down the hall.

"She's got stitches so she can't have puppies. She's not allowed to chew them. Come and see my room!"

Adele could hear the two of them moving in her direction.

"Did you paint all of these?"

There was pride in Saffy's voice as she introduced James to each family member's portrait along the hallway.

"You're so very clever." James' words were still soft, but closer now—easier to make out.

Adele closed her eyes tight as their footsteps neared, boxing her in even further.

"This is Mum's room."

Nothing from James.

"Do you like it?"

"Yes, it's very pretty." James' voice came from the hall—formal, but still with that faint, underlying Aussie twang, making pretty sound like 'priddy.' "Especially this."

"I did Mum's portrait in pastels. I like them best because they're so bright. But they're messy. Mum says they get everywhere."

"Your mum's fond… She was always went for bright things, too. It's a good likeness, Saff. I love how you've drawn her so happy." In contrast to his cheery words, James' tone was flat and even.

"Come and see the backyard. I can do a backflip on the trampoline." Saffy hesitated. "Can *you* do a backflip?"

James laughed. "No. But I'll take it as a compliment you asked."

"Mum can do a forward flip and land on her feet."

"Why does that not surprise me?" came James' sardonic reply.

Footsteps ebbed, the over-excited dog followed, and finally silence was restored. Adele opened her eyes and allowed herself to breathe again. "See? That wasn't so difficult, was it?" She muttered.

Taking a tissue, she pushed it into the corner of each eye, soaking up the wet that was threatening to ruin her mascara.

When stepfather and daughter eventually came back through the ranch slider after checking out the backyard, Adele was poised and ready for them in the kitchen.

"Holy sh… *Wow*." James appeared to do a genuine double-take. "You look so—" He glanced quickly at Saffy, then back to Adele again, clearing his throat. "Blue still suits you."

Yep. Blue was definitely her colour.

Adele knew she looked nice. She didn't need *James* to tell her she looked good. Yet something in the sincerity of his reaction helped put her shoulders back, and lent a touch of sass to her strut.

"Thanks," she breezed. "I'm not sure if you've eaten, but there's lasagna and garlic bread in the oven, and the makings of a salad in the fridge. Enough to share. School night, so eight-thirty bedtime, and if I'm home late, feel free to sleep on the sofa."

Adele grabbed Saffy and stole a quick smooch.

"We'll have to tidy these up a bit in the morning." She tweaked one of Saffy's cornrows, where the shorter baby hairs were escaping to frizz along her hairline. "No more than two cookies." She touched a finger to her daughter's nose, then turned and pointed the same digit at James. "That goes for you, too."

Taking her keys out of her handbag and grabbing her coat, Adele headed to the front door, realising only when she reached it that James was right behind her.

She turned, eyeing him somewhat warily.

"He's not picking you up?" James was frowning when he looked from the keys in Adele's hand, to the door behind her.

Like she'd trust a total stranger at her door when she lived here alone with her nine-year-old daughter? What did James take her for?

"You're *assuming* I'm dating a man."

James' eyes snapped back to her face. "Ah, yes?" His neck began to take on a faint tinge of red. That was twice she'd made him blush in one day. A new record. "I did assume that."

It was quite fun putting him on the back-foot.

"Mmm. Maybe I'm over men." Adele neither confirmed nor denied as she sashayed out.

Let him work that one out for himself.

"Ruby is Kana and Uncle D's baby, and she has one more chromosome than everyone else," Saffron explained. "Sometimes that happens." She took a micro-break from marathon talking, just long enough to steal the last piece of garlic bread from James' plate, stuff it into her mouth and swallow it down. "I'm teaching Ruby to roll over, and it might take her a bit to learn, but she's pretty determined."

Saffy licked a dribble of melted butter off her thumb before launching into further details about her extended family.

"Uncle D says I'm 'determined' too. I like that word. D-E-T-E-R-M-I-N-E-D. Obāchan is Kana's nana, but she's more like a mum, really. She grows all their veggies in the garden and has enormous radishes called *daikon*. We use them in salads. They're white, but otherwise they look like carrots. Big, white carrots that taste like radishes."

Saffron Fergus was a chatterbox, as bright and colourful as a box of felt-tips, and James had missed her daily presence like an amputated limb.

They'd reheated the lasagna and garlic bread, added a chunk of cucumber to their plates as a nod to greens, and sat out under the willow on an old wooden slat-chair. It was just large enough for two.

"Did you know Kana's real name is Kanako? *Ko* means girl. Kana-girl. I know that because sometimes Obāchan teaches me Japanese words when we're cooking. There are chickens up at the farm now, *niwatori*, and I'm allowed to collect the eggs."

"How many hens?"

"Ten. They're called red shavings."

"Red shavers," James corrected automatically.

"Yeah, them. When Mum used to get sad…" Saffy trailed off, looked down at the remnants of her lasagna, then up at the willow branches above them. "This tree's probably older than Obāchan, don't you think?"

"Probably twice her age. What were you saying about your mum?"

"Um…" Saffy turned to look at him, her features fine like her mother's, but under much darker skin. Her birth father, Moses, was Sudanese, and other than the fact Adele had met him in Wellington, that was practically all the information James had ever been offered about the man.

Secrets upon secrets.

"Mum doesn't like me talking about her," Saffy whispered.

"Ah, right. Yes." James nodded seriously. "But if there was ever a problem, and you needed to talk about it with someone, you could talk to me. Or Kanako, or Obi Wan."

Saffy cracked up, as James had meant her to. "Oh-*baa*-chan, not Obi Wan!"

"I stand corrected." He smiled. "I'm pretty sure *I'm* allowed to talk about your mum though. I mean, I have a lot of stories." And for once James knew for certain Adele wasn't listening in—just out of sight, and more than ready to cut the conversation short. "When we met, you were tiny, so you wouldn't remember all the crazy things she used to get up to. Like the time she got her foot stuck in a rickety old elevator. Has Adele ever told you about that?"

"No. How do you mean, stuck?"

Adele had never told Saffy the story of how James and herself had met? Well, no, of course not. Why would she?

James cleared his throat. "Well, there was an elevator she was anxious to get into. The door began to close as she ran up with a box of files, so she stuck her pretty little foot in to hold it. Unfortunately, it didn't register her there, and closed on her. Her heel got stuck in the gap." He smiled at the memory. "Luckily, the guy already in the elevator saw what'd happened, and he had the foresight to press the emergency stop button before it started moving. That gave him a couple of minutes to get to know the angel with curly-wurly hair through a little ankle-sized crack in the doors."

"The elevator guy was you?"

"Why, yes." James grinned. "How did you guess?"

"Just a hunch." Saffy sniggered, making him laugh. "I thought you met at work."

"We did. Sort of. I was in Wellington speaking at an agricultural conference, and Adele was there supporting her boss in an admin role."

"Admin?" Saffy queried the word.

"Administration. Office," he reiterated.

"Did she like you straight away, too?"

James turned to look back down at the nine-year-old. In some ways Saffy seemed so grown up, but her concept of connection and affection were still so childlike. He pulled a yellowed willow leaf from where it had caught in a midnight cornrow. "Not exactly. Not in the beginning, anyway."

And not in the end, as it happened.

Time to change the subject.

"How would you feel about hanging out together this weekend?"

"Cool! But we'd have to ask Mum first. Can you help me paint my room? The landlord said one feature wall is okay, and I want teal. Teal's *so* sick."

"Is it? Right." They didn't own this place? James mulled on that for a moment. "But we should probably start small. Work our way up. Ask Adele if we can paint something somewhat smaller, first. Like this." He patted a hand to the chair they sat on, and a few little flakes of yellow paint came away.

"Somewhat?"

"A bit. Something a bit less full-on. Once we've sicked the hell out of this, she might trust us with a wall."

Though James wouldn't be holding his breath.

Saffy stared at him for a long moment before nodding, and beginning to smile. "You're right. I'm glad you came to see me."

James smiled back. It was better than breaking down, which was what the gravel in his throat was threatening all of a sudden. "Me too. I'm just sorry it took me so long to get here."

4

WĀ KĀINGA - TRUE HOME

One's place, though it may be far.

It was all very well for Adele to leave the date early, but she couldn't exactly go home. Not yet. It'd look like she'd had a rotten time, and though she hadn't had a *great* time, her ex-husband needn't be made aware of that fact.

The blind date had ended up being with Tony, who Adele already knew—sort of. The upshot of living in a small town.

Tony did some maintenance work on the houses Adele cleaned and managed for a branch of Spic'n'Span, the hire-a-holiday syndicate. He was an okay guy, really. Pretty harmless. He just wasn't Adele's cup of tea. Not that she was particularly sure what her beverage of choice was. The two men she'd been with in any serious capacity were poles apart, and neither had eventuated into long-term partners. Nothing like her parents, who were approaching thirty-five years of Yorkshire-blend Ceylon, with a splash of cream.

Adele was pretty sure what she *wasn't* looking for, and that was growing old with Tony Tregonza. The man was ploddingly predictable, promising as much excitement as watery chamomile.

Taking the lake road to see if Kana was still up, Adele was delighted to see the light still on in the studio when she pulled off onto the shingle access road. Her cousin's partner had become a close friend over the past year, and Adele was craving her calming company.

"You're working late," Adele stated the obvious, pushing open the ancient barn door to the combined scent of wet clay and woodsmoke.

Kana looked across the re-purposed space and grinned. "I know. Isn't it cool? Ruby's sleeping, and Daniel's on bottle duty. I feel like a teenager, sneaking out of the house at night to do something illicit."

"It's nice and warm in here with the pot-belly on."

"So, take your coat off then, and give me a spin," Kana directed.

Adele complied, showing off with a bit of a catwalk strut while swinging her coat over one shoulder.

"*Ooooh*, very sexy! Who had the pleasure of this ensemble tonight? One of the new skydiving instructors?"

"No." Adele wrinkled up her nose. "Tony."

Kana's nose followed suit. "What, *Maintenance* Tony? With the…" Kana wiggled her clay smeared fingers near her ears, and Adele nodded.

"Hairy ears, yes."

"I wouldn't call those things hairy, there's something else going on in there." Kana thought for a minute. "*Forested*."

Adele choked on a laugh.

"I'm amazed you thought he deserved to be graced with *this*." Kana waved her hand in Adele's general direction, and a couple of blobs of wet clay landed on the floor not far from her multicoloured wedge-heels. "Oops, sorry."

Adele took a step closer to the pot-belly, out of range from the wheel where Kana sat potting. The studio was kept relatively clean, surfaces wet-wiped daily, but when Kana was actively potting there was no telling where clay could end up.

"Not exactly. It was a blind date set up by my boss."

"Oh, what a bummer. You got a sitter and everything? You should've asked, you know one of us can always—"

"No. I didn't need a sitter. James is visiting," Adele interrupted.

Kana blinked somewhat comically, like a possum in the headlights. "Your ex-*husband*, James?"

Adele nodded.

"He's *staying* with you?"

"God, no!" Adele frowned. "Actually, I don't know where he's staying, he just turned up to deliver my jewellery, and to see Saffy."

"Nice." Kana gave the word an upward ending, making it sound like a question.

"Yeah." Adele couldn't help rolling her eyes. "Saffy will be 'Dad this,' and 'Dad that' for a while, but he came to see her, and I'm glad he bothered. I mean, it's good for her."

"Did you know he was coming?"

"Nope. Out of the blue." Adele chewed on her inner cheek. "Very unlike him, now I come to think of it. He's usually meticulously organised." Within their marriage, Adele had always been the impulsive one—the fly-by-the-seat-of-her-pants one. James was a lot more measured in his movements. Usually.

"Oh." Kana hesitated. "Saffy says they still talk every week."

"Yeah, they do."

"They're close." It wasn't a question, so Kana obviously knew it to be true.

A faint prick of envy jabbed. "Saffy talks about James with you?"

"Sometimes. You know Saffy. She talks about everything. When she's potting here, she's told me about her trips to Sydney. She was hoping she'd be allowed to go back after she turned nine, but that didn't eventuate." Kana looked up almost guiltily. "Entirely up to you, of course."

"Of course," Adele muttered, feeling like the world's meanest grinch.

"Sorry, I just assumed it was on the cards. Five, seven... then nine."

Adele sighed. "We had it pencilled in, but had to sideline it due to Poppy and Clem's wedding this summer."

"She misses him."

"I know." Adele turned side-on to watch the orange glow behind the smokey glass of the little pot-belly.

"How do *you* feel about James just turning up here? Have you actually seen him in person since you split?"

Adele looked down at her frivolous shoes, out of place in the potting studio, and way too breezy for an Otago autumn. "No. First time in the same room since I walked out. It was a shock, actually. I wanted to feel nothing, you know?"

"But you felt… something?"

"I felt *everything*," Adele whispered. Shivering, she slid her arms back into her coat.

"Poor you," Kana commiserated. "First the shock of James, then Tony's forested lugs. It's a wonder you're still upright. Let me just finish pulling this one up, then we'll steal a quiet cup of tea in Obāchan's kitchen, eh?" She put her head down and got her hands working on the clay again.

Very quickly, what had looked like a rough cylinder when Adele entered the studio became a large V-shaped bowl.

"You never cease to amaze me," Adele decided aloud.

"Right back at you." Kana laughed as she scraped the bulk of the muck off her hands into a bucket of similar slime, before heading toward the sump-sink to wash up. "You take it all in your stride. Saffy. James. Tony. All of it."

"Really? Is that how it comes across to you?"

Kana took her time to answer, and when she did it sounded like she was deep in thought. "That's how you make it look from the outside, yes."

Adele had a knack of making four walls and a roof into a place that felt homely.

James wandered around the bungalow lounge, touching pottery pieces and picking up frames after Saffy was finally asleep. It'd taken him a lot longer to tie her hair into tight little French braids than it used to. One, because his fingers were out of practice, and two, because Saffy had a lot more hair now than she'd had as a preschooler.

Cornrows were beyond James' capacity, but braids were doable.

It felt a little odd to know his face wouldn't be in any of the pictures in this communal room. There wouldn't be any visible trace of him here, nothing he'd bought or gifted, nothing he'd built or repaired. It was as if he'd never existed in Adele's life at all—never meant anything to her.

Perhaps he never had, after all?

James resisted the urge to go back to Adele's room and take a closer look at the bright portrait Saffy had done of her vivacious mother.

Privacy where privacy was due.

They came from different backgrounds, with different expectations and family dynamics. That'd caused some friction even in the initial stages of their relationship, but nothing they couldn't handle with conversation and compromise. Adele was as stubborn as she was proud, and had a way of showing James' choices up as if they were all owing to his privileged ignorance. Perhaps some of them had been, but he'd never forgotten his yo-yo childhood; continent to continent and feast to famine.

Born in Switzerland, James had immigrated to Quebec with his family for a brief time when he was a child, then shifted to Australia when Canada had proved 'unwelcoming.' His father, much to his mother's disgust, had invested heavily in a farm way out in the red dust. Nothing like the wealth they were accustomed to in Switzerland, nor the civilised four-seasoned climate of eastern Canada.

By the time he'd met Adele, James was waist-deep in the little empire his father had begun to build, pulling the family finances back to what was considered comfortable. He'd been forced to head the family-owned farming consultancy after his father's death, refocussing to specialise in I.T..

With eighty-hour weeks more common than not, business had been steady. The Montagues were a far cry from sustenance farming when James had inconveniently fallen head over heels for a much younger, strawberry-blonde Kiwi, with a zest for life that'd shaken him right out of his solitary cycle.

Love at first sight—on his part, anyway.

With twenty-twenty hindsight, the whole thing had been a powder keg, just waiting to go off.

James had been forced to re-evaluate his priorities and choices over the past few years, after his marriage and his father's business had imploded, one after the other. A shift in attitude was long overdue. The money was incidental, more pride lost than anything else. But losing the love of his life through his own stupidity? Nothing could ever fill that gaping hole.

He ran his fingers down the spines of the books on the shelf, unconsciously searching for anything familiar from Adele's bookcase in their Sydney home. He'd teased her about it at the time, because the paperbacks seemed to mean more to her than the real life dramas of her new neighbours.

James realised now it had been Adele's only form of escapism. He'd had work, his father's all consuming company, whereas Adele had survived the loneliness of a new country by climbing into those happy-ever-afters.

He'd gone ahead and botched that bit up for her, though, hadn't he? No happily ever after. No bed of roses.

He'd been no knight in shining armour for Adele, that's for sure.

James had found Adele's non-fiction books on how to handle grief when he'd finally packed up the house. They'd been so unfamiliar within her shelves of romance, he'd stopped and leafed through. In the most dogeared one, just about every page had something highlighted, and Adele's tiny, tortured script had filled the margins.

Try not to assign blame.

Moving on doesn't have to mean forgetting.

There is no guilt in seeking happiness for yourself.

If you are the leopard, the spots you are wearing are optional.

There's no point trying to erase another's spots, they're there by choice.

Adele's books had never been packed and sent on to her with her clothes and other belongings. Her lawyer had said they could be donated as James saw fit. But in those first few months after she'd gone, he'd thought she'd be coming back, so had held onto them.

He'd actually believed Adele was taking a much needed break with her family until he'd been served with divorce papers.

The boxes of books had moved with him to his single-room rental when the house in the leafy suburbs had sold. James had even pulled some novels out and read them after the initial stages of Farmtech's takeover. Overseeing the operation until Montague Holdings ceased to exist had required a thick skin and studied numbness, and in the evenings, alone in his poky city-flat, James had craved some escapism of his own.

Perusing Adele's new collection of books up and down, James found some familiar authors. Catherine Robertson, Nora Roberts, and Michelle Holman.

He chose a name he hadn't heard before: Natalie Anderson. Adele had presumably bought this contemporary romance brand new, because the original pricing sticker was still on the back. Unusual for her, as she tended to trawl second-hand bookstores.

A gift?

James toed off his shoes and sunk onto the sofa, thumping the cushions into a comfortable lying position and welcoming the dog's company when she trotted over.

The paperback had been signed by the author with a personal note on the title page.

'Dear Adele, Best of luck, Warm regards, Natalie.'

Best of luck with what? Her new beginning? Single life?

When Adele arrived back at the bungalow, she let herself in and tiptoed out of pure habit.

Saffy's usual babysitter, Maddie, was a light sleeper, and if Adele stayed out after twelve, the twenty-year-old often stayed over. But tonight, the long-limbed body on Adele's sofa wasn't the bubbly barista. Not by a long shot. The young café worker's golden-cherub curls had been replaced by a flop of dirty-blonde hair, a couple of days worth of stubble, and a masculine, thirty-six-year-old jawline.

James wasn't exactly snoring, but his breathing was heavy enough to denote he was deeply under. A paperback lay open on his chest, rising and falling with the slow rhythm, and one of his arms was flung over the side.

Adele stood in the lounge archway, under the unsightly seventies scalloped plaster, and scowled at the dog lying replete under James' dangling hand.

"Traitor," she admonished Winger in a whisper, and the one-year-old border collie had the grace to look slightly bashful in response. "Some guard dog you turned out to be. Rolled over for a pretty face, didn't you? Definitely the right choice to get you spayed, if that's how you roll."

Winger let out a light whine, and James re-shuffled in his sleep.

Yeah, well. Adele couldn't really blame the dog. She'd rolled over for the same pretty face herself, once upon a time.

Slipping down the hall to Saffy's room, she checked on her daughter.

Saffy was clutching a soft toy Adele didn't recognise. Something fluffy and probably new from Australia. An owl? Definitely an animal with a beak.

She pressed a kiss to Saffy's forehead. "I love you. Sleep tight."

Used to the routine, Saffy hardly stirred, and Adele gazed down at her daughter's sweet features all softened in sleep.

They were happy, weren't they? Her daughter and herself?

Nicely settled into their habits and routines.

Adele frowned. Saffy's hair had been plaited tightly into James' signature French braids. The sight made her downright titchy, because it didn't fit in with her plans. Admittedly *unlikely* plans, in which she got up at the crack of dawn to deal with her daughter's hair.

"What the hell am I supposed to do with your stepdad now, asleep in the lounge?" Adele muttered. She hadn't exactly thought this bit through.

After climbing into her nightie, she washed her face free of makeup, still mulling on it.

The least she could do was get the man a blanket. The nights could get bitterly cold this deep in the southern Lake District. Feeling vaguely naked and out-of-sorts with a man in the house, even a very familiar one, Adele pulled a housecoat over her short cotton bed-wear and took the heavy patchwork quilt off the end of her bed.

James was still asleep, though the dog had gotten up and was now waiting patiently at the back door. Adele padded over to let Winger out. "Go do your business, but make it quick," she murmured.

There was a faint buzzing she didn't recognise. The last of the summer bumble-bees, caught inside?

No.

James' phone, with the sound turned down to mute. It lay face-up on the table next to his jacket, and Adele craned her neck to see who might be calling him at past twelve on a weeknight.

Mother.

Figured. James had always been expected to be at Isabella Montague's beck and call any time of the day or night. Adele picked up James' phone on a whim and snuck out into the cold, pulling the slider closed behind her.

"Good evening, Isabella, what a *lovely* surprise," she laid it on thick.

There was the hiss of an indrawn breath on the line, before her name was thrown back at her in the form of an accusation. *"Adele?"*

She couldn't help chuckling at the sheer distaste the other woman managed to give two syllables. "I can hear the pleasure's mutual."

"Why are you answering Aksels' phone?"

Adele hadn't heard James' first name in so long, it threw her for a moment.

"He's… otherwise indisposed." Adele added a decent splash of innuendo, shivering violently as the cold began to seep in. There was no point attempting to wrap herself more warmly in the quilt she'd dragged outside with her, because the ice was emanating from inside herself.

Sparring with old enemies did that to a person.

"Don't play me, Adele."

The scaly tone in Isabella Montague's accented warning brought back memories of a time Adele would rather forget, a time when she'd been rendered practically obsolete, and reduced to a lesser version of herself. She shuddered, wishing she'd let the phone ring.

"I wouldn't dream of it." Answering smoothly took some doing, but she managed it.

"So you've crawled back into Aksel's life, after all this time. I can't say I'm surprised."

"I don't *crawl*, Isabella, I walk with my head held high. James came seeking *us* out, not the other way around."

"Only because he feels indebted, surely. You've run out of money?"

"I don't need his bloody Montague money," Adele growled, losing her cool.

"I must ask you to desist, whatever it is you think you're doing." Perhaps sensing she'd won that round, Isabella switched to a more queenly tone. "Go back to New Zealand."

Adele had her mouth open to retort, but she closed it again after that little morsel of information. Isabella assumed Adele was in Australia, so must believe James was still there, too?

"What makes you think I would take orders from you?" Five years and a truckload of experience under her belt meant Adele was no longer willing to let Isabella, or anyone else, bulldoze her.

Isabella made a sound of derision that sounded like a French curse. "Release James from whatever ties he's promised, and let him find a suitable wife. Produce children to carry on his father's name. Now the business is gone, that's all I have left."

Now the business is *gone*?

In the past, Adele would've bitten her tongue to keep the peace, but she had no marital locks on her opinions now—no reason to fold.

"Is that misogynistic crap about carrying on the family name a dig at me having a miscarriage?"

Isabella snorted in an unladylike manner. "Don't you mean *abortion*?" she muttered.

Adele's feet were freezing on the concrete slab and she was shivering in her cotton nightwear, but her fury was suddenly red-hot. "No. I mean miscarriage. A bloody soul destroying *miscarriage* Isabella, you heartless bitch."

There was silence on the line, and Adele assumed Isabella had hung up. Which was just fine and dandy. She needed her ex-mother-in-law's brand of poison like she needed a swig of arsenic.

Adele was readjusting the quilt on her shoulders when Isabella's hesitant words reached her from far off.

"But... that's not how I heard it described."

Adele expelled a puff of air and watched it form a little white cloud, reaching out faintly toward the willow tree but disappearing well before it got there. Her teeth chattered together the instant she closed her mouth.

Isabella had a lot to answer for, but within that moment she just sounded like a slightly bemused old lady.

"Then James has wilfully misinformed you," Adele whispered.

Disconnecting with a decisive press of her thumb, she snuck back into the warmth of the lounge to contemplate her ex-husband.

Adele had never met James's father, he died well before she'd married into the Montagues, but in sleep, the son suddenly looked very much like the photos she'd seen of the patriarch, Luka. Bold cheekbones and brow, and a high-bridged nose.

James' features appeared somewhat vulnerable in sleep though. Less culpable.

Anyone could be forgiven for assuming him completely blameless.

Adele settled the phone back where she'd found it, taking the pointless precaution of turning it on its face. One conversation with her ex-mother-in-law was quite enough for the night.

For the year.

For the decade.

5

PAPANGARUA - QUILT

Bone-warming protection from the ever present cold.

Adele's fingers had trouble doing what they were told, and she fumbled to get the multi-coloured quilt off her shoulders and over James as he slept on her sofa. His eyes flickered open as she drew the weight up to his chest. "I was dreaming of you," he murmured sleepily, motionless but for the soft lips and roving eyes. "With your hair out, just like that."

Adele stepped back, the welcome in James' smile sending off all sorts of alarm bells.

"You can stay over if you want." Her voice chose that moment to emulate Marilyn Monroe; an invitation and a half.

Completely unintentional, and totally inappropriate.

"I mean *here*, on the sofa, or there's a pull-out," she flustered, indicating the direction of the sunroom.

"Mmm? No, that's okay. I'll get going." James smiled again, still a little on the muzzy side, and Adele's body automatically responded, tugging her towards his bedroom eyes.

Cut that out.

This man was bad news. He'd proven that once already.

James swung his legs down and planted his feet on the floor, rubbing one hand over his jaw while the other moved to grab the sliding book.

"Sorry, I didn't intend to fall asleep. Is it late?"

"Around twelve-thirty."

"You could've stayed over... *Out*... longer." James cleared his throat and looked down at the book under his hand, as if surprised to find it there, then leaned over to place it on the side table. "Did you have a good time?" He hesitated before turning to assess her.

Adele squirmed under James' scrutiny, suddenly aware her housecoat had fallen open and her pink cotton nightie shouted *I DOUGHNUT CARE*, with a picture of a heavily iced pastry to prove its point.

"Absolutely. Yes, of course," she breezed, wrapping herself back in the relative safety of her housecoat.

"Good." James nodded, reaching for his shoes. "That's really good," he muttered to himself, not sounding entirely convinced. Dressed much more casually than he had been this morning when he'd turned up at her door out of nowhere, he still managed to make dark pants and a sweater look expensive. "Saffy was asking about a bake-sale tomorrow down at the school. She invited me, but I said I'd ask you first."

"No. I'd feel weird about that." The honest answer jumped out before Adele had tempered it with niceties. It was a direct snub, and she took a moment to feel a little bad about it. After all, the man had just done her a favour. "I mean, it's in the school hall, so everyone will be there." Which made it sound worse, like she was embarrassed to introduce him to anyone.

But Adele had already fielded multiple questions from the other single mums who'd been at the school gate when Saffy's 'hot dad' had turned up as a surprise, and had no inclination to re-enact that intrusive carry-on.

"Fair enough." James seemed to have been expecting no as an answer, and Adele breathed a sigh of relief. "Your call," he added, pulling on his shoes, one by one. "Could you let her know, though? So she doesn't think I'm a no-show."

James looked up at Adele again from his lower position on the sofa, incredibly poised and softly spoken for having just been woken from a deep sleep. He'd always been like that, calmly prepared for whatever life threw at him next.

"I'll tell her," she promised.

"Dell, I can go." James hesitated. "I mean, I can leave Wānaka if you want. I get that it wasn't on the cards, me turning up—it wasn't what you wanted."

They stared at each other in silence, Adele the first to look away.

"You took some time off?"

"Yes."

No explanation. No, *'The company's gone,'* or, *'I don't have a job to go back to.'*

Then again, there was no guarantee Isabella had even been telling the truth. Hadn't James said he had business in Otago?

Adele shrugged, pretending it didn't matter to her either way. "You don't have to rush off on my account. Saffy missed out on spending time with you this summer. She'd love to see more of you, and you may as well see the sights while you're here."

"Okay." James got up to stand, and Adele was once again struck by his woodsy scent, like the forest after rain. "Thanks. If you're sure. Saffy has my New Zealand number, and I've pinned it to the board." James gestured vaguely toward the chock-a-block cork board in the kitchen, next to Adele's weekly planner. "So you can get hold of me if you need me."

If she *needed* him? Fat chance.

Adele thanked James for his time, which he brushed off as nothing, then let him out the front door. She watched him tuck his phone into his pocket and knew she should tell him his mother had rung—but chose not to. There was an awkward moment on the porch when she didn't quite know the best way to farewell him.

Shaking his hand was pompously formal, waving childish, and hugging out of the question. She reached one hand out to touch his forearm, but was saved from the contact by the dog.

Winger raced between them wagging her tail, excited about being out so late and having company. Adele stooped to take the collie's collar in her hand, relieved to have her as a distraction.

"Did she chew on her stitches at all?"

"No. Not that I saw. She was great. Saffy was great, too. You're doing a fantastic job, Dell. She's a lovely kid."

Adele's hackles went up, affronted James felt he had a right to say. She opened her mouth, then shut it again, resentment building.

How the hell would James know what kind of job she was doing?

"She tells me you're both learning Sudanese?" James continued.

"Not that it's any of your business," Adele snapped, finding herself incapable of conducting any more small-talk with this man, when there was so much gigantic-talk they'd never addressed.

"No, right." James' mouth tugged into a sad little half-smile. "Of course not. Goodnight, then."

James turned and moved into the darkness beyond the porch, and Adele heard his car door close with a quiet 'pop' a few moments later. She stared at the empty patch on the gravel drive long after the sedan had disappeared, trying to come to terms with the fact her ex-husband still affected her too much, and brought out the worst in her.

She hadn't even thanked him for taking the time to plait Saffy's hair so diligently.

What was the significance of James showing up in Wānaka in person, when his family clearly had no idea where he was?

Winger whined, breaking Adele out of her reverie. She was bone-tired and craving bed, but when she returned inside, still found herself drawn to the kitchen noticeboard. Her fingers came to rest on a small rectangle of paper that hadn't been there this morning. A Wanderers Café receipt flipped on its face, with James' name, and a loopy scrawl of numbers on the back.

James M.

As if she might get him mixed up with all the other James' in her life who drank short-blacks?

Adele was able to laugh about it as she climbed into bed and snuggled deep under the covers.

Adele followed Daniel and Kana into the school hall, her eyes adjusting to the dimmer light as she automatically searched the bake-sale trestles. She found Saffy's dark head easily amongst the others, her hair tightly bound into the skinny braids James had perfected when his stepdaughter was just three years old, heading off to preschool three days a week with a backpack almost as big as her.

Saffy beamed her welcome. "Is Dad here?"

Adele hadn't had time to discuss the details of the bake-sale in the morning rush, other than shoving the re-purposed ice-cream containers full of cookies into Saffy's hands as she'd exited.

They'd both slept late, and Adele had never been good at mornings.

"No. I... I actually asked him not to come by today." The instant the words were out of her mouth, Adele could see she'd made a really bad call. Saffy's face fell, her chocolate eyes swimming with disappointment. "I'm sorry. I just thought..." It'd be too hard to explain to all the other parents who the stunning blonde man was, and where he fitted into the picture. "I thought it might be easier to keep the two of us separate."

"Easier for who?" Saffy's eyes glittered.

"For all of us?" Adele hazarded.

"I find *that* somewhat hard to believe." Suddenly sounding like a teenager instead of a sweet, assenting almost ten-year-old, Saffy turned and stalked back to the table where her classmates waited, leaving Adele floundering in the centre of the large, open space.

"You okay?" Kana wandered toward her with Ruby in the front-pack. The little one was a magnet for the school children, who all knew her by name and fluttered up to say hello, or touch the chubby little fists she liked to swing with wild abandon.

'Mōrena, Ruby. She's smiling at me! I like your kiwi socks, Ruby!'

"I should've said yes to James coming today." Adele murmured the words as her cousin, Daniel, moved over to join them.

Daniel offered Kana a chunk of the muffin he was in the process of demolishing.

"Saffy's so disappointed he's not here," Adele added. "And that's on me."

"You don't have to rearrange your life for someone who couldn't be bothered doing the same for you," Daniel disagreed firmly.

Adele had informed him of James' arrival yesterday, and the former rugby player seemed particularly put out by the impromptu visit.

"The guy's a waste of your time." Daniel may've been speaking with his mouth full, but his tone invited no argument.

It went against Adele's grain not to push back, and defend.

"You're judging James unfairly," she muttered, incensed her cousin assumed he had any say when he hardly even *knew* her ex-husband. "He's here to spend time with Saffy, and he's welcome."

She was even more riled by her own actions. It'd been petty of her to keep James away from Saffy when he'd soon be gone. After all, James had always been generous to both of them. Not so much with *time*, but when they were married, he'd always made sure there was cash in Adele's wallet, along with a cashed-up credit card.

Even so, she'd tried to be reasonably frugal. It might've been a pipe dream at one time in her life to be a lady of leisure, without a job or financial worries to stress about, but in practice it'd felt incredibly powerless to be so dependent.

Within James' cloistered family, 'There's no need for you to work' had begun to feel a lot more like 'It would be considered offensive if you chose to work.'

Adele had always stood on her own two feet before James—admittedly with some family support after Saffron was born, but not like a *bank*. It had sat all wrong.

Less input felt like less entitlement, and therefore less of a voice than she was used to.

"We could make James up a doggy bag," Kana suggested quietly, brushing a few of her own crumbs off Ruby's downy head. "Ask him to pick Saffy up after school so she gets to gift them herself."

"Why would you even bother to—"

"Great idea." Adele cut Daniel off and brushed past his obvious affront, heading towards the baked goods and dragging her cousin's surprised partner-and-baby duo with her.

Put that in your pipe and smoke it, Dante D.

They may have grown up more like brother and sister than cousins, but that didn't mean Adele was going to let Daniel bloody Dante boss her around and tell her what to do.

6

TAHETOKA - AMBER

What was once liquid, now hardened and fossilised.

James wasn't sure if he was seeing things when Adele walked past the coffee shop at ten past five, dressed in a navy business suit. Her hair was pulled back from her face, but once up in the ponytail, she'd left it to its own wild and crazy devices. It seemed to be her only concession to wild and crazy today, as the rest of her ensemble had 'serious stuff' written all over it.

She reminded him so much of when they'd originally met, it was almost as if he'd conjured her up as a mirage. That little fitted suit took him back eight years…

"Dell!" He called after her as he loped across the street to catch up, and she was smiling as she turned towards her name.

Not just serious stuff, seriously *hot* stuff.

When she realised who was hailing her, Adele's face dropped. If James had ever had a sense of how little he'd come to mean to her, the knife struck home in that one, awful moment.

She'd wished he was someone else.

Anyone else.

James stared, first at the all-too-familiar amber beads in a choker line around Adele's neck, then down at his ex-wife's naked hands, before forcing himself to concentrate once more on the translucent topaz of her eyes.

He had no reason to feel the blade twist under his ribs.

Of course Adele would wear the amber, it had always been her favourite. She'd probably never touch her rings again, let alone wear them. Giving them back to her after all this time would've just come across as a token gesture. A simple acknowledgement of ownership.

Not love. Not longing.

He asked after Saffy instead. What else was he supposed to do?

"She goes to Daniel and Kana on Thursdays after school, and they'll drop her home after seven. Then it's homework, bath, and bed." Adele didn't say it, but James could read clearly between the lines. They had their routine, and Adele was buggered if she'd let him get in the way.

"I could bring you guys something for dinner? Take-aways?" James offered, not holding out much hope.

"No. Saffy will've already eaten. Obāchan's teaching Saffy to cook, Japanese style, so she brings me home a *bento* every Thursday. It's kind of a tradition."

"Obāchan's their cook?"

"No, James." The way Adele intoned it, it sounded like 'wrong again.' "Obāchan is Kana's grandmother."

"Right." Saffy had told James that already, and he wasn't usually this obtuse. Nor was it commonplace for him to be scrabbling around in his loafers for his self-esteem. "Of course. Well, nice to see you." James went to turn away, then remembered what he'd wanted to ask Adele last night. "One last thing. The wooden seat, under the willow?"

"The love-seat?" Adele frowned.

Was that actually what it was called?

"Yes, the… ah… that. Saffy and I were going to paint it, but I said we'd ask you first. She may have mentioned it?"

"No."

When Adele didn't elaborate, James sought to clarify. "No, she didn't mention it?" He rubbed his jaw between thumb and forefinger, faintly surprised to find the rasp of bristles there. "Or, no, you don't want it painted?"

"No, she didn't mention it. What colour?"

"Teal."

"Really?" Adele blinked.

"She likes teal right now." James grinned at her. "It's so *sick*."

Adele rolled her eyes comically, then shrugged. "I don't care. Do what you like, but don't make a mess."

"Great." He clapped his hands together then rubbed the palms, excited to have a new project.

Adele frowned at him again. "You need a shave."

"Mmm," James hummed noncommittally.

Admittedly, Mountain Man was an unusual look for him. Since he'd graduated University and joined Montague Holdings at twenty-one, he'd shaved daily for work, seven days a week. The aim of running the company one day had taken over every living, breathing moment of his life after his father's death. Everything he'd done was in order to cram himself into the stipulations in his father's will.

Everything until Adele.

The distinct lack of anything resembling Montague Holdings and the consequent collapse of his shaving routine were symbiotic, and James found, with some surprise at first, he was highly enjoying the freedom from both.

"What've you been doing all day?" Adele continued to eye him suspiciously.

"Ah, having a look around." James slid both hands in his pockets, trying to look nonchalant.

"When are you flying back home?"

"Oh, soon." He nodded with what he hoped looked like confidence. "Sometime after the weekend."

"Your P.A. must be frantic," Adele added snidely as she stalked off.

His P.A.? Didn't Adele know he worked alone, now?

As soon as Adele disappeared into the nondescript office building, James realised he hadn't thanked her for the bag of baking Saffy had handed him at the school gate yesterday, or checked in with her about Saffy's invitation up to the family farm.

Forgetting what he'd been aiming to say was an effect Adele often had on him, and he wasn't overly enjoying the return of it.

It was her eyes that did it, cool crystal that turned him into a blithering mess.

Today he'd eaten chocolate brownie for breakfast, blueberry muffins for lunch, and Adele's own chocolate-chip cookies interspersed throughout. Not the most nutritional fare. He'd have to counteract all the carbs and sugar with some extra laps in the pool, and something seriously green for dinner.

James would've known those chocolate-chip cookies anywhere. Adele had always been heavy handed on the vanilla, and no matter how many others he'd tried, they never tasted quite the same.

She'd made a batch of chocolate-chip cookies the night before she'd left, five years ago. James still didn't know if that had been purely coincidental, or a concession on Adele's part to help ease the hurt. But before she'd taken Saffy and flown from Sydney without any indication they weren't ever coming back, she'd filled the baking tins.

On edge after seeing Adele without time to prepare or buffer himself, it slipped James' mind he'd actually driven into the township. He was halfway back to the lakefront motel on foot before he remembered he'd parked his new four-wheel-drive outside the café.

Never mind. It'd keep. The walk would do him good, as high doses of sugar tended to affect him like caffeine, and Adele tended to affect him like crack cocaine.

He could walk the length of the South Island, and still be buzzing.

When they'd originally met, what seemed like a thousand years ago, he'd felt the potential like static electricity throughout his entire body. His mother had discounted the first-time phenomenon as common lust.

In the heat of a particularly ugly argument, Isabella Montague had referred to Adele as money hungry, and James as slumming it.

Needless to say, James disagreed on both points.

Isabella kept any further offensive comments about James' wife to herself. Smart woman. Though his mother's vulgar assertions from eight years ago still hung between them, vaguely tainting the air.

James had chosen Adele's engagement ring immediately after he'd met her. The 'ostentatious' square-cut diamond.

God, what an idiot.

He'd wanted the largest they'd had; wanted to dazzle Adele into overcoming any trepidation about how fast he wanted their relationship to move, and what it would mean to shift her small daughter to Australia.

He'd been wrong, he realised later. Wrong on so many points.

Wrong to not realise flashy gifts only pushed Adele further away, and steadfastly supported his mother's hypothesis. Wrong to assume it had to be Adele making all the concessions; uprooting her and Saffy from everything they'd thought of as home. Wrong to not include his young wife in what was going on with the company, and his mother's mental health. Wrong to stay silent on the loss of Rosetta, when the grief was obviously tearing Adele apart.

Checking the time on her phone, Adele was pleased to note bumping into James had only lost her five minutes. She entered the counsellor's office right on time.

"Nau mai, haere mai, Adele. Lovely to see you. I'm just grabbing us each a glass of water. Hot, isn't it? Gets me all flustered."

Adele was flustered too, but it had little to do with the unseasonable heat of the day.

Her counsellor, Fran, could be considered a touch overweight, and a touch over-opinionated by some, but Adele valued the down to earth, no-nonsense woman immensely. The sessions didn't always sit comfortably within Adele's slim budget, but missing one would be tantamount to missing her daily walk along the lakefront.

Soul food, that's what Fran offered. Last year, they'd pared it back to a single half-hour session per week—just the right amount to keep Adele's head above dark water.

Adele had talked a lot about her failed marriage and miscarriage with Fran in the early days, and again when Daniel and Kana had moved back to Wānaka with one-month-old Ruby. Having a new baby within her direct family unit, and seeing Daniel and Kana together as a loving couple had been incredibly difficult at first, but it'd helped Adele to offload all her turbulent emotions into an independent ear.

She couldn't talk to Kana about Rosetta. Though she'd been on the verge of doing so many times, the moment never seemed quite right, and her mouth point-blank refused to comply. Kana and Daniel had their own series of mountains to climb with Ruby, and it didn't seem fair to tangle her own loss up in that.

But as Ruby had grown, the sweet girl had launched a healing offensive all on her own. Repairing scars with her gummy smile, and soothing hurts with her gurgling laugh and chubby fingers.

Adele and Fran had long since moved on to discuss more current concerns; solo parenting, juggling work with Saffy-time, positive self-image, and figuring out what Adele wanted to do with her future self. They weren't necessarily saving the world, but the sessions were incredibly helpful in solidifying Adele as her own person again, something that had all but imploded during The James Years.

"What's new?" Fran cut to the chase as soon as they were seated, her eyes a warm, welcoming brown. There was no point beating around the bush—they both knew they had little time for small talk.

I had the courage to go on a blind date. I had a breakthrough at the law office, and might be offered more permanent work. I'm thinking it might finally be time to invest in a house, with a B&B option attached—put down some permanent roots. I got my jewellery box back.

All of those thoughts popped into Adele's head, but what jumped out of her mouth was, "My ex-husband's in town. Dropped in out of nowhere."

"James?" Fran scribbled something in her notebook, the detailed moko on her chin contracting as she pressed her lips together in concentration.

"Yes, James."

Aksel James Montague.

A.J.

"How do you feel about that?" Fran wondered.

"I would've preferred him to stay on the other side of the Tasman, of course. Seeing him is incredibly unsettling."

"How so?"

Adele stared at her glass of water, still on the side table. "When I see James, I'm hurt all over again. About the affair. About the pipe dream. About Rosetta."

"How did the loss of Rosetta affect James?" Adele could almost hear Fran's pen hovering above the paper.

"I don't know. We never discussed it."

There was a moment's hesitation. "Not even when the miscarriage actually happened?"

"No, not really." That sounded awful, but it was the truth. They hadn't talked about it. Adele hadn't wanted to—hadn't allowed it.

Now Fran's pen was scribbling furiously, and Adele took the time to sip her water.

The coolness failed to soothe her throat.

"Perhaps you could broach the subject while he's here?" Fran suggested with a small smile.

"No. Absolutely not. James comes from a long line of stiff-upper-lips and private grief. I can't talk to him."

"You must've been able to talk to him at some stage?"

"When we were first together, we talked about everything."

It had felt like that, moving so fast. An all consuming connection. So much so, Adele had hardly had time to catch her breath. They'd agreed on some things, and argued furiously about others, but were so hungry for each other the differences of opinion hadn't seemed to matter. Not until they were all encompassing, suffocating all else.

"Everything?"

Well, no. Not exactly.

"Everything except Moses."

"Why was Moses taboo?"

Adele hesitated, her fingers reaching to touch the amber resting warmly on her neck. A gift from Saffy's birth father, long ago, along with the compliment her hair glowed with the same light as the ancient sap.

"James suspected I was still in love with him."

"Were you?"

"I'm not sure." Adele ran her tongue over her teeth and looked away from Fran's all seeing gaze.

The tattoo inked on the counsellor's chin denoted her status within her iwi, but she was a woman first and foremost. A woman who was dead good at reading other women. Adele took her time studying the less confrontational bookcase, which was full of children's picture books, the odd psychology text the exception rather than the rule.

"I was in love with the idea of him… So, yes. Maybe. Initially, anyway," Adele finally conceded.

"And why did Rosetta become taboo?"

Adele looked back smartly, meeting Fran's warm gaze. "Because I lost her."

"You *both* lost her," the counsellor reasoned, leaning forward in earnest.

"But she was in my body. I was supposed to be keeping her safe."

"You blamed yourself." Fran settled back in her chair as Adele nodded. "Hmm. You've never admitted that openly before."

Adele swallowed, suddenly incapable of speech.

Of course she'd blamed herself. It was nobody else's fault.

"And you believed James blamed you as well?" Fran continued gently.

"I don't know," Adele whispered.

"I think you could ask him that."

Could she go ahead and ask him that? After all the oceans of silence?

"No. I don't think so." She hated that her voice came out reedy, and weak.

"Would it help to have a mediator? Someone to help facilitate the conversation. Or would your ex-husband feel threatened by that?"

"James never feels threatened. He's the world's coolest cucumber. Do you mean, like couples counselling?"

"Yes."

"But we're *not* a couple. Nothing near a couple. Not even close."

"No, but you were when you both went through the loss of Rosetta. That's a shared experience—shared grief—and if you want support discussing it, I could help you both with that."

"No."

Fran performed an exaggerated two-handed shrug. "It was just an idea, Adele. You don't have to decide right now."

7

WHAKATUMA - CHALLENGE

In defiance against what stands.

Adele wore a silky white top with a halter neck. Not because she particularly wanted to, it wasn't exactly practical for applying copious amounts of pizza sauce, but because Saffy had insisted they 'dress up nice' as James would be there.

At least the autumn weather had complied with an extension of the unseasonably warm sunshine.

She needn't have bothered. The only thing James saw was her pale skin on display, and the potential for sunburn.

In fact, the first sentence out of his mouth when Adele got out of the car at Kana and Daniel's farmhouse was, "Have you got sunscreen on?"

"That's not your concern." Adele eyed him with a coolness she hoped was cutting.

James' nostrils did that little flare. "You'll burn," he muttered.

"Mind your own business, Nord," she bit back. "We can't all have pretty olive skin."

"Your skin's pretty, Mum."

Adele had forgotten Saffy was within earshot. Slipping out of the car looking gorgeous in the garnet-red jumpsuit that would look garish on anyone else, she came to stand beside her mother.

"I think so too, Saff. You've both got beautiful skin," James murmured, and his eyes told the truth.

Adele looked down at Saffy's dark hand on her own freckled arm, and felt a sense of shame for behaving like the colour of anyone's skin would mean anything to James. He'd gone ahead and complimented her daughter with the same comment, so she couldn't refute it now without sounding obnoxious.

She chose to completely ignore it instead.

"What does Nord mean?" Saffy grabbed James' hand, and practically skipped him to the front door.

"It means north. From the north. My father was French, but Nana Isabella's Finnish."

"Finished?"

"No." James laughed, and Adele hung back, purposefully dawdling by the car so she didn't have to be party to their little tête-à-tête. "Finnish. Originally from Finland."

James had brought paint, and somehow the wooden love-seat as well. Adele hadn't noticed it missing, but James must've had it for some time because it looked like it'd been stripped, sanded, and undercoated.

"I wonder how much he paid someone to do that?" she muttered, as she watched James arrange newspapers, brushes, and overalls for himself and Saffy so they could 'attack the topcoat' before dinner. Their overalls both looked brand new, and although clearly a smaller size, Saffy's had to be rolled at the sleeves and ankles to accommodate her nine-year-old frame.

Almost *ten*-year-old… Time was catapulting forward way too fast.

"The undercoating? Oh, I'm pretty sure he did that himself."

"What makes you say that?" Adele turned to Kana, frowning.

"I make it a point to look at a man's hands." Kana answered cryptically, a little smile playing on her lips.

"Are you being crude?"

"Have you ever *known* me to be crude?"

"No," Adele grouched. "But there's a first time for everything."

Kana laughed as she walked away, her dark hair out of its thick braid and swinging freely down her back.

They set up on the back patio next to the new pool fencing,

Adele's daughter and her ex, so the paint could dry in the late afternoon sun.

Adele watched the proceedings, not because she wanted to, but because they were right in her view. And it was *her* chair, goddamnit. She'd bought it at a garage sale a couple of years ago, fully intending to paint it herself.

And she *would* have, at some stage. When life wasn't so chocked full of work and commitments.

Adele did go outside, just the once, and only to check that Saffy's coveralls really were covering everything. The jumpsuit had been a gift from Aunt Poppy, and was kind of special.

It wasn't a bad thing Saffy loved her ex-stepfather, nor was it surprising he loved her back, but it *was* hard watching them getting on like James had never screwed it all up.

"What do you think of the colour, Dell?" James turned to her, the wheaten highlights in his hair catching the last ochre rays of sunlight.

It was just like old times, that easy smile and well polished charm making her want to smile back, and be a part of it all.

The colour of the chair wasn't bad actually. Deep teal. It'd look good when finished.

Adele stared at James' hand, wrapped around the dripping paintbrush, and remembered it flying over the keys of the piano that used to reside in the front room of his house in Sydney. Those long-boned fingers had the ability to draw sublime imagery with music, and charm passion from every centimetre of her body, but right now all she could see was the tell-tale white paint settled around every cuticle.

She shivered, suddenly missing her sweater.

What was James Montague even doing here?

"Don't call me Dell," she found herself snapping in self-defence against the fact she'd been wrong about the undercoating. "I don't like it."

That wiped the smile off James' face, and Saffy skidded a look from one parent to the other, clearly discerning trouble.

Recovering himself, James gave Saffy a playful nudge. "See? I *told* you we should've gone for something brighter," he quipped.

After scrubbing up with Saffy in the laundry, James settled back to watch the unfamiliar family group. On the periphery, he kept finding himself in the company of the dogs. Both were a working breed—sheepdogs—but although well-trained, appeared to be essentially pets. Not the kelpies he was used to from Oz, but the black and white border collies Kiwi sheep farmers favoured.

The dogs had clearly chosen pack leaders. Wherever Saffy went, Winger's eyes followed, and whichever direction Kana moved in, the older collie, Halfback, was watching from a respectful distance. Daniel Dante's focus was also on Kana, as if he had no other purpose in life other than scoping out potential dangers approaching his partner and child.

That was preferable to Daniel's attention being trained on James.

The ex-rugby player had a glare that could strip skin, and there was clearly no love lost on that front. James was yet to have a full conversation with the New Zealand icon. It was Saffy who'd called and formally invited James to family pizza night, and Kana who'd okayed the painting of the chair up at the farm.

If Adele and himself had been married in Otago, James would've no doubt had more of a foothold with her family, but they'd chosen a quiet registry office in Sydney.

Yet another thing he'd do differently, given the chance.

James knew Adele's sister and parents a little, from their early visits to Australia. They lived a few hours drive from here in Adele's hometown, Dunedin.

The small city had given off a vaguely Scottish atmosphere when he'd driven through it—the austerity of the hillside cathedrals and the harbour glistening in the forefront like a legend-filled loch. Maybe that's why Adele's Scottish ancestors had felt so at home there, and set down roots?

As well as the family of three living in the farmhouse, Kana's grandmother, Obāchan, occupied the annex down by the potting studio. The Japanese woman was a tiny white-haired firecracker, full of energy and mischief, and appeared to have all of the other pizza-night attendees firmly under her thumb.

Daniel's mother—Adele's aunt, Poppy—was married to Clem, a

neighbouring farmer. If James had his information right, it was Poppy's second marriage, and Clem's first. A very recent event. The two behaved like they'd been together forever, though, finishing each other's sentences and answering questions their partner hadn't even asked yet.

James began to wonder if he'd gotten the timeline of the story mixed up.

"Did you—?" was interrupted by, "I did try, love. But the bugger wasn't taking offers under a thousand."

A muttered, "Damn!" was answered by a snappy, "They're on the table right in front of you, you blind old barn owl."

Clem meandered over towards James, slightly bow-legged but with a spring in his step. "You've been relegated to the dog-box?" the older man quipped, adjusting his glasses on his nose.

"These two are good company." James sunk his fingers into the thick fur of Wingers ruff, warmed by the outdoor gas heater.

The evening was cooling off sharply—still and crisp.

"Only if they judge you fit for the job." Clem grinned.

"My brother and I had a kelpie-cross when we were kids." James could remember Blue's face, clear as if it were yesterday; all-seeing eyes and a speckled white muzzle. She'd come with the farm, and had made the shift from Canada bearable. "Kept us out of trouble on the farm."

"Is that so? Took you for a city-fella. Boys and dogs are a good mix. Both need a good run and a firm hand. I bred these two myself."

"Did you?" That was a surprise. "Beautiful dogs. Is that a sideline, or your main focus?"

"Run sheep, mostly."

"Right." James knew sheep. He could talk bovine too, at a pinch, but he knew sheep better. "What breed?"

All the while he kept Clem talking about his farm, James watched Adele. She was wrapped in a pale blue cardigan now, holding the baby, cuddling into her and sniffing the hair on her dark head. She was also chuckling at Saffy's antics. Handstands and wonky cartwheels, funny faces and little ditties to entertain Ruby. A lump formed in James' throat as his mind touched on little Rosetta.

She'd have been five years old now, if she'd lived.

The thought threatened to climb up and choke him.

Daniel abandoned his post at the outside pizza oven and came to join the men over with the dogs, striking up a conversation with Clem about a hunting trip they had planned next month. He turned to James, ostensibly playing host by including him. "Do you enjoy hunting?"

James shrugged and met the man halfway. "I like fishing."

Clem chuckled. "A man after my own heart. Fishing's more to my liking, too."

James wasn't aware their conversation was being monitored until he heard Adele bark a single laugh from her newly appointed station beside the pizza oven. "Ha! James would no more go hunting than climb Mount Everest," she called out, levelling a loaded pizza bat at him. "No dry-cleaners."

James stiffened, then looked down at the tailored clothes he'd taken care to protect with the coveralls earlier. He hadn't been sure how formal to go with the dinner invitation, so had played it safe.

Was that how Adele saw him? Lost without a well-pressed shirt? He'd never given her reason to believe otherwise, he supposed, and the omission didn't sit very well.

Ignoring Adele's disparagement, James turned back to Clem and Daniel, lowering his voice a little. "I was never keen on hunting roos. Seemed to me they had more right to be there than I did." He'd immigrated to Australia at seven, so was new blood to the ancient continent. "We shot rabbits, but we couldn't eat them." James studied his hands, still flecked with paint even after a decent scrub. "Myxomatosis," he added by way of explanation.

Clem cleared his throat. "Hell of a disease, that."

James and his brother had spent their hard earned pocket money on live ammunition. More to put the poor little buggers out of their misery than hunting for sport. The grey-pelted leporidae had been well sick with the disease, pustulated and bloody.

Even now, the thought turned James' stomach.

He looked up, catching Clem's eye as he swallowed. "I hear the deer and boar over here are good eating, though."

"Yep. Too right," Clem agreed wholeheartedly. "Cured and cooked right, bush tucker beats it all."

"A deer fills a freezer," Poppy added her two cents worth,

twisting around in her chair beside the nearby table to smile at him. She'd taken ownership of Ruby now, and had wrapped a blanket around both herself and her grandchild to ward off the evening chill. "Takes the strain off families financially."

"Of course." The more James thought about it, the more it made sense. "Do you like venison, Saff?" He turned to include his stepdaughter in the conversation. She was lying on the grass, trying to prove to Ruby by example just how easy it was to roll over.

Saffy pushed up onto her elbows and wrinkled up her nose. "I guess it's okay in sausages with Aunt Poppy's plum sauce. I like pork better."

Right. Wild pork. How hard could it be? A slab of meat would be the antithesis of an 'ostentatious' gift.

"Pepperoni and Hawaiian are done," Adele announced. "Let's head inside to eat, it's getting cold out here."

James had been expecting the third degree from Adele's wider family, and he wasn't disappointed in the end. On the pretext of showing him the gym shed, and the half-finished in-ground pool, Daniel took James aside after dinner to ask him what the hell he was doing in Wānaka.

"I had some business with a couple of the wineries, and I came to see Saffy." That was the safe answer, but James was far beyond the safe-zone now. "Both Adele and Saffy," he reiterated clearly.

He'd come for his family. Let Daniel take whatever he wanted from that.

"As you can probably guess, I'm not a fan." Daniel laid the statement bare as he folded his considerable arms across his considerable breadth, and stood with a wide stance. "Adele took a long time to adjust, being back here. You must've realised how hard it would be for her to go back to solo-parenting. It took you five long years to show up. Why now?"

James took a cooling breath, pissed off Daniel felt the need to assert dominance, but unwilling to show it. He was also gaining a grudging admiration for this man who was backing his cousin, one hundred percent.

"I was tied up, before."

"Yeah." Daniel snorted derisively. "Sounds like you spent most of your marriage in that state."

"I was running a company." James managed to hold his temper in check and feign an almost bored tone, refusing to be intimidated by the rugby player, or his reputation.

"Much to Adele's unhappiness. That speaks volumes for your priorities." Daniel's verdict landed like a fist in James' solar plexus, winding him before creeping lower to settle as a knot in his gut.

Daniel wasn't wrong. James had come to the same conclusion after Adele's departure.

"You had your chance. Why don't you leave them be, now." Adele's cousin added another verbal punch with a softness that did nothing to dispel the underlying sadism.

James had fucked up—been a fool to let his relationship with Adele falter, thinking they had all the time in the world to make things right.

He should've been Adele's rock, her foundation, but instead he'd let her go. And now there was an unscalable chasm wedged between them.

"Looks like you can afford to keep yourself well enough," Daniel continued dryly when James remained silent, "but you left your wife and stepdaughter high and dry. I don't know what kind of divorce settlement you call that, and as Adele won't discuss it, I have to assume you had a prenup that cut them off."

"No prenup. Adele got half." Admittedly it'd come very close to being half of nothing—their Sydney house mortgaged to the hilt to refloat a floundering Montague Holdings. But James had managed to salvage what he could, pulling the company back from the brink of extinction to sell it. It'd been a decent sum after the Chinese buyout had come into effect, and if Adele chose to live relatively frugally, she'd never have to work again.

"Like hell. Adele's one proud mother, and she's worked her knuckles to the bone to give Saffy a decent life here. Did you know she holds down three jobs? Cleaning, managing properties, and legal work. That's three jobs too many for a mother trying to raise a kid on her own." Daniel stepped forward to angle a finger towards James' chest with a narrowed stare, and it was suddenly clear how much underlying anger Adele's cousin was holding back by the struggle on his face. "Saffy calls you Dad, but that's a name reserved for people who give a damn shit. Not once every two years, but every bloody day. She deserves better. They both do."

James didn't have to be told Saffy and Adele deserved the best. Did Daniel think he wasn't aware of that—hadn't tried to set it all to rights?

What kind of monster had Adele portrayed him as to her family?

8

WHANGAONO - DICE

With which games of chance are played.

After setting cups out on the farmhouse bench, Adele flicked on the kettle and hunted around for the lemon-infused green tea Kana and Obāchan favoured. The kitchen was large, the pine table by the patio doors still carrying the spoils of a successful family pizza night.

She found the box of tea hiding under a discarded tea-towel, and wished every mystery in her life were as easy to solve.

If only…

Adele turned with a start when she heard the hall door open and close, bringing with it a murmur of voices from the lounge. She'd been daydreaming, gazing out through the window above the butler's sink at the mānuka scrub, painted silver by the moonlight.

But it wasn't Obāchan entering the kitchen on the hunt for her delayed tea. It was James.

Adele watched warily as her ex-husband stalked towards her, clearly wound up by something Daniel had stirred up. Her cousin's direct manner had a habit of rubbing people up the wrong way.

James' demeanour struck Adele as a little unhinged—an unusual look for a man who was always in control. She bit her lip to cover her smirk.

"Why Wānaka?" James shot at her.

"What?"

"Why did you choose this place, hours away from your family in Dunedin? Your sister? Your mum?"

Her amusement dissolved.

She hadn't been able to face them, day in and day out. The questions. The failure. The defeat.

"It was safe, and far from you," she answered with honesty—though it emerged sounding flat, and somewhat heartless. "It was a new start, and Daniel made sure we never wanted for anything."

"That cuts, Dell."

"Why, because *you* want to be the one to pay for everything?"

"No, because you're deliberately trying to bait me."

"Get over yourself. Daniel's family."

"That's all he's ever been to you? Your cousin, or something more?"

"It's none of your goddamn business who anyone is to me!" Adele's voice rose along with her temper. "And I have signed divorce papers to *prove* it."

"I never wanted the bloody divorce!" James stopped walking and dug his fingers into his hair. With his arms akimbo like that, he looked almost vulnerable.

Adele spun away, annoyed with both his accusatory tone and the view out the patio door. The love-seat James and Saffy had painted together. She'd have to deal with seeing that on a daily basis, and be reminded how he'd looked in overalls, all scruffy and enthused.

"You haven't touched your divorce settlement."

"How the *hell* would you know that?" She snapped back to face James. The reproof in his eyes was as clear as the finger-tracks through his hair. "That's my own private business!"

"Daniel confirmed it."

"Bloody *interfering*—"

"And your annual statement turned up in my mail."

"Addressed to *me*! You opened it? That's tampering with something you have *no* right to. That should've been forwarded to my P.O. Box along with the rest of my post!"

James shrugged. "No doubt. What I want to know is, why? You want to forget so much, you won't take what's rightfully yours?"

"Rightfully mine!" Adele scoffed. "You never let me work. None of it was *mine*."

"We were married, in every respect. To have and to hold—"

"Through depression and infidelity," Adele interrupted tritely.

James' lips thinned into a white line. "Don't try to pin that line on me. I failed you in many ways as a partner, but I was faithful to you, one-hundred percent." His voice was dangerously quiet, but Adele chose to ignore it. Perhaps James hadn't changed so much, and perhaps she wanted to have this blown out in the open once and for all.

"I *heard* you making a date with Tiffany the day before I left for Katie's wedding," she hissed the words. "So there's really no point in denying it ever happened."

James' eyes narrowed and he stepped swiftly towards her again, covering the last few metres in milliseconds. Reading the play, Adele scooted around the kitchen bench—manoeuvring to keep the central island between them and James directly opposite, no matter which way he moved.

"You *heard* me? That's impossible, Dell, because that *never happened*."

James lurched again, and she evaded.

"Stop *calling* me that! My name is Adele. You don't get to have a special name for me, because you revoked 'special' when you treated me like an imbecile and slept with your assistant!"

James lent across the bench top and deliberately planted his fingers down one by one, widespread, like the roots of a mangrove. "*Dell*, Dell, *Dell*, Dell, *Dell*," he mocked her with a chanting singsong lilt.

"You're behaving like a bloody five-year-old."

"*I'm* behaving like a five-year-old? You're the one telling tall tales to make yourself feel better about walking out on me when the going got tough. It'll be unicorns and mermaids next."

"I didn't *walk out*. I went to my sister's wedding—which you may recall you were *also* invited to, but never bothered to show up for!"

"It was an unavoidable clash. I apologised." James grated the words out.

He'd resumed stalking her around the kitchen island with eyes as green as a feral cat, and was changing direction swiftly to try and catch her out.

Adele took great care to counter his every move, adrenaline pumping.

"That makes it alright? You *apologised*?" she retorted. "My only sister's wedding, and you ditched me for a honeymoon flight to Asia with that silicone stick-insect. How *could* you?"

James growled, and Adele realised an instant too late that there was another, much more efficient way to reach her.

Over.

James leapt the countertop in one swift movement, his hand braced like a farmer clearing a fence, and had her up against the pantry door before she could even squeak.

Her upper arms were in James' unrelenting grip, and his body wedged her in without compromise. There was no escaping the pure passion on his face.

"I was trying to save my father's company from the dogs. *Not* fucking around with my P.A.!" James' face was right up in hers, and Adele had nowhere to look but into his eyes. The usual leafy-green was replaced by a raging ocean storm.

"Don't!" She wasn't afraid of James' uncharacteristic show of temper, but was severely pissed off with his vice-like hold, and the way her body was responding to his proximity.

Nerve endings singing, skin buzzing... Heart rate through the roof.

James laughed. Just a single bark, without humour. "Don't what? Don't *touch* you?" He drew her up until she was on tippy-toes, then pressed his forehead against hers in a forced hongi. "Don't *feel* anything for you?" His voice softened. "You *destroyed* me, Dell." He enunciated each word, torment clear, before bringing his mouth down hard on hers.

No mercy. No leeway. No relent.

Nor did Adele want any. Her pent up emotion was just as volatile as his, and the way he'd chosen to express himself was goddamn perfect.

She'd show the man destruction.

James' taut body was smack-bang against Adele's as they wrangled for position, and a faint rip denoted the fabric of his shirt had come apart at a strained seam.

Want.

Hands, lips… tongue. The scruff of James' unshaven jaw, foreign against the smoothness of her own, pushed Adele over the edge of self-preservation. Her low moan of acceptance was immediately reciprocated—the ache of not getting what they needed fast enough shared in one unified sound.

She wanted him. God, she wanted him.

Somewhere in the heat, somewhere in the agony of letting fly with both body, and deep-seated betrayal, Adele became aware of a soft click.

The patio door.

"You okay, Adele?" Daniel's cool stare slid from Adele to James, then back again, assessing the situation in seconds flat.

Adele was up against the pantry door, both legs wrapped around her ex-husband's hips, with one hand in his hair and the other thrust aggressively through the buttons of his shirt.

Uh-oh.

"Yeah," she finally croaked, shamefaced, unhitching her ankles.

James re-adjusted his grip on Adele's butt and let her toes slide down to meet the floor, but his eyes never left her face.

Adele came back down to earth gently, not entirely convinced it was the same planet she'd lifted off from moments earlier. Neither was she particularly clear on who'd been destroying whom, though she recognised this form of detonation all too well.

Almost instantaneous, just like in the past, but today the perfect storm of past love, hurt, and loss had swung the weathervane directly towards cyclone warning.

A warning they'd both ignored.

If Daniel hadn't just walked in…? Heaven only knew.

Adele groaned. She should've been more than aware it was inadvisable to go within a mile of James and his bloody magical lips. What *had* she been thinking?

Not that she'd been offered an iota of choice, to be fair.

At least she wasn't the only one affected. James' eyes were

dark with lust, the familiar bulge thrusting into her belly was *not* his belt buckle, and he hadn't quite gotten his breath back either.

She slid her palm off James' pec—hardened nipple, muscular plane—and eased her hand out of his shirt.

"Just discussing old times," she murmured, registering belatedly she was verbalising to an empty doorway.

Daniel had gone.

"But we're all done now," she added for James' benefit.

James slid his hands to her hips, clenching her tight against himself for one last, agonisingly hot heartbeat, before she was suddenly freed.

He was looking down at her, and for once, no matter how hard she tried, she couldn't fathom his expression.

Maybe she couldn't beat him at poker, after all.

James had arranged to take Saffy to her seven-a-side training game the next day, and out for a treat afterwards. Saturday mornings were Adele's sleep-in day, her own particular form of indulgence, though it was usually Daniel, Clem, or Poppy helping on sports duty, not her confounding ex-husband.

Any minute now, James would be turning up on her front porch, and she'd only just crawled out of bed.

Crap.

Still in her nightie, Adele heard James pull up the drive. She scrambled to make herself presentable, yanking on leggings and dragging her curls into a quick ponytail. Catching sight of herself in the mirror by the front door, she immediately turned back to the hooks in the hall, covering the slogan on her sleepwear with a cardigan.

Saffy loved choosing the cheesiest quotes.

Adele argued with herself, even as she slid her arms into the cheap merino knock-off. Why should she care what James made of it? But touting, *'I believe in LUV!'* after last night's lip-lock was definitely a step further than she was willing to go.

All she'd proven by kissing James back, as opposed to kneeing him in the family jewels, was that they were still volatile. Nothing more, nothing less.

Mark it up as a dodgy bit of experimentation.

With their history, and the type of man James was, keeping away from him on a physical and emotional level was an absolute no-brainer. The man could *not* be trusted.

And neither could she, apparently.

He'd soon be out of her hair. She could hang her future sanity on that.

On opening the front door, Adele did a double take. She hadn't exactly been expecting a three-piece suit, but neither was she ready for the sight of James in a beanie and puffer jacket. He looked comfortable, if a bit rough around the edges—still unshaven and sporting mud on his walking boots.

"You're wearing jeans," she noted with some bewilderment, wrapping her cardigan a little tighter around herself.

"Yes?"

As Saffy bowled up, sports bag in tow, James beamed a thousand-kilowatt smile at the nine-year-old, white teeth flashing against the spiced-caramel of his stubble. His expression had lost all trace of tension, and Adele took a conscious step backwards into the dim hallway.

Could *not* be trusted.

Him.

Her.

Neither of them.

"All good to go?" James aimed the question towards Saffy as Winger launched herself at him, front paws landing solidly on his midriff. "Down," he suggested calmly, then scrubbed the back of the collie's neck when she complied, curling her densely furred body around his legs.

Jesus, dog. Find a molecule of self-respect.

"Boots, headgear, mouthguard, socks, uniform shorts—?" Adele aimed the checklist at the back of her daughter's head, as Saffy knelt to tie her sneakers.

"Yeah, yeah, Mum. Water bottle, and oranges for half-time. Got it."

Adele didn't need to see Saffy's face to know there was some eye rolling going on.

"Is Winger allowed down at the park?" James turned to Adele.

She hadn't been expecting that.

"On a leash, yes. But she'll take a dip if you let her anywhere near the lake," she warned.

"You swim with her?" James appeared surprised, and Adele was suddenly acutely self-conscious of her shortcomings in the water.

"God, no," she muttered, squaring her shoulders under his scrutiny.

James swam like a fish, while Adele avoided full immersion at all costs.

"It wouldn't want to scare the locals with my lily-white ass," she muttered, before raising her voice to legible levels. "I throw the stick, *she* swims." She turned to grab Winger's lead from the coat rack.

"I meant—"

"It doesn't matter. Here." She shoved the lead towards James and grabbed a dog towel, too.

Winger completely lost the plot at the sight of her lead—favourite item on the entire planet—and began scrabbling around on the wooden floor with ecstatic little yips. She raced up towards Saffy's room, turning on a dime to flash back towards the trio at the front door.

There and back. There and back.

Adele could definitely relate to the motion, she was feeling a bit like that herself.

Saffy and James looked at each other and laughed.

"I guess she's coming too, then," James decided, taking the offered lead and seen-better-days towel. "Thank you." He reached his other hand out and brushed it down Adele's arm in a seemingly casual gesture, his eyes meeting hers.

She stiffened and whipped her arm away smartly, glowering at him with the unspoken message, *hands to yourself.*

There was definitely *not* going to be any more touching.

"Dog-poo bags are in the pod on Winger's collar." Adele took some pleasure in delivering that little aside, and watching it wipe James' smile right off.

9

PUTIPUTI - FLOWER

The precious, the delicate, and the truly colourful.

"So, how is Aussie rules different from rugby?" Saffy licked the icing off her fingers, and James smiled, glad he'd at least made her wash her hands before taking an outdoor seat at the café. She still had a fair amount of mud on her from the game, but her digits looked relatively clean. Even cleaner now she'd sucked on them.

He tried to imagine his mother allowing such behaviour at the table, and couldn't. Isabella would've insisted on a knife and fork, even for a doughnut.

"It's played on an oval field, for one thing, and there are eighteen a side."

"Oval?" Saffy frowned. "Like cricket?"

"Just like cricket," James agreed, as Saffy leaned forward, her elbows on the table. Another no-no in Isabella's strict book-of-etiquette. "I think you'd smash Australian Rules, to be honest. I was incredibly impressed watching you today. You're strong on the ball, quick with it, and can take a solid hit."

The 'hits' had been what crunched him as a parent though. Standing like a useless tit on the sideline, watching as Saffy hurled herself at moving targets, or was felled as she ran. He'd curled his fists in his jacket pockets each time, stomach in knots while he'd waited for her to bounce back up, distinctive fuchsia mouthguard flashing as she grinned.

"Uncle D taught me," Saffy declared proudly. "But he says I'm only allowed to play if I wear headgear."

James looked down into his dark, bitter coffee. "He's a good uncle," he conceded.

"Yep," Saffy agreed staunchly. She had a smear of mud across her cheek that ended at her temple where the headgear would've been, and a hint of crusted blood under one nostril testifying to the bleeding nose she'd received from a random elbow just before full-time. "He's the best. Uncle Cam can build stuff though," she added as a quick aside, perhaps wary of showing a clear favourite. "He rebuilt Poppy's old treehouse up at the farm for me, Levi, and Tobias."

James cast back in his memory. "Cam is Daniel's brother, right? Younger?"

"I don't know." Saffy shrugged. "They're both old."

James barked a laugh. "I guess that makes me old, too?"

"Yeah. *Real* old." Saffy grinned mischievously.

"And Levi and Tobias are…?"

"My cousins. Second cousins." Saffy frowned at him, as if he should know the names. "They live in Dunedin. Levi's three. Tobias just started school, and he's got a little brother, Ethan."

"Right, Tobias and Ethan." James vaguely recalled Saffy's stories about Adele's sister, Katie, coming to stay in Wānaka with her dinosaur-mad little boy. "Katie and Rue's kids. The T-rex and the ballerina, right?"

Which had to make Levi Cam's boy.

"Yeah." Saffy laughed. "Tobias wears a Dorothy the Dinosaur tail most of the time, and Ethan has all my old dress-ups. Fairy tutus are his favourite. Levi is the bossy one. He likes to tell everyone what to do."

One of the café's young staff members slipped out to clear the outdoor tables, and came over when she saw Saffron, flashing a wide grin complete with pretty dimples.

"Hey, Sweet-pea! Long time no see!"

"Hi, Maddie." Saffy turned back to James, and he could see by her smile she genuinely liked the bubbly blonde. "This is Maddie. We hang out sometimes when Mum's out."

James assumed that was Saffy's round-about way of explaining her babysitter.

"James Montague, Saffy's stepfather." He stood to hold out his hand, and Maddie did a coquettish sideways thing with her head as she took it in hers.

"*So* nice to meet you. Adele said you were in town." Maddie giggled, then removed her fingers ever-so-slowly, so the tips stroked James' palm as she turned again to Saffy. "How's it going with Zane?"

"Okay. He asked to meet me at the school disco, and I said yes."

What? Surely it wasn't boys already? Saffy was only nine, for pity's sake!

James must've been glaring, because Saffy chided him under her breath a little huffily. "What! I have friends who are boys."

"Good call, Saff." Maddie gave James a slow-mo wink. "*I* have friends who are boys too. And men." She was laughing as she sauntered off to collect a stack of cups and plates. "You can never have too many friends." She slid James a loaded look before she moved back inside, opening the door with her shapely butt, then rolling through.

"Maddie already has lots of friends, Dad." Saffy sometimes came off as older than her age, and this was one of those times. She eyed him knowingly. "*Loads*."

"Okay, I get the drift." James chuckled a little self-consciously at Saffy's not-so-subtle warn-off. She'd matured so much since he'd last seen her, it was a bit frightening.

Boys. He shuddered.

The skip in age had hit him hard last time, too, when she'd visited Sydney as a seven-year-old. Every two years, he'd taken the measly holidays owing under his contract with the Chinese supercompany, and spent them with Saffy. When Adele had originally relented and allowed Saffy across the Tasman at five years old, James had tried to keep it simple with beach trips and wildlife parks, not knowing how comfortable or relaxed she'd be without her mum. He'd even gone so far as to hire a part-time nanny, just in case.

But by the time Saffy arrived at seven, he'd known for sure he could be more adventurous without any fear of her freaking out. It seemed to be in his stepdaughter's nature to throw herself wholeheartedly into the next unknown, be it a helicopter trip over Kata Tjuta National Park, or drinking cocoa from the campfire billy. She took after her mother in that respect.

James had arranged with the new owners to take Saffy to his childhood farm, and they'd gone bush for a few days. It was a toss up as to who'd enjoyed themselves more.

The cancellation of their biennial summer trip a few months ago had hit him hard, and he knew Saffy had been disappointed, too.

"I've been wondering." Saffy ran a finger across her plate to pick up the last smudges of pink icing, then slid it into her mouth. "What does the 'A' in A.J. stand for? Mum used to call you A.J.."

"Yes. She did." James was surprised Saffy remembered that. She would've been four... Almost five? "My full name's Aksel James Montague."

Though Adele had reinvented his unremarkable initials, informing him loftily they actually meant 'Adele's James,' and always would. The memory of that ownership, and the love lost, still had the power to sting.

"Your real name is *Axel*? Like a wheel connector-thingy in Lego?" Saffy frowned, clearly unimpressed. "You *so* don't look like an Axel."

He shrugged. "Not spelt the same, but yes. When I started school in boondocks, Australia, it became clear it was better to blend in, not stick out—so I went with James. Aksel's not a common name Downunder, but James was tolerable."

"I can't even *pretend* to blend in," Saffy lamented, and James experienced a shot of remorse for speaking so glibly.

Saffy had told him about the trouble at school last year, the racist taunts and snide asides about the colour of her skin. The school had dealt with it, but the fact it had occurred in the first place boiled James' blood.

"Why would you want to? You stick out in all the best ways."

"Ha! You're just saying that because you're biased." Saffy was smiling at least.

"Well, of course I'm biased. I can't help that. You're the best nine-year-old winger I've ever seen play."

"Almost ten."

"Almost ten," James agreed mildly.

"*Waaait* a minute." Saffy was immediately wise to him. "Am I the *only* nine-year-old winger you've ever seen play?"

"That too." He dodged a light thump from Saffy and stood, laughing. "Let's go. I told your mum I'd get you home by one."

"I like the colour of this car better." Saffy touched a hand to the 4x4's paintwork as they stepped up to it, and climbed in. "Mouldy green."

"Charming."

James smiled. *Mouldy green*. Saffy had a refreshing way of stripping things down to their visual elements.

He liked the colour of this car better, too. Though the grey sedan he'd hired to drive across from Dunedin had served its purpose, buying the second-hand four-wheel-drive was a much more practical idea. He could garage it when he wasn't around, and go off-road anytime he needed to. The more he explored the back roads around the lake, the more he wanted to.

"How would you feel if I was able to see you more often?" he asked as he settled in the driver's seat.

Saffy swivelled towards him, her seatbelt poised to click. "*How* often?"

"Maybe once a fortnight?" He cleared his throat before ploughing on. "I mean, it'd be more for me than for you. I get that. Your mum's made a great home for you both here, and I know you've got everything you need."

"I miss you, Dad." Saffy said exactly what James needed to hear, reaching one hand over to squeeze his arm painfully hard, digging narrow fingertips in.

Had she gotten more empathetic, or was he just incredibly see-through? James couldn't be sure, nor could he be prouder of the person Saffy was growing into. Strong, funny, and uncommonly caring.

"I miss you, too. So what do you think? Once a fortnight?"

"Do we have to get Mum's permission?"

James' blithe optimism took a solid hit, because therein lay the snag. Adele would never agree.

Saffy offered him a cheeky grin. "We'd better ask for once a *week*, first."

"So we've got some leeway to negotiate?"

"Exactly."

"I like your style, Saffron Fergus." He grinned and started the engine. "You've got serious smarts."

"No. I just know my mum."

A car pulled up the drive in the early afternoon, and Adele peeked out the open front door, knowing it would be James, but needing to check anyway.

He'd exchanged cars at some stage, and was now driving a more robust looking 4x4, liberally splattered with muck. Unfolding himself, James moved to stand in the V of the open car door, lounging his arms on the roof.

She hadn't fussed or primped the interior of the cottage. Just the usual weekend spruce-up interspersed with some yoga stretches Kana had been teaching her. Well, maybe she'd indulged in a *little* more nervous tidying than usual, and perhaps she wouldn't have been wearing her new fitted athletics top if she hadn't been expecting her ex.

When James spotted Adele in the doorway, the grin he'd been sharing with Saffy slowly left his face, like the batteries on a torch giving out.

"One nine-year-old, pretty much in one piece. Only slightly grubby round the edges," James called across the space between them with a hint of his old humour. "And one border collie, in similar condition."

Saffy walked around the nose of the car to squeeze James in a goodbye hug, and he slung an arm around his ex-stepdaughter's shoulders as he handed over Winger's lead.

Both child and dog looked totally spent, but happy.

Adele had to turn away when Saffy looked up, and James kissed her forehead. There was so much tenderness and understanding between them, it almost hurt to watch.

"Thanks, Dad. That was fun." Then Saffy was running up the path toward her, Winger prancing alongside.

"Yes. Thank you, James," Adele added more formally, raising a hand in a clear farewell.

Better not to get any closer.

James must've had a similar thought, because he didn't attempt to move either.

"Why don't you call Dad A.J. anymore?"

"Oh." Adele hesitated before she answered, trying to drag Saffy through the front door by the arm, out of earshot. "He's not my A.J. now, sweetheart," she muttered.

"He's someone else's A.J.?" In contrast, Saffy spoke at regular volume—loud and carrying.

"Quite possibly, yes." Adele lowered her voice, barely whispering as she glanced in James' direction, hoping he was too far away to hear. "That would be his business though, not mine."

"Because of the divorce." Rather than allowing Adele to hurry her, Saffy dumped her boots and bag and turned to wave at James, blowing him a kiss from each hand.

That had always been their custom and it tore at Adele, because although Saffy had only been a preschooler when they'd split, she still remembered the routine and insisted on doing it.

Adele didn't wait to watch James pretend to catch the airborne affection and plant it on his cheeks. She refused to see that.

"Yes. Mostly because of the divorce," she muttered, stepping into the hall.

She could hear James' big-tyred rental backing out, pinging stones as Saffy swung inside with Winger.

"And because of Rosetta," Saffy stated matter-of-factly.

"Mmm-hmm." Adele couldn't speak through the sudden lump in her throat, so the hum of agreement would have to do. Tears smarted, but were blinked away as quickly as they formed.

Rosetta. Their sweet dream that never was.

Adele had told Saffy the honest truth about the miscarriage when it happened. There hadn't seemed to be anything to gain by hiding it from the then three-and-a-half-year-old. After all, it had been Saffy's loss too.

A little sister.

But she didn't realise Saffy had held onto the memory all this time. Unless James had brought it up with her recently, without Adele's say-so? Highly unlikely, but not out of the question.

Dropping to the floor, Saffy began rolling around and goofing off with Winger, until it became difficult to see where girl ended, and dog began.

Adele began to feel distinctly like a third wheel in her own home.

James and Saffy were thick as thieves on the phone, arranging to see each other every spare moment. James had picked Saffy up from school on Monday, helped paint the feature wall of her room on Wednesday evening, then stayed on afterwards for dinner.

Admittedly, Adele had okayed everything, defrosting a decent sized slab of salmon and harvesting the last head of lettuce from the veggie patch with the sole intention of inviting him to eat with them. But she was merely being convivial for Saffy's sake.

Initially, James seemed as hesitant as Adele, nervous of tripping over ex-marital grenades. But he agreed to stay for the simple meal, all the same.

So far, he'd adhered to Adele's dagger-eye rules of physical engagement—strictly no touching of any kind—and she began to relax a little more. This was something she could pat herself on the back about. It was commendable to be civil while occupying the same room as an ex, let alone sharing a few laughs over a family meal.

She deserved a gold star, and another glass of this excellent Pinot Noir.

Saffy was over the moon her everyday life was overlapping with her stepdad's, and that should be payment enough for Adele. But the nine-year-old was also insistent on a board game after dinner, which her mother was less enthused about.

"Mum hates board games," Saffy complained.

"I remember." James leaned in toward Saffy, as if imparting a secret of great importance. "She's a particularly bad sport when losing at Monopoly."

"Don't talk about me like I'm not here. I can hear every word, and it's not doing anything for your cause. If I pull out, there's only two of you, and what are you going to play then?" Adele flicked the light off in the kitchen and wandered through to the lounge with her wine glass topped up. "Another for you?" She held the half-full bottle towards James, and he took it.

"No, thanks. Nice drop though. Local?" James appeared to be studying the Lake Taimana label in minute detail, chewing on the inside of his cheek.

"Very. Next property on from Clem and Poppy." And usually way beyond Adele's price range. But this one had been a gift from a legal client, who happened to own the winery.

"Ludo!" Saffy was on her knees by the bookcase, pulling out her game of choice with aplomb.

"*Nooo.*" Adele groaned, pulling her feet up under herself as she commandeered a corner of her slightly shabby sofa. "Anything but that!"

"*Any*thing?" James teased, his hand reaching around Saffy's shoulder to tap on the single pack of cards.

Adele cleared her throat. "Not cards," she flustered, turning her face a little aside and pretending to peruse the meagre range of board-games herself.

Her first-ever game of Strip Poker had been with James—an evening she'd never forget. Even now, years later, she couldn't pick up a Jack-of-hearts without flushing.

"Scrabble?" James offered instead, all false innocence.

Saffy obligingly pulled the word game out next.

James and Adele had played it as a date-alternative when they'd first met, because Adele had been pretty much immobilised at the time with a sprained ankle, and bored out of her tree. She'd been more than a little dubious when her Aussie-elevator-man had come calling, with a large bouquet of lilies and a board game tucked under his arm. But James had managed to keep it on friendly terms, issuing zero pressure, and she'd liked him more due to the impression the ball was totally in her court.

The man's unchanging resolve when presented with the

evidence Adele was a single mother on his second visit was another major point in his favour. But it was his willingness to play along with her silly games, and his lack of prowess at Strip Poker on his third visit that had expedited how fast their relationship had careened forward.

All that toned, tanned skin...

Their one-on-one Scrabble games had been fully clothed though, and involved fierce rivalry, with hotly contested rules and stipulations. James had a tendency to hold onto his high scoring pieces, pulling last-minute miracles out of nowhere, and extending on existing words to utilise triple word scores.

He also cheated. Adele was sure of it. He made up scientific words and botanical names that *sounded* feasible, but were inconclusive when looked up.

"Bring it on." Adele met James' challenge with a hard stare, rising to grab the Oxford Dictionary off the shelf. She plopped the hefty tome in his lap on the way back to her seat. "But if it's not in there, you don't get the points. Plus, no looking up words *before* your turn." She'd show the cocky Aussie.

James won. Convincingly.

Adele didn't know quite how he did it, seeing as English wasn't even his first language, but he was miles ahead of herself and Saffy right from the get go with 'zygotic,' which he lengthened to 'polyzygotic' on the next turn. Glad became 'gladiolus'—which James insisted was the singular form of gladioli. Squid became 'squidgygate'—a phone scandal involving Princess Diana, apparently. And if James' quietly stoic opinion was to be believed, zap was able to be transformed into 'zapodinae'—a Chinese jumping mouse.

"You must've cheated," Adele muttered, admittedly without much conviction, as Saffy packed all the pieces back into the box under an hour later.

"No," James returned softly. "I didn't cheat. I never have, and never would."

Adele met his serious eyes across the coffee table and swallowed the last centimetre of her wine in a single, unladylike gulp.

Okay, so they clearly weren't talking about board-games anymore.

Her fingers were shaking when she returned her glass to the coffee table.

Adele could no longer be sure on the infidelity front. Not after James' level of conviction on Friday night. It had shaken her, his uncompromising refusal to shoulder any wrongdoing of that nature, making her re-hash every detail in her head and second guess herself.

No longer comfortable sitting directly across from him, Adele rose again to put both of their glasses in the kitchen sink, her cheeks hot. "Time to get ready for bed now, Saffy."

Saffy moaned about it, totally missing the undercurrent flowing between her parents in her self-absorbed state, which was probably a good thing. James responded by getting ready to leave, making it ten times easier to convince Saffy she wouldn't be missing out on anything.

Another trait in his favour was his ability to read the room.

It had beed a lot easier to hate James when he wasn't around. Sure, he'd been constantly underfoot this past week, but essentially proving himself to be a decent human being. It made Adele feel a little better about her initial fall for him, something she'd beaten herself up about after the breakup.

Though she didn't have to condone how fast, or how completely, she'd let her infatuation for James take over, she could admit he presented well. Articulate and confident, he was smoking-hot then, and he was smoking-hot now.

If she hadn't known the man back-to-front already, it'd be easy to go all gooey over the way he looked and smelt.

But she did know him.

Saffy had gone to brush her teeth and hop into her P.J.s, and James was hovering by the bookcase, fingers trailing along the spines of the paperbacks.

"I was wondering if I could borrow a book?" James' hand came to rest on one, but Adele couldn't see which, as his wrist hid the title. "I started a story the other day and keep finding myself wondering…" he trailed off.

"What happens in the end?"

"Yes." James turned and smiled, but the light didn't quite reach his eyes. "What happens in the end."

"They get together, regardless of which one you pick." Adele gestured, including all bookcase occupants with a sweeping hand. "Guaranteed."

Knowing exactly what James thought of her favourite genre, she steeled herself against the inevitable flash of humour—or negativity.

"Really?"

"Yes, really. That's the whole point. Reader satisfaction. Probably not something you'd enjoy." Adele moved to draw the book out of James' hand, but he didn't release it, instead increasing the strength of his grip. She frowned. "Didn't you once call my romance books fluffy-love?"

James did an uncomfortable little half-shrug and looked away. "I was misguided. Preaching before practicing. Jerk move."

Aksel James Montague, taking the low road?

Adele hesitated before conceding, "Well, as long as you've seen the error of your ways."

James chuckled, the warmth of their shared humour suffusing a section under Adele's ribs—a part that had been in the chiller for a very long time.

Finally getting a look at the title, Adele wrinkled up her nose.

"Great author, but not my favourite trope, that one. Love at first sight always seems a bit of a stretch of the imagination. A bit ridiculous."

"I'd have to disagree." James' voice was soft and velvety. "That's the bit I could relate to best."

Adele stared at him for an agonising heartbeat.

For her, love for James had grown over time, like ivy over a wall. Just a few tendrils at first, then a rush of summer growth, until the entire masonry was covered in lush leafiness.

It had only taken one drop of poison at the root to kill off the whole damn plant.

"Mum!" Saffy called from the bathroom, her voice echoing down the hall. "We're out of toothpaste!"

Oh, that's right. So they were.

Adele huffed out a sigh and moved toward the archway. "Borrow whatever you like," she offered over her shoulder to James, grabbing the kitchen shears on her way. "But I want it back after you're done."

In the narrow, communal bathroom, Saffy stood in her pyjamas squeezing the toothpaste tube for dear life, with very little to show for her effort.

"Here." Adele took the emaciated tube from her daughter and cut it across the midriff. "Jiggle the head of your toothbrush around in there and you'll get enough. Payday tomorrow. I'll pick some up on the way to work."

"Tha' wa' fun tonigh'." Saffy spoke with the toothbrush in her mouth, eyes earnest in the oval mirror.

"Yeah," Adele admitted, then kissed the back of her daughter's head, drawing in the familiar scent.

She only knew two people who indulged Saffy with hints throughout a game; keeping the competitive nine-year-old's score up, while being subtle enough to let her think it was her own skill holding her there. The second cousin Saffy affectionately called 'Uncle D,' and James, her 'dad.' Both males were forces of nature, with more in common than either of them were ever likely to admit.

James wouldn't be in New Zealand for much longer, which was probably a good thing. It wouldn't be smart to get too used to having him around. After all, he'd told her he'd be leaving after the weekend, and it was Wednesday already.

Soon, they'd all be getting back to some semblance of normal.

10

KŌRERO - NARRATIVE

A story spoken, and heard.

"Adele. Fancy seeing you here." If James was going for a nonchalant tone, he missed the mark, coming off as tongue-in-cheek as he jumped into step beside her.

It was Thursday, so once again Adele was racing to her after-work counselling session without much leeway in her schedule. And for a second time, James was flagging her down on the street, making her heart jump.

"*You*," Adele muttered. Refusing to stop and chat, she continued to breeze along. But James didn't seem at all put off, and kept pace. "Did you leave a tube of toothpaste and a bottle of wine on my doorstep this morning?" A very expensive Lake Taimana Pinot Noir reserve.

"What if I did?"

She glanced his way. "I don't want anything more from you. No presents. No nothing."

"You're upset about a tube of toothpaste and a replacement bottle for the one I helped drink?" One of James' eyebrows twitched upward.

"No. *Yes*." Adele took a deep breath in through her nose and attempted to attach all her tension to it before blowing it out between pursed lips. "A little bit."

"The toothpaste was for Saffy." James grinned. "Can't have her teeth crumbling, and falling out."

It was one of Adele's more ingrained stress dreams, as James well knew. So convincing, she used to make him check they were all still present and accounted for before she could go back to sleep again.

He'd never once complained about being woken up to reassure her.

"Right. Hmm." She paused again, trying to find some semblance of manners amongst her mixed emotions. "Well, then. Thank you." Maybe it came off as grudging, but that's all she had to offer today. Work had been a slog, chasing up signatures, re-issuing unpaid invoices, and verifying bank accounts—the worst part of admin.

She was beat.

Truth? Her heart had melted a little at the sight of the lonely grocery items on her welcome mat in the morning chill. It had wedged a lump in her throat to imagine James sneaking it there without setting off the dog.

Someone looking out for her—for both of them. Someone on their team, listening in to the background noise and making their day run a little smoother. Making it all seem a little easier.

"Anytime." In contrast to hers, James' voice was soft.

"You said you'd be gone after the weekend, and it's now *Thurs*day." Adele didn't bother looking at James sideways this time, just kept her focus front and centre.

"No. I said I'd be gone sometime after the weekend. As it turns out, work negotiations stalled, so I decided to take a slightly longer break."

"How *much* longer?" Adele lost the fight with herself, sneaking another look towards him, then away. James still hadn't shaved, and a weeks worth of auburn beard, with hints of ginger, was tantalisingly different on his chiselled bone structure. "You need to give Saffy plenty of notice so she can prepare herself."

And Adele was getting fidgety with her own need to know, growing daily.

James paused. "Sometime after the weekend," he finally answered, exactly as he had more than a week ago.

Adele stopped stock-still. "You mean this weekend coming, right?" She turned to stare, seeking something concrete in James' demeanour.

He always had a solid plan, he was the quintessential man-on-a-mission. But instead of putting her mind at ease, his cryptic little half-smile made her belly flutter.

"Maybe."

She watched in morbid fascination as James reached one hand up to worry at his earlobe for a moment. Not willing to outright lie, but not being entirely honest with her either.

"Longer?"

"Perhaps." His eyes were crinkling at the corners, ever so slightly.

"God, you're infuriating! Wānaka is *my* place, right? *My* home. And you're treading all over my toes on a daily basis. I've been *more* than accommodating—"

"Oh, *more* than," James interrupted in agreement, and she couldn't tell if he was being sardonic or not.

"Are you actively trying to piss me off?"

Because it was definitely working.

James' hint of a smile turned into a grin, and Adele had the urge to shove him. Hard.

She fisted her hands, all too aware of how sexually charged any form of touching was between the two of them. It had always been that way, right from the get go, but the pent up emotion due to having him right up in her grill over the past eight days had been building to a crescendo.

Especially after that bone-melting kiss.

"I was hoping you'd have a minute to talk."

"No. I don't." Remembering her objective, Adele began to hurry forward again, irritated all over again by James' singular ability to pull her off focus. "Are you stalking me?"

"Of course not. I just happened to be having a coffee, and you walked past." James stated evenly, pointing in the vague direction of Wanderers Café behind them.

Wait a damn minute…

"At exactly the same time and place as *last* Thursday?" Adele added some saccharine to her tone.

"Exactly." James wasn't even trying to hide the fact he was laughing at her, now.

As she stopped at the commercial building and went to open the door, he moved to stand slightly in front, blocking her way.

"I'd like your permission to visit with Saffy on a regular basis." James' eyes still carried the punch of his humour, but his lips weren't smiling anymore.

Adele narrowed her eyes. "What's your definition of 'regular?' Because right now it's looking a lot like hourly."

"After this initial break, if I were to come back to Wānaka once a week, could Saffy stay with me?"

"Stay with you where?"

James moved a touch uncomfortably. "Ah, wherever I was booked in? A hotel?"

"No!" Adele shook her head as well, in case the spoken word hadn't conveyed her vehemence strongly enough. "Nine-year-olds need *stability*, James. Not pie-in-the-sky." She discounted the idea with a flick of her hand. "And the next school holidays are booked up with family-time in Dunedin, so if you were thinking of taking her on that make up trip to Australia, you'll have to wait till spring, or the summer holidays in December."

"One night a week, always at the same property," James counter-offered. "Always during term-time, and not interfering with school. Two weeks over the summer holidays to travel to Oz." He scratched at the fuzz on his jaw. "I know I don't have any right to ask… But I'm asking."

Adele stared at her ex for a long moment, trying to figure out if he was for real.

"Ongoing?"

James nodded. He looked serious enough, unblinking, like he should be wearing a three-piece suit to carry out these negotiations rather than jeans and a cable-knit sweater.

"I don't have time for this, seriously." She brushed James off, annoyed it actually sounded like a feasible arrangement—presuming Saffy was keen to go along with it.

"Will you think about it?"

Adele made a noncommittal sound, wishing James would drop the subject. She wasn't nuts about changing anything in her life to suit him, or anyone else. "James? No offence, but I've got a meeting, so you need to get out of my way, now."

James squinted over his shoulder at the signage on the door then back into her face. "What kind of meeting?"

There was a moment's silence, where they simply stared each other down, trying to gauge the other's underlying objective.

"I come to talk to someone here—"

"I can't stop thinking about kissing you again," James slid in at exactly the same time.

"What? Don't say *that*!"

"Why not? It's the truth." James' eyes slid to her mouth. "I wanted to apologise about the way I went about it, though. I hadn't planned… It was too…" He cleared his throat. "Rough."

Adele touched her tongue to her top lip with the memory of that kiss. Not rough exactly, but desperate—out of control. Very un-James-like, in retrospect. Unusual for *both* of them to be totally off-piste.

James groaned, one hand sliding under Adele's elbow to draw her forward.

"You're killing me here. Tell me you want it too, Dell. When I sleep, I dream you're beside me." His voice was ragged. "It's hell waking up."

They stood toe to toe, breathing the same air, Adele shivering when James brought his free hand up to run a featherlight finger down the length of her neck.

She wanted it too.

When her ex had been asleep on her sofa, she'd totally wanted it. He'd smiled at her with paint on his overalls, and she'd wanted it all too much. James could walk all over her and she would *still* want it. That's why she'd had to leave in the first place.

It wouldn't take much to be right up against James, right now. Place her lips on his and take this moment for her own pleasure.

"No." The negation came out breathy, and a smidgen on the wobbly side, but clearly audible.

"Then stop sending me those come-get-me looks," James growled.

"Who, me? I think you must have me confused with someone else."

"Dell—"

"*No*." She was trying to convince herself as much as she was warning James. "This is a really bad idea. *You're* a really bad idea."

James blinked once, his eyes sparking before he dropped her elbow as if it'd scorched his fingertips. He was in the process of taking a step aside when the door behind him swung open.

"Kia ora kōrua! Right on time. And this must be James? Lovely to see you both. I can't tell you how pleased I am that you decided on a joint session, Adele. Ka pai! Good for you!" Fran beamed, waiting until James took the weight of the door for her before striding back down the hall, clearly intending for them both to follow. "Nau mai, haere mai. Come on in."

Intrigued beyond measure, James trailed after Adele and the much more rounded behind of the woman in front.

'Dr Fran Hoani,' according to the signage on her interior office door.

His ex-wife was hissing at him under her breath like an eastern brown snake, disturbed from its sunbath, but James chose to pay no heed. For some reason, Adele was deferring to Dr Hoani and allowing him to sit in on this 'meeting,' though she clearly wasn't enthused by the idea.

Once settled in the snug confines of the desk-less office, it took about ten seconds flat for it to become abundantly clear what kind of tête-à-tête James had just stumbled in on, and he initially felt nothing but deep shock.

Over the time he'd known her, Adele had gone from an open, incredibly gregarious and bubbly personality, to private incarnate—holding her innermost thoughts tightly to her chest. But she bared her soul to this woman on a weekly basis?

No wonder she was all contorted about him bowling in.

Too intrusive. Too invasive.

James didn't know whether to go with the flow or bolt, and was guessing by the haunted expression on Adele's face she was experiencing a similar set of emotions.

"Please call me Fran," Dr Hoani beetled on after their basic introduction. "I feel I should first inform you I know a little about you already, but only with regards to your history with Adele," she continued, appearing to skim over her notes.

Possibly grizzly details she'd written down about their short-lived marriage? Questions to cane him with, should he ever be bold enough to show his face.

"Do you prefer Aksel, or James?" the counsellor wondered aloud.

"James is fine."

"Right. James. I want you to know zero information leaves this room." Dr Fran nailed him squarely between the eyes with a look, and he wasn't sure he liked the mixture of sympathy and doggedness he saw there. "Patient confidentiality is my priority. Forgive me for bolting right in, but we have a limited timeframe. Today we're talking about the loss of Rosetta."

James balked, turning to blink at Adele, who was sitting primly on the very edge of her seat at the other end of the sofa. The room was set up like a mini lounge, and 'Fran' had settled herself in the opposing armchair.

"Are we?" he murmured.

Adele refused to meet his eyes, staring wide-eyed at Dr Fran instead. "Yes," she whispered, crushing her fingers between her knees.

Discussing Rosetta, after six years of deathly silence on the subject, and in front of a total stranger.

"What would you like to know?" James asked mildly, ignoring the urge to jump up and pace.

Taking a leaf out of Adele's book, he angled the question at Dr Fran, careful not to stare too long at the tattoo the woman wore with pride on her chin as he pondered the perfect symmetry of the swirling design.

"James, could you tell Adele, in your own words, how it was for you to lose Rosetta?"

How it *was*? The day he returned home from work to find an unknown neighbour mopping blood off the staircase?

Adele's blood? Saffy's?

He'd panicked, following the trail toward the kitchen, where Adele's cellphone lay on the floor with congealed russet fingerprints smeared across the screen. The dread had risen to clamp his chest in a death grip.

James cleared his throat, placing his hands palm down on his thighs.

"It was hell on Earth."

James had no idea how he got through the counselling session. He went ahead and answered the questions and prompts Dr Fran gave him to the best of his ability, but his voice was far from steady. Possibly due to the fact his head didn't feel like it was on entirely straight.

Rosetta had been fifteen weeks along. Old enough for them to have presumed her out of the danger zone, but too young to be considered a viable foetus, or even stillborn. Adele had named her Rosetta, after her maternal grandmother, Rosa.

James had insisted on seeing his daughter, though he'd been warned the event would be distressing.

Not seeing her would've been worse.

Her name suited her inconceivably tiny frame. Rosetta of the minuscule webbed-fingers and semi-formed butterfly lips. Rosetta furled and compact, like a pale little rosebud.

All they were given from the medical profession was that tests confirmed her to be female, and there was no known reason.

No reason at all.

When Adele woke in the recovery ward, pale and shaky, she kept repeating she was sorry. She'd thought she'd strained her back and gone back to bed after taking Saffy to preschool. But the pain had grown unbearable, and she'd realised too late she was bleeding.

Miscarrying. Haemorrhaging.

That was the one and only instance Adele had been willing to discuss it. By the time she was home again, the door to all personal communication had been padlocked shut. Rather than crowbar it open, or seek help, as James clearly should've done, he'd thrown himself back into his work to blank out the loss and all consuming regret. Trying desperately to save something from the carnage, even if it was just his father's legacy.

He blamed himself. If he'd gotten Adele's messages earlier. If his phone hadn't been turned off for his I.T. negotiation meetings. If he'd been at home with Adele, or taken more notice of how tired she was getting—how run down.

"How horrific for you James. Your baby, gone." Dr Fran finally spoke again, making James realise he'd been silent for some time.

"When they told me Adele was stable, I cried with relief. I still feel guilty about that, because part of me was glad. So much blood..." James had discovered as a boy, if he dug his thumbnails into the soft pads of his forefingers, it gave him something else to concentrate on as he spoke, removing the threat of showing too much emotion. "My father's death was, ah... relatively gory." Gruesome. *Grotesque*. "It reminded me..." His father's words reverberated in his head. *Man up, son. Show weakness and you're fair game.*

"Adele and I have been over this, but you should be made aware too, James. That much blood-loss during a miscarriage is unusual. Not at all common. Some women will have little more than spotting to indicate a loss."

He swallowed. "I immediately assumed the worst."

"What would've been the worst?" Dr Fran pushed for a complete picture.

"Adele." James glanced towards his ex-wife for the first time, having been actively avoiding the confrontation. "Or Saffy."

He was unprepared for the evidence of how his account had affected Adele. She had tear tracks down her face, and her eyes were red-rimmed.

So alone, he almost lost the battle within himself not to reach out and pull her in.

If he could just hold her.

"Adele..." James repeated, stumbling over the concept of her death. Looking back down, he studied the much less agonising view of his own hands, gripped in his lap. "I don't think I could've borne that," he admitted to himself, and the room.

James hadn't realised until much later he'd actually lost his wife that day, too. She may've stayed on for another year of marriage, but after the loss of Rosetta, Adele was no longer with him.

"I loved Rosetta, but she was just a dream. When I said goodbye, she was already cold… and so, so tiny." James paused, gathering himself. "It was my wife I missed the most," he concluded quietly, slanting another look sideways as he felt the cushions on the sofa shift.

Adele was bum-shuffling towards him, her rained-off eye makeup leaving little grey tracks down to her chin. Then she opened her arms and invited him in for a hug.

"Thank you," Adele croaked into his shoulder, arms tightly wrapping around his ribs and hair smelling like a tropical sun-shower.

"For what?" It was hard to get the words past the overwhelming sense of loss gripping his throat, but James knew he hadn't done anything worthy of her thanks.

"For talking. And for loving her too."

"Well, that part was unavoidable. She was half you, wasn't she?"

The counsellor leaned forward, making her armchair creak, and James was surprised to remember there was a third person present. "You mentioned your father's death, James."

"Suicide. Shotgun. He'd just been diagnosed with pancreatic cancer." He parroted off the facts as dispassionately as possible, but still felt Adele stiffen in his arms.

"Ah, I see. Very traumatic. How old—?

"Fifty-one."

"No, James. How old were *you* when your father took his own life?"

Adele pulled back to look at him too, so he had both women staring at him intently.

"Oh." James ran a hand over his eyes, but it didn't erase the vivid picture of the farm shed wall—painted in his father's blood—or the unrecognisable body slumped on the ground. "Eighteen? No, nineteen. I was in university, but home for the term break."

"I would like to discuss this further at some later stage. Your father's death, and its impact on you, but I'm afraid we're out of time."

James' relief was immediate, and he blew out a breath.

Done. Finished.

"Excellent session from you both." Dr Fran wrapped it up. "Te kōrero tino pai. If we could all meet at the same time and place next Thursday, that would be superb."

11

WAIATA AROHA - SONG OF LOVE

Conveying meaning without the necessity of actions.

Leaving Fran's office was incredibly awkward, and Adele spent some time in the toilet cubicle tidying up her face before joining James at the main door. He stood with his back to her, gazing out through the glass paneling. So still, he could've been carved from greenstone.

He turned with a start when he realised she stood behind him.

"I wanted to apologise—"

"Don't." Adele winced, unwilling to carry on such an emotive topic in such a public place.

Not here. Not now.

James' face clouded, and for a moment he looked as if he were about to carry on, regardless.

The lump in Adele's throat rose in anticipation, but to her relief James appeared to think better of it.

He pursed his lips, nodded, then held the main door open for her. "After you," was all he murmured.

Then he walked her home.

Unnecessary, but chivalrous all the same. Adele wasn't about to keel over, but she knew she looked a mess because the mirror in Fran's bathroom didn't lie.

Washed out and hollow, like a well-weathered hunk of driftwood.

"So, I gather you've been invited for family pizza night again tomorrow?" Adele hazarded as they walked, trying to drum up some semblance of normal conversation.

She felt, rather than saw James glance her way, then back to the lake spread out before them as they angled down through the township. The water changed with the mood of the weather, white capped and stormy one day, and reflective calmness the next.

Whatever the weather, the body of water seemed to breathe solace, and tonight it glittered like a crown jewel—a deep-blue diamond, clasped between rusty mountains.

Traffic had all but disappeared in the half-hour they'd been inside, and they had no trouble jaywalking across the main street.

"Actually, I wanted to talk to you about that." James shoved his hands into his pockets. "Saffy and Kana were both insistent, but I don't want to insinuate myself into Daniel's family home; his private space. Neither do I want to make you feel uncomfortable."

James made her uncomfortable all the time. That's just how it was.

"Daniel warned you off." Adele had guessed as much.

James didn't bother quantifying exactly what had been said, but issued an irritable grumble Adele took as assent.

"Look, I'm a big girl, and keep company with whoever I damn well please. You should come. For Saff," she quantified belatedly.

They turned down Adele's street, parallel to the lakeshore, but far enough away to warrant slightly cheaper rents.

"I could show up for Saffy's benefit, then leave before you all eat," James decided aloud.

"Alright." That wasn't such a bad plan. Giving everyone breathing space—herself included.

"Can I get you an ice cream?" James gestured to the corner-store they were passing, Tip Top logo emblazoned across the front.

"No, thanks." Adele's stomach was still churning from the counselling session.

James paused, as if undecided.

"I'm happy to wait, though, seeing as walking past without

buying something is tantamount to sacrilege to you." Adele allowed herself a small smirk.

Her ex-husband's face split into an unexpected grin before he swung into the store, and she was immediately taken back to another time, when all between them had been humour and love, laughter and acceptance. Her eyes smarted.

What had happened to them? What had happened to her?

She knew James' habits and vices as well as she knew her own. He'd be in there, having a hard time choosing between double chocolate-chip, and cookies-and-cream. She wondered if he'd still offer her the first lick, and if there'd be a not-so-secret chocolate bar poking out of his pocket when he came back out.

It wasn't exactly easy between them, but it had become almost normal having James around again, and that was due to him barging in without asking. She hadn't thanked him at the time, but did owe him something for that. The initial confrontation between divorcées was over, like a bandaid being ripped off, and it boded for a better future now the sting was wearing off.

Healthier for Saffy. Healthier for all of them.

James exited the store with a single scoop of orange chocolate-chip in a cone—Adele's favourite—and what looked to be a rope of raspberry liquorice in a paper bag. He offered the ice-cream towards her a little sheepishly.

"Want a taste?"

She did, actually, now it was right there in front of her. Holding James' hand steady on the cone, Adele took a good lick from the lower curve.

"Mmm." She hummed in the back of her throat, tastebuds singing. "That's yum."

"Here, you have it."

"No, thanks." She straightened. "My metabolism isn't anything like yours, and ice cream isn't usually in my vocabulary. Not anymore."

They began to walk again, side by side.

"Well, whatever you're doing, it's working. You look phenomenal."

Adele whipped her head around to check if James showed any

signs of having made that admiration up. Green eyes stared right back with just a hint of a smile, but no subterfuge.

"It's none of your business how I look," she countered huffily, turning from him again.

It *wasn't*, but that didn't mean she didn't feel the urge to preen a little.

"Not my business, no." James chuckled. "But neither am I blind or made of brick. Wānaka suits you. Your lifestyle here suits you. You look… happier."

"We *are* happy here."

"Yes."

"You, on the other hand, surprise me."

"I surprise you? How so?" James sounded a bit put out by the observation, and Adele hid her amusement by bringing her fingers to her lips as if in deep thought.

"I mean, a *single scoop*?" she queried in the most serious tone she could conjure. "What is the world coming to?"

James gave an almost inaudible laugh, self-deprecating and a little sad. "Look, I know you don't want to hear this, but for what it's worth, I *am* sorry. I promised you one thing, and it turned out to be something else entirely. I should've admitted to myself it wasn't healthy, the way we carried on as if nothing had happened after Rosetta. It's a hand-me-down from my mother and father, I suppose. The Montagues never mention the unmentionable." He rubbed a hand across his eyes. "None of us even knew Father was sick until his autopsy results came through, and the hospital started calling, wondering why he wasn't keeping his oncology appointments. I can see now it was incredibly damaging—my systemic lack of communication. So I wanted to apologise. Officially."

Adele was silent for some time as she digested that, and they walked on in a companionable lull.

"It wasn't just you," she finally conceded. "I shut down." It was hardly surprising they'd grown so distant in such a short time. She hadn't wanted to let James into her private pain. Fran's counselling sessions had been able to show her that, after much unpacking. Pain left unattended could fester, and become septic… "Have you ever really talked with anyone about your father's death?" she wondered aloud.

James stiffened up.

"I talked with you," he murmured.

"I mean *other* than me," she carried on with stubborn intent. James was right about the Montague tendency to bottle stuff up. How much had that damaged him over the years? "Someone who could help."

"I don't think you realise how much help you were. Just listening."

They'd been sitting on a Gold Coast beachfront one evening, the air heavy with humidity and salt. Saffy had fallen asleep under a mosquito net in the pram next to them, and Adele asked James what had happened to his father.

She'd known by the residual waves in James' family that Luka Montague's death had been a tragedy, but was unprepared for the point-blank nature of what James had experienced.

"Yes, but, I'm not—"

"I don't want to discuss the details with anyone, Dell."

Luka Montague had selected a shotgun for the job. Due to access, or for the full after-effects? Not having known the man personally, Adele wasn't at liberty to judge. She was, however, uncompromisingly horrified he'd gifted his nineteen-year-old son that nightmare visual to live with for the rest of his life.

"Fran's impartial, discreet, and so far from your family it's not funny."

"I get that you trust her, but no. Thank you." James offered Adele the final bit of his ice cream, waiting until she shook her head before polishing it off and tucking the paper wrapper neatly into his jeans pocket. Careful, precise movements, almost masking his agitation with Adele's choice of conversation topic.

Almost.

Adele shrugged. "Just an idea." They reached the hedge that cordoned her rental property from the street. "Are you still taking your antioxidants and vitamins?" Not exactly her business, but suddenly on her mind.

James' genetic testing had come back as negative for pancreatic cancer mutations, but that didn't mean he couldn't get sick, and his sweet-tooth was a bit of a worry…

"You're concerned about my health?" James mused, looking at her a bit too searchingly for her liking.

"You eat a lot of junk," she counter-accused.

"I get an annual check-up. Everything's fine." James didn't openly laugh at her, but she could hear the smile in his voice, and easily discern the glint in his eye.

Adele cleared her throat and looked away, feeling exposed.

"Thanks for opening up with Fran today—that can't have been easy for you. And thanks for walking me home."

"You're not going to invite me in?"

The hint of humour was still in James' voice, and when she turned to face him again it twisted Adele's heart, that soft half-smile tugging at the corners of his mouth.

"No, I'm definitely not," she assured him, unable to help returning the smile.

"I could make it worth your while." James finally grinned outright, making her laugh.

"Oh, I know damn well you could, James Montague, but I'll not be tempted by your body, or your bloody booty call." She took a step backwards.

"Just before you go." James readjusted his stance, feet a little wider, shoulders a little back—serious-mode. "I wanted to spell something out in black and white. There was never anything sexual between myself and anyone else during our marriage. I assumed you knew that, but I realised after our, ah… our conversation on Friday night, you had some doubts."

'Some doubts' didn't even begin to cover it.

Adele chewed on her lip and tried to quell the panicky feeling rising in her chest. She hadn't wanted the conversation to swing back to this, and frankly the less she talked with James about sex, the better.

"If that's true, Tiffany has a hell of a lot to answer for," she muttered under her breath.

"What?" James' expression turned to laser-intent.

"Oh, nothing." Adele looked down at the footpath and kicked a random stone. "Just bemoaning your choice of staff." Perhaps prudent to change the topic completely, rather than engage in the whole 'what constitutes cheating' debate. "So I've been thinking…" She opted for something she knew James would grab with both hands. "I don't see a problem with that one day-a-week thing with Saffy, if she agrees to it."

She'd been turning it over in her head since he'd brought it up. Space for herself, while nurturing the connection between James and Saffy. She'd have to be blind not to see how much the proximity of James had meant to her daughter over the past couple of weeks.

Adele was right about James grabbing it. He grabbed her as well, closing the gap and dragging both her hands to his chest in his excitement. She hadn't counted on the full body-against-body tingle, and had a bit of trouble keeping her voice steady.

"I'm assuming you mean if you're over here for business? We could have a trial run next term and see how it feels. Surely you didn't mean you'd fly over, week in and week out?" Managing to retain an even tone took some doing. "With all my contacts here, I should be able to find you a decent rental property. The same place each time. Not a hotel. Something a bit more homelike. Give me the dates, and I'll work it out."

"*Thank* you." James kissed her soundly on each cheek, French style. His scent was warm and leafy, heightened by a faint but delicious tinge of orange-chocolate-chip, and his bristles tickled her skin with the brief contact.

Adele squeezed her eyes shut. "No problem," she choked out. "You're good for her. You're good for each other."

Her hands clenched as James went to step back, fists closing convulsively around the soft fabric of his cable-knit to keep him close. Just for a moment more. Just for two. When she peeked up at James through her lashes—heart pounding, he was staring at her with every ounce of want mirrored back.

"You're wearing your come-get-me look again," James whispered, eyes darting to her lips.

"Am not," Adele refuted softly, fingers still locked in his sweater.

"Definitely are." The words were little more than a murmur as James' forehead eased down to rest against hers.

Still a bad idea, no matter how well her senses remembered him; no matter how badly her body wanted him.

Disentangling herself, Adele pulled back until there was a good metre between them. "I gotta go." Then she turned and high-tailed it up her driveway.

"Adele?" James called after her, and she turned when she figured she was a safe distance from him.

"Mmm?"

"About that booty call…" His grin was wide and wicked.

"In your dreams, Aussie." She smiled too, making light of the fact they were still more than compatible on the pheromone scale. "I'm *far* too busy for an ex-on-the-side." And she had no way of tempering where her heart would take it from there, either.

Friendship, plus physicality, equalled in-way-too-deep with this particular man. She'd been down this route before.

Adele walked away from James' low chuckle—away from his particularly addictive brand of magnetism, his joking invitation to make it worth her while, and his assertions of fidelity.

12

WHARE - HOUSE

More than just a place of residence.

This hadn't been a smart move on his part. James knew it the moment he set foot on the property. He shouldn't have come back to the farmhouse, should've instead listened to his inner voice, loudly petitioning for distance.

Thank God he'd given his excuses for the actual meal.

"Dad! You came!" Saffy ran up and hugged him as he entered the kitchen.

He'd been ushered in by Kana, who'd smiled when she met him at the front door, but was clearly on edge.

"Yes, I did. Can't stay long, but I wanted to drop by and say hi."

"*Hi*," Adele offered dryly in response. She looked to be wound tight, standing with her back against the sink and a tea-towel gripped in one hand, high spots of pink on her cheeks.

In light of Adele's comments last week, James had gone for more casual clothes this time—chinos and a black polo shirt.

Poppy and Clem seemed to be missing this evening, so it was just Daniel scowling from the table where he was grating cheese, and Obāchan jiggling Ruby on her hip. The white-haired woman beelined over, and to James' astonishment pointed to her cheek, asking for a kiss of welcome.

James couldn't begin to guess why the octogenarian had chosen to champion him at that particular moment, but the show of solidarity helped, and he performed his duty with perfunctory care. She seemed to get he was there for Saffy's benefit, not to stir up trouble.

He looked down at Adele's dark-haired daughter, an angel in French braids, and smiled. "Missed you," he mouthed silently.

Saffy grinned and gripped his arm, dragging him backwards toward the hallway again. "Come and see," she enthused, all lit up about something.

More than happy to be leaving the kitchen and the steel-trap atmosphere, James followed along with Obāchan, who was still hoisting a grizzly Ruby. He waited until they were out of Daniel's line of sight before offering to hold the baby. Her weight couldn't be easy on the older woman, who was fine-boned and looked like a light breeze might blow her over.

"No. I'm stronger than I look." Obāchan chuckled. "Anyway, Saffy has a job for you that needs both hands."

In the lounge, up against the interior wall, stood an upright Bechstein in highly polished rosewood. James hadn't spent much time in the room last week, but he could've sworn the piano hadn't been there. He ran his hand over the smooth-panelled front.

"Open it!" Saffy was fairly bouncing on the spot.

James turned to Obāchan. "Where did this come from?"

"I bought it," Obāchan smiled. "I read that music therapy has a lot of ties to speech and language skills in children."

James blinked at her, uncomprehending.

"Especially those with a special need," Obāchan reiterated.

"Oh, right." He looked down at Ruby, who was sucking on the sleeve of her great-grandmother's shirt, eyes wide and interested. "Of course. So you play?"

Obāchan shrugged. "Only tolerably."

James lifted the lid and stroked his fingers soundlessly over the keys.

Alabaster and jet—good memories, and bad.

"It's a beautiful instrument."

"Yes," Obāchan agreed with minimum emotion. "Saffy says you play to a very high level."

He glanced at his daughter. "Well, I—"

"Please, James." Obāchan was settling Ruby on the floor and offering the piano stool, her eyes beseeching. "Something soft."

Even as James sat, his fingers were already running up the E-major scale. He played slowly, transitioning into chords as the mood took him.

C# minor, G#, E.

The piano had been well tuned, ringing clear as a bell. Looking up, he caught the expectant glow on Saffy's face.

"Maybe shut the door, Saff?" he murmured. Saffy raced to do as she was bid, then arrived back at his shoulder, all excited. "Here." He shuffled sideways, making room for her to fit on the long stool with him. "This is your note." He showed her the key. "It's a low E. When I nudge your knee, you hit that, okay?"

"Okay." She grinned.

They used to do this often when Saffy was little, her need to be involved had been so great. But James had played less and less as time went on, the pressures of other things taking over.

Obāchan sat on the floor with Ruby snuggled in her lap, and a calmness settled over James as he closed his eyes. The first notes of Claude Debussy's *Clare De Lune* eased out from beneath his fingers, as if they'd arrived there of their own volition.

One of his Father's favourites.

James had learned it by heart in his weekly lessons as a child, over and over again until Luka Montague was satisfied with the rendition. Just like his father's regimented collection of records, everything had to be perfectly ordered.

James had thought at the time his father must've owned every recording the Swiss Philharmonic Orchestra had ever made.

It was necessity that had forced Luka from Switzerland in the first place, and then from Canada. The business of escape had pushed the highly educated man to drag his young family to central Quebec, then outback Australia to start fresh, where no-one knew them.

You could take a Swiss-French man from his homeland, but the homeland remained strong.

James sighed, the notes hovering and hanging. Not tentative, but delicate. Debussy wrung out every emotion and left him hollow, straining for the next bar. Saffy gave up halfway through the piece, easing both arms around his midriff as she listened, her head resting lightly against the swaying movement of his shoulder.

It was the calmest, most beautiful moment James could remember since he'd arrived in New Zealand, just under a fortnight ago. When the last notes faded, he turned to kiss Saffy's smooth forehead—everything suddenly crystal clear.

"I love you," he murmured against her textured hairline.

He hadn't necessarily expected to, not in the beginning. Sure, he'd been ready to *care* for Saffron Katherine Fergus, and stand as her stepfather; accepting the role of financial support and co-parent to Adele's toddler. But that was before he'd gotten to know the precocious little heart-stealer.

It hadn't even taken one day, and he'd been a goner.

There was a movement in his peripheral vision, the sigh of skin on wood, and James turned to take in Adele leaning on the door frame. He didn't know how long the door had been open, or how long she'd been standing there, but her arms were wrapped tightly around herself and her eyes held the shimmer of unshed tears.

And I love you, too.

James left the words unsaid, waiting until the last note faded before he stood, placing a hand on Saffy's shoulder to give it a quick, farewell squeeze.

"Don't go."

Ignoring Saffy's entreaty, he forced his lips to comply with a smile. "I'll see you soon, short-stuff. Enjoy your pizza."

"Thank you, James." Obāchan nodded as he passed her, still on the floor with Ruby cosy in her lap. "That was beautiful."

"My pleasure." And it really had been.

Adele remained in the doorway when James moved towards it, forcing him to stop. Her oversized T-shirt was knotted at the front—pulled tight around the waistline of her jeans. The wide neck sat asymmetrically, leaving one shoulder and sculpted clavicle exposed.

Feminine, unstudied, and incredibly sexy.

"You don't have to leave," she whispered.

James glanced towards the kitchen, then back to Adele's conflicted expression. Her eyes were glassy, and her cheeks still rosy from whatever disagreement had been ensuing in the other room.

"I beg to differ, Dell. Time I made myself scarce, I think."

"Let me walk you out, then."

"Sure."

The evening was cool, with a brisk wind off the lake.

Adele turned from closing the front door behind her, and the breeze stirred the curls around her face, getting tendrils in her mouth and flicking corkscrews across her eyes. She raised her hand to wipe them away just as James did, their hands colliding mid-motion.

Rather than pull away, as James had expected, Adele laid her hand over his, pressing it to her cheek.

"Thank you for coming."

"Thank you for seeing me out." He didn't want to break the spell by moving, and they stood together for seconds that felt like minutes, Adele's cheek soft and warm under his palm.

When Adele turned her head and pressed her lips against his fingers, as light and fleeting as the wings of a moth, James closed his eyes against the want for more.

He burned for all of her. Every. Single. Piece.

When she stepped back, James' hand dropped to his side, tingling.

"Why now?" Adele pinned him with a speculative look. "We both know the jewellery box was just an excuse. I wasn't expecting you here. No one was. At first, maybe. But not after all this time."

Possibly what Daniel had been interrogating Adele about in the kitchen?

"I thought you liked surprises?" James sidestepped the question.

"I do, yes. Generally," Adele agreed solemnly.

She was giving him the opening he needed, but was it too early to drop the full weight of his dreams on her?

After Adele had left, there'd been nothing but bitterness for a long time. Bitterness towards her for having walked out without so much as a conversation, and bitterness towards himself for not realising abandonment was on the cards. James had needed time to re-stabilise, both emotionally and financially, and to lick his wounds.

James was more than aware he had less to offer Adele now than what she'd originally walked away from; less than what she'd already said no to. Nothing drastic had changed to morph him into a more appealing package, and the fact he could add loss of income, business prospects, and property to that equation was a depressing thought.

"I needed to see you." James paced the words carefully, trying to navigate the tricky waters of loyalty and expectation. "Both of you. I missed having Saffy in Australia this summer." An understatement, if ever there was one. He understood the timing hadn't worked, but her absence had left a gaping hole. "There was a window, and I took it."

Working for Farmtech, the Chinese super-company, he'd been expected to be present at a moment's notice. They'd all but held Montague Holdings hostage on the money front. Fifty-one percent at the signing of the deal, and the remaining forty-nine at the conclusion of James' fourth year as their software CEO. But the deal had been too good to pass up, considering the state of his father's company at the time. Washed up, compromised, and haemorrhaging customers, it had held a mere shadow of its former potential.

The restrictions had been punishing, and the work increasingly soulless, but it was over now.

"By window, you mean in your work?"

"Yes." Though the true catalyst for this trip had been a once-in-a-lifetime window into Adele's world, and the fact she'd clearly never spent a cent of her divorce settlement.

He hesitated. 'Self employed' didn't have a particularly attractive ring to it, and the last thing he wanted to do was repel Adele even further.

He settled on a vague explanation. "I was under obligation to a super company, Farmtech, under contract—it's a bit complicated… " he trailed off, unsure if she'd even be interested.

"Ah." Adele's mouth took on that little downturn of disappointment, and James felt her defeat like a shaft under his ribs. "Of course. Your work takes precedence over… Well, everything else, I guess."

"No. Not at all." Did she believe that to be true? Was that how he came across? Business was merely a means to an end, supporting his family the only way he knew how.

Adele touched her fingers to his arm, briefly re-connecting them. "You don't have to explain yourself to me, James. I'm sorry I asked."

"When your diamonds turned up, I knew you hadn't pawned them," he blurted as Adele turned to leave. "Then I knew you couldn't have married me for the…" He balked before uttering the word 'money,' and left the space blank.

But Adele picked up on the omission, and ran with it, sucking in an affronted breath.

"You really thought I married you for your *lifestyle*?" she hissed, eyes flashing.

"I didn't know *what* to think. You wouldn't speak to me. All I knew was Montague Holdings was going down the toilet, and suddenly you'd run back to New Zealand without a backward glance, slapping divorce papers on my table as an afterthought. Money was the only thing that made any sense."

"I don't think you realise just *how* insulting you make that sound."

"Look, I know I had no right to open your bank statement, but the fact is, I've never stopped caring, Dell. Caring you were looked after; comfortable. I had to see for myself. Saffy tells me all about her life here, but I needed to make sure." He shrugged. "So, I delivered your jewellery box myself."

"And saw I was *perfectly capable* of looking after *myself*, without feigning love, or scamming a single unsuspecting man into marrying me!"

Then Adele was gone, slipping in through the front door and closing it firmly behind her.

"Of course," James muttered to the slab of painted wood he was left facing. "Of course you are."

He stood on the verandah, the word empty not even coming close to conveying how he felt.

He'd gone about it all wrong; should've explained his growing interest in the organic viticulture businesses, and told Adele about the wineries he was looking into on this side of the Tasman. He should've explained how he'd hoped his induction into the New Zealand market would secure time with Saffy—time with both of them. Time to see if there was any hope left of building anything from the ashes.

Wading through his own thoughts, James jumped when a wet muzzle was shoved into his palm without ceremony.

"Oh, hey, Winger." He gave the collie a good neck scratch and ear rub, glad of the temporary company. "You watching over Saff out here? Head of security? Good girl. Good dog." She was still sitting on the verandah, watching the front door, when he drove away.

Once again, Saffy was putting James' own painting skills to shame with her careful brushstrokes and attention to detail. He looked out the window of his newly purchased cabin towards the lawn, where Saffy had just finished the final coat on Adele's outdoor love-seat, and smiled.

It didn't look half bad.

James tried to envisage how the bright colours would sit under Adele's willow tree. A bit childish perhaps? Too obvious a bid to appease his ex-wife? It was hard to tell how she'd take it.

James grimaced.

Some surprises definitely went down better than others.

He was finishing washing up the brushes in the metal laundry tub when Saffy called him upstairs.

"Dad! Can this be my room?"

When he reached the loft, he found Saffy plopped on the wooden window seat in the smaller of the two upper bedrooms, her face turned to take in the view of the lake. James was presented with her profile—so like her mother's.

Beyond Saffy, through a cluster of native trees, light glinted off crystal water.

"*If* Adele agrees to you staying at this property, you have dibs on this room," James agreed with a slow smile, surveying the light-filled space with an eye for improvement.

It was just a shell, with nothing in the way of built-in furniture bar the window seat. The high ceiling needed repainting, and new blinds would have to replace the tired curtains.

Scuffed, used, and in need of a major update, the roomy cabin was definitely a project, but one James was looking forward to getting his hands dirty with. He'd never had the time to really take a property in hand before. Never *made* the time, he corrected himself. Adele had said 'homelike,' and this wasn't even close. Not yet.

"You think she won't?"

James' smile faded as he turned his focus back to Saffy's strongly set jawline, and pert, Adele-like nose. "Jury's out on that one."

"What does that even *mean*?" Saffy turned around to stare at him.

"It's a judicial reference."

There was no change in the blank expression his daughter was lancing him with.

"Courtroom. Jury of twelve people. Still deliberating whether the answer is yes or no for the accused." He brushed his hands on his thighs, attempting to dry them off.

The cabin was in desperate need of some hand-towels, and a shit-ton of other household essentials.

"What are you accused of?"

"Hmm...?" That was actually a good question. "I'm not entirely sure what the full list is." James aimed for a light tone, not wanting Saffy to think he was locked in an eternal battle of wills with her mother.

Stupidity. Neglect. Product unfit for purpose. After that interlude in the farmhouse kitchen, James was pretty sure he could add 'suspected infidelity' to that list as well.

God only knew what else.

He cleared his throat. "On second thoughts, perhaps it's better if *you* ask your mother about this place for a sleepover," he joked, then changed the subject purposefully. "Do you still have that picture of you with a python around your neck?"

James had taken to talking with Saffy about the life they'd shared in Australia, because his daughter was so little when they'd met she wouldn't remember much of it, and it was worth remembering. He wanted her to know how much fun they'd had in those blissful two years before the miscarriage—how it had felt to be part of a close-knit family where everything was shared. He needed her to believe that kind of connection was something she could choose for herself when she grew older.

He also needed her to know there had been real love and mutual respect there, once.

"Yeah." Saffy grinned.

"That's one of my favourites." In fact, he'd had a copy made before Saffy's belongings had all been shipped to New Zealand.

Adele had talked James into muscling a short family trip to the Gold Coast in between his Australia-wide consultancy schedule, and there'd been a reptile handler at the night market, touting photos for the tourists. Saffy, true to self, had been fabulously fearless, and James was incredibly proud of how the then four-year-old had handled herself around the shy, cool-blooded creatures.

While Adele had squirmed, unable to stomach watching her daughter gently stroke and hold a small, black-headed python, Saffy had asked the handler a multitude of pertinent questions.

What's her name? Where's her mummy? Does she sleep in your bed?

"Do you remember when Adele found a green tree snake in the backyard in Sydney? She screamed so loud I heard her all the way down in my city office."

"You did *not!*" Saffy snorted a laugh.

"No, maybe not." James chuckled. "But I bet the neighbours still talk about the crazy Kiwi chick with beautiful hair, who called the cops on a harmless reptile minding its own business in the washing basket."

Saffy left a beat of silence. "You think Mum has beautiful hair?" she asked softly.

James thought Saffy's mum was the most stunning woman he'd ever laid eyes on, but that was dangerous territory to step into.

"Of course, don't you?" he answered mildly, schooling his features into a bland expression.

"*Yeeeeees.*" Saffy was eyeing him suspiciously, and James looked down at the toe of his boot rather than hold her stare, finding a loose floorboard that would have to be dealt with at a later stage.

"Better get you home for dinner, I guess." He turned on his heel and started back down the stairs. "Come on, snake charmer."

13

HĀNEANEA - SOFA

All the comforts of home.

Adele put her hands on her hips and surveyed the pristine leather sofa and two-chair set, now residing on the driveway of one of her regular cleaning jobs. Her excitement grew. It would look perfect in her lounge with a few colourful throw cushions to break the monotony of honey-brown, and had to be infinitely more comfortable than the secondhand suite she already had.

"You're sure?"

The client shrugged, her designer jacket slipping on bony collarbones. "Absolutely. As long as there's no trace of it by the time my husband gets home this afternoon, it's all yours."

The client's name was Margaret, and she had a tendency to change the decor in her five bedroom monstrosity of a house on a whim. This particular day, Adele had been polishing the glass dining table to a gleam when Margaret's new lounge suite had been delivered.

Adele had been eavesdropping with one ear, so had heard one of the delivery people ask casually, 'Would you like us to dispose of the old one for you?'

She'd nearly swallowed her tongue when Margaret had replied eagerly, "Oh, would you? That would be *fabulous*."

Adele had never moved so fast in her life, almost shouting in her haste to say, "I'll take it off your hands, Margaret. I'm in the market for a new lounge suite, as it happens!" Then she'd fired dagger-eyes at the removal guy.

He hadn't looked too pleased about her interference, and Adele guessed he'd pretty much had the same idea himself. He *did* help carry the suite out to the driveway though, so no sour grapes there.

Out with the old, in with the almost-new.

Adele just had to figure out a way of getting it off Margaret's damn driveway before the woman's husband came home to find his favourite armchair languishing in the open air.

The first half of Adele's workday complete, she rang her time into the office while sitting on Margaret's luxurious, newly-appointed outdoor seating, contemplating who she should phone for backup.

Daniel wasn't answering his phone, and Kana said she had no idea when he'd be back at the farm. Clem was still up the valley, fishing. Kana's new electric-blue SUV didn't have its tow-bar fitted yet, and Poppy was over in Dunedin for a few days.

Adele groaned, tapping her phone to her temple in frustration. Her work vehicle didn't have a tow-bar. Clem had a trailer, but wasn't home. Daniel's truck had a tow-bar, but no space for Ruby's car-seat if Kana were to help with the lifting.

None of the combinations worked.

Adele could drive to the farm, pick up Daniel's truck, then go and get the trailer from Clem's... But couldn't manoeuvre the suite on and off the trailer by herself. It was no use asking Margaret to help. Apart from the fact she was a client, the woman looked like she might snap in two if she lifted anything heftier than a champagne flute.

Adele needed help, and it looked like James was it.

She'd been avoiding him since pizza night, unprepared to witness him seated at the piano, totally wrapped up in his music. Staying away from the lilting score filtering through to the kitchen had been more than she could pull off, though she regretted watching him after the fact.

It was just too easy to let her heart rule where James was concerned.

When they'd first been married, James used to get home from work and take Saffy directly to the piano to play, and Adele had always been drawn there to watch, listen, and daydream.

Back before Montague Holdings was *all* James could think about. Back before he'd come to the conclusion his wife must've married him for his bank balance.

Sitting for another minute, her head back on the plush cushioning, Adele went over all her options again to be sure she hadn't missed anyone.

Maintenance Tony.

Tony would absolutely *love* to help. Adele could ask him to shift a whole house-load and he'd be totally down with that. She picked up her phone to search for the handy-man's number in her contacts, finger hovering over the call icon.

Her gut began to seriously question her actions. Did she have any idea what the man would expect in exchange?

Adele sighed, placing a resigned call to her ex-husband instead.

Better the devil you know.

"James Montague," he answered after the second ring, sounding out of breath.

"Hi. It's me."

There was a moment's hesitation. "Dell?"

"Yeah."

James chuckled. "To what do I owe *this* pleasure?"

She didn't much like that he was laughing at her. Alright, so she hadn't actually called him on the phone for a number of years, but he *had* left his number, and he *had* said if she needed help...

Should've called old forest-lugs.

"Actually, I'm in a spot of bother."

"Are you okay?" James' tone lost all hint of tease, and Adele could imagine him leaning forward, eyebrows snapped together in serious mode.

"Yes. Not that kind of bother. I just need a tow-bar, a trailer, and an extra pair of hands."

There was another pause on the line as James digested the information.

"Please," she added as an afterthought.

"It just so happens I can assist with those particular

requirements." James spoke the words slowly, as if gauging his ground. "Where are you?"

"Not going to bloody fit," James huffed, his face flushed with exertion. "Backdoor." He nodded his head in the direction of the path around to the back of the cottage and lifted his end of the three-seater again.

"Said the prostitute to the well-endowed vicar." Adele snorted at her own questionable joke. "Not so fast, Superman. Let me get the feeling back in my fingers first." She held her digits up and wiggled them, still recovering from manhandling her end of the heavy-framed sofa.

"Lightweight." James grinned.

"Overachiever," she hassled him right back, plumping her ass down on her end of the leather cushioning. "God. I need a glass of wine after this."

They'd left the three-seater till last. Both of the wide-armed chairs had fitted through the front door side-on, albeit with some manoeuvring. There wasn't a hope in hell the three-seater would follow suit, though. That fact had become apparent after three false attempts, some cursing, and a lot of grunting from both parties.

James mirrored Adele's action, easing his end of the sofa back on the porch and plonking himself down mid-way along it. He slid his arms along the back before laying his head on the cushions with a sigh. "It's a big bastard, but it's damn comfortable. I'll give it that." He drew an empty hand out in front of him, and stared at it. "I'm going to imagine I've got a cold beer, then this would be just about perfect."

They sat for a few minutes in silence, and Adele closed her eyes to bask in the blissful autumn sun.

"You bought the car, didn't you? It's not a rental." Rentals didn't come with tow-bars and visible dents.

"Yes. I bought the car." James may've hesitated before answering, but the words seemed honest enough.

"And the trailer?"

"And the trailer," he conceded.

"*Debussy.*" The composer's name popped into Adele's head and out of her mouth. It had been bugging her—on the tip of her tongue all day.

"Mmm. Claude Debussy, *Clair De Lune,*" James agreed. "Moonlight."

Adele sighed. "It *sounded* like moonlight. All dreamy," she murmured. "Swiss composer?"

"No. French."

When she turned to look at James, her mouth open to ask him what kind of beer he was 'drinking,' she realised he'd been watching her. Head to the side, he was wearing the saddest expression.

"Have I changed much?" she asked without thinking.

"No." James' answer was immediate. "Not one bit." The hand behind her gave her ponytail a light tug. "That's the hardest part."

Adele snorted, because she knew she *had* changed. Immeasurably.

Grown up. Wised up. Hardened up.

"Bullshit," she chided him softly, looking at the curved lips that lied so glibly. The beautiful lips that kissed so magnificently, and made her forget everything else.

"Well, *this* is new." James touched one finger gently to the stud on her nose. "Very cute. Very sexy."

One beat in time turned into two, the air between them heavy with all that remained unsaid, and unresolved.

James stood abruptly, brushing his hands down the seat of his jeans as he cleared his throat. They moulded his butt and showed off his quad muscles, and Adele looked away, not wanting to see.

Some things did stay the same.

James was beautifully built, and always had been. Unfair when you considered the man's dietary habits. She supposed he still swam everyday, and wondered if he'd found the public pool at the Rec Centre, or braved the frigid water of the lake. Her own swimming skills were crappy at best, made jerky and ineffective by her tendency to panic-gasp for air. More of a natural dog-paddler, she half-assed swam, with her head well clear of the water.

The French doors around the back made for an easier fit, and

Adele's new three seater joined its matching armchairs without any more cursing.

Adele was fairly pleased with the results of their efforts, though she was now sweaty and overheated; in dire need of a drink and a shower—in that order.

"What are we doing with this one?" James clamped a hand on the back of the older sofa, taking up valuable space and looking a little worse for wear, but still with some life left in it.

Adele groaned. "God, I hadn't thought of that. Garage?"

James scratched at his new beard while he checked the sofa over. "I could take it."

"Take it where?"

James looked up suddenly, blinking as if she'd caught him out. "Ah… Away?"

She shrugged. "Okay. If you don't mind? There's a last-chance shop at the dump that would accept it. I can help you load it at this end, and the staff will help you once you're there."

"Sure." James touched a finger to his earlobe, not looking her directly in the eye.

The old sofa was much lighter, and James knew from experience it was comfortable enough to sleep on. Adele helped him load it and the chairs onto the trailer and strap them down, then he moved to leave.

"Stay for a drink?"

James's hand was on the car door, and he turned slowly to eye Adele. She looked almost shy, standing in her worn jeans and cleaning logoed T-shirt.

'Elbow grease is our middle name.'

"Sure." He let his hand drop. "You happy to have company?"

"*Sure.*" Adele shrugged, mimicking him.

"Maybe just a quick one, then." He didn't want to overstay his welcome, but as always, was thirsty for time with his addictive ex-wife.

Adele was already on her way back to the house, but she threw a smirk over her shoulder. "Not to be confused with a quickie," she joked.

"God forbid," James muttered under his breath, following at what he deemed a safe distance.

During their first couple of years of marriage, they'd perfected the art of the 'quickie' in numerous situations, and James tortured himself sometimes by trying to remember the fevered intensity of each and every one.

Ten minutes before Saffy's preschool pickup. Five minutes before he had to leave for work. Two minutes in the bathroom at the restaurant, because they just couldn't keep their hands off each other…

It was Adele who drew him into it, every time. Off the cuff, opportunistic, fun-seeking Adele. She'd broken him out of his stuffy, ordered life and stirred in heavy doses of fly-by-the-seat-of-your-pants spontaneity.

In the beginning, anyway. Before he'd managed to all but snuff out that iridescent sparkle in her.

If the thought of quickies made him hot around the collar, it was best not to even touch on the memories of long tropical nights with the windows open, making love to the sound of night frogs and cicadas. They'd had all the time in the world to explore each other, then.

"Beer?" Adele asked, stepping through the open front door.

"No. Better make it water." His judgement was already well-clouded by this unexpected Dell-infusion.

James followed Adele through to the lounge and stopped in the archway, checking out her appropriated lounge suite in its new habitat. "It fits well in here."

"Yes, it does," Adele called through from the kitchen. "But my favourite thing about it is still the price."

James barked a laugh.

Adele had always been one to covet a bargain, even when she'd had his entire cashflow at her disposal. How had he bought into the idea that money had been her objective all along?

He chose one of the new armchairs to sit in. Best not share the sofa again after the porch incident, when he'd wanted to kiss his ex-wife so badly it hurt.

He'd sneaked a touch of her hair though, sliding his pinky into one of her tight corkscrews as they sat together on the sofa, and marvelling how the little spring of sunshine wound and furled its way around his digit as if it had been designed for that very purpose.

Then Adele had opened her eyes and asked him if she'd changed.

Maybe on the inside. Maybe they both had.

When Adele returned with two glasses of water and handed him one, clinking with ice, she perched herself on the wide arm of his chair and eyed the opposing sofa with her head cocked to the side.

"What colour cushions do you reckon?"

"Ah, something bright?" James muttered. Adele always chose something bright. Rainbow was her favourite colour.

How the hell was he supposed to think about cushions when Adele's thigh was resting up against his arm, and her cheeks were all flushed and pretty when she laughed? He just wanted to bury himself in the scent of her and forget the last five years had ever happened.

Six. The last six years. The year after losing Rosetta had been hellish, watching Dell fold in on herself like a lone atoll. Solitary; surrounded by shark-infested waters.

James took a giant mouthful of water as Adele leaned forward, a small frown between her brows. "Do you still have that black linen lounge suite in the formal sitting room?"

He shook his head. He'd gotten rid of everything when he'd sold up.

"Shame," Adele mused, a faraway look in her eyes. "I remember christening that one."

James choked as his water slid down the wrong way, well into his windpipe.

Fuck. Now she mentioned it, so did he.

14

RUA - TWO

Infinitely trickier than one.

Adele walloped James a few times between the shoulder blades, concerned. He was hunched forward in the armchair, still coughing as if his life depended on it.

"Steady on," James rasped the words between bouts of hacking. "I might need my spine later in the week."

"You're alright now?" She stopped hitting and rubbed the spot with her palm instead, up and down. Turning back to the sofa, she refocused on what she'd been thinking before she'd been rudely interrupted. "I'm imagining red through to yellow. Sunshine colours, you know? Or maybe cooler tones—green and leafy. Yes! Tropical. Fiji-style would look *great* in here."

"Adele?"

"Mmm?"

"Stop."

"Stop what?"

She turned to James in surprise, and realised she still had her hand on him, stroking the contours of his shoulders and back. Gently up, then massaging down in the valley between his blades where he had a tendency to hold tension. Soothing the musculature that alluded to the amount of swimming the man did; sheer power in the strength and breadth.

"Oh!" She withdrew immediately, red-faced and flustered. "Shit! Sorry."

It'd felt so natural, so normal. For a moment she'd totally forgotten…

James leaned back against the cushions and slid his hands behind his head, lacing his fingers there as he closed his eyes. "Let's get something straight."

"Um, okay."

"You don't want me to touch you, right?"

Was that right? Why was she no longer sure if that was right?

She should be positive. *Right*?

"Right. Yes." Adele bit down on her lower lip, staring at the tanned skin of James' exposed neck, and marvelling at how the new beard petered out to give way to corded muscle. "I mean, I guess so."

James' eyes flew open. "You *guess* so?"

"That's the best plan, with our history, and your, your… You know. I can see it going somewhere fast."

James hesitated before answering, his eyes on her lips. "Or we could take it *real* slow," he offered, eyes darkening. "And see where it leads us."

The devil inside agreed. Could Adele twist 'real slow' into having few consequences and little meaning? Highly unlikely. But then again, real slow might just be the only way to scratch the infernal itch that was keeping her up nights and infusing her working day with shots of pure want.

Her body was already choosing, twisting towards James' frame below her in the armchair. He remained statue-still, the only hints at his emotive state the shallow rise and fall of his chest, and the muscle twitching in his jaw.

Knees settling into the enveloping snugness either side of James' thighs, Adele stayed crouched above his lap, but allowed her head to lower until their foreheads met for a brief re-connect.

Then he shifted.

Adele jerked her head up, peripheral vision warning that James was readjusting; sliding his hands out from beneath his head.

"Don't move," she whispered, sure if he touched her, they'd both go up in smoke. "Not a goddamn muscle."

Groaning at the order, clearly not within his own game-plan, James nevertheless re-laced his fingers securely out of harm's way. The action left his arms akimbo, torso at Adele's mercy. To make sure it stayed that way, she brought her hands up to press his tensed forearms into the cushioned leather.

Adele hadn't meant to make a sound, but it was with a whimper her mouth touched James'. Soft and tentative—the antithesis of the last time these body parts had met.

And oh, oh, *oh*. The taste of him, the bittersweet memories of all they'd been, and all they'd gone through.

James remained a non-threatening participant through all of it— meeting Adele at her own pace without pushing for more. He let her pick her own way through the sadness of loss to the bliss of the physical realm, where each breath was a miracle of exquisite sensation.

Each whisper of lip against lip ignited an explosion of light against the back of her eyelids.

A.J.... Her James, and the goodbye kiss she'd never allowed herself.

Her breath hitched on a single sob, and she pulled back from him, blinking away the wetness. Realising how tightly she was gripping his arms, she released them too, noting the colour flowing back into her white fingerprints with a strange sense of detachment.

Not a good idea, after all. Not the least bit smart. Rather than smothering something, that kiss had re-lit a whole bag of Tom-thumbs. Not only could Adele see it burning in the intensity of James' eyes, she could feel it fizzing and pulsing through her own body with a heat akin to pain—like freshly warmed blood to long-cold extremities.

A reminder. A warning.

A frickin' fog horn of a wake-up call.

Adele struggled up to standing. Pushing away from the armchair in self-disgust, she began wringing her hands to keep them busy. Better than chewing on her nails, which was her instinctual go-to at times like these.

In her mind's eye, she could see James and herself christening her new sofa in record time.

"You don't want it to go anywhere, fast?" James picked up their previous conversation softly, as if the earth hadn't just moved beneath them. As if she hadn't just kissed him blind and lost all her senses.

He didn't move from his seated position, but his hands were now gripping the arms of the leather chair.

"No," Adele squeaked in a voice very unlike her usual one. "I told you I wasn't interested in your booty call, and I... I meant it."

At least, she had at the time. There was way too much history between them for a fling, and too much hurt and distrust for a relationship.

"Do I scare you?" James' voice was low, almost too soft to discern the words.

"*You* don't scare me, but my reaction to you does. I don't want to feel anything for you, James. Not ever again."

"Ah, I see." There was a fleeting sadness in James' eyes, a shadow of torment before he closed them against her again. "I already knew that, to be fair," he murmured.

"I can't go back there—be that person. I don't even know who that woman was. Your wife. Dell Montague. I'm only just figuring myself out now... It's taken me that long. I don't mean to say I'm not really happy to have some level of connection with you, though. Oh, I don't mean what just *happened*," she flustered, again at odds with herself. What had she meant to achieve by kissing her ex-husband again? "I mean a kind of, ah... peace," she pushed on, her voice still pitchy as she faced him. It was a laughable concept. She was feeling anything but peaceful right now. "For Saffy's sake. She loves you, and I—Well, I had doubts we'd ever be able to be in the same room holding any semblance of polite conversation." Jabbering on in her nervousness, she threw her arms wide to encompass the room. "But here we are."

"Yes." James opened his eyes and studied Adele, and something about the raw hunger in his look made her take a step backwards. "Here we are." He looked down at his white-knuckled hands, then brought them back to his thighs. "So, you've forgiven me for turning up here unannounced? Long overdue and treading all over your toes?"

"I guess I have," she whispered after a beat of silence. "It was past time for us to talk, face to face."

Talk being the operative word.

She'd had no way of knowing how she'd react to seeing James until he'd knocked on her door, forcing her to confront her past in all its grisly details. She definitely owed James for a measure of closure, along with how much his presence had meant to Saffy. Her daughter had been more confident, more *grown up* about James being here than Adele ever would've expected. Much more mature than she found herself behaving.

"Would you like to pick Saffy up from school today?"

"Consider it done." James was quick to agree, but hesitated before continuing. "Could we talk about the long-term now, Dell?" His voice was soft.

"Long-term?" She experienced a moment of sheer panic.

"About Saffy, and visitation," James reiterated.

"About Saffy," Adele echoed, nonplused. "I'm still thinking about the ins and outs of it. The details. Thursdays would still be Daniel and Kana's—things like that. We do an online course together on Tuesday nights, which I wouldn't want to compromise on. Sports training… There will be weeks where it just won't work."

"Right." James' eyes took on a more watchful slant.

"Don't look at me like that. I'm taking it all into consideration, alright? It's just there's more to this than you realise. After school art classes in terms two and three… Family pizza nights… I don't want Saffy pulled a thousand ways. I want her to be settled; confident in who she is and where her roots are."

James spread his fingers in supplication—his articulate, clever digits. "We're in agreement, then."

"Sort of." Adele chewed on her stubby thumbnail, realised she was doing it, and shoved her hand deep in her jeans pocket instead.

Disgusting habit.

Being confronted with a regimented time-plan from James could prove even more problematic than Adele had first supposed, owing to the fact she was having trouble keeping him at a safe distance.

"I'm not looking to take over your life here, Adele. Tell me how much you're willing to give, and I'll work around that. I just don't want you to give me a flat no."

"It won't be a flat no," she promised, sure of that at least. "But this term's chocka already, and the holidays are problematic."

"Forget the holidays. Next term is fine." James seemed to pick up momentum. "We'll make sure there's no interference with her learning, sports, family nights, anything like that. I want what you want for her, Dell."

James' style of being was good for Saffy. Grounded. Organised. Methodical.

"Once a week or once a fortnight would be doable, most of the time," she murmured, almost to herself. "Mondays before and after school are a bit more quiet. Maybe Mondays." She thought of Monday as James' day anyway, because he'd always video-called from Oz on the first day of the week... "But weekly is not remotely feasible with you in Australia."

"Let me worry about that side of it."

Turning to look towards the teal love-seat stepfather and daughter had painted together, Adele realised it'd been moved out of her line of vision again. She frowned.

Where—?

But the thought was interrupted by the doorbell.

Startled, Adele glanced towards the dimness of the hall, the kitchen clock, then back to James. Twenty minutes until she needed to be back at work for her afternoon shift.

"You can sneak me out the back if you like?" James quipped at her obvious indecision, just the hint of a smile tugging at the corners of his mouth.

"Don't be ridiculous." She laughed.

"I'll get going, though. Don't you have Spic'n'Span again this afternoon?"

"Yes. The Property Management side, though. Not cleaning."

James scratched at his jaw. "Right, and you prefer—?"

The doorbell sounded again.

Torn, Adele began moving backwards toward the hall. They hadn't finished talking, and she wasn't ready for James to leave just yet. "You don't have to go, I've still got a few more minutes before I have to head out."

But James stood as she spoke, and followed her down toward the front door.

Maintenance Tony stood in the open doorway, casting a huge shadow and twirling his cap on one finger. Catching sight of Adele, her co-worker beamed. "Candy-Floss!"

Adele winced, hating the nickname Tony had settled on due to her crazy hair.

"I gather you need some furniture moved?" he continued, full-of-beans and talking way too loud. "Sorry, I missed the message, I was out on a job."

God, the man's timing was abysmal.

"Ah, actually, it's all done and dusted, Tony, but thank you so much."

Who'd left a message for Tony? Clem, probably. The two occasionally fished together, and small-town grapevines were speedy.

"And who might you be?" Tony was staring over Adele's shoulder at James.

"James Montague." Ever the businessman, James stepped forward and offered his hand with a tight little smile. Adele noticed Tony wiped his own palm on the seat of his blue overalls before thrusting it forward, indicating it may well have been fixing something unsavoury moments ago. "Saffy's stepdad."

Tony turned to look at Adele sharply.

"My ex," she murmured.

"Oh!" Tony's face cleared. "You're the ex. I'm Tony, the boyfriend." He aimed the statement at James, and Adele felt, rather than saw her ex-husband start.

Tony had an affable manner, but an annoying tendency to jump the gun.

"Actually, we only went on one—" Adele tried to interject.

Her voice clashed with James, who was already answering with, "Good to meet you. I'm afraid you'll have to excuse me, I was just heading off."

James was through the door and down the porch steps before Adele could even get her head around him going. She put a hand up to halt Tony, who'd already launched into a product analysis of the bleach he'd used today, and skipped down after James.

"Hey!"

James hesitated, then turned to regard her with hooded eyes.

"I wanted to thank you for today. I really appreciate your help."

"Anytime." He had his poker face back on, but she could see by the set of his jaw it was beginning to take its toll.

"It was really good of you to come and be my... You know."

"Backup plan?"

"What? No!" Adele laughed, but James didn't follow suit, and she began to wonder what had miffed him.

Surely he wasn't actually jealous of Maintenance Tony?

Well, now. *That* was interesting.

"I was going to say 'brawn,' but it sounded a bit sexist in my head." Adele took another step closer, and lowered her voice. "I didn't call Tony. He must've heard a rumour I needed help. So I wasn't using you as my backup plan." She mock-punched James' shoulder in slow-mo. "I was just using you, full stop."

The corners of James' mouth eased into a self-deprecating smile, changing the angle of some of the whiskers in his beard. "I'm not sure if it should, but somehow that sits better with me." His green eyes sparked with an undercurrent of something else. "Use me all you want."

Adele chuckled, remembering her thoughts about christening the sofa. "In my experience ,James Montague, you're *much* more suited to some things than others."

"Like what?" One of James' eyebrows tweaked upward.

She admired that, having never been able to achieve it herself. How did he manage to get them to move independently? Laughing again, she leaned forward to swipe her thumb across the suddenly puckered skin on James' forehead. It smoothed out only momentarily before the lines reformed.

"Like sofas," she answered cryptically, not willing to give him any more of a heads-up than that. Then she turned and flounced back towards Tony before James could come up with a response.

15

WHAKAOHOMAURI - SURPRISE

The least expected is not always welcome.

When Adele opened her front door later that same afternoon she'd already finished her second shift at Spic'n'Span, wading through booking requests and cancellations, and was hard pressed to find the energy to get up and be sociable. Her older sister stopped her persistent knocking and stood, hand raised and fisted on the bungalow's porch, all five-foot-five of her arrested in unnatural stillness.

Katie's hair was longer than she usually kept it—wild and a bit on the wooly side, auburn chunks obscuring her ears as if she hadn't bothered to style it. "Hey, sis." Her voice was almost a whisper, and she remained static as if unsure of her welcome.

"Katie!" Adele threw her arms around her one-and-only sibling, surprise instantly overruled by pleasure. She was relieved to feel Katie's out-of-character reserve melt a little under her tight squeeze, and held on until the pressure of her sister's hug matched her own. "What's wrong? What are you doing here?" A sudden fear gripped her. "Mum and Dad?"

"They're fine," Katie assured her, pulling back to give Adele a plastic smile that did nothing to dispel her growing trepidation. "I tried calling you a number of times, but I couldn't get hold of you."

"My phone was flat. I just got in from my afternoon job and plugged it in." As if on cue, somewhere in the house Adele's phone began to bleat.

She blinked at Katie—eighteen-months older, and usually a thousand times bolshier—trying to fathom the context of her sister's unscheduled arrival. The skin around Katie's eyes seemed thinner somehow, showing the faint blue of her veins, and Adele could see by the redness there had been tears in the not too distant past.

"Where are the boys?"

Katie's car was pulled in behind her own up the driveway, but there was no sign of five-year-old Tobias, or Ethan, his little shadow.

No sign of Katie's husband either.

"Mum's got the boys." Katie set her teeth, as if willing Adele not to ask.

So she didn't. Not aloud, anyway.

Where's Rue?

The husband and wife team were usually joined at the hip.

Why this sudden appearance, when the sisters hardly spoke on the phone anymore, let alone drove three and a half hours to see one another?

"Come on inside, Kit-Kat. You look like you could do with a coffee." Adele had the distinct impression she wasn't going to like what Katie had to say, and held the door frame for support a moment longer than necessary. It needed a good sand and paint, and little flakes of white came off in her palm. Stepping back into the hall, she rubbed one hand off on her jeans, gesturing with the other for her sister to follow.

It turned out it was Rue, not herself who was in trouble, but Adele's relief was short-lived. Katie was really pissed off—ranting angry—and it was all aimed at the genteel Englishman who'd fathered her two children.

The sisters sat facing each other across the coffee table, both settled on the new lounge suite. Katie occupied the chair James had been sitting in earlier in the day, and Adele's palms got more and more sweaty as she tried, without much success, to forget that kiss.

Her discomfort grew to another level as she listened to Katie's story unfold. Her sister suspected Rue of having an affair at the University, finding he'd lied by omission about his new workmate.

Apparently Rue had met the young English professor years ago, when they'd studied together. No problem, except they used to be lovers, and he'd helped the woman get her teaching position in Dunedin.

Katie would've been none the wiser if the dean—stupid, ineffectual pencil-pusher that he was—hadn't lauded on about the acquisition of such a fine, Cambridge educated professor at a faculty dinner. From there, it had just been a matter of squeezing a few of her husband's more inebriated colleagues for information.

Domestic-level interrogation and lie-detection were tasks Adele's sister was more than adept at, being the eldest, and the mother of two young boys.

"Does he want out? Is he having some kind of mid-life crisis now we've got two underfoot, and another one on the way?" Katie fumed.

"He told you he wants out?" Adele blinked. Rue was a hands-on father, and from what she'd seen, more than content with a household full of dinosaurs and dress-ups. "Wait. Do you mean you're pregnant, again?"

"Yes, *pregnant*." Katie looked less than enthused, so other than leaning over to place a hand over her sister's, Adele let the subject drop. "He says he didn't tell me about their past because he *knew* I'd get irrational about it. Me! Irrational!"

"Well—" Actually, Katie did look to be going down the attack route without much in the way of ammunition.

"I am *not* irrational!" Katie warned, shaking her hand free.

"Of course not. But you're saying Rue denies any wrongdoing?"

"Essentially, yes. But he went behind my back. He didn't tell me about their history, and he had ample opportunity. That smacks of guilt right there."

"I don't want to play the devil's advocate here—"

"Then, *don't*," Katie growled.

Adele hesitated for a moment more before continuing. Her sister could be wild-cat fierce, so she picked her way carefully. "The thing is, I kind of understand Rue's reluctance to tell you about his past connection with this… this woman. You're absolutely sure they used to be—?"

"Fuck buddies? One-hundred percent. Got that juicy tidbit from the horse's mouth. They were at it all through their honours year." With that statement, Katie's anger seemed to abate, and pure dejection oozed.

"Well before he met you, Kit-Kat," Adele breathed out the old pet name, feeling her sister's pain. "What if he was trying to save you from this hurt by not telling you? Try to think what might have been going through his head."

"You mean other than, 'Shall I pop some condoms in my desk drawer, just in case?' "

Adele pulled back in shock.

Not Rue, who gave every indication of being totally in love with his wife. Her heart made a sickening lurch downward, along with her positivity.

If it looks like a duck, and walks like a duck… The chances are in favour of it being a damn duck.

Katie waved a hand in irritation. "He says they're from ages ago; before we were married and just seeing each other. He *says* he forgot they were even there."

"But you don't believe him?"

"It's possible." For the first time, Katie looked unsure.

It wasn't a far-fetched idea, the forgot-they-were-there part. Adele had seen the way Rue kept his poky office at the University. A jumble of books and English Literature papers stacked high on the old oak desk, keeping company with stuffed bookcases and a dilapidated old printer on the sideboard.

It looked like Rue hadn't cleaned out his desk in years, if ever.

"Same brand?" Adele wondered aloud.

"Yes."

"Expiry date?"

"I don't know. See? I knew you were the right person to come to." Katie gave her a twitchy smile, and a surge of pure guilt shot through Adele, rendering her speechless for a moment.

She'd never afforded her sister the same—never spilled her guts when she'd desperately needed someone on her side as her marriage went up in smoke.

Because she'd had an underlying suspicion, even then, she didn't deserve the support. She'd believed herself guilty of losing Rosetta, and single-handedly failing at her marriage. Guilty of abandoning her family and hiding her growing unhappiness from them, while blaming herself for James' suspected infidelity.

"What if Rue felt it would hurt you less—not knowing she was there at his workplace, hanging over him like a potential threat?" Was that feasible? "It could be seen as him trying to protect you."

"*Protect* me? Hurt me *less*? By *lying* to me? It's sordid. Incestuous."

"I'm pretty sure 'incestuous' means carnal knowledge of a family member," Adele muttered.

"*Ew*." Katie screwed up her face. "I mean on a workplace level. From the sound of it she's slept her way through half the bloody faculty in the space of a year, and I'm sure the other half have considered it."

"Even Professor Argyle?" Adele couldn't help bringing up the loud, proudly gay Shakespearian specialist.

"Christ, Adele!" Katie fumed. "Whose side are you on, anyway?"

"Yours, Kit-Kat. Of course, yours. I'm just trying to help you see it from another angle. You see, when I was in Australia…" Adele trailed off.

Katie leaned forward, suddenly all ears. "When you were in Australia, *what*?" she prompted.

Adele looked down at her hands. "Moses came to see me. I never told James, because I didn't think he'd understand."

"Oh, my God. You cheated on James?"

"No! I didn't *cheat* on him. It wasn't like that. See?" She flushed. "That's exactly how James would've seen it."

"So, you met Moses secretly."

"Yes."

"But didn't do the funky-monkey."

"No monkey business at all."

"How long did this go on for?" Katie reclined back, bringing one forefinger up to stroke the hollow of her cupid's bow.

"Three times, over the course of a week." Adele had only needed the once, for closure. But Moses had needed more, for Saffy. "He was there for a human rights conference. I met him in the park during his lunch break, so he could watch Saffy play."

"So, Saffy's actually met Moses?" Katie's eyebrows disappeared under her bangs.

Adele nodded, a bit choked up to remember Moses' face; his wonder in everything Saffy did, and said. "I introduced him as a friend, thinking it would be less confrontational. To be honest, Saffy was more interested in the other kids than the man I was sitting with." And considering how contact from Moses had petered out after that, Saffy's initial reserve had probably been a good thing.

"I see." Katie's lips flatlined, a sure sign of her disapproval.

"You think I should've told James." Adele didn't bother posing it as a question. She could read Katie's censure loud and clear.

"That depends on what Moses was to you at that stage."

"Saffy's birth father."

"That's all?"

Again, Adele nodded.

Katie cocked her head to one side and looked her straight in the eye. "Hun, if that were true, wouldn't you have invited James along to meet his daughter's birth-daddy?"

"I… No." Suddenly wrong footed, Adele stumbled on her words. "James was so busy at work," she finished lamely.

Taking in a deep breath, Katie let it out in a long huff. " 'Oh, what a tangled web we weave…' " she quoted with a sad little laugh.

"Love's complicated." Adele tried to wave away the self-doubt with a flick of her hand, but the feeling remained, sticky and unwanted. "James is here, actually." She shifted the subject sideways to escape the moral grey-area she'd just found herself floundering in.

"Here?" Comically, Katie did a double take and glanced over her shoulder.

"No. Not *here*, here." Though he had been, only a few hours ago, in that very armchair. "In Wānaka, visiting Saffy."

"I bet that's not all C.E.O. Montague's got on his agenda." Katie wrinkled up her nose in a clear show of distaste. "Since when are you comfortable being in the same town as your ex-husband?"

Same town. Same room. Same armchair.

Adele cleared her throat, which suddenly had a frog residing in it. "Since now."

"If he's crowding you and Saffy, tell him to bugger off. Who the hell does he think he is, following you here?"

"He didn't. It's not like that," Adele scoffed. Though James kind of had, and it kind of was. She was no longer sure of James' motives, and the longer he stayed, the blurrier his reasons became. "He loves Saffy." That was a sure truth. "If you and Rue ever split, you wouldn't keep him from the boys, would you?"

"It's not the same. Nowhere *near* the same."

"Oh, tomato, toe-may-toe. You're beginning to sound like Daniel, and not in a good way."

"Because we both have your best interests at heart?"

"How did we end up talking about me and James?" Adele muttered, peeved her big sister could turn up out of nowhere and still manage to put her squarely in the wrong. "You never liked him."

"Of course I didn't *like* him! He sauntered across the Tasman with his smooth-talk and promises of Utopia, stole my niece *and* my sister's heart, then dumped her back three years later missing that very vital organ! I've never seen you so lost and alone, so wiped of self-confidence, and I hope to never see it again."

A strained silence hung between them after Katie's angry outburst, and they stared at each other over the coffee table.

"I didn't know you saw it like that." Adele finally filled the awkward space. "You know that *I* left *him*, right?"

"Oh, tomato, toe-may-toe," Katie copied Adele's taunt. "That's the *only* thing I know. You've always been so clammed up about the whole bloody thing."

"I wasn't ready to talk."

"Yeah? Well I'm still waiting, five frickin' years later."

James hadn't been able to get Adele on the phone, so he dropped by the bungalow again on his way to pick up Saffy from school. He still had the trailer attached, along with the lounge suite and a load of building supplies he'd picked up from the local Mitre 10, so he parked out on the street.

There was an unfamiliar station wagon on the driveway, but he still did a double-take when he recognised the pocket-rocket opening the French doors to him.

Adele's sister, Katie, ushered him in with an exaggerated bow and flourish.

The siblings were alike, and not. Katie's hair was darker than Adele's—more auburn than strawberry-blonde, more wavy than corkscrewed, and her curves were set on a shorter frame.

"Speak of the Devil," she drawled with a steely edge.

"Katie. You're visiting from Dunedin?"

"And it would appear you're very much visiting from Oz," Katie returned with a twitch of her lips, closer to a snarl than a smile. "Better late than never, I guess."

James'd be obtuse not to expect derision and suspicion from Adele's family, but the all-inclusive nature of it was wearing a bit thin. At a guess, her parents would feel the same way about his sudden reappearance in Adele and Saffy's lives, convinced he was back to cause further damage.

A sense of heaviness prevailed as he moved deeper into the lounge and caught sight of Adele in the open-plan kitchen, making coffee. If his ex-wife's heightened colour and flashing eyes were anything to go by, the sisters were mid-scrap.

He looked from one Fergus to the other. "Ah, congratulations on your..." Marriage? Children? There were two boys now, right? "Business success." At least he was sure on that point. Katie had made a name for herself with her organic skincare products, moulding her cottage-industry into a commercially viable enterprise in a notoriously tight market.

Nuggety and smart, just like her sister.

Katie didn't bother to answer other than to shrug, eyes still narrowed. The silence in the bungalow intensified.

"Sorry to interrupt." And James was positive he just had. Returning focus to his ex-wife, he got on with his agenda. "I couldn't reach you on the phone. I'm on my way to pick up Saffy, and wanted to check in with you about what time you want her home?"

"Oh. Yes." Adele glanced at the wall clock, then back to him, her whole demeanour fidgety. "Something's come up." Again with the secrets, settling around her like mist in a valley.

"Your parents okay?"

"Yes. Nothing like that. But I need to spend some time with Katie."

Katie snorted. "Bugger off. I'm heading back to Dunedin."

"Over my dead body." Adele's voice rose, confirming James's first impression. He'd clearly walked in on what the Fergus household called 'a lively discussion.' "You're tired and emotional, and it's a long drive."

Katie made another sound of derision, opening her mouth as if she was going to refute every word of that, and not in a polite way.

"No! Absolutely not," Adele cut her sister off before she'd actually spoken. "Mum'll be fine with the boys for a couple of days, and everyone could do with the space to calm down." Her voice took on a softer edge. "Plus, you and I? We're not finished here." Something passed between the siblings, an understanding James wasn't privy to, before Adele turned back to him. "Are you in a position to have Saffy for a sleepover?"

"Tonight? Sure." There was something serious going on if Adele had suddenly decided sleepovers at unknown destinations were a good idea.

"Good." Adele flicked a look towards her sister, as if daring her to protest, then back to James. "You get Saffy from school. I'll be in touch." Her tone was decisive—authoritative.

"Christ, Adele," Katie muttered. "I get you're a sucker for a pretty face, but do you have to drag Saffy back into this again? The poor kid must be confused as hell. He should take her up to the farm," she aimed the directive at Adele, though the message was clearly meant for James. "At least Saffy knows she can trust Daniel."

James clenched his jaw to withhold his retort. Who the hell did Katie think she was, ordering him around and stirring in insults?

He turned to leave.

"Saffy knows she can trust James," Adele interjected as she came around the island bench to stand arms-length away, chin lifted. "We both can." Her cool-as-cucumber comment was met with stony silence.

James faltered on hearing the unexpected support, turning to re-gauge Adele's mood.

Calmer now, she seemed immovable on this particular point, though her face was still flushed in rosy splotches.

"Just because you're in a crappy mood, doesn't mean you get to take it out on James," his ex-wife added quietly.

Katie visibly squirmed under her little sister's regard.

"Wait!" Adele moved toward James, cutting off his exit as he headed for the French doors. Reaching out, she gripped his forearm and spoke in a furious whisper. "You'll need Saffy's sleepover stuff." She began to drag him toward the hall, stopped, groaned, then slapped her palm against her forehead. "Oh, *crap*. It's disco night. I completely forgot. Bloody *disco night*, which is really important to her. There's a boy—"

"I know about the boy."

"You do? Of course you do." Adele was leading him towards the stucco arch as she spoke, then down the hall at a brisk trot. "She's chosen most of her clothes already, but we were going to paint her nails and... Here." Adele entered Saffy's light-filled bedroom, collected the pile of clothing that was laid out on the single bed, and shoved it into his arms. Then she was rummaging for shoes, nail polish, and hair trinkets, cramming all of it all into a sports bag. "Don't let her know Katie's here. She'll want to know where her cousins are, and... Oh, *double* crap. I completely forgot I promised Saffy that Obāchan could be here for the getting ready bit."

"No worries. I'll pick her up on the way."

"Do you have time? I don't think—"

"Is Katie in trouble?" he interrupted.

"No. I hope not. Just a marital speed-bump." Adele hesitated before adding, "I think."

"And you're going to counsel her with your vast experience?" The quip came out sounding a lot more sarcastic than James had meant it, and he caught Adele's little flinch.

"You're right. What the hell am I doing?" She dropped the bag with a thump, bringing one hand up to swipe across her mouth.

"No. I'm wrong. I shouldn't have said that," James murmured, recognising Adele's building anxiety and pissed off with himself for adding to it. "Katie needs you. It's clear she's—" What... In a snit? On the warpath? He went with, "Wound up." It sounded less judgemental. "Saffy will be fine. I'll keep her safe and make sure she has a good time, okay? She can stay with me tonight. No worries. Longer if you need." He went against protocol, dropping his armload back on the bed before pulling Adele in for a hug. The hand that had been trying to wipe the tremble from her lips shot around under his ribs to squeeze him back, and was immediately joined by its twin.

Adele hugged like a vice. She always had. It was like having all the breath squeezed out of him by a human-sized fairy, while she transferred the scent of tropical flowers and coconut milk onto his shirt.

James' hand naturally found its way to the back of Adele's neck to rub out the knots. Her nape was soft and warm under the thick fall of hair.

Fragile.

Much more vulnerable than she liked to pretend.

"Right. You'll keep Saffy safe, and I'll tame the Kit-Kat." Adele took a deep breath before releasing him. "I'm so sorry, she had no right to—"

"Forget it. She's got Saffy's best interests at heart." James recognised that as the truth as the words came out of his mouth. "I get I'm not exactly on your family's Christmas card list." He attempted a laugh, but it didn't come off sounding very natural. "Let's focus." Easier to do without Adele's body smack-bang against his. Taking her by the shoulders, he placed her sweet curves a little further away from himself. "What does Saffy need for a sleepover? P.J.s, toothbrush, change of school clothes for tomorrow. Socks and undies?"

The worry in Adele's eyes lifted a little as the list began to form.

"Sleeping bag." Adele puffed the words out. "Pillow," she added more decisively.

"Great. Okay, let's get that sorted."

"Better take the owl, too. She's been sleeping with it." Adele held out the latest soft toy.

"Kookaburra," he corrected.

"No shit?" Adele brought the bird in closer, frowning at its soft, furry features. "So, *that's* why she calls it Kookie," she muttered. "I thought it was a comment about its state of mind."

By the time they exited Saffy's room, Katie was perched on the arm of Adele's new sofa with a cup of coffee, looking less like she wanted to rip anyone limb from limb. Nevertheless, James took the hall to the front door, keen to remove himself from the equation.

Adele surprised him by trailing after him; seeing him out. Once on the porch he reshuffled the strap of Saffy's sports bag on his shoulder.

"If you need me, I'm right here." He tapped the phone in his top pocket. "I can bring Saffy back after school tomorrow. Either here, or up to the farm. Or keep her with me. Let me know about the timing."

"Can you take some pictures of her dressed up, and send them to me?"

"Sure. Of course."

"Thank you." Adele breathed the words out on an exhale.

"Hey, what are uninvited exes for?" James countered softly, looking away.

This time, it was Adele who stepped forward with a hug of her own volition.

James pressed a firm kiss on her forehead, breathing in the aching loveliness of her through the constriction on his lungs, and trying to convey the level of his support through the simple gesture.

Don't let your sister get to you. You've got this. You're amazing. I've got your back.

"God, I must look a fright." Adele's voice was devoid of its usual humour when she stepped back, fingers fidgeting with her work T-shirt.

James didn't have to look Adele over to know nothing could be further from the truth. Her hair was trying to escape from its hair-tie, and some wildly curly strands were framing her cheeks. The fitted blue jeans he'd admired on her earlier were still hugging every curve and sway, but it was her sweet face that caught his attention and had him murmuring, "No. You look beautiful. Might want to change out of the 'elbow grease' T-shirt, though, if you're planning to go somewhere upmarket for dinner." He smiled, and got a twitchy one from Adele in response.

16

WHĀNAU - FAMILY

Some chosen, and some gifted to you.

Obāchan and James were eight minutes late to pick up Saffy from the school gates, but the on-duty teacher was standing with her. His little girl's face lit up when she saw him, and the almost ten-year-old proved she wasn't too grown up to run up for a slam-hug, making his day.

"So sorry I'm late." James directed the apology to the teacher over Saffy's head. "We've been planning a special night, and time got away on us." He looked to Obāchan to support his story, and Kana's grandmother stepped up admirably.

"What do you say to a sleepover at James' place tonight, Saffy-ko?" Obāchan injected a decent amount of enthusiasm into her voice.

"On a weeknight?" Saffy sounded incredulous, looking from one to the other as they moved away from the school. "Mum said yes?"

"It was actually her idea." The irony of it wasn't lost on James.

Adele suffered him to be around for Saffy's sake, and these past couple of weeks the exes had managed to rebuild the foundations of a passable friendship, alongside the inevitable fireworks. But Adele would no doubt prefer him off the scene and out of her hair. She'd allowed a couple of slips—kisses that went above and beyond the realms of possibility, but that's as far as she would ever let it go.

She'd made it plain she saw their physicality, their chemistry, as a problem. A glitch in the system.

Besides, she was seeing someone else. Brawny Tony.

Five years they'd been apart, and all that time Adele had known exactly where to find James, had she wanted to. But she hadn't. Be it five years or fifty, she would never have come for him, because in her mind they were over. Truly over.

It was beyond time James admitted that to himself.

He'd have a hard time forgetting that wild, untamed lip lock against the pantry door, though. A kiss that had wrenched all his inner longing out into the open. The contact had opened him up, slicing through everything he'd tried to close off and cauterise after the divorce. Like a fresh wound, pumping fresh blood.

It hadn't been the same for Adele, though. What had she said to Daniel?

'Just discussing old times, but we're all done now.'

All done. So why the soft, pillowy dream of longing she'd planted on his mouth just today?

He wouldn't try to fool himself into believing Adele was beginning to feel as much as he did—there was too much angst still left in her for that.

More than likely she was just testing herself. And him.

Adele trusted him with Saffy though. Against her family's advice she trusted him to look after her daughter, and somehow James had to figure out a scenario where that would be enough.

"Crazy, eh? We're having fish and chips and doing a nail salon before the disco. Right, James?" Obāchan picked up the conversation in James' place, ad-libbing whilst giving his forearm a fierce pinch to break him out of his morose reverie.

James cleared his throat. "Right. Yes. A nail salon. And I'll give you three guesses what I've got in the trailer." He aimed for a playful tone, but Saffy was giving him a strange sidelong look.

She slipped her hand into his as they walked, as if in silent support for what he was going through—almost too good at picking up on the emotional undercurrents of those she cared about.

"A pony," Saffy decided.

"Nope." He managed a smile. "That's one down, two to go."

"A swing for the willow tree." Saffy's eyes were round and expectant.

"*Noooo*. Is that something you'd like?"

Saffy shrugged. "Maybe."

"Third and final guess…"

"Dirt."

"*Dirt?*" James found himself laughing at her unexpected prediction. "Why would I have dirt?"

"To build a veggie garden at your place. You need fresh vegetables, five-a-day to keep you healthy and strong."

"I see. Not a bad idea, but wrong again."

They turned the corner and approached the 4x4 and trailer.

"Our sofa!" Saffy crowed.

Even under the stack of strapped down dress-wood, the dark fabric was distinctive.

James cracked a smile at the ridiculous serendipity of it. "Yep. The most comfortable sleepover sofa in the history of sleepovers."

Obāchan surprised James with her energy and stamina, not to mention tact. As Saffy relentlessly dragged the older woman around every inch of James' new cabin and grounds, Obāchan made all the right noises, avoiding any mention of how uninhabitable the place was.

Furniture-less—carpet all ripped up—zero soft furnishings.

While Saffy and Obāchan stood on the lawn, earnestly discussing the best spot for a boxed veggie garden, James did his best to rectify the furniture situation by unloading the building supplies, and piling them against the wall of the lounge where he was planning to construct a built-in bookcase. Then he manoeuvred the two armchairs off the trailer. They weren't particularly heavy, just awkward to grapple with.

Though he returned for the sofa, it was no use. He wouldn't be able to get it off the trailer and into the lounge without potentially breaking its back, or his own.

Obāchan was a tiny wee thing, no bigger than Saffy, so he wouldn't be asking for her help.

It was true James didn't have much, but he did have a fridge with a carton of milk residing in it, so he went ahead and made hot chocolates all around. God knew he needed the sugar to combat the bitter aftertaste left by the whole Katie confrontation, let alone the whole Adele situation.

James had idiotically watched his marriage set sail five years ago, with everything he loved on deck. By the time he'd figured out what was going on, he'd been too late to strike out in the direction Adele had taken, freestyling it towards her in the hope she'd somehow find a reason to drag him back on board.

A reason he was at a loss to see himself.

But recently there'd been two pinpoints of hope in his overwhelmingly bleak sky. Two reasons to believe he'd somehow got Adele's story wrong. Her jewellery box coming to light had been the first, crumbling his theory of her long-planned escape. When the insurance assessments were complete, James had planned to secure-courier her belongings, along with her boxes of stored books...

But that was before he'd seen Adele's bank statement.

James owed some postal worker a huge favour for the simple hand-scribed mistake at the on-sending service. A single piece of folded A4 had revealed her completely untouched divorce settlement in black and white, left in a high-risk, high-earning account to languish and multiply.

It didn't make sense for a single mother, in a new town, setting up a new life for herself and her daughter. It *definitely* didn't make sense to continue lying to himself about the possibility of Adele having been in it for the money.

James was no stranger to bitterness. He'd all but bathed in it after the divorce. Disbelief, anger, and self-flagellation had played their part, too, but it was the bitterness that had enabled him to carry on and fight for his own future.

He was worth something, dammit, and if Adele had merely seen him as an opportunity to set herself up financially, he was better off without her. But Adele's diamonds, and that figure at the bottom of her bank statement, had smattered droplets of doubt. Doubt that had been pooling into a veritable lake of unanswered questions since his arrival in New Zealand.

He'd made a vow to himself not to leave until he got to the bottom of it... Only it hadn't been an easy mission so far. Getting to the bottom of *anything* where Adele was concerned involved holding your breath as you dove past old secrets and intricacies; past hurts and sunken wreckage.

James cast his eyes around the dark-tiled kitchen. The potential he'd seen on buying the place settled into hopelessness when he considered the sheer amount of time and work needed to bring it up to scratch as a home.

Time he didn't have.

He'd bought it on a whim, buoyed by his conversation with Adele about somewhere 'homelike' for Saffy to stay. He'd jumped in boots and all when he'd realised what a secure property in Wānaka would mean to Adele—how it could change her perspective on his time and connection with her daughter... Perhaps even his time and connection with herself.

'Nine-year-olds need stability...' And Adele was right. Why should Saffy be subjected to a series of motels and rental properties when she could have a room of her own, set up with things she loved?

James had gotten used to living off the cuff the past few years, after selling the Sydney house. He'd travelled where Farmtech needed him, and pretty much lived out of a suitcase, returning to his soulless one-bedroom in Sydney periodically to regroup. That didn't mean his daughter had to experience that kind of lifestyle.

He'd been mindful of that when she'd come to Australia on visits, and rented furnished apartments rather than hotels, trying to make it at least seem a bit more solid.

The cabin was 'solid.' Chunky and deep-rooted.

A potential boulder around James' financial neck.

He'd broken the cardinal rule and bought something he'd fallen for, rather than something fitting his immediate needs. But the property had gripped him from the moment he laid eyes on it, the view of the lake from the verandah phenomenal. Spirit soothing.

Taking a sip of his hot chocolate, James leaned his hip on the kitchen bench behind him and took in the much more domestic view through to the main lounge, rubbing out the crick in the back of his neck with one hand.

Saffy and Obāchan had drawn the two lounge chairs together and settled themselves in companionable cosyness, facing the warmth of the log burner. The property had come with a mountain of firewood, neatly stacked almost to the eaves around three sides of the garage.

Chatting excitedly, Saffy was holding her mug in one hand and keeping the other spreadeagled for Obāchan, who was applying electric blue nail polish. Firelight warmed the scene, and James could appreciate the glow from where he stood as an outsider, looking in.

Saffy was happy here in Wānaka, needing nothing from him. He was pretty much a non-requirement.

Just as the deadening thought entered his head, Saffy looked up and gave him a wide grin.

"Come and see. Obāchan knows how to do polka dots."

James meandered over to take a look. There were, indeed, polka dots. Obāchan was blobbing neon purple onto the blue base with what appeared to be a toothpick. The combination of colours was eye-popping, and Saffy was having trouble sitting still in her excitement.

The connection between these two was beautiful to watch. He didn't have to dig far to see the underlying trust and mutual admiration.

James ran a hand over his jaw, suddenly exhausted.

"Saffy can paint yours next, if you like," Obāchan offered sweetly, waving her toothpick.

"Oh, *please*, Dad! We can be matching!"

And that is how, at four o'clock on a Wednesday afternoon, James Montague got his nails painted for the first time in history. With purple polka dots, no less.

It was actually quite uplifting to be involved in the getting ready part, sliding neon beads onto Saffy's freshly braided hair, and being consulted on clothing choices. Silver sparkly leggings, or the ones with the musical notes on them?

Decisions, decisions.

James took down Saffy and Obāchan's fish and chip order, and didn't bother disconnecting the trailer before taking the short drive into town to pick up their early dinner.

The busy take-out shop was bright, and way too social, so he slipped outside to wait, taking the time to check his phone for the email he was expecting from the Organic Wineries Collective.

Nothing yet. They were probably still in discussions about his second proposal.

The supermarket over the road had a small selection of homewares, so James grabbed some towels, bowls, utensils, and plug-in nightlights, along with tomato sauce, milk, bananas, and a breakfast cereal that looked like the kind of thing Saffy would like. At the checkouts, he leaned over to grab an obligatory chocolate bar, and caught the eye of someone he recognised.

The blonde from the café had turned in the queue, and was giving him a conspiratorial smirk.

"Well, hi!" She didn't try to hide the fact she was openly checking him and his groceries out, and judging both.

"Hi... Ah, Maddie, isn't it?"

"Yes!" Maddie beamed. "I like your nails." She touched a finger to James' colourful thumbnail, still gripping the Crunchie bar.

"Oh. Thanks." James had forgotten all about the polish, and dropped the Crunchie into his shopping basket before shoving his hand in his pocket, disconcerted. "We were getting ready for the disco, tonight."

"Of course." Maddie fluttered her eyelashes a little too conspicuously. "The disco. Young love."

James frowned. "The Zane thing?"

"I'm only teasing you, it's all totally innocent." Maddie grinned, then turned to pay for her groceries—two bottles of red, a bunch of grapes, and a round of camembert. It was the antithesis of James' collection of random goods, scattered on the checkout conveyor-belt like a sad reminder of the state of his life. "They've been friends since they started playing rippa-rugby together, years ago. Tonight they'll just meet there, and dance in a big group. Plenty of supervision." She picked up her jute bag, and the wine bottles clinked together. "I was thinking I should give you my number." Maddie let the suggestion hang, and the checkout woman scanning James' items slid him a knowing look.

"Ahh..." James looked from Maddie back to the checkout woman, whose name tag announced her as 'Sylvie.'

"In case you need me to watch Saffy, or anything?" Maddie prompted.

"Oh, right. Yes, of course." James relaxed, pulling his phone from his back pocket to input the babysitter's details. They moved away from the checkouts together after he'd paid, Maddie asking what he thought of Wānaka so far.

"It's smaller than I'm used to." He thought of Sydney's bustling intensity in comparison—energy incarnate—and laughed aloud before smiling down at her. "Smaller and prettier."

Maddie flicked her hair back and giggled, and James realised belatedly that could've come across as a bit of a line.

Moving to put his groceries in the 4x4, Maddie stuck to him, wanting to chat more about Saffy. "Oh, you've got a sofa on the back," she stated unnecessarily, perhaps recognising the furniture as Adele's, and seeking context.

James didn't give her any.

"Yeah," was all he muttered, scratching at the beard which was finally growing beyond itchy, into the softly tactile stage. He joined Maddie in contemplating the trailer and its contents. "God knows how I'm going to get it into the house."

"I could help you?"

James turned and looked at the little blonde, smiling sweetly at him with her dimples flashing.

That was a great idea. A bloody fantastic idea.

"No, that's cool. Thanks for the offer, but I'll figure it out." James offered Maddie a tight smile to try and compensate for the clear rejection. "Sorry to race off, but I've got to get going. I ordered take-outs, and they must be about done."

Raising a hand in farewell, he jogged across the road to where the fish and chip shop beckoned... Literally ran from her. Because God forbid he actually found someone attractive. Someone to connect with. Someone who showed an interest.

His ex-wife was *dating*.

The thought made James slightly nauseous, because after five years apart he still felt like he was cheating even looking at another woman sideways.

"We don't go in, just sign her in at the door. Then you pick her up in two hours." Obāchan tugged on James' arm at the entrance of the school hall, drawing him away from the bottle-neck.

"Right. Only…" James craned his neck, trying to see the interior of the school hall a little clearer through the sea of moving bodies.

Saffy waved. "Bye, Dad!" Then she was swallowed by the crowd moving inward, all spangles and excitement.

James would've felt a lot better if he'd checked out this Zane kid before he left, though both Maddie and Obāchan had assured him there was nothing to worry about.

"Oh! There's the person I need to talk to. Can you wait here for me? I'll be quick." Then Obāchan was off, weaving through a swathe of parents who all seemed to know one another—milling about on the netball courts.

James eased back into the shadows, shoving his hands deeper into his pockets. The evening had a bitter edge to it, and the feeling of being an outsider grew with each minute he stood alone.

The duty teacher from earlier in the day deviated off course to speak to him, her smile shy, but friendly nonetheless.

"You're Saffy's father, right?"

"Yes, that's right." He tugged his hand out of his pocket and offered it. "James Montague."

The teacher laughed as she took his hand. "Yes, I know. You're all she's talked about for the past fortnight. Aksel James Montague, software engineer and designer of farming and horticultural apps, if I'm not mistaken."

James blinked at her in surprise.

"I'm Talulah Opie."

"Miss O?" James put two and two together from Saffy's description. This had to be the part-time librarian and art teacher.

"The very same." Smile-crinkles emerged under the woman's glasses, softening her somewhat angular face into sweetness.

"She enjoys library time, and your Tuesday after-school art class more than anything else in school."

Miss O beamed. "Reading and the arts are her happy places, and I totally get that. They're mine too." She glanced back toward the hall. "I should really head back to the mayhem."

"Right, well, nice to meet you. Properly, I mean."

"Yes." But Saffy's teacher hesitated again, not making a move towards the large, sprawling building.

She wore an eye-popping necklace, flashing like Christmas lights, and a series of glow-in-the-dark bracelets up her arm. It was bling to rival anything James had seen on the students.

The unmistakable strains of the Makarena eddied out of the open door, and James wondered if that's why Talulah Opie was hanging back.

"Can I ask…? It's not really my business to delve into your personal life, Mr Montague."

"It's James. And ask away." He could always choose not to answer, or evade.

"James," she conceded. "Are you planning to stay in Wānaka?"

Good question, though totally dependent on outside factors. He went with a vague answer. "I'm planning to divide my time."

"Between Australia and New Zealand?"

"That's right. But I'll always be around for Saffy, if that's what you're meaning. I'm hers for the long haul."

The positive answer seemed to satisfy Saffy's teacher, and she flashed him another smile before moving off.

James had another thought, and jogged to catch up. "Ah… Miss O?"

"Call me Talulah."

"Talulah. A quick question. A boy called Zane?"

Talulah Opie laughed. "Welcome to parenthood, the 'tween' version. Scary, isn't it? He's a nice kid. They're good friends, who look after each other in the playground and bond over witches and wizardry. I believe their wands were mastered from the same oak tree." She pointed towards a huge specimen not far from the main gate.

"Okay." James drew the word out, not entirely convinced.

"Remind me, and I'll introduce you to his parents on pickup."

"That'd be great. Thanks."

Then Saffy's teacher was gone, weaving through to the pulsing dance music.

"Look what I found!" Obāchan scooted over, wearing a wide grin and wheeling a sack barrow almost as big as her.

"Wh—?"

"It's a sack barrow." She wiggled the handlebars from side to side.

"I know what it is." James looked around himself. "Where the hell did you get it from?"

"The caretaker's lending it to us."

"The school caretaker?"

"Yes. You can bring it back when you pick up Saffy tonight, after we've moved the sofa inside."

The older woman's reasoning suddenly dawned, and James took Obāchan by the shoulders and smacked a whisker-full kiss on each of her cheeks. "You little perla!"

Obāchan giggled. "I did good?"

"You did *great*!"

17

KUIA - FEMALE ELDER

A grandmother's wisdom teaches many generations.

After they'd moved the sofa into the house, with Obāchan in charge of steering and James on brawn duty, they took the squabs off all of the seating and took them upstairs to the largest bedroom.

"There. That looks cosy." Obāchan stepped back and admired their handiwork.

"Not too bad," James agreed, though it wasn't exactly the Hilton. They'd pushed together the squabs to make something resembling two single mattresses, and James and Saffy's sleeping bags lay side-by-side on them. Saffy had her own pillow, with Kookie planted firmly on it, and Obāchan had fetched James a small cushion from the sofa and covered it with one of his T-shirts.

"Where have you been sleeping up until now?" Obāchan wanted to know.

"I was in a motel until I bought this." James looked around himself. "And the last couple of nights I slept in the car," he admitted.

"Too *cold*," Obāchan remonstrated, giving a dramatic shiver. "You need a bed."

"You think?" James chuckled at the face Obāchan pulled.

"And some curtains."

James tapped his temple. "All on the list."

"Do you have a wife on that list, too?" Obāchan slid in knowingly, and he shrugged off the astute little jibe.

After detaching the trailer and storing it away in the garage, James drove Obāchan home to her compact little annex off Kana's pottery studio, while she pumped him for information.

Appearances could be so deceiving. Anyone meeting Kana's grandmother for the first time could be forgiven for thinking the diminutive, white-haired woman was sweet as apple-pie, and just as flaky. It was probably a demeanour she put across on purpose.

Underneath that coquettish daintiness ran girders of pure steel, and a quick-fire intelligence.

When Obāchan invited James into the annex for a cup of tea, he saw no reason not to. He backed himself to keep what was sacred to him close to his chest. So it was with some surprise he found the words, "We lost a child… A pregnancy," coming out of his own mouth just fifteen minutes later, when Obāchan asked him outright what he thought had started the disconnect within his marriage to Adele.

They were sitting at Obāchan's kitchen table, a pot of green tea between them and a finely-thrown handleless cup each. James looked deep into the dusky liquid instead of into the wise, knowing eyes, wondering just what kind of truth serum the octogenarian had served him.

Kindness? Acceptance? Whatever it was, it had loosened his tongue.

"I did know that, actually," Obāchan returned gently. "Not through Adele, but through Saffy. She likes to talk."

"She does, indeed."

They laughed together, and James met the truth-serum maker's eyes—so dark, they appeared black. Saffy trusted this woman, and confided in her. It was another major point in her credibility.

He cleared his throat. "I think something broke in Adele when we lost Rosetta, but I didn't see the extent of it. Not at the time. I wasn't there for her. I thought we were coming right, and by not talking about it, I was helping. I thought we had every reason to…" He ran a hand down over his jaw, then pinched at the flesh on his neck, still furious with himself for being so fucking obtuse. So arrogant he hadn't seen how deeply Adele's unhappiness had run, or how far apart they'd grown. He should've been able to see the danger looming a mile off.

"We planned to come over to New Zealand for her sister's wedding, spend some time together while Adele's parents looked after Saffy. Both of us were feeling the weight of having split her from her grandparents and wider family. Adele and Saffy had moved to Sydney due to my work," he elaborated, unsure how much Obāchan knew.

He didn't add, 'to their detriment,' but it hovered on the tip of his tongue.

"But you didn't come to the wedding?"

"Adele and Saffy flew over. I didn't."

"Why not?"

James groaned, sliding his head into his palms. "Work took over, the company was flailing, we had an inside leak and our software was compromised. Clients were bailing, left, right, and centre. I pulled out of the wedding trip to follow up on a last-minute takeover bid by a Chinese super-company." He looked up, catching Obāchan's eye. "I regret that. Always will."

"Adele never came home?"

"I guess that depends on what side of the Tasman you're on." He smiled without seeing much humour in the situation. "She came home to New Zealand, but never came home to me."

"Home is where the heart is," Obāchan stated matter-of-factly.

"Ha." There was no humour in that, either.

James turned his attention back to the beautifully sculpted teapot, with a dainty little Taj Mahal style knob on the lid. It was pale-blue, glassy and translucent, but with a depth of colour that went well below the surface.

Very like Adele's eyes.

"Do you think Wānaka has always been home to me?" Obāchan spoke softly. Her diction and vocabulary were exemplary, though her accent denoted the fact she'd lived in Japan for her formative years. "Or New Zealand, for that matter?"

There was an exotic edge to both her clothing and style, and James looked around the annex kitchen a little more carefully. There were photos of friends and family on the fridge, hand-dyed blue fabric at the windows, and a dainty sake set artfully displayed on the bench-top.

"This is the farmlet I grew up on." Obāchan stood to take down a magnetised picture from the fridge, and handed it over. The low, white building sported wide eaves, with dark, decorative roof tiles. "It was in my family for five generations, but Kanako was settled here in New Zealand, making a name for herself with her pottery. Then Ruby arrived. She's the light of my life, that child."

"Don't you miss Japan?"

"With half of my heart," Obāchan touched her fingers lightly to her sternum, bird-like in her grace of movement. "But Kanako and Ruby are my true reasons to be on this earth, my true destiny," she answered simply, re-magnetising the photo before returning to her wooden dining chair. "Buddha says, *'Your purpose in life is to find your purpose, and give your whole heart and soul to it.'* "

James nodded, understanding all too well the pull of loved ones. "I thought it was my purpose to save my father's legacy, his company. Now I'm not so sure." He spoke almost to himself, admitting to the sense of loss, but no longer dwelling in it. "He built Montague Holdings from the ground up. As a smallholder, a sheep farmer, he had ideas on how to improve agricultural systems." The company became his father's whole existence in the end. "It's strange to have it gone. It was all I lived for after he died, keeping ahead of the competition, keeping pace with digitisation, and the massive A.I. boom that was taking over agriculture and horticulture."

Obāchan leaned forward. "Your father has passed?"

"Yes." Accidentally on purpose.

James eyed the hand that had reached out to lightly touch his. Obāchan's skin was paper-thin, and seemingly fragile, but he knew better.

"It's a long story," he warned.

Obāchan squeezed his fingers. "I have time." Then she swivelled her head to check the clock on the oven. "And you have just over an hour before you have to go back and pick up Saffy. More tea, I think." She stood again. "A long story needs a fresh pot of tea."

"Is that another Buddhist quote?" James wondered aloud.

"No." Obāchan laughed. "It's common sense."

Obāchan came to stand next to James near the front door of the annex while he pulled on his boots, getting ready to leave. Then she handed him a brown paper bag.

Peering in, James could see something wrapped in Japanese newspaper.

"What's this?"

"A teapot."

"Oh, no. I can't accept that." James balked, passing the bag back. "Your teapot?"

Obāchan laughed. "I'll get Kana to make me another one." Her voice took on a sly tone. "The celadon glaze is beautiful, isn't it? Adele's favourite."

James snapped his head up at the mention of his ex-wife. "Yes, beautiful," he murmured.

Obāchan offered him a small smile. "Saffy talks about the special things you send her in the mail, so I gather you're a gift person. This is a housewarming present, so you can invite me to tea. I'll help you wherever I can, smoothing the family's ruffled feathers."

"Why?"

"I've been where you are, chasing home. And I believe your heart's in the right place. Daniel is against it, of course, but that's not about you. I think you remind him of himself, and he can be a stubborn *oni* when the mood takes him."

"Thank you." James took the re-offered bag, wondering where he'd heard the word used before. "An *oni* being a…?"

"Devil." Obāchan chuckled as she pressed her fingers to James' arm. "He's very protective of his family, but his bark is worse than his bite, usually." All hint of laughter left her dainty features, like the tide slowly ebbing out. "Adele's very important to us."

"She's very important to me, too." James spoke softly, and Obāchan relaxed enough to smile again.

That's when Daniel chose to slam in through the annex door, all boots and bristles.

"I've just got off the phone with Katie…" Daniel began before catching sight of James. "*Christ*. You again?" The border collie, obviously having been told to wait outside, gave a sharp bark on hearing its owner's combative tone.

Obāchan took her hand off James and moved between the two men with her chin up. "I invited Saffy's father in for a cup of tea." She eyed her grandson-in-law stoically.

Daniel muttered and grumbled, but left James alone. "Kanako and Ruby? I thought they were down here."

Obāchan shrugged. "Out for an evening walk on a beautiful night like this would be my guess." She slid into Daniel's exit-path and pointed to her cheek, directing him to kiss her on his way back out.

Daniel clearly wasn't stupid, nor one to rock the boat when it came to family. He bent to kiss his wife's elderly grandmother perfunctorily on her cheek before turning back to eye the other man in the hallway.

"You on your way to pick up Saffy from the disco?"

Daniel must've been informed of the evening plans, and clearly felt the need to make that known.

Obāchan rolled her eyes at the proprietary tone.

"Just leaving," James conceded, squashing the touch of humour that wanted to tweak at his own mouth.

He wasn't stupid either, and didn't allow the smile to fully emerge until Daniel had turned and left through the annex door.

"See? *Oni*," Obāchan muttered.

Adele wrangled Kana into joining her usually solitary lakeside walk the next morning, with Ruby chortling a happy up-down sing-song in the stroller, and Winger trotting obediently alongside. Being a Thursday, Adele should've in principle been at the law office by now, but she didn't have the head for it, and had taken the morning off.

Katie was still snuggled up in Adele's bed, stealing a much needed sleep-in.

It was difficult to know where to start as they strode out. Adele had woken with the urgent need to share, but there was also the conundrum of confidentiality. The private lives of Katie and Rue were not hers to share—not even with sweet, discreet Kana.

The lids to several of Adele's own cans of worms had been well and truly ripped off during her in depth conversation with her sister last night, and she was juggling a mountain of emotions that'd crept out of the dark to poke at her.

"Katie drove over yesterday." Adele hesitated before adding, "Needed a break from family life for the night."

That statement broke no confidence.

"Yes. Daniel said." Kana craned her neck forward to check on Ruby over the rain-hood. "Has she still got both her socks on?"

Adele scooted forward, and Ruby made a delighted *'Ahhh!'* sound when she caught sight of a familiar face.

"Both present and accounted for."

"Great." Kana picked up the pace again. "Is she going to be okay?"

"Ruby?"

"No. Katie." They were back to walking side by side, and Kana caught Adele's eye. There was an understanding gleam there.

"Yes. I think so."

"Good. And you?"

"Well..." Adele still wasn't sure on that point. Her discussion with Katie had lasted through a simple dinner of cheese toasties, and well into the small hours. Then they'd curled up together in Adele's bed, like chicks in a nest. "We covered a lot of ground," she hedged.

For a while they were silent, with just the crunch of fine gravel underfoot and the sound of Ruby's sleepy cooing. The day was still and bright, one of those unexpected autumn gems that blows the forecasted temperature right out of the ballpark, and Winger wasn't the only one panting.

"Saffy?" Kana finally queried as she navigated a bend in the path. The view from this point included Ruby's namesake island, standing much greener than the dry backdrop of hills, far beyond.

"Stayed with James."

"Right." Kana didn't look directly at her, choosing instead to gaze out towards the island. "Poor James," she murmured.

"No, not at all." Surprised, Adele lost concentration for a

moment, scuffing the toe of her sneaker on an uneven bit of path before righting herself. "He wanted to."

"No. I don't mean looking after Saff. I mean falling all over himself to please you."

"What?" Adele flustered. "No. He's just here for... He wants to spend time with Saffy."

Kana cleared her throat with a little '*ahem*.' "If you say so."

Adele frowned at her. "James and I are done."

"Yes, Daniel told me about that too, in the kitchen on family night." Kana chuckled, but her laughter died away when Adele didn't answer right away. "Not that it's any of my business."

Adele grasped her arm. "It's not like that. I just... I don't know what to tell you. I have no idea what I hoped to achieve with that. It was a dumb move."

"So you're *not* back together with him?"

"God, no. We're not *together*." But the word and the thought weren't nearly as abhorrent as they would've been a fortnight ago, and Adele turned that over in her head for a moment—what 'together' would look like with James. Up-close and personal. Skin on skin.

The visual was in no way conducive to clear thought, and she pushed images of her ex aside in irritation.

"Is that what you thought?"

Kana gave a half-shrug. "That's what it looks like from where I'm standing. The sexual chemistry between you two pings around like an overextended rubber band."

Adele sighed, "Tell me about it. But, no." Her hesitation was loaded with self-doubt. "Not that I haven't been thinking about it— the sexual side of it." That had always been their fallback. Her body knew James' as well as it knew itself, and she'd be lacking all senses not to recognise the pull of him. "I'm hoping it's *residual* pinging, if that makes sense? Unfinished business."

"Right," Kana huffed a wayward strand of hair out of her face. They were heading up the incline, and it was steep. "Though I think James still has feelings for you."

Feelings that were in danger of becoming mutual.

The rush of warmth to Adele's face was more than the small hill warranted. Blushing had been a constant embarrassment since childhood, a window into emotional states she'd rather not broadcast, but the paleness of her skin left her no defence.

Where was she supposed to house these emerging feelings for James? They no longer fitted in the black box of regret she'd kept aside for him in her memories.

The path evened out again, and Adele looped Winger's lead over the pram before jogging back to pick up the sock Ruby had just dropped.

"I'm not under his jurisdiction, anymore," she reminded Kana *and* herself, passing the tiny piece of clothing over while avoiding the dog's investigative muzzle.

"Though he'd like you to be." Kana wrangled the sock back on. When her daughter promptly toed it off again with a chortle, Kana groaned. "I don't think I'm going to like this game, Rubes."

Winger *loved* the game, yanking on her lead to try and reach the sock first.

When Ruby's feet were re-clothed, they started back down the path, a single row of deciduous autumn trees between them and the water.

"We'd never work. We failed at that already. A clear message from the fates," Adele muttered.

"You don't think either of you have changed?"

"Oh, undoubtedly. We both have."

"Then you prefer it solo." Kana issued it as a statement, rather than a question.

"It's not that I *prefer* it. There's nothing fun about going it alone," she grumbled.

"You're a good advertisement for going it alone, if you ask me." Kana spoke with sincerity, and Adele appreciated the shot of moral support aimed her way. Kana had been a single divorcee too, once. "You're a strong, can-do-anything woman, and a kick-ass mother."

"Thanks. Really."

"Careful though, your other exes might've caught wind of that pheromone bomb you've dropped, and be on their way around to your place right now."

"No chance of that." Adele snorted, though her mind naturally skipped back to a high-school boyfriend she hadn't thought about in years, and a few short-term try-outs. "The only other serious ex I've got is Moses."

"Saffy's birth father? Where's he now?"

"England." Moses' contact details were tucked into Adele's address book, getting musty. "So, I think I'm fairly safe on the ex front. Though now you mention it, he's overdue to get in touch."

"See? What did I tell you? Pheromone bomb." Kana laughed, and Ruby gave an answering chortle, setting off a chain reaction.

It was better to joke about the situation than to take it too seriously. Adele had a tendency to panic if she allowed herself to get bogged down in the semantics of it all.

18

TIKA - TRUTH

Honesty is not always the easiest path.

Adele breathed deeply in, then out. The golden poplars were a perfect backdrop, the nut-scented leaves underfoot a pleasant reminder of the season, and Kana's company second to none. She was loath to finish their walk.

"Have you had breakfast? Daniel made a batch of muffins this morning," Kana offered.

Adele checked her watch. She wasn't due at the office until twelve, and Katie was probably still asleep. "Sounds perfect. I'm starving. Can I text Katie and invite her if she's up? We're out of milk at my place, and she'll be ropeable without her morning coffee."

"Of course."

Adele slipped her phone out of her pocket to text her sister.

They took the short route back, everything fought about with her sister last night crowding Adele's mind, and the sweat creeping down her spine only added to her itchy mood.

"You said Moses is due to get in touch," Kana broke the silence some time later. "He writes?"

Adele sighed. "Every now and again. I didn't know where he

was for the longest time, and it all got a bit complicated after James came on the scene." She looked out to the far shore of the lake, the pretty scalloped edge where mountains met with deep water. "Everything's a bit more complicated with James on the scene." Drawing her hand down from where she'd been using it as a visor, she turned it over to assess the damage she'd done to her fingernails over the past couple of days. She hadn't chewed them this bad in years.

Kana finally gave up on following the trajectory of Ruby's biffed socks, and shoved them both into the pram bag. "He adores Saffy," she mused.

"Yes. He does." Adele could admit that without any qualms. James and Saffy's father-daughter connection had nothing to do with herself, or the divorce. The two just clicked. "I can see how much this time means to him, but I've only agreed to it because it also benefits Saffy. She has to come first."

"When was the last time *you* came first?"

"What do you mean?"

"Do you want to be with Moses?" Kana spoke softly. The cooing and snuffling from the pram had been replaced by silence. Ruby was finally asleep.

"With *Moses*? No." The answer came easily to Adele's lips without her having to think about it.

It'd been so strange, seeing Moses in Australia. He'd been shorter than she'd remembered him, but just as charismatic. Older, but with an agelessness of spirit that defied his years. Moses had always been magnetic, with a lot to say about the world. He'd become even more of an advocate for those with little voice, and Adele admired him for it, but she hadn't been gripped by that all consuming need to be near him.

Not like with James…

James—worming his way into her thoughts again and making Adele question her own sanity. How had she let herself get back into this situation? *Not* smart.

Reaching the turnoff to Ruby Island Road, Adele and Kana were on the home stretch, the lake now behind them.

"Moses, was…" This topic was harder than Adele had imagined.

More involved. More confronting. "He was seeking political asylum here in New Zealand when I met him. I was doing work experience for a lawyer who specialised in immigration law."

Kana nodded. "How old were you?"

Of all the questions, she'd had to pick that one.

Adele hesitated, fiddling with her hair tie and attempting to pull her ponytail tighter. "Eighteen," she finally conceded.

"And he…?"

Adele allowed herself another faint hesitation. "Forty-two."

"Hmm."

A pair of swallows shot past, swooping over the farm fence and in between poplar trees.

"It's not how it sounds." Adele tracked the trajectory of the agile birds. Raking over the past was a slow and painful exercise, like picking gravel out of a graze. "I was the one chasing him."

"I'm not passing judgement. I'm older than Daniel by five years."

"And, yet?"

"Eighteen to forty-two. That's a big age gap."

"Yes," Adele conceded. "Though it didn't seem so at the time."

The road came into view, a narrow dual-carriageway with grass verges, and they slowed pace by unspoken consent.

"And he'll be touching base with you again, soon." Kana sighed, as if it were a romantic notion.

"With Saffy," Adele corrected her.

"If you say so." Kana checked in on Ruby again, appearing to spend some time wording the next question just right. "You're sure he's not just interested in re-kindling…?"

"Does he want me back?" Adele took in a deep breath and looked up at the bluer-than-blue sky as she expelled it slowly. "No. He knows I'd never take on the role of the other woman again."

"He's already with someone?"

Adele squeezed her eyes shut and wrinkled up her nose, loath to tell Kana this bit. "He's *always* been with someone. Married to someone," she finally admitted in a whisper. "Not my finest hour, I'm afraid."

"Again, not judging."

Adele fixed Kana with a solemn stare. "*I* judge it. Moses and his wife were separated by war and hardship. For months he didn't even know if she was..." she trailed off. "But they were married, nonetheless. I disrespected that. In the worst possible way."

Kana brought one shoulder to her ear in a sideways shrug. "Youth and entitlement go hand in hand. Add lust to the mix, and you've got a potent cocktail of don't-give-a-shit." She chewed on her lower lip for a bit. "That doesn't excuse Moses, though. I'm not willing to allow him that, considering he was a grown assed man who'd already made promises elsewhere."

"In his defence, he had no idea if she'd survived. Not at the time. But they found each other again. There's a Red Cross initiative that brings divided families together." Adele looked down at the dust on her sneakers. "So he left."

"He left," Kana echoed. "Just like that? Does that mean Saffy has half-siblings?"

"No." Actually, Adele wasn't a hundred percent sure. "Not that I know of," she reiterated with slightly less confidence. "I'm not naïve to extra-marital flings, but it didn't feel like that with Moses. I knew it wasn't entirely right, but I also knew there was something special between us. It seemed fated to happen, somehow." She sighed. "I've learned to regret my behaviour without regretting it happened, because without it, there'd be no Saffron."

A lark was ascending, disturbed by an approaching vehicle. The bird warbled upward and onward to the background sound of tyres crunching on gravel, as the car emerged from a long driveway and turned towards them. Women and dog pulled off to the verge to let the hatchback past, and Kana stilled the motion of the stroller beside an out-of-place advertising placard.

"I never imagined how it would feel for her," Adele murmured. "The wife. Not until the shoe was on the other foot and I suspected my own husband." She gave Winger's ruff a rummaging pat, old guilt still able to dispense a dose of self-disgust.

"*He* wasn't unfaithful, though. Not *James*." Kana pulled a prune-face. "I thought, after I'd met him..." she trailed off, glancing sideways to where a shingle drive joined the road. There was a red sticker overlapping images on the for-sale sign, boldly pronouncing the property '*sold.*'

"I thought he was, with someone at his work. Convinced myself it was a concrete truth." Adele pulled up the hem of her T-shirt to mop sweat off her forehead. "The stick-insect put forward a pretty airtight case."

"The stick-insect?"

"Tiffany." Adele gave up the name as she studied the details on the signage. Three bedrooms, two lounges, and multiple outbuildings. A serious doer-upper by the looks of it, with million-dollar views. Why hadn't she seen this advertised? Huge potential as a B&B if you converted one or two of the garages into cabins. First time on the market in seventy-five years, and already gone to another buyer.

"I guessed as much, to be honest."

Adele's head snapped back towards Kana. "How?"

Kana shrugged. "When we watched Love Actually over Christmas, you emptied your tear ducts."

"Everyone bawls over that scene," Adele discounted with a flick of her hand. "Joni Mitchell backing Emma Thompson. It's inevitable."

"No. Most of us get choked up. We don't lock ourselves in the bathroom and sob for half an hour."

"Thin walls," Adele muttered.

"Incredibly thin. Don't ever have noisy sex in the guest bedroom. When Cam and Shal stay, I've been known to employ earplugs so I can look them in the eye over breakfast."

Adele laughed again, then remembered Ruby was sleeping and slapped a hand over her mouth.

Her cousin, Cameron, couldn't keep his hands off his life-partner. Which was hardly surprising. Shal was stunning, and only had eyes for him.

"You'd hear those two even if you had Led Zeppelin blasting from every speaker in the house," she whispered.

Kana rolled her eyes. "*Tell* me about it!"

Adele kicked at the gravel, creating a little divot before raising her eyes and gazing up towards the 'single owner' property again. "I've since realised she might've lied."

"Who? The stick-insect?"

"Yes." Adele turned to look back at Kana—back to eyes full of consternation. "Some things just don't add up, you know?

"What kind of things?" Kana leaned down to lock the wheel-break on Ruby's stroller, then grabbed her water bottle and took a long draught.

"James is really partial to curvy, for one. Natural. I know his type, because I was his type."

Kana snorted. "*Are* his type."

Adele worried at the hem of her T-shirt, ignoring the aside. "But if you were given a lineup, you'd know exactly who your guy would go for on a physical level, right?"

Kana thought about it for a moment. "Right." Moving a little off to the side, she planted her butt down on the grassy embankment.

Winger clearly thought that was the best idea ever, and followed suit.

Adele took the offered water and removed the lid to take a sip, then poured a handful for Winger to lap at.

"But I could name several other single women in James' company who'd have been more his demographic, and more than receptive to the idea."

Kana hesitated again before asking the next question. "Maybe just convenience, then? Vicinity, or dare I say it, personality?"

"That's just it. Personality a definite no." Having had five years to mull over the details, Adele was pretty sure on that point. "Type-A. Organised, efficient, and cold as a fish. Incredibly focussed on climbing the corporate ladder. Tiffany was what *I* found threatening, because she was everything I wasn't. The female version of James. Single career woman. Immaculately presented. Leggy, with perfect silicone boobs."

"There's no such thing as perfect silicone, it's perfectly gross."

Adele finally sat on the tufty grass, too. "You know what? I love you, Kana."

"Why, because I have trouble filling an A-cup?" Kana's mouth twisted wryly, making Adele grin. "You're saying if James was horny at work, there'd be other options more to his taste." She mimed bigger boobs with her hands.

Winger, realising they were settling for the long-haul, lay her muzzle on her paws and relaxed.

"Yes, but that's another thing. I've always found it hard to figure why he'd compromise his father's business, or its reputation, with such an open affair." Resting the water bottle between herself and Kana, Adele began plucking randomly at the wild grasses, removing seed heads. "James *is* his work. He's consumed by it."

So why was he spending so much time in New Zealand? Two weeks just hanging with Saffy... What was *with* that? If Isabella was to be believed, Montague Holdings was no longer trading. Did that mean James was unemployed?

Adele waved the idea aside as ludicrous. James was an incredibly driven individual, with cutting edge IT designs...

"He denies cheating. And that first pizza night, when he came to the farm..." Adele's eyes slid in the direction of Daniel and Kana's property, not five minutes walk along the main road.

Where James had kissed her, and she'd kissed him back.

"I actually found myself believing him," she finished in a whisper.

Adele's hand made its way into her mouth again, and before she knew it, she was gnawing at her already tender thumbnail. Yanking the digit back out, she wedged her hand securely between her knees.

"So, what made you think James had strayed in the first place? You saw them together?"

Adele made a small sound denoting the negative—because she hadn't.

"They were in each other's pockets all the time, working all hours. I could tell something was off. Something had changed between them. Intensified. But most of the red flags were from Tiffany, not James," she admitted. "I thought at the time he'd become a master at hiding his indiscretions, but I'm beginning to realise it's all too clean, too clear cut. I got the confession from *her* mouth, swallowed the evidence *she* gave me."

And the more Adele thought about it, the more it grated on her. She'd been so quick to believe Tiffany's word over her husband's.

"I think James' P.A. was trying to get rid of me," Adele confided. She'd never said that aloud before, and it sounded strangely elemental in the open air. "She wanted him all to herself."

Kana nodded, but was still sporting a light frown. "So, ask him."

She stood and dusted off the seat of her leggings. "It's a valid query."

"Yes, it is." Adele sighed as she followed Kana's movements, easing up to stand. "Give me ten minutes with that man and a lie detector."

Kana laughed. "Sure you wouldn't prefer to spend that ten minutes focussing on something else?"

"Ha!" No. Adele *wasn't* sure. "The thing is, James and I were in trouble well before the Tiffany fiasco." Adele steepled her fingers to quell the shake, and combat the urge to chew on her nails. "Two years after we married, I got pregnant, but I... *We*." Taking a deep breath, she eased it slowly out again before continuing. "We lost it."

There was a beat of pure, shocked silence.

"Oh, hon, I'm so, so sorry." Kana was hugging her awkwardly with one arm, her drink bottle wedged in the crook of her other elbow. Winger pushed her wet nose between them, perhaps sensing something was off.

"I couldn't talk about it." A single tear escaped, running down Adele's cheek to plop off the end of her chin and onto Kana's shoulder. "I was just too raw. Some women live through miscarriage after miscarriage. Then they pick themselves back up and try again. I wasn't strong like that."

Kana pushed back to squint at her. "You're one of the strongest people I know, and the loss of a child is..." She got a wobble in her voice as she took Adele's hand in hers, crushing the remaining grass-seed heads. "Thank you for telling me. I can't imagine how hard that had to've been. Daniel and I could've been a lot more sensitive, what with Ruby and everything."

Adele closed her eyes and took another deep breath, again letting it ebb slowly before speaking.

"Daniel doesn't know."

"But you..." Kana slid a look towards her sleeping baby, safe in her stroller, then back to Adele's face. "You're so close. You talked to your mum about it?"

Adele shook her head miserably.

"Katie?" Kana offered Adele's sister's name almost hopefully.

"Not until last night. I was so proud. So miserable. So *stupid*. I realise now, after counselling, I was deeply depressed at the time. I didn't want anyone to know I'd failed Rosetta." Adele held her free palm over her stomach. Relatively flat now, but once upon a time it had held the miracle of Saffron, then Rosetta. "Or failed to keep my marriage alive."

The hand still resting in hers squeezed tight.

"Then, after a while, it got too hard to bring up."

"Yes." Kana let go, sliding her water bottle back into its holster on the stroller. "I know what you mean. The habit of secrets."

"It helped talking to Fran. She's been amazing." Adele suddenly realised how that sounded.

'I could talk to a stranger, but not to you…'

"I want to apologise. You mean the world to me, Kana, and I'm sorry for being so—"

"No. Don't do that. You told me when you were ready, and that's how it should be. We all have untold things." Kana moved her weight from one foot to the other, then waved a hand towards the property they'd been resting in front of. "Speaking of which, I hear Iris, the real estate agent, is crowing about this particular sale." There was something close to regret in her tone. "Sold before it was even on the market. Not really worth putting up a sign, though the self-proclaimed queen of property does like seeing her own name posted everywhere."

Adele narrowed her eyes, suddenly on high alert. Kana was chewing on her lip, definitely having trouble holding something in.

"I hope they're not planning to develop the crap out of this for lakeside holiday accommodation?" Adele tried to get a finger on what Kana's problem might be with the speedy change of hands. Because clearly, something was bothering her.

"No. Nothing like that." Again Kana glanced at the partially hidden house, then back to Adele with a touch of sympathy. "More like a family bolt-hole."

From the pictures, the place was a sprawling two-story, with extensive garaging and land, screened from the road by landscaped stands of established trees.

It was no 'bolt hole,' unless… "Big family?"

As Adele tied Winger's lead to the pram, Kana cleared her throat.

"No. Just the one guy at the moment."

It took a second for the penny to drop.

"You're shitting me!" Adele's growl was fierce enough to rouse Ruby. "*James?*"

19

KANIKANI - DANCE

Dance around your nemesis, or with them?

James' day was shaping up to be a strange mix. Waking up to a breakfast date with his daughter before school had been the highlight—a shiny gem of normality. They'd had Coco Pops and sliced bananas with milk, sitting together on the lounge chairs they'd pulled out onto the verandah for a grand view of the lake.

He'd kept his side of the bargain, not breathing a word to Saffy about her aunt being in town. If the almost ten-year-old knew something was up, she was a good little actress—all bubble and squeak about the dance the night before.

Once his daughter was safely deposited at school, keen to digest events with her friends, James sped back to the cabin. He got there with less than a minute to spare to keep his nine a.m. with the interior designer.

More than an hour spent pouring over colour-ways and fabric samples was tedious, but necessary. He deferred to Simone's professional opinion to speed things up, but requested more colour in the upstairs bedrooms. "My daughter, Saffy, is an artist," he explained.

And rainbows were her mother's favourite.

"Sorry, but I need to cut this short." James checked his watch again after agreeing the downstairs bathroom walls could mimic the white subway tiles they'd chosen for the kitchen splash-back, as long as the towels were bright and there were indoor plants and wood accents. "Think Fiji style." He echoed Adele's words, and smiled, remembering how it'd felt to have Adele's hand absently stroking his back as she'd talked him through ideas for her own lounge. "I'm afraid I've got a video conference kicking off in a few minutes. Would you be happy to leave the colour boards here?"

"Sure. But tomorrow's going to be final-call on the sofa covers and window-seat fabrics if you want them completed within the month. The upholsterer has a cancellation, so time is of the essence there." Simone tapped her pen on her clipboard. "How does four o'clock suit you?"

"Tomorrow," James promised, shaking her hand.

His online meeting after Simone's departure was nowhere near as straightforward. It had already been decided Lake Taimana Wineries would play guinea pig on the trial run, as they were by far the smallest of the Organic Wineries Collective, and had the most data collected with regards to soil samples and organic pest control.

The problem was the price.

The Collective wasn't keen to pay tens of thousands of dollars worth of research and development on new tech that might potentially aid only one vineyard, and Lake Taimana was ostensibly refusing to foot the bill alone.

Quibbling was the word for it.

It wasn't a new complaint to be fielding in James' line of work. Everyone was looking for someone else to pick up the financial shortfall, that was the nature of business. Though it was fairly unprofessional and disorganised for the various heads to still be arguing when their contractor, James, was still in the virtual room.

He zoned out of the heated e-conference debate, and was actually daydreaming about Adele when she stormed around his wraparound verandah, eyes flashing fire.

"Of all the bloody nerve!" Adele pointed her finger at him like she was sighting a rifle, though it appeared to be a touch on the shaky side. "That's *my* chair!" Dressed in walking gear and sneakers, she had dust on her T-shirt and her leggings hugged every beautiful curve of her.

"Sorry, did you say something, Mr. Montague?" The chairman of the board leaned forward with a frown.

No, James hadn't. Though he may well have grunted in surprise swallowing his tongue.

It was as if he'd conjured Adele up by thinking about her, all hiss and brimstone, and it was all he could do to stare at her with his mouth gaping open.

"What the hell are you doing, buying this? You *bought* this! Without asking me first!" she continued at volume. "Like I have *no* say in what goes on."

There was a moment of complete silence from the other five microphones on the video call as they digested her words.

"Pardon? I think we may have some audio crossover. Is anyone else hearing—?" one of the vineyard owners on James' screen finally ventured.

"You'd better have a bloody good explanation," Adele continued over the top of the woman, still firmly in 'Fergus-lively-discussion' mode. "This is *my* space. *My* place. *My* life! You can't just waltz in here, buying everything and taking over!" Adele stomped closer to stand a mere metre away, hands fisted on hips.

Ready for battle, and stunningly in charge of herself. So reminiscent of days past, Adele took James' breath away.

"Ah, excuse me." He scrambled to grab at his laptop, which was in imminent danger of sliding off his lap. "My wife—" the slip was unintentional, but unforgivable.

"*Ex*-wife," Adele almost screeched.

James flinched. "*Ex*-wife," he amended, and before Adele could continue with the verbal lashing, swiftly added, "Adele Fergus, meet the Lake District Organic Wineries Collective."

Adele blinked, then narrowed her eyes.

"Bull*shit*," she muttered as she yanked the laptop from him and turned it around to face her. The look on her face when she clocked all the faces staring back at her was priceless. "Oh, *shi*... Sorry! I didn't realise." She cleared her throat, and if possible, flushed an even deeper shade of crimson. "Ah... Hello there, Mr Kaihanga."

"Adele! Kia ora! Whaea Tania and I were just saying we missed you when we dropped into the law office this morning. Such a friendly face. You're not unwell, I hope?" The owner of Lake Taimana Wineries eased over the awkwardness with a relaxed smile.

"Um, no. I just… I took the morning off. I'll pop back in this afternoon." Adele made a nervy little *'ahem'* sound. "Well, I'll let you get back to it, then."

She one-eightied the screen back to face James, and backed off as soon as he had hold of the laptop again.

He held up five fingers, just out of camera-view, and caught Adele's eye with a silent plea. If she would just give him a few minutes to wind this up, she could rake him over hot coals to her heart's content.

Adele rolled her eyes and stomped off the way she'd come, and James grinned after her retreating back.

It actually took ten minutes to lock in another meeting time to suit everyone, and wrap the rest of the agenda up. By then, James had no idea where Adele had gone. There was no sign of her car when he checked the drive, but he hadn't heard one arrive, either. Had she come on foot? That would explain the sneakers, the rosy cheeks, and the light sheen on her skin.

James headed back to the comfort of the verandah armchair, demoting his laptop to the timber floor and digging his phone out of his pocket. Adele's cell number was back in pole-position on his contact list after five long years of absence, and he took a moment to stare at the deceptively simple letters of her name before he texted.

Meeting's over. Are you still here?

It only took a moment for Adele's reply to come through, and it was so snappy and in-character, he chuckled aloud.

You can't put this green textured tile in the upstairs bathroom. It's all wrong.

So, curiosity had gotten the better of his ex-wife, and she'd stayed on to investigate. Along with a strong opinion on his decision to purchase the property, she appeared to have its interiors under a microscope. Why was he not surprised?

Alternative? James texted back.

Glossy white, like the kitchen. But they should all be herringbone, not linear.

Herringbone, like tweed? Angular?

Adele was probably right. She was right about most things.

James ignored that nagging thought for the present, and fired back a passive-aggressive, *Anything else?*

Adele's next text was much longer. She took him literally and listed her dislikes. She hated the navy master bedroom scheme. Of course she did. Too cool for the south side of the house, and too masculine. Neither was she a fan of the kitchen layout. The sink needed to be situated with the view in mind, and was presently too far from the dishwasher plumbing to promote a 'workable triangle.'

The nitpick-list continued to ping through as consequent texts, right down to the colour of the skirting boards, and James smiled at each one as he reclined in *her* armchair with a calming view of the lake.

There was something comforting about visualising Adele moving from room to room behind him, taking an interest and demanding her say. He stayed seated until he could hear her footfall in the main lounge behind him.

Shoving his phone back into his pocket, he took one last look at the glinting water before strolling through the open door separating them.

Adele was standing with the wood burner at her back, hand on hip as she surveyed the space, her phone at the ready. She didn't look at him as he entered, but James knew she was aware of his presence by the way her chin rose in that proud little tilt.

"Overall?" His voice sounded remarkably expressionless considering how his chest was crushing in at the sight of Adele in his space.

"It's big. Has a lot of potential. How much did you pay for it?" This time Adele turned and pinned him with a look. It was a contemplative stare that told him in no uncertain terms he was still firmly in the furnace for buying the damn thing.

James shrugged in mild discomfort, knowing Adele was well within her rights to be majorly pissed. "Probably too much."

Adele loosened up enough to emit a short chuckle, the sound warming and curling around him. "No doubt. What's your budget for the refurb?"

"Not enough." He glanced away as he skirted the answer. His present funds were already stretched.

"If you've got any leeway, you should put in a walk-in wardrobe in the downstairs master, and both upstairs bedrooms would benefit from bigger built-ins."

James scratched at his eyebrow. "Possibly?"

"Definitely. There's also a great spot past those ngaio trees to extend a boardwalk off the verandah and add a hot tub." To someone who didn't know her, Adele would appear calm, but her even tone didn't match the fact one of her fists was still clenched at her waist, and the other was strangling her phone.

"Maybe at a later stage," James decided aloud. If there was any money left over from the winery deal. "Would you like me to pick Saffy up today?" He changed the subject, nudging it away from dollars and cents.

"No. It's Thursday. Kana and Daniel's day."

"I realise that, but I was thinking with Katie here, and you taking the morning off work—"

"No," Adele restated firmly, then seemed to remember her manners. "Thank you," she added coolly.

This polite, icy version of Adele reminded James too viscerally of the last year they'd spent together-apart in Sydney. Adele aloof and unreachable, quietly furious and achingly sad. He was experiencing withdrawal for the finger pointing, openly hostile version of her on arrival at the cabin. Regardless of whether it kept him square in the firing line, he preferred her argumentative, deeply opinionated mode. At least it was heartfelt.

"You're angry I went ahead and bought in Wānaka, without consulting you." James purposefully opened himself up for hunting season. "And you have every reason to be."

"Angry doesn't even *begin* to cover it." A touch of heat had crept back into Adele's voice, and James tried to hide the fact he welcomed her temper.

"Would it make you feel any better if you had free rein with the interior designer?"

"Yes," Adele answered instantly, then frowned. "No," she amended.

"Which is it? Yes or no? She's back onsite at four p.m. tomorrow, and I could really do with your input. I'm drowning in colour swatches."

Adele blinked at him, clearly drawn off target.

"You know what Saffy likes—what would make her feel at home," James continued in what he hoped was a reasonable tone.

"You can't fob me off with a project, James. You wilfully came to Wānaka without telling me, and now you're literally buying property on my doorstep." Adele waved her phone around, swinging her arm wide to encompass the house, the property, and the view through the large picture windows.

"For Saffy." James scratched at his earlobe and took a step towards her, drawn toward the heat, rather than away from it. "You said pie-in-the-sky wasn't good enough, and I agreed."

"I meant a rented *holiday* home, not a bloody lakefront mansion!"

"I'd hardly call this place a mansion in its current state," he pointedly looked around the dim interior. "But given a few months, Saffy will be more than comfortable—"

"You think you can pull that one over on me? This is all for Saffy's benefit?" Adele growled.

"All of us, then," James admitted aloud for the first time, even to himself. He moved another step closer.

"Honesty. Finally." Adele began to pace, more than likely to remove herself from the touch-zone that kept drawing him in. "I have nothing to offer you, James. Least of all a scenario where we contemplate *living* together." She turned to face him again, stationary at the window. The light streaming in from behind her suffused her hair in fire tones. "Our marriage obliterated everything I was, all of my self-esteem and self-belief in a very short space of time."

The raw hurt behind that statement was a direct slap across the face, and James flatlined his lips to deal with the sting. "It was never my intention—"

Adele threw one hand out towards him. "I'm not blaming you. Not entirely. As you said, it takes two to tango. But you can't really believe I'd willingly go for that again... *Any* of it?"

"None of it?" He lowered his voice in suggestion.

"Oh, there's no denying my *body* wants yours." Rather than angry now, Adele sounded a touch despondent.

James' libido shot an electrified jolt directly to his groin, merely on hearing the confession come out of her mouth.

In no way helpful.

"Don't try to cheapen what we had," he cautioned. "Yes, it was physical. Inescapably so. But I *loved* you Adele." He hesitated before continuing quietly, "And I like to think you loved me back."

"Then why did you never come?" Adele whispered, leaning back on the window frame, her profile suddenly a picture of pain. "You let the divorce go through without contest…"

James moved swiftly towards her again, frowning. "You told my lawyers I was never to contact you!"

"And you took that and ran with it," Adele countered with a sigh.

"Christ, Adele, I can't keep up with you. You *wanted* me to disregard your wishes and get up all in your face, demanding answers?"

"I wanted to feel *some* sense of worth."

"Worth? You and Saffy were *everything* to me."

"It didn't feel like we were even in the running, at the time." Adele offered him a sad little half-smile that kicked him squarely in the gut. Each little dig she came up with was beating him black and blue, without her ever laying a finger on him.

Had James dealt with Adele's request for a divorce all wrong? Complied when he should've pushed hard in the other direction? He'd been so shocked, sledge-hammered she would choose to leave him without so much as a phone call to explain.

He'd seen the divorce papers as Adele's final word. Unexpected or not, the woman had spoken. She didn't want him—would rather settle back in her home country without him. The thought still had the ability to sink fierce claws into his soft tissue, as did the fact he'd never been unable to give her the happiness she deserved.

No unicorns. No rainbows. Just storm cloud after storm cloud.

"I followed your instructions to a T, because I had no other recourse. I have no legal ties to Saffy, and if you'd decided I didn't deserve to see her—" James grabbed at Adele's free hand when it looked like she was aiming to slide past him and swing out the front door, and her eyes flashed at the uninvited contact. "Don't leave now," he pleaded. "This is something we should've discussed a long time ago."

Adele stepped in close, eyes sparking with blue fire. "You came to Wānaka when it suited you in the fiscal sense, and I will *never* put myself or Saffy in the position of runner-up to your work again."

"That would be understandable, if it were true," he growled back, finding it suddenly difficult to breathe with the faint brush of Adele's breast against his arm, and her sweet and salty scent all around him. "But it's not. I came when you cancelled Saffy's trip on me, and your bank statement arrived. Then I *knew* I'd misjudged you, been misguided as to why you left."

"Misguided?" Adele rapped her phone against his chest with an angry little *tap, tap, tap.* "Tell me, James, what exactly was happening at Montague Holdings while your marriage was going under? All those clandestine evening meetings you couldn't *possibly* get out of to spend time with your family?"

"The business was going under, too," he admitted. "Flatlining. Everything, including the house, was mortgaged to the hilt."

Adele hesitated, and the sudden pucker between her eyebrows showed James that hadn't been the answer she was expecting. "And you couldn't share that information with your wife?" Her voice cracked a little on the last word.

"I should've told you everything." He rubbed his free hand over his eyes, swiping redundantly at the twenty-twenty hindsight.

"Why didn't you?" Adele whispered, standing so close he could feel her breath faintly on his neck.

"I didn't want to put more on your plate, when you'd suffered the loss of Rosetta." James swallowed. "I failed, Dell. No one wants to admit that, do they? I wrecked it, lost it, mismanaged the problem."

"What problem?"

"We had a leak. Someone was undercutting us and selling my designs to our own customer bank. Owen, as it turns out."

"Owen." Adele repeated, stepping abruptly back from him again. Their hands were still connected—opposite arms pulled taut in the space between.

Reluctant to let go, James took a risk in bringing Adele's hand ever-so-slowly to his mouth. But although her eyes widened and her grip tightened, she didn't resist as he kissed one abused fingernail after the other.

"I was wrong not to tell you," he murmured against her skin. "I was wrong about a lot of things."

Their eyes met.

"What are you doing?"

"Kissing your hand," he answered in a perfectly judicial tone, considering his blood was threatening to pump right out of his chest, and pressed his mouth to the next pale fingertip with the tang of Adele's salt on his lips.

Adele cleared her throat when he touched his tongue to her pinky before he kissed it, her own tongue darting out to moisten her lips. "Cut that out."

"You don't like it?

"I didn't say that. But you know what it *does*..." Adele berated.

Yes, he knew very well what it did—what it used to do to her. And he could see by the widening of her pupils she was no more immune to the sweet tension building between them than he was.

James had noted Adele's nails were chewed down painfully short. The tell-tale damage didn't sit particularly well with him, and self-reproach eddied. She always nibbled on her nails when she was distressed, and he knew without a doubt he was the cause this time.

He growled his regret, deep in his throat.

"Just one more?" Adjusting her hand slightly, he brought her thumb topside.

Adele hesitated, then nodded, her teeth catching at the fullness of her lower lip.

James mimicked her by nipping at the fleshy tip of her thumb gently, watching her reaction all the while. She closed her eyes briefly, opening them with a sigh when he finished and turned her hand again, this time to expose her wrist. He arched one eyebrow in query, holding his breath until Adele conceded with another faint nod.

Her wrist, silken skin with a tracing of azure veins just under the surface, begged to be taken into consideration, and he did just that with his mouth. By the time he was done, Adele was right up against him, her shallow breath mingling with his.

It was a mutual movement, the kiss. A slight lowering and angling of his head, Adele rising onto tiptoe... Instant intergalactic travel.

Adele yanked on his hand, still locked in hers, pulling it from between their fused bodies and dragging it towards her shoulder. "Do that thing," she muttered against his lips.

Which thing?

"This thing?" He slid his suddenly freed hand into the hair at Adele's nape, gently manoeuvring through tightly furled corkscrews until his fingers were widespread and super-slowly massaging her scalp.

He caught her responding moan with his mouth.

Yep, *that* thing.

"Ohhh…" The sound came from deep within Adele like a purr of contentment, melting James' bones. Sliding his free arm around her waist, he pulled her in against himself, luxuriating in her softness.

When Adele's tongue teased across his, James almost lost the plot. His body was screaming for more of her. More skin, more depth, more release. He contented himself with the silkiness of her back, his free hand finding the gap between T-shirt and leggings, stroking the bare contours of spine and muscle in broad sweeps.

The self-assurance of Adele's mouth urged him on in the way only she could, her palm on his jaw, angling him where she wanted him as her fingers slid up to frame his ear.

From the deep recesses of James' mind, he could hear tinny music, but it didn't register until Adele jerked in his arms and something clattered to the floor. They pulled apart, staring at each other.

"My phone," Adele noted, her voice breathy and rough.

"Right," James agreed, not removing either of his hands from her person.

"I dropped it," Adele reiterated, still gazing at his lips in some sort of daze.

"Right," he agreed again, then lowered his head. Their mouths were drawn back together as if by magnetic force, and Adele sighed. It sounded so fatalistic, James tightened his grip on her back, holding on as if he never meant to let her go.

"You've always been too good at making me forget myself," Adele murmured, a hair's-breadth from his lips.

"*You've* always been too good at making me forget *my*self," he corrected gently.

"Mmmm..." Adele conceded, rocking her hips from side to side in a minute movement against his hard-on, building exponential static between them.

Adele's cell kicked in again, somewhere in the vicinity of James' feet, and she was suddenly pulling back—enforcing distance by pressing on his chest. James let her go, detangling his fingers from her hair and T-shirt. Limbs suddenly heavy and benign, he shoved his hands into his pockets to stop himself from dragging his wife back against his chest.

Ex-wife.

Adele bent to answer the call and the intensity of the moment was swallowed by awkwardness.

"Katie? Yup. On my way."

James could hear a faint voice on the other end of the line, raised in disbelief, or anger. He couldn't quite make out the words spoken.

"Of course not!" Adele glanced up at him, blushed rosy on the apples of her cheeks, then lowered her voice to little more than an indignant whisper as she moved backwards towards the waiting doorway. "I *know*." She hung up and blinked across the room at him, suddenly out of reach on all counts. "I've gotta go."

20

TĀTORU - THREEFOLD

A rope woven with three strands is stronger than two.

Stupid, stupid, stupid. Why couldn't she keep away from James? Like a blowfly to a blue-light, she kept flying too close and zapping her wings. Adele's sneakers kicked up dust on the gravel road as she broke into a run in her haste to be gone from James' vicinity. Berating herself all the way did nothing to kill the buzz of touching him, though. Kissing him.

Adele let out a deep-seated moan.

She was always too quick to let her heart rule, leaving her brain floundering two strokes behind. Her common sense was finally jumping in to tell her how futile this reconnect would be, but her physical body was far from agreeing. Nerve endings and pleasure centres lit up all over whenever James was within reach, and lately he seemed to be within reach *all the time*.

She was heading for serious trouble, no matter how much she refuted the fact to her sister.

What had happened to the guidelines she'd set down for herself, the single-mum rules that protected Saffy and herself from harm? She was a glutton for punishment where her ex-husband was concerned. Even now, her unconscious self was filling her head with raunchy images of James.

James with his shirt off, eyes darkened with lust—James all over her, one with her, inside her. Oh, *hell*, those little groans he made when he was losing his grip threw her straight in the deep end.

She was losing her *own* grip. This wasn't some blind date, this was the man she'd chosen to *divorce*, for heaven's sake.

A.J., the little voice in her head insistently argued. *Adele's James*.

Adele moaned again, tears of frustration brimming. The ache to be with him was becoming unbearable.

She scampered to the farm, where Kana and Katie sat speculating, eating bran muffins while dipping their toes into the new swimming pool.

Ripping up the rotten flooring in the downstairs bathroom was more than cathartic for the mood James was in, but he still found himself obsessively checking his phone for messages from Adele.

She'd told him his services weren't required for Saffy's afternoon pickup, so he had no reason to expect a text, but they'd left everything else up in the air when she'd scuttled out after Katie's phone call.

The builders arrived after eleven, helping take James' mind off Adele by forcing him into the practical realm.

"Would it be feasible to enlarge those built-ins in the two upstairs bedrooms? And maybe add a walk-in in the downstairs master?" James wondered aloud.

"You've been talking to a woman." Mike, the head carpenter, chuckled at James' reluctant nod. "I'm surprised she didn't want an ensuite in there, too. There's plenty of room, if that's her next question. Pipes run directly past for the main bathroom, so it wouldn't be as expensive as you'd think to squeeze a small one in."

James managed a smile, but the builder had a valid point. Distracted or not, all thoughts seemed to lead back to Adele.

"While we're on the subject of pipes…" he brought up Adele's concerns about the kitchen layout to get the builder's take on it.

When the head plumber arrived, James ran the ensuite idea past her, and ended up signing on for that too. Yet more capital invested, yet more locked into this pipe-dream venture. He rang the council to wrangle an extension on his current consent, and pitched in to rip up even more floorboards for the new sewer connection. The physical work took the remainder of the afternoon.

James didn't have any idea if Adele still wanted him to attend her counselling session with Dr Fran this evening. It'd be the height of rudeness to turn up to her booked slot and take her time.

She'd taken the morning off from the law office, which could only mean she needed a break.

Flip-side? It'd be inexcusable not to be there. He'd been invited by the therapist, and anything he could do to help Adele...

He owed her that at the very least.

Perhaps best he hadn't gotten around to asking when she'd turned up this morning. It hadn't been the right platform to discuss practicalities due to her mood, and the mind-bending nature of that kiss. She probably would've disinvited him on principle.

James decided to just turn up at Dr Fran's at the appropriate time. Available, but ready to leave if Adele wanted him to. He showered and changed at the pool, due to his water being off, and was so mind-bent on not being late he managed to arrive fifteen minutes early, again.

Just as much of a time-wasting exercise as the alternative.

'If you can't manage your business effectively, you have no business being in management.'

Even as a grown man, James still found it hard to get his father's voice out of his head. Concrete habits were hard to break, no matter how unnecessary. He had no wish to follow his father's absentee mentorship, but the tenacious Montague punctuality was deeply ingrained.

James headed to the café to grab a coffee while he waited, and as usual, Maddie greeted him like a long-lost friend.

Perky and talkative, the barista's banter always bordered on flirtatiousness, and usually made him laugh. Not today though. James had trouble cracking a smile and wondered if it was any indication of how much he needed this shot of caffeine.

Sugar? Maybe some sugar.

Perusing the options, the pink jelly-crystals on the Belgian biscuits caught his eye. "And three of these to go, please." Then he remembered Dr Fran would be there, too. "Better make it four."

Maddie pursed her lips and eyed him over her food tongs. "You're not having these for *dinner*, are you?"

"No." Not exactly. "More like afternoon tea."

Maddie smirked. "I couldn't fathom how you stayed in shape with the amount of biscuits you eat, but I saw you at the pool on Monday. You *swim*." She said it triumphantly, like she'd figured out the missing link in Darwin's theory.

"I swim. And I don't eat junk *all* the time."

Only when he was stressed.

"Most of the time," Maddie countered.

Maybe she had a point there.

Though James had ordered take-out, he sat at one of the outside tables and waited, sipping on his short black and keeping his eyes peeled for Adele.

When his cell rang, he checked the caller first.

Kaihanga - Lake Taimana Vineyard.

His finger hovered over the green icon.

No. He'd call the man back. Plenty of time to negotiate terms.

When it rang a second time he assumed it'd be the vineyard trying him again, but the notification stated otherwise.

"Mother?"

"Aksel. Just letting you know there's a trust meeting on Friday evening."

"Tomorrow?" James barked.

"Yes, six p.m. at my solicitor's office."

James mulled on that for a moment, fuming.

"I'll be there," he finally replied with forced geniality.

"Oh, *good*. And one other thing—"

"Sorry to cut you off, but this isn't the best time to talk. I'll see you tomorrow, and we'll touch base then."

James rang off before his mother could fill his ear with saccharine niceties, or demands. It was very difficult to tell how genuine Isabella Montague was being from one moment to the next, and James had given up trying to read her. He knew for a fact this meeting would've been planned well in advance, and it was by no means a coincidence he was being informed of its existence just a day out.

A strategic move on Isabella's part, no doubt. But to what gain?

Without James present, his brother Owen could assert as much pressure as he liked.

Owen had proven he was anything but trustworthy when it came to money, and Isabella had proven she was anything but impartial when it came to her youngest son.

James switched off his phone and turned his full attention back up the street. The little lakeside town was growing on him. Small enough to be cosy, but large enough to hold all the amenities you'd need to build a comfortable life. Incredible scenery and outdoor opportunities, but also rich in agricultural and horticultural possibilities. One of which was viticulture, and a gaping hole in the market when it came to technological management.

With the first flash of strawberry-blonde, James' mind stopped wandering.

Adele emerged from the law office further up the street, fresh, confident, and stunningly out of reach.

She checked her watch and seemed to relax some, even pausing for a few minutes to look in the travel agent's window, before threading between traffic to cross the road.

Italy? France? The Maldives? What destinations was Adele dreaming of with that far-away smile on her lips?

She'd changed since this morning. Easy to follow in her red coat, she was in and out of the chemist before bee-lining it to the commercial building housing the independent doctor's offices.

That was James' cue to stand—almost forgetting to grab the bag of take-out biscuits in his haste to cross the road and intercept.

The black knee-high boots Adele wore were sexy in their own right, but next-level when worn by her. There was something about the way the leather hugged her slim ankles and muscular calves that made it difficult to swallow.

Coffee, sugar, and Adele Fergus. Three habits James couldn't seem to quit.

"Still here, James?" Adele drawled as he approached. "Leaving sometime after the weekend?"

God help him, she was wearing something glossy on her lips, and they looked totally kissable. He couldn't stop his eyes from returning to her slight pout, and imagined stepping forward to taste her.

Adele's eyes narrowed and her mouth flickered with a one-sided smirk.

She knew damn well what he was thinking, and it clearly amused her.

"No, much earlier. Tomorrow."

That wiped Adele's smile clean off, and James experienced a moment of perverse satisfaction. Even after all her pushing, Adele didn't seem particularly keen for him to go.

He took a chance and moved right up in her space, registering the flicker of trepidation on her face before he lowered his head to kiss one smooth cheek, then the other.

This was how they should greet each other, with respect and kinship over Saffy, and it soothed his sense of disconnect that Adele had just allowed it.

She'd showered too, and it was beyond him not to linger for a moment and inhale her fresh scent.

Adele stepped back first. "Did you just sniff me?"

"When you smell that good, you've got to expect a guy to inhale, Dell."

"Don't call me Dell," she muttered, but there was no heat in it.

"Turns out, that's a hard habit to break." James shrugged. "Along with a couple of other things. Would you like company in your session today?"

Adele stared up at him, and the moment stretched.

"No pressure, I just wasn't sure if you needed me," he added.

Of course she wouldn't. Adele would want to use her time with Dr. Fran to go over her scrap with Katie. Hell, for all James knew, the redhead might even be co-piloting this particular counselling session.

He looked behind himself, but saw no sign of Adele's confrontational sibling.

"Alright." Adele surprised him by conceding. "But I warn you, I have some points you're not necessarily going to like."

"Your prerogative. Your session."

"Yes, it is."

James held the outer door for her, and Adele inclined her head just a smidgen as she slipped through.

"Stop *sniffing* me," she muttered.

"Stop smelling good," he countered.

Dr Fran was waiting for them at her office door, all smiles. "Kia ora kōrua! Kei te pehea kōrua?"

This seemed to be a question requiring an answer, and James looked to Adele for confirmation. He was guessing Māori, but had no grasp of it.

"Kei te pai ahau," Adele answered evenly. She turned to James. "I'm fine, how are you?"

"Oh, good. Not bad. Fine, thanks." Suddenly nervous on seeing the sofa where he'd spilled his guts last week, James rubbed his palms down his pants and waited for the women to sit.

"Tino pai. E noho. Please have a seat." Dr Fran frowned, and Adele laughed, when he remained standing.

"He won't sit until you do. It's a throwback, but you get used to it." Adele once again took up the furthest corner of the sofa.

"A throwback?" Dr Fran cocked her head to one side and considered him standing by the door as she plopped into her armchair with a soft '*oof*.'

"Old European manners. James' parents immigrated to Australia when he was…" Adele stopped and turned to watch him sit on his end of the sofa. "How old?" she checked.

"Seven."

"*Seven*," Dr Fran repeated, flipping open her session notebook to scribble that in. "And how much English did you have back then?"

"Minimal," James admitted, recalling the total lack of comprehension, the panic of being left in a classroom where the only language spoken was inaccessible to him. "I spoke French. Mostly Swiss-French, though I'd spent a couple of years in Canada. Quebec."

Owen had fared a bit better, being younger.

"Character building," he stated aloud. That's how his father had seen it back then, citing full immersion was the only way to go. He'd commanded everyone to stop speaking French on the farm, so James had spent that first year in Australia practically mute.

"Anxiety inducing," Dr Fran countered, her eyebrows raised in question.

"That too," James mused, loosening up enough to smile at the good doctor's astuteness.

"It can be an incredible learning tool to a young mind, though. You quite possibly retain new languages faster than most, and I bet your observational skills were well-honed as a result."

Adele snorted.

Dr Fran turned to her. "You disagree?"

"I disagree," Adele confirmed.

"Okay." Dr Fran took the bait. "Let's run a quick experiment then. Both of you close your eyes, please."

James complied immediately, though he wondered what the counsellor was up to.

"All the way shut, Adele," Dr. Fran intoned. "Now, can you tell me what I'm wearing today?"

Adele hesitated. "A dress?"

"Don't open!" Dr. Fran warned. "Now James, your turn."

He cleared his throat, remembering Dr. Fran opening the door to them a few minutes ago. "A white cotton dress with yellow daisies on it, and a black cardigan."

"Anything else?"

"That's not fair!" Adele interrupted.

"Not your turn." Dr Fran had the hint of a smile in her voice. "Keep your eyes closed." Her voice took on a softer tone. "James?"

"Black shoes—no heel, and a circular pendant like a swirl."

"A koru."

"Now you're *giving* him the answers!" Adele wailed in affront.

"Shhh. And how about Adele? What's she wearing today, James?"

That was easier. James imagined Adele standing in front of him and described her red wool coat with the wide lapels, the buckles on her boots, and the way she'd tied her hair in a bun, with tendrils loose at the sides.

Lip gloss, silver loops in her ears, and a fiery opal pendant she'd splashed out and bought for herself in a secondhand curio shop in Coolangatta, long ago.

There was silence after he finished.

"Can I open my eyes now?" he ventured.

"Not yet." Dr. Fran's voice was very, very soft. "Adele. Your turn. What is James wearing today?"

"This is silly," Adele huffed.

"*Don't* cheat." Dr. Fran sounded very much like she was holding back a potential chuckle.

"Black. He's wearing a black top."

"Anything else?"

"He needs a shave," Adele added mulishly.

"Okay, you can both open your eyes now."

The first thing James saw was Dr. Fran's grin. The second was Adele's frown.

"That doesn't prove anything," Adele grumbled.

"No, of course not. But it's food for thought," Dr. Fran breezed. "Now, you said on the phone you'd like to discuss—"

"No," Adele cut in, blushing. "I've changed my mind."

Because James had just gate crashed her counselling session? Or because he'd known what colour lip gloss she was wearing? He stared at Adele, but got no immediate lock on her pissy demeanour.

"I want to discuss Moses."

Moses.

James watched the flush on Adele's cheeks slowly ebb, and experienced the very real sensation of sinking to the bottom.

"Saffy's birth father," Adele reiterated for Dr. Fran's benefit, and James closed his eyes against her breathy tone.

As a child, new to Australia, James' family had been invited around to a neighbouring property with a pool. He didn't remember much about the day, except it had been hot and still—the water incredibly inviting.

And the sinking, he remembered that.

His father had dragged him out by the scruff of his neck and given him mouth to mouth.

Swimming lessons promptly followed. Years upon years of them. But no amount of swimming tuition could abate the sensation of drowning—right here, and right now.

Moses was Adele's unicorn; the mythical one that got away. The man was also Saffy's biological father, and that covered a lot of bases right there.

"Absolutely." Dr Fran waved her hand in a generous flapping motion, as if she were discouraging flies. "You go ahead."

Adele cleared her throat. "When I was in Sydney… When James and I were married…"

What?

Adele hesitated for so long, the suspense began to eat at him.

Adele finally continued, her face in solemn lines. "Moses came to see me. To see Saffy."

Was that all?

James let out the breath he'd been holding, the whoosh loud to his own ears. "I know."

"You... You *what?*" Adele's mouth actually dropped open.

"For the humanitarian conference?" he reiterated, checking he had the right timing.

Adele nodded, clearly dumbfounded. "How did you...?"

James lifted his palms slowly upward in a shrug. "Saffy."

Adele's face was a picture of shock, and though she opened and shut her mouth a couple of times, no sound emerged.

"We'd fought about your independence, your need for trust, and privacy," he reminded her. "I tried to respect that." He frowned. "That doesn't mean to say I didn't have him checked out." He looked down at his hands, fisted on his thighs. "And I'll admit I followed you to the park a couple of times to make sure you and Saffy were safe."

"You... You... Didn't you think... Weren't you afraid I'd leave?"

He had been. More than anything.

"You did leave," he answered instead.

"No," Adele huffed. "I mean with Moses."

"What I thought I was seeing was you weighing up your options. I had to trust you wanted a future with me more. Wanted *us* more. There was no point in trying to make it my decision, it had to be yours, without any external pressure." And from a distance, things had looked blessedly stilted between Moses and Adele, sitting on a park bench with acres of space between them. She hadn't even hugged the man goodbye.

James had convinced himself there was nothing romantic left between them.

Adele put her head in her hands. "I felt so *guilty*."

Guilty for what, exactly? Had there been more to Moses' visit than James realised? The humanitarian conference had been two years into their marriage, at a time when he'd thought them relatively strong—able to face anything together.

"Fuck," he swore under his breath. The lump in his throat was rising, threatening to choke him, and he looked up at the ceiling, seeking calm.

Not enough. Of course he hadn't been enough against the draw of Saffy's birth father. Where the hell did that leave him now?

"Was there a reason for you to feel guilt?" Dr Fran intervened softly.

"No!" Adele sounded so adamant, James risked another sidelong look at her. "I mean yes, for the *deception*, for not saying anything. But not for anything else. Nothing *happened*. We talked, we exchanged addresses…" Adele's fingers worried at the opal pendant at her throat, flashing orange and red, and she turned to make eye contact. "I never lied to you," she promised solemnly.

"You went behind my back."

"Yes, but for your own good."

James didn't comment, but raised a single eyebrow at the statement.

"What?" Adele huffed. "Haven't you ever held back from telling me stuff?"

He considered that. "Yes."

Adele cocked her head to one side, a sad little half-smile once again tugging at the corner of her mouth. "You'll have to tell me about it, sometime."

James ignored the little side barb. "I waited for you to talk to me about Moses, but you didn't." And that had killed him a little—the lack of faith. "So I told myself it must've been nothing. Tying loose ends, maybe. You met with other friends all the time and didn't feel the need to tell me about it, why was Moses any different? You seemed content at the time. Saffy was settled at pre-school, and you…" he broke off.

"I was pregnant with Rosetta," Adele finished for him.

"Yes." He frowned as another thought came to him. "Was that why? You chose to stay because we were having a baby?"

Adele rolled her eyes. "We were *married*, James. I was *with* you," she admonished, clearly pissed off at the assumption she would wiggle her way out of a vow. "I didn't choose to go with anybody else, because I was in love with you, you noodle."

"Right. Of course." James attempted a smile, though the words hurt. The past tense, 'was,' sounded a thousand times worse than he'd expected. "I just wasn't so sure on that point, looking back in retrospect," he murmured.

The last of the sun's rays slanted through the window and highlighted the detailing on Adele's water glass as she picked it up to take a sip, refracted light sending a crystal design over her bare hand, like cut stones.

"But you know *now*, because I told you that's how it was? You're ready to believe nothing happened just on my word?" Adele made no secret of the fact she was dubious as she clunked her glass back down onto the wooden side table.

"Yes. If you say so."

Still appearing uncertain, Adele narrowed her eyes at him. "The truth is, Moses tracked me down, and I arranged to meet him so he could see Saffy. I kissed him on the cheek, but that was it."

James slowly nodded his agreement, watching as Adele chewed diligently on her thumbnail.

It was easy to gauge the instant she realised what she was doing, because she yanked her hand away with a muted sound of disgust and sat on it. The action made him smile, being so incredibly familiar.

21

PŌURI - REGRET

Inability to change the past does not inhibit remorse.

Adele laid out the facts in plain English in a vain attempt to make herself feel better for keeping them hidden for so long. "Saffy and Moses keep in touch the old fashioned way—by mail. He gets the odd drawing and photo, and she occasionally gets a letter in exchange. It's intermittent, but it seems to work." She studied James' face for hints on his emotional state, her hands wedged firmly under her thighs to keep them out of her mouth. "That doesn't bother you?"

"No. I see any connection with Saffy's birth father as a positive for her. Either as closure, or a step forward." James answered evenly, his boardroom face giving nothing away. "Whichever works for her."

"I thought you'd freak out," Adele muttered.

"I'm not saying I don't have a gut reaction to it. I do. But it's not my place to interfere with Saffy's connection to her birth-father, or who you choose to be with, and I'd like to think it detracts nothing from what Saffy and I have together."

"I'd be jealous, if it were me," Adele mused, still studying his face in case she caught him out. "*Super* jealous."

"We're different. I tend to spread-sheet the situation, whereas your reactions are more emotional."

Emotional?

"Trust a Montague to make this a bloody competition," Adele huffed, her cheeks scorching as she looked away.

Emotional was a word bandied about to belittle females. She'd seen it in court, and she'd experienced it in everyday life. It pissed her off James would try to use it against her, even in the midst of a disagreement.

"Dell…" James started.

She spun her head back to him, her mouth open to correct him, but he bet her to it.

"Sorry, A-dele." James offered her a twitchy smile in apology before turning to meet Dr. Fran's warm brown gaze. "I tend to be analytical, whereas Adele's a lot warmer. An optimist, a believer in the brighter things. And sometimes she's proven right. Like with Moses. If you can dream it, you can live it—that sort of thing."

He made her sound like a ridiculous girl-child, prancing through a make-believe fantasy-land.

"What's Moses got to do with it?" Adele snapped, not giving Fran a chance to respond.

"You know…" James raised his hands in a helpless gesture. "Follow your rainbow," he reiterated, ending the sentence with an upward tilt that made it sound like a question.

"Moses? My *rainbow*?" Adele rolled her eyes. "He *left* me, eighteen and pregnant, and went back to his *wife*. I stopped believing there was a pot of gold waiting for me a long time ago, James. And *our* little foray into marriage did nothing to relieve me of that view."

James flinched at her caustic tone. Or was it due to the fact he'd just realised Moses had been married all along? Adele gnawed on the inside of her cheek as a whirlpool of distemper eddied around, leaving her high and dry on her own private island of regret.

"One hurtful experience needn't put you off seeking your own happiness, Adele," Dr. Fran slid in.

"Two," Adele corrected, pointing a finger at James without looking at him. "*Two* hurtful experiences."

"Regardless, it's all about believing in yourself, and what you're capable of. You've created a little pot of gold here for yourself and your daughter." Fran waved one arm around in a wide, expansive arc. "Look at what you've built here, and be proud of it."

"I *am* proud of it. And I was doing just *fine* until James waltzed into Wānaka with his fancy clothes and began taking over Saffy's life. *My* life. I can't even walk down the street without tripping over you." Adele turned back to glare at him. "You've ruined it by turning up and reminding me what I can't have! What right did you have to do that?"

"None. None at all, except I love her. I love you both," James stated, calm as bloody custard.

"Love?" Her voice rose in incredulity. "*Love*," she hissed again, incensed. "You wouldn't know love if it jumped up and bit you on the—"

"Time out," Fran stated, firmly unflappable as she formed a capital T with her hands like a referee. "When this discussion turns into all out scrap, I'm intervening. It strikes me, having listened to your communications for a while now, you two have a tendency to speak *at* each other, without ever hearing the underlying message from the other person. You're both going to work on that, okay?"

Adele swallowed. "Okay," she complied in her meekest tone, her voice overlaying James' murmured assent.

Fran shuffled a little forward on her seat. "I'm going to do an exercise I call 'In Summary,' where I sum up what I've heard. Please raise your hand if you believe I've misinterpreted your meaning." She focussed on her notes. "Adele, you believe your relationship with Moses and your marriage to James were both hurtful experiences?"

"Ah… yes?" Though that made it sound like their marriage had been *all* bad. Adele pursed her lips before continuing. "But just the last year with James, the rest was… It was mostly good."

"James?" Fran queried his take on it.

"Agreed," James conceded. "Though, I knew nothing about Moses, or that breakup. I always assumed it had been Adele's choice to leave him. No one in their right mind would leave Adele, let alone if she was pregnant with his child."

Gobsmacked, Adele turned to James and stared. His nostrils had that little flare going on, but he seemed to have everything else in check.

"Adele," Fran continued mildly, "you also expressed guilt, and I would go so far as saying *regret*, that you met with Moses without telling James."

"Absolutely."

"Even though the meetings were platonic in nature." Fran pushed the point home.

"Yes."

Fran turned to James for his input.

"It would have been…" James appeared to be searching for the right word. "Ah, *comforting* if you'd come to me about it at the time, but I realise you would've felt some trepidation about doing that. I wasn't exactly dispassionate on the subject, and know you hated my possessive streak. You don't have to feel guilty on my behalf."

"I don't *hate* it," she muttered.

"My possessive streak? You *do*," James countered.

"No—"

"How many times did you tell me off for putting my arm around you at a bar, or whisking you away from some bloke who was showing too much interest? How often did we fight about the way you thought I vetoed your independence, and made you feel trapped?"

"You didn't trust me to deal with it in my own way! I wasn't even flirtatious, I was just getting on with people," Adele huffed. "Being friendly. Having *fun*."

"No. I know. You're right," James agreed in an easy tone. "It was my issue, not yours. You were so much younger than I was, I thought I had to protect you all the time. But I see now it cramped your natural sociality; intensified your claustrophobia. I suppose it increased after Moses' visit, looking back. I wasn't sure how to read your silence, and I guess I was trying to protect myself against potential hurt."

Adele's mouth was open, ready to rebut what she'd assumed would be another point against her behaviour, but she was once again left speechless. She closed her trap without saying anything.

Was James just being magnanimous because Fran was there,

presiding? Or was he also looking back at their past relationship and actually finding fault in himself?

Fran checked her watch. "Moving on…" She smiled apologetically. "James, you've indicated you trust Adele's choices for herself and Saffy. You would willingly stand back and allow Adele to take her shot at happiness with someone else, taking Saffy with her."

James cleared his throat. "Yes," he replied gruffly.

"Because you love them both," Fran reiterated.

Respect had been growing back over the past couple of weeks, sure. But, love?

"That's not even remotely—" Adele began, still incensed James would play that highly reactive card.

That level of emotion was long gone between them. Right?

Fran pointed a finger at Adele, stopping her in her tracks. "Not your turn, I'm afraid. Raise your hand if you wish to contradict your own information. This is James' truth, and it's only fair you take the time to listen to it."

Adele closed her mouth again, blinking at Fran and her faint reprimand.

"Yes. I love them both." James didn't look at Adele when he said it, nor did he seem particularly happy about the fact. He was focussed on Fran, his mouth set in a flat line.

"Right." Fran consulted her notes again. "I also have here that Adele doesn't like your clothing, the fact you're in New Zealand, or the amount of time you spend with Saffy and herself." The counsellor turned towards Adele, her eyebrows raised in faintly questioning arcs.

Adele raised her hand again, quick smart. "I didn't say any of that."

Again, Fran turned to James. "What do you remember about the conversation?"

"Ah, they were doing better before I came? My clothes are too fancy. I've taken over."

"Right." Fran nodded.

Adele left her hand raised, though she possibly *had* said all of that.

"I'd like to retract," she decided aloud.

"Which part?" Finally James turned to pierce her with a bottle-green stare. Like a cat eyeing up a thoughtless bird.

"Oh, all of it." Adele huffed out a breath, no longer angry. The Fergus streak was infamously fiery, but just as commonly short lived. "I'm glad you came to Wānaka, but it was hard to see you again. Difficult to come to terms with what I... What we lost. Your clothes... You look like a magazine article on lakeside living, which makes me feel like a scruff in comparison. And Saffy needed this time with you to know you were still there for her. That you, um... Let's use the word '*care*' about us both. But I can't be comfortable with you buying a house here. I feel overshadowed by you. It feels a lot like you're taking over again, lording it over me."

"The plan was only to be here for a short time, then intermittently. I would never have bought a property if you hadn't planted the idea in my head. Somewhere more homely where Saffy can really relax and be herself. Can't you see us... Couldn't you see me as someone who could help you out, rather than someone angling to be your, ah... Overlord?" The way he repeated the description of himself made Adele snort, and James pursed his lips.

"If the shoe fits..." she murmured, leaving the accusation hanging and taking some comfort in her ex's scowl.

Again, Fran checked her watch. "Sorry to cut you short, James, but we'd best move on. Well done, both of you. Tino pai. Try to remember what you've learned from this exercise next time you're conversing, and watch that tendency to blame one another." The doctor's eyes gleamed with what looked suspiciously like held back humour. "Next topic, Adele?"

"Next topic." Adele tapped her finger on her bottom lip. "I want to know something," she frowned as she contemplated James. "And I want an honest answer. Even if you think it would hurt me."

"Of course." James raised one eyebrow in a faint, twitchy arch.

Adele wrestled with herself. It wasn't an accusation. Not *blaming* exactly... Not if she posed it as a question.

"Did you ever have an affair, have feelings, or a connection with anyone else when we were married?" She tried to tone down her usual snap and snark, but in doing so her question came across as sounding a lot more vulnerable than she would've liked.

Her stomach fluttered as she waited for James' response, too hollow to be comfortable.

James looked Adele dead in the eye, clearly determined she would believe his innocence on this point. "I told you before. No. I did not. My story won't change, Dell, because it's the truth."

Adele's vulnerability still existed where James was concerned, locked and twisted painfully deep. She'd believed for so long he'd wronged her, and carried it around with her as a righteous stick to beat down any tender feeling towards him.

"Would you swear on a bible?" she whispered.

"I'd swear it on any book you cared to present," James' frown lifted, and he actually smiled as he motioned towards Fran's bookcase, full of children's stories.

"Inadmissible without a lie detector test," Adele muttered.

"I'd swear on my life," James added, more seriously this time.

Adele broke eye contact first, looking across at Dr Fran. "I was afraid he might say that," she murmured.

The counsellor's soft features were much less confronting than Adele's ex-husband's, who she'd just decided was sitting too close for comfort. On the same sofa, in the same room, in the same country—too close.

James refuted any cheating within their marriage, and to all intents and purposes appeared to be telling the truth, the whole truth, and nothing but the truth. No twitches or tells, just pure, bottle-green eye-contact and a sexy little upward curve to one corner of his mouth.

Which placed Adele wholly to blame.

For everything.

She swallowed down a rock of self-disdain for her younger self, a discomfort compounded by the fact James had given *her* the benefit of the doubt over Moses. It was true the majority of her husband's outward possessiveness had emerged after Moses' visit, which was understandable if he'd just been presented with the evidence his wife wasn't always upfront with him.

Why couldn't she have confronted her husband about her own suspicions before running away with her tail between her legs? Too afraid to face him and hear the ugly truth?

Yes.

Too fearful of seeing the disconnect on James' face—the features that had once glowed with so much admiration. Too afraid to hear the words, 'You've changed, this isn't working,' or even worse, 'This was a mistake, I'm in love with someone else.'

Just like Moses.

Adele had tried to protect herself with a fortified shell, assuming one day James would move on. What he'd so actively pursued in the beginning would prove to be a fast-burning, temporary inferno, and dissipate once out of fuel.

After the loss of Rosetta, the shell Adele had formed around herself was all she had left. A painfully brittle defence mechanism, all too ready to crack under the pressure. She couldn't possibly pass muster, not in James' world of precise presentation and tidy lines. Not with his mother lobbing verbal grenades. Not in a relationship where laughter had turned to long silences, and all the light had turned concrete-grey.

"Not even with Tiffany," Adele asked the all-burning question as she looked down at her hands in her lap, noting her nails were well-and-truly munted, and a great deal of remedial moisturiser was in order.

Her skin had always gotten more high-maintenance as winter approached, lately made worse by the abrasive cleaning products associated with her job.

"Not even remotely."

"Oh." The single syllable came out sounding vaguely disappointed, because Adele had a sinking suspicion her younger self might've been wrong about every damn detail. "So, she wouldn't have chosen my engagement ring then, thinking it might be for herself?"

"Not unless she was in Wellington the day I met you, hiding around a corner." There was more than a trace of satire in James' voice, and perhaps a touch of self-depreciation, too.

Adele swallowed audibly. "You can't possibly have bought it that first day," she argued, her brain refuting the feasibility.

"Check the receipts in your insurance file if you don't believe me." James sighed. "I told you, for me, it was love at first sight."

"It doesn't exist," Adele whispered, eyes flicking to meet his, only to skitter back to her hands again.

Love at first sight was a phenomenon she'd never trusted—had in fact been incredibly fearful of—because it gave the sufferer all the more potential to be disappointed.

The more James actually got to know her, the more likely he was to realise his mistake.

"Explain that to my heart, because the moment I saw you, I knew you were it for me."

"But Tiffany said—"

"Adele, could you please explain your obsession with my P.A.?" James' voice was still smooth, but when Adele looked up, the last vestiges of humour in his eyes had given way to rising coolness, and his nostrils were beginning to flare.

"Ah, you see..." A wash of true regret threatened to overpower her. "I was under the impression it was *you* with the obsession."

"That's in no way funny."

"I can assure you, I wasn't laughing when she informed me she'd been having an affair with you since our miscarriage." Adele allowed herself to feel a touch of pride, because her voice came out clear; without trace of emotion.

"She *what*?" James jumped to standing as if he'd been kicked from his seat by an invisible boot, startling both women backward in their seats.

"Tiffany took me aside and explained it quite simply." Adele could remember the moment in excruciating detail—right down to the gem detailing on Tiffany's pearl nail polish. "She said it was out of kindness she was letting me know, because everyone else did, and she didn't want me to make any more of a fool of myself than I already had."

It was getting hard to breathe in Fran's poky little lounge-office, with James now pacing to the door and back like a caged dog. He had a wired edginess about him, and an easily recognisable fury building between his brows.

"That vindictive little... Why would she do that? What possible gain could she have had from it?" James was muttering the words to himself, but when he turned and faced Adele again his finger rose to point in her direction. "*You*. You believed her."

It wasn't a question, and Adele shrunk back further into the sofa's cushioning—away from the intense hurt she could read in the accusation.

"E noho," Fran calmly interjected, correctly pinpointing the catalyst for Adele's sudden compulsion to fidget, and reasserting her authority. "Please take a seat, James." She eyeballed him when he didn't immediately comply, and roughened her tone. "*Sit.*"

James sat, as if in slow motion. Then he rested his head against the wall behind him and covered his eyes with one hand. "You believed her, without even coming to me," he repeated in no more than a whisper. His desolation sunk through Adele's skin more than his anger ever could, and ate at her.

"Yes. I believed her," she finally conceded, studying the neckline of James' sweater. Not black after all, but charcoal grey. A perfect combo with those inky-blue jeans, and a perfect analogy to prove how wrong she could be—how off-piste with her beliefs and observations. "I wanted to hear the details. The when and the where. It seems strange now, sordid, to need to know all that. I guess I was desperate to prove her wrong, catch her out. But Tiffany had all the answers. Dates and times I knew you weren't with me. Weren't home."

Adele had held it together until the last, putting up a stony face of denial against Tiffany's assertions of late-night trysts and business trips with very little 'business' attended to.

"I was leaving Tiffany's office, telling her she was crazy and hoping like hell I was right, when her phone rang, and she held it up to show me it was you." Adele slid her gaze back to James' face, and their eyes locked and held—his with little flecks of gold in the green. "It was you, James, on her private cell, not the office line. She put you on speakerphone, and I heard you tell her…" she broke off, squeezing her hands into fists on her knees. "You asked her to come with you on a trip to China, told her you wouldn't be taking the trip to New Zealand with your wife after all, that this trip with her took precedence over everything else."

Tiffany had covered the mouthpiece and mouthed 'I'm *so* sorry' to contradict her not-so-sorry smirk before answering James in the saccharine affirmative of a lover.

It had hit Adele full force then, the enormity of James' betrayal.

James froze as if he'd suddenly gone still inside. "Then she would've said something like, 'A.J., *sweetie*. You know you can always count on *me*,' " he hazarded aloud, his voice low and slow. "Trying to imitate my wife to piss me off." He was so pale under his Aussie tan, he looked like he was about to be sick.

"Yes," Adele breathed out the single word, pressing her own eyes closed for a moment. "That's when I ran." Ran from the office, and ran from Sydney.

With tears of anger and frustration dredging her face as she'd packed, Adele had come up with the somewhat hazy strategy to leave for Katie's wedding as if nothing had happened, and never return.

"I was only twenty-three, James. I wasn't equipped to deal with it."

"Jesus, Adele. You couldn't *talk* to me about it? At least give me the decency of a hearing before you found me guilty? You may've fallen out of love with me by then, but I was still your husband!"

"I was wrong not to—"

"Too bloody right you were wrong not to!" James interrupted, slapping his forehead. "You thought because we were no longer intimate—because I was giving you time to heal—I had to be getting sex at the *office*?"

"You couldn't even *look* at me!"

"I didn't want to break you!" James all but shouted the words.

"Intervening!" Fran interjected when she could get a word in edgeways, waving one hand aloft.

They both ignored her, Adele with blood thumping in her ears, and James with veins popping on his neck as he strained forward.

"*Break* me? I'm not a bloody crystal vase! I needed you, James, and you wrapped me up in cotton wool and all but locked me in a padded room!"

"You needed *time*," James ground out.

"I needed *you*," she re-stated firmly, sure of that now.

"I couldn't run the risk of getting you pregnant again, and putting you through another potential miscarriage."

So, that had been the root of James' disconnect. It suddenly made a lot of sense.

"There's no evidence to suggest I have a higher chance of miscarriage due to Rosetta." Adele spoke with studied calmness, having had to talk herself into believing this truth. "I carried Saffron to full-term, and don't have any underlying health issues. What's more, I had every intention of trying again with you, though I had serious doubts the wider family dynamics would ever work."

James was still leaning forward into her breathing space, elbows on his knees and eyes glittering. "Serious doubts? What do you mean? I tried to create a life where you and Saffy would be happy. A safe home. A *loving* home." Perhaps in consideration to Fran, he kept a handle on his tone.

"You're not going to like this next part," Adele hazarded.

"Ha!" James aimed his bark of laughter at the roof, but turned back to sear her with a pained look before he continued. "I'm not sure you can top that Tiffany clanger."

Oh, yes. She could.

"I don't know if you're aware that Isabella asked me quite early on to, um… to step aside." Adele hesitated, swallowed the spit that was threatening to choke her, and ploughed on. "For someone more 'suitable.'"

James continued to stare at her, his chest rising and falling in a deep sigh.

"Christ, this just gets better and better."

"I warned you."

James reached a hand out toward her. "Yeah, Dell. You did."

Adele took the peace-offering at face value, slipping her fingers into James' palm, and squeezing. The contact, and forgiveness implied, eased some of the tension constricting her chest.

"Sorry to interrupt again. Isabella being…?" Fran queried, pen at the ready.

"My mother," James supplied, in a growl.

"James' mother," Adele confirmed with a sigh as Fran scribbled the name down in her notes. "She was always hissing at me, but rather than easing off as we got to know each other, it became more of a concerted effort over time. Eventually, I was hacking my way through a forest of self-doubt." She allowed herself one *tiny* nibble at her thumbnail before continuing; a single morsel of self-soothing. "Part of that was on me. I was pretty green, and I let her get to me." She turned back to James, meeting his gaze dead on. "It started off with comments about how you were already married to Montague

Holdings, about how you needed someone who understood the business. Always in a sweet tone—"

"Like a passive-aggressive missile," James muttered.

"Exactly like that," Adele agreed. "Then later, it switched to comments about how unhappy you seemed to be. How close you were to your P.A.. How indispensable Tiffany was to the company, and to you." Adele swatted away the bitter memory that still had the capacity to sting.

James spluttered. "What a crock of shit. Any assistant, trained in the job, would've been fine. Yes, Tiffany made noises about extra-curricular activities when she *began* at Montague Holdings, but I made it clear that was never going to happen."

"You did?"

"My mother had no business putting that rubbish into your head. What was she thinking?"

"She made me uncomfortable all the time," Adele admitted. "It felt like Australia was crawling with poisonous things. Cane toads and snakes in the garden, crocs and bluebottles in the water, a septic mother-in-law in the kitchen…"

James groaned. "I'd chosen to spend my *life* with you, Adele. It's not like I could shield you from my mother forever."

"No? Not even a heads up?" She studied James' expression as it slid from anger to one of remorse—his lips shifting from flatlined to slightly downturned as he clenched his jaw—and actually felt sorry for him. After all, he'd been caught between an inexperienced, small-town rock, and a well-polished diamanté of a hard place. "I suppose not. But it wasn't until recently, *very* recently, actually, she mentioned one of the reasons she became so anti at the end of our marriage."

"You've spoken to my mother?" James took on a more alert look, shoulders back and eyes sharpening. The hand still gripping Adele's gave a couple of convulsive clenches. "Recently?"

"She, ah… She called you, actually. The first night you were here in Wānaka. You were asleep on the sofa and your phone… Anyway, she was under the impression I chose to have an abortion." The words seemed so alien, the action so far from the truth, Adele's voice wobbled. "Did you tell her that, James? That I chose to get rid of our baby?"

James made a choked sound of surprise as he slid across the sofa, slinging his arm around Adele's shoulder and pulling her bodily into his heat with a fierce, sideways grip. He lay his forehead against her temple.

"Of course not." His answer rumbled from within his chest, stirring the hair escaping her hair tie, and she shuddered at the unexpected deliciousness of it, skittering along the nerve endings behind her ear. "I'd never do that. I don't know how she misconstrued that so badly."

Adele let out the breath she'd been holding in relief, not realising how much emotion she'd had riding on that one piece of misinformation until it was out in the open. Sliding one arm around James' ribs, she squeezed him back.

"I didn't think so, but I couldn't be sure." They sat like that for a moment, the silence calming, rather than uncomfortable.

The session had gone a lot smoother than Adele had anticipated, asking James about Tiffany, and exposing his mother's behaviour. In the back of her mind, she'd been expecting him to defend Isabella's actions, or side with her in some way.

Bringing up Moses' visit to Australia had been both necessary and cathartic. Because in talking it over with Katie, Adele had felt deceitful, with a residually dirty feeling about *not* telling James. She owed him that honesty; that clarity.

She owed herself.

"Would your mother have any reason to... to not want us to work out?"

James pulled back from her. "No."

But by the flash of something icy in his eyes, it looked like he was no longer sure on that point. Adele opened her mouth, then shut it again.

These were conversations she should've insisted on having with James before she left for Katie's wedding, the reckoning she'd avoided for five long years because it underlined every insecurity she'd ever had. The fear she wasn't good enough for James, that his infatuation had been just what Isabella Montague had always believed it to be; a cheap, short-lived lust.

Adele's knowledge she'd pulled her two-year-old from

everything she'd ever known, placed her own desire above the needs of her child, all for nothing? That had been the worst.

Being young and inexperienced wasn't reason enough for what she'd put James through—put them *all* through.

"We're out of time, I'm afraid." Fran sounded truly sorry. "But in summary of that last bit… James, would you agree your mother and Tiffany's involvement was incredibly misleading, and malicious towards Adele?"

James groaned. "That doesn't even begin to cover it. As for Tiffany and myself being involved? She was only ever involved with Owen, though I have no idea if she had a hand in getting him access to the locked files, or if he figured that out all on his own. The information was keyed out under my own login."

Adele shot her hand up, but waited for Fran's nod before asking, "Owen and Tiffany were involved, as in, *with* each other?"

"Yes. Though not for long."

"Oh." That was news to Adele, although not particularly shocking. Owen was a flirt, and Tiffany an opportunist.

"Owen?" Fran interjected.

"James' younger brother," Adele informed the counsellor as an aside.

Perhaps James' mother and brother had both wanted Adele gone. The entire family, in fact. Suddenly hotly aware her hand was still on James, she slid it off the heat of him and back into her own lap.

"I don't understand what you said about your locked files, either," she added.

James sighed. "Owen downloaded my latest I.T. designs a week before they were scheduled to be promoted. Undersold them to our original customers from a bogus sister-company."

"But, why?" Adele floundered.

James shrugged. "The usual reason. Money."

22

TŌURANGI - RAIN

Washing dirt from the day, ready for a fresh start.

It had started to rain in earnest while they were in Fran's session, so Adele conceded to James driving her home in his big, warm 4x4. It was an older model than she'd first assumed, well-used, though relatively clean inside.

If James was still upset, he didn't show it. He just sat, cool and aloof behind the wheel, never taking his eyes off the slick road. As if he hadn't just had to defend himself over allegations of infidelity and overlord tendencies, his choice of streetwear, and the basic moral fibre of his entire family.

As if he hadn't just told her he still loved her.

Adele gazed out the passenger window, the familiar landmarks of the low-rise township cruising by as they turned off the main road.

James was leaving tomorrow, so she was going to have to bite the bullet and apologise now, before they reached her bungalow. Right *now*, or at least before the next intersection.

They passed the designated roundabout, and still the words stuck in her throat.

When Adele finally blurted the opening line, "I really screwed up," one block from her rental, she was overlapped by James' much more formal, "I can't begin to apologise enough," said at the same time.

They both stopped, glanced at each other, then looked away.

"This isn't on you," James continued gruffly. "My family and staff mistreated you incredibly badly, and I ignored the warning signs and compounded the issue by making you feel isolated and unwanted. It's clear to me now why you left."

"I should've talked to you," she whispered. "I should've trusted you."

James paused before answering mildly. "I've been told I'm not one of the most, ah, *approachable* people, and I was focused on everything but us. Your happiness should've been my first priority, and I failed you."

"I don't *blame* you. Not anymore."

James huffed a single laugh, with zero trace of humour. "You don't have to. I blame myself. It must've been even more of a nightmare for you than I first supposed, me turning up here unannounced." He flicked on the indicator to turn into her driveway.

"Do you mind not driving in?" Adele blurted. "I mean, park here on the street. Katie will be waiting, and I don't want…"

"Don't want her to think you've gone back to the dark side?" James finished for her when she trailed off, and Adele was relieved to see the shadow of a smile twitching.

"Something like that," she muttered.

"She thinks I cheated on you." James parked, then turned in his seat to face her. Reaching out ever so slowly, he tucked a spring of wayward hair behind her ear. "I suppose they all do."

Adele shrugged the uncomfortable knowledge off. "She knows I suspected. She also knows I've been questioning it."

"Have you?"

"Yes. Katie was adamant you and I should've talked it through, which is rich considering her current situation…" Adele trailed off, knowing Katie would hate having her private life discussed. "But on that point, she's right. I *should* have approached you, James. At least got your side of it. I'm sorry. This all could've been worked out if I'd just—"

"If I'd just trusted you with what was going on at Montague Holdings. Confided in you. Told you what I suspected."

"About Owen?"

"About Owen," James agreed, appearing to mull something over. "Tell me, what do you think of my brother? How does he strike you, say, in the realms of trustworthiness?"

"Well..." Adele checked James' expression before she continued, not sure she should go ahead and insult both of his living relatives in one day.

Owen was too handsome for his own good. A playboy with little care for the consequence of his actions, and a litany of minor offences and financial blunders to show for it. During Adele and James' short-lived marriage, Owen had been constantly looking to his brother to bail him out in one sense or another. As if it was the younger's due to live the high-life off the elder's back, while vaguely hitting on his wife.

"He's flamboyant," Adele summed up the younger of the Montague brothers with a relatively innocent adjective.

James laughed, and Adele relaxed a little.

"Put it this way, I wouldn't be giving him my lunch money to look after," she added.

"No. Me neither." James smiled with a rueful twist to his lips. "Let alone the family finances. You're aware Owen wasn't a shareholder in Montague Holdings by the time I met you? When he turned twenty, he was given the choice to opt out for a lump sum. Against legal advice, he took the payout. The business grew, as predicted. But Owen no longer had any financial ties to it, except through my mother."

"I'm not following you."

"My mother's more than happy to be manipulated when it comes to her youngest son. How she spends her money is her own concern, but Owen's unbelievably skilled at playing her sympathies. It's a lethal combo," James mused. "Do you remember Mr Wickham?"

The question came out of left-field, and Adele hesitated.

"Umm..." Thinking James must be referring to some random suit she'd been introduced to in Australia, Adele racked her brains, unable to place the name. Unless...

"You're not meaning *Jane Austen's* Wickham?" Incredulity lent a quiver to her voice.

"Jane who?"

"Austen. The author."

James narrowed his eyes slightly. "If she writes historical novels, then, yes."

How the hell could James know the characters of Pride and Prejudice, but not recognise the writers name?

"Not 'writes.' *Wrote*, during the Regency period. Don't tell me you've actually read her work?"

"Yes, I've actually read it." James pulled back, looking a little put out. "*It is a truth universally acknowledged*—"

"Stop." Adele held up a hand in case the word wasn't enough incentive.

She needed a moment of silence to process. Because, how could that *be*?

"Who *are* you, actually?" she muttered, questioning her own memory as much as she was James. "And what have you done with my ex-husband?"

The James she remembered read books about farming machinery, livestock, and irrigation systems. He studied dry tomes on computer code and copyrighting. Did she actually know this man at all? Surely he couldn't have changed that much in such a short window of time?

James' jaw flexed, all affronted. "You left it lying around. I got bored and read it."

"You got bored." she parroted inanely. "You mean, when I left Sydney?"

"Yes, when you *left*. It was in your nightstand drawer. You've missed the point entirely. Owen is like Wickham—likeable, easygoing, but fatally flawed in the fiscal and moral sense."

"Oh, right. I get you." Adele dragged herself back to topic. "He wanted more?"

"No matter what it is in life, Owen always wants more."

"Fleecing people along the way," she added, no longer concerned to voice her honest opinion after her ex-husband's Wickham analogy.

James' eyes twinkled. "The more the merrier. Why he didn't

come to me with his money worries at the time, I don't know. Possibly too much needed in a hurry? A boat he liked the look of, or a horse he thought was a sure bet."

Adele became aware her mouth was gaping open, and carefully closed it.

"I'm assuming Owen masterminded it, but it's difficult to tell if anyone else benefited. Tiffany, for example." James brushed a hand down Adele's arm, his eyes apologetic. The glancing touch sent a shock wave down to her fingertips and back. "It's got his means-to-ends style written all over it. Sell the tech—instant cash. Sell the company—even more cash, drip-fed through my mother."

"When you said Tiffany and Owen were together..." Adele was trying to fit all the pieces together, and kept coming up short. "Do you think it was his idea to create a bogus affair?"

"I doubt it." James sighed. "I'd put that down to Tiffany's own vindictive game-playing. I don't think my brother has it in him to come up with that amount of background noise for a simple theft. But if there *was* a set target, it would've been me, not you. Owen has made it his life's work to get me on the back-foot. I guess by creating tension between the two of us he could shove me off-task while he got up to no good, but I can't prove that." James rubbed the heel of his hand into one eye socket, then the other, suddenly looking every one of his thirty-six years.

"But you were always so generous—"

"Father stipulated I was to take over Montague Holdings in his will," James interrupted in a quiet, even voice. "As the youngest, Owen was put in charge of the farm."

"The *farm*?" Adele shook her head, unconsciously vetoing the concept. Owen was the furthest thing from farming material.

James blew out a long, deep breath. "Right. Disastrous idea. You can't *make* someone love working the land. Either it's in you, or it isn't. Owen hated it. Everything about it. He always had. The drought, the dust, the rains, the livestock, the isolation... Everything. It should've been the other way around. I don't mind getting my hands dirty, it gives me a sense of purpose. That's why I always check the tech onsite, rather than send someone else out to implement the running of it. But I was the eldest, so Father shoved me forward to follow in his footsteps."

"So, who's looking after the farm now?" Because Owen certainly wasn't.

James' quiet smile held more regret than amusement. "Owen sold it out from under us. He'd been surreptitiously trying to push Mother to sell for years. Sell the farm, sell the company... "

"But isn't it counterproductive to sell company assets if you're in the black?" Adele was in no way an expert in property management, but she knew that much.

"Except Owen wasn't part of the company, merely an overseer for the rural property attached to it. If Mother's shares of Montague Holdings were liquidated in say, a takeover—"

"She's an instant cash machine," Adele finished the thought for him.

James shrugged. "I'm just guessing, of course. Owen's choices make little sense to me. Ever since Father died he's been…"

"Narcissistic." The negative description slipped out on a tart note.

"Yes." James grimaced. "Self-absorption swings towards self-destruction. It's a shitty mix. Throw alcohol abuse in and he's a bloody Molotov cocktail." Lips pressed together in a firm line, he stared out of the windscreen at the low-lit street vista, streaked and muted by rivulets of rainwater. "I never expected that level of mutiny from him, but somehow it didn't surprise me. He's been making himself scarce these past few years, spending a lot of time in the States. I've hardly seen him unless he's been wrangled into position by my mother." He shook his head. "Owen's finally achieved a fallout large enough to feel some culpability."

"I think I can say, without offending you, you've got some seriously screwed up individuals in your family."

"I should never have put you in the firing line in the first place." James sighed, a deeply desolate sound, before shifting his eyes from the softening drizzle and settling them back on Adele.

What would the outcome of their relationship have been if they'd removed those outside influences? Adele's own family may've been dubious about James, and the speed with which he'd rocketed into Adele's life and shaken everything up, but they would've come around soon enough. On seeing her and Saffy happy, they would've understood.

Why *had* Adele let James' family take over so completely?

"I know it's not Monday, but would you mind if I took Saffy to school tomorrow?" A heaviness lingered around James' eyes—forest-green in the evening light. It made Adele wonder if he was sleeping alright. "That is, if you intend for her to go to school while her aunt's here? I wanted to touch base with her about my travel plans, let her know I have to go," he expanded.

Adele had almost allowed herself to forget James would be leaving tomorrow, and berated the loneliness sluicing through her nervous system. It didn't mix well. She was a competent, single mother. She didn't need James in her life. But she was beginning to want him there, warming everything up with his own personal brand of annoying.

The thought was disconcerting to say the least.

"You need to be here at eight-fifteen, then."

"Done. I'll video call on Monday afternoon, as usual."

James leaned towards Adele, and she blinked at him and drew her head back until it met the passenger window with a light bump.

James chuckled. "I'm not going to jump you. I was just going to kiss your cheek."

"Oh." The heat of a blush crept up Adele's neck. The thought of being jumped by James had a real deliciousness to it. "Of course." She offered her cheek, but rather than kiss it perfunctorily, James took his damn time about it. She felt every breath—every whisper of touch. The tips of his fingers on her neck and the scent of his warm-toned soap in her nostrils.

"Do you still have it?" she blurted, her thoughts jumping and scattering like skittles.

James managed to make any intimacy feel a lot like romance.

"Have what?" James' voice was a low rumble dancing along her nerve endings.

Adele swallowed audibly. "My copy of Pride and Prejudice."

"As a matter of fact, I do."

Taking her chin gently in hand, James turned her head, meeting her eyes for one hot moment before paying just as much attention to the other cheek.

Almost nuzzling…

Adele held her breath tight in her chest, and tried in vain to slow her pounding heart rate.

"Goodnight, Dell." James murmured against her skin, his whiskers tickling.

A shiver of pure want shuddered down her spine.

No.

Fumbling behind her, she managed to open her door and slide awkwardly out, relatively unscathed.

"Goodnight. Have a good trip." She conveyed the mundane sentiment through the open door as her phone began to chirp from her handbag. "See you when… See you later," she amended, unsettled by how badly it rankled she didn't know exactly 'when.'

"I'll be back as soon as I can," James assured her, and she nodded in response, not wanting to come across as too eager.

"That'll be Katie texting, checking up on me, again." Adele grimaced, glancing toward the house, then back to James.

When they were married, it used to be James' phone constantly butting into their conversations and eating up all their precious time together.

"Weird it's my phone that keeps interrupting," Adele murmured, shivering in the damp evening and belting her coat a little more firmly around herself. "What did you do, drop yours in the lake or something?" She felt comfortable enough to mock James a smidgen, now she was out of his direct breathing space.

"I turned it off."

"You *what*?" Laughter bubbled up and escaped in a disbelieving chuckle.

The corner of James' mouth quirked up into a self-deprecating smile, too. "I discovered there's an off button on the side. It's genius."

"Oh, shut up."

The smile turned into a grin. "So, tomorrow morning?"

"Eight fifteen. Don't be late."

Not that he ever was.

Adele went to close the door and walk away, but James called her back.

"Dell?" Leaning across the console, James was looking at her from under those long, lush eyelashes. The way he shortened her name and rolled it around in his mouth, it almost sounded like the common Aussie endearment, darl.

There was something sensual about the way his sweater pulled taut across his shoulders and chest with the sideways strain, and Adele was drawn to stare at his unshaven jaw. Tactile. Just begging to be touched, stroked, and played with.

"Here, have these." James handed over the paper bag he'd had with him at Fran's.

Adele snapped out of her reverie, unrolling the top to have a peek in.

"Belgian?"

"Mmm-hmm."

"Lethal," she decided aloud. "You'd better take one back. Otherwise me, Saffy, and Katie might just launch world-war-three over the extra one." She drew out a single pink-encrusted biscuit, and handed it back.

James playfully wolfed a bite the instant she held it within range, and she laughed at his lack of self-control and the rakish twinkle in his eye.

"There's one more thing I'd like to ask you." James wiped the back of his hand across his mouth and whiskers as he accepted what remained of the cookie with his other hand. His face again settling into more serious lines. "A favour. I know the cabin is not exactly within your, ah… comfort zone. But, I won't be able to make that four p.m. meeting with the interior designer tomorrow, and I was wondering if you'd consider taking Saffy to meet with her? I think she'd love having a hand in it, and I wanted her to have some say in how it all looks. Make it hers. Give it her stamp of approval, you know?"

So, he planned to keep the cabin?

Adele contemplated James, his beseeching eyes, with just the trace of a smile left on those totally kissable lips.

He would taste of Belgian biscuit; all sweet, cinnamony, and decadent.

She cleared her throat. "All right."

Again James broke into a full grin—a devastatingly attractive look on him.

"But you owe me one," she warned, closing the door with a flick of her wrist before sauntering away.

It wasn't true. James didn't owe her anything. She'd been dying to put her stamp all over the lakeside property ever since she'd caught sight of it this morning.

23

KAHUKURA - RAINBOW

All colours together, forming one collective.

The next morning, at precisely eight-fifteen, James shut the driver's door on his 4x4 and caught a glimpse of his reflection in the tinted glass.

He was looking decidedly unkempt, in dire need of a shave. Almost unrecognisable.

He ran a hand over his chin, deep in thought as he made his way to Adele's front porch.

"You didn't bring it?" Saffy exited the bungalow and all but hurled herself at him, not bothering with a greeting, and clearly expecting an early morning delivery of the little painted love-seat.

Adele was nowhere to be seen, and James didn't know whether to be disappointed or relieved he didn't have to soldier through another goodbye.

Disappointment won, as it always seemed to if he missed a chance to see his ex-wife.

He walked back around to the driver's door and slid back in before answering.

"No." After the session with Dr Fran, he'd chickened out and decided it was probably best he wasn't present when Adele saw what they'd done to her chair. He'd left it wrapped in a tarp on the trailer, back at the cabin.

"When will you drop it off, then?" Saffy asked as soon as she'd climbed into the front passenger's seat, and secured her seatbelt.

"Today. Soon. I can slip it out the back while you're at school and Dell's at work." He cleared his throat. "There's something else I wanted to talk to you about. I'm afraid I'm going to have to skip to Sydney for a while. Today, actually."

"Can I come?"

"No, sorry love. Not during term-time, and not without Adele's say-so." James backed out of the driveway, glancing back at the house.

Still no sign of strawberry curls, or lush-limbed curves.

"Did you talk to Mum about me spending some more time up at the cabin with you?" Saffy threw an arm out her open window as they drove towards school, pointing in the general direction of his property.

"I did, yes."

"And?"

He hesitated. "She's thinking about it."

"That's a big, fat 'no,' then," Saffy muttered mulishly.

"Not at all." James scratched absently at the stubble on his neck. "She's figuring things out, and there's no rush. There's a lot for her to take into consideration, but she didn't seem against it. Maybe even a make-up trip to Oz at the end of the year."

Though that had been discussed before everything had come out about his mother and Owen.

"Really?"

James turned and gave Saffy a half-smile as the engine idled at the give-way. "Yes. Apparently your social calendar's booked up till then."

Saffy snorted.

"So, while I'm away, there'll be a bit of work going on up at the cabin. Adele's meeting with the interior designer later this afternoon… Did she talk to you about that?"

"Yeah."

"Good." James smiled, imagining them together, thick as thieves. "It'll be great to get your take on it." He nosed the 4x4 onto the roundabout, heading towards Saffy's school. Further and further from Adele.

Everything about that felt wrong.

"Can I actually choose colours and stuff?"

"Yes. Whatever you two like. Your mum has the final word. Are you going to pizza night tonight?"

"Uh-huh. Are you coming to play piano for Ruby? You could bring your togs! We're having our first pool party. Uncle D says it's warm enough now, and Mum needs someone to teach her. He says it's *imperative*."

Clearly another new word for his daughter, who was collecting vocabulary like a little dictionary.

"No. I'll be long gone by then."

Saffy nodded, looking a touch despondent again.

"Do you want to see the piano I'm looking at for the cabin?" Imagining that might cheer Saffy up, James dug his phone out of his back pocket and flipped it onto her lap, keeping his focus on the road. "There's a screenshot saved in photos."

It was a secondhand maple upright.

Playing Obāchan's piano had brought it home to James how important it could be to have an instrument to take his mind off Adele—within reach, but as elusive as panned gold.

"What's this shelf thing?"

James sneaked a look phone-ward. "A bookcase I'm building in the lounge."

"You *made* this?"

"With a bit of help, yes." The stripping, sanding and varnishing of the recycled rimu had been surprisingly easy, and though he'd needed one of the carpenters to help him put it together, James was pretty chuffed with how it'd turned out.

Saffy eventually found the photo of the piano, and sounded her approval with a hum. "Will you give me some lessons?"

James glanced across in surprise. "You'd like to learn?"

"Maybe." Saffy shrugged.

"I'll research local teachers," he murmured, concentrating back on the intersection ahead. Someone with good qualifications and a proven track record.

"I don't want any old teacher. I want you."

James laughed. "Then you won't get the best instruction."

"I don't care." He could feel Saffy turn to stare at him. "You're not going to leave me, are you, Dad?" The question came out of left-field.

"You mean this trip to Oz? I'll only be a few days, Saff. A week at most. I'll video call on Monday, like always, and we can keep in touch by phone. Call me whenever you like. I don't think your mum will mind."

"No. I mean *leave*."

He parked the car in the nearest available car park to the school and wrenched on the handbrake, finally able to concentrate on Saffy's expression. Her eyes were pooling.

James' heart clenched in a tight fist, making his own eyes smart.

"No. I won't." He blinked rapidly. "I'll be back soon, and I might be able to stay a bit longer, next time. There's some unavoidable stuff I have to tie off in Sydney, that's all."

"I mean, I know I'm not yours," Saffy stated with a hangdog expression, eyes lowering to James' chin and refusing to rise and meet his.

"That's not how I see it." James reached for the hands that were clenched tightly together between Saffy's knees and gave them a squeeze, voice low with feeling. "You'll always be my little Sass-a-frass, my snake charmer, the best nine-year-old winger on the planet."

The collection of pet-names tweaked a smile before they said their final goodbyes, and Saffy clambered out of the car. James was grateful for that. Parting was hard enough without contending with those soulful eyes.

He watched Saffy hesitate on the corner by the lollipop crossing, and was glad he'd waited when he caught two thrown kisses and planted them on his opposing cheeks. She grinned before joining ranks with her school friends and strolling off.

Alone again.

The thought came unbidden, an unwieldy brick for James to carry around as he prepared to catch a flight he didn't want to take, for a meeting he'd rather not attend, in a country where he no longer felt at home.

His phone was in his hand before he'd even thought about it, and he fired off a quick text to Adele.

Saffy safely at school.

Unsure if that warranted a reply, he drove towards the cabin to pick up his gear and lock up for the week, but found a safe spot to pull over on the gravel verge when his phone pinged with a notification a minute later.

Thanks.

No 'goodbye?' No 'safe travels?' James thought a moment before texting back.

Maybe she'd forgotten he was leaving?

My flight leaves at 10am.

This time Adele's reply was longer, and imminently shittier.

Don't have to tell me all your comings and goings. Thanks for letting me know about Saffy, but the rest is your business.

In other words, don't drag her into it.

James took the missive on board with a sigh of resignation. Adele didn't want her ex clogging up her phone with unsolicited information, nor did she like getting yanked sideways into his life any more than she had to for Saffy's benefit.

Best to forgo reminding her of her four o'clock meeting with the Interior Designer, then?

The devil in James had other ideas, though, and he rattled off another text.

The design team is expecting you at 4pm. Head of interiors is Simone. Saffy knows where the key is.

They'd always left the spare key in a combination lock-box at their Sydney house, but country living had demanded a more immediate solution. James *had* shown Saffy where, though admittedly she'd been distracted at the time...

In the left gumboot. He slid Adele another text, just to be sure.

STOP! TEXTING! ME!

James chuckled over Adele's snotty reply as he drove back to the cabin, but left her alone after that.

As soon as Adele got her daughter home from school, Saffy scrambled out of the car and raced out of sight around the corner of the house, leaving her school bag on the driveway and her car door swinging.

"Saffy, wait! What are you…?"

But it was no use, the extra pair of helping-hands had just disappeared into thin air.

Adele sighed, emptying the backseat of overflowing supermarket bags on her own. She'd just piled herself high, multiple handles hanging from each arm, when Saffy bounded back.

"It's here! Come and see!"

"Nope. I've just got to put these… Hang on. *No*. I need to…" but Adele was shoved around the corner of the house, shopping bags and all, in Saffy's exuberance.

"There!" Saffy grinned and spread her arms wide like a three-ring circus master, presenting a fantastical performance.

Adele took in the willow, the grassy bank, and the repainted love-seat.

Each rung had been carefully coated in a different colour, forming a multicoloured rainbow.

"Oh! You changed it!" It was all she could think to say. The handle on one of the supermarket bags chose that moment to give way, and a large tin of Saffy's favourite baked beans and two corn cobs thumped to the ground, and rolled.

Saffy was studying Adele, concern written all over her face. "You don't like it?"

"Oh, no. It's lovely. It's just… I thought you chose teal."

"We did. But when you didn't like the colour, Dad said maybe we could repaint it for you as a surprise."

"Rainbow?" she whispered.

"Dad said you used to say, 'Rainbow is my favourite colour,' and he never gave you enough rainbows." Saffy blinked, swallowed, then scrambled to pick up the fallen groceries. "I'm sorry, Mum. Don't cry. I'll paint it back, I promise. Any colour you like."

"I'm not upset."

But she was. Tears were distorting Adele's view, overflowing, and she didn't have a free hand to wipe them away.

She'd fought with herself, but eventually chosen to avoid James this morning because she hadn't wanted to see him go. She'd even stooped low enough to bitch at him in text-form when he'd insisted on putting his imminent absence out there in black and white. Now there was a bloody hand-painted rainbow love-seat in her backyard, with her ex-husband's vibes all over it.

It was too much for her bruised, battered, and ridiculously optimistic heart to bear.

After the crisp autumnal weather in New Zealand, Sydney's humidity hit James like a wall of wet, and his shirt stuck to a strip down the centre of his back in a matter of minutes. Though he had precious little time to sweat the details, he definitely needed an overhaul to get himself up to scratch.

Visiting the barber in the bustling central city, he walked in without an appointment and strolled back out thirty minutes later, clean-shaven and sporting a decent haircut for the first time in months.

A fresh collared shirt bought off-the-rack completed the surface transformation.

It was only a family trust meeting, but the appearance of having it together went a long way with the Montagues, and today it was even more imperative than usual to show no chinks in the armour.

"Mother," James greeted Isabella with the formal label she preferred when he entered her solicitor's office, bending to kiss both of her cheeks, compressing his lips against the litany of allegations that threatened to eddy out of his mouth.

The office was large and dim, old fashioned, but positioned on a corner affording it an expansive view of the park.

"Ms Ermine." He greeted his mother's white-haired solicitor with affection when he spotted her on the other side of her massive mahogany desk, glad she appeared to be the only other person present.

His brother, Owen, was nowhere in sight.

"I hope you're well?" The woman never aged. She'd seemed ancient when he'd met her as a first-year university student, during the tying up of his father's will, and she looked exactly the same now. Neat as a pin, and all in lilac. "I'd like to be signed out of the Montague trust at your earliest convenience."

"Opt out?" Ms Ermine's voice cracked like a whip, the volume at odds with her tiny size.

Aptly put.

"Yes. Opt out. I no longer want any part of it."

"Oh, Aksel!" Isabella scoffed. "Don't be so dramatic. The little that's left is all locked in property, term deposits, and bonds. At *your* insistence, I might add. What's brought this on?"

Securing Saffy's financial future and wellbeing, that's what had brought this on.

James ignored his mother and continued to focus on the solicitor. "Can it be done?"

Ms Ermine pursed her lips. "Of course, but it will cost you—"

"I don't care. Do it."

"All of it?"

"Anything where my name's attached, determine the current worth, split it down the middle, and get me out."

Isabella made a small guttural sound, perhaps realising he was dead serious. It was unlike her to play with her jewellery or show any other outward signs of disturbance, but right now her fingers were worrying at the plain platinum band she was wearing on her right hand—twisting it to and fro.

Something about the ring, and the action, drew James' attention away from what the solicitor was saying.

Isabella flushed, quitting all movement to stare back at him, and James watched the tell-tale pink creep up his mother's neck with a gnawing sense of déjà vu. The appearance of guilt jarred him, like a door swinging open from the past, and his conviction grew.

The ring?

Surely not. Even Isabella Montague wouldn't be that brazen.

"I'm sorry, what did you say?" He angled back at Ms Ermine.

"Liquidate half?"

"Half, yes. Excluding my mother's apartment," he agreed. "That should be hers to do what she wants with. The farm's gone, and I don't care about the rest. Hold or reinvest mother's shares as she chooses."

"What do you mean by this... this *ridiculous* idea!" his mother spluttered.

"You have no reason not to agree to it." James shot her a look, but managed to keep his voice even by sheer force of will. "You lose nothing, and gain the full deed to the penthouse."

"And the legal fees, etcetera?" Ms Ermine continued on, taking her cue from James and overriding Isabella's outburst.

James shrugged. "Take it out of my share."

"Alright. That's a lot of valuation and paperwork though, so let's set the follow-up for next Friday. I'll have the legalities printed up and ready for you to peruse and sign. The liquidation of any property will of course be subject to sale, so that will be a longer process. Bonds and shares are less of a problem. It's not a seller's market—"

"I'm afraid I have to be out of the country on Thursday. It's imperative." James spoke with quiet conviction. "I need this wrapped up tight by Wednesday at the latest, though I can return the following week if that helps. No sales necessary, just market valuations."

"What could *possibly* be that important?" Isabella snapped, clearly miffed at being ignored. The meeting she'd instigated had just been hijacked, and James could see it was going down like a truckload of sheep shit.

"I'm contracting out to a winery in New Zealand. Several to be exact." James turned back to pin his mother with a narrowed look, skirting the truth with a secondary reason. No need for Isabella to know anything more than she already did about his contact with Adele.

"What if *I* want to be involved in a wineries deal?"

James shrugged. "Your prerogative, but no longer any of my business."

"No longer...?" Isabella looked horrified. "But your father's *trust!*"

"Should've been overhauled years ago, when Owen managed to sell the farm without authorisation through a bloody loophole," James added to Isabella's train of thought, and she screwed her face up as if the memory left a sour taste in her mouth.

It hadn't been James' favourite Owen-ism either.

Owen could be totally one-eyed when he was desperate for cash, throwing one hare-brained money making scheme after another.

James had always thought selling the farm was the worst of his brother's double-crosses, even more selfish than selling Montague Holdings' designs for a quick injection of cash. But that was before he suspected Owen of having a hand in his marriage breakup.

Had his mother been complicit in that affair too?

"Time you stood on your own two feet in the business world, Mother. I think you'll find you're actually quite adept." James' voice dipped a few degrees cooler as he glanced at his mother's hand again. "But before I head back over the Tasman, I'm going to need a couple of things from you."

"What kind of things?" The wariness in Isabella's voice had in no way abated.

"That ring, for starters."

"What?" The blush was gone, and Isabella Montague was suddenly deathly pale, wax-figure-still, gripping the arms of her wing-backed chair.

"My wife's wedding ring," James stated, suddenly sure without a shadow of a doubt. "I'd like it back."

Isabella swallowed. "Adele gifted it to me." But the waver in her voice contradicted the truth in that statement.

"I don't think she did," he growled softly.

A look of studied hurt crossed his mother's face as she readjusted her features. "Are you calling me a liar?" Isabella was an excellent actress, but James was more than wise to her tricks, catching the little cracks in her demeanour—the nervy twitch of her lips and white-knuckled hold on the highly polished wood. "Because I don't appreciate it, Aksel. After all I've done for you."

After all she'd done for him? The irony wasn't lost.

"I'm saying you must be *confused*." James re-angled the accusation with the loaded word, strolling over to where she sat.

Reaching out to take her right hand gently in his, he touched his forefinger to the little platinum band she'd been worrying at. Rolling it slowly sideways, the uniform row of diamonds that had been hiding against his mother's palm became visible, one by one. They winked up at him, like a row of familiar stars, and he released a heavy sigh.

The bigger part of him had still wished himself wrong; had wished Isabella innocent of this particular betrayal of trust.

"I gave this to Adele, and I don't think she would've given it away," he murmured.

Not in the beginning, anyway.

He remembered Adele's words on getting her engagement and eternity ring back, and experienced a nauseating lurch. *'Buy something new for your next wife.'*

His next wife? How had they slid so far apart?

"You're so much better out of it, Aksel. Adele was clearly in it for the pay-check."

"What did you say?"

"No need to take offence. You're happier without her." Isabella seemed desperate for that to be the truth, taking Adele's wedding band hostage by clenching her hand into a fist,

"With*out* her? Losing Adele and Saffy all but ripped me apart. How could you have been blind to that? She was everything to me. The only person who ever saw me as myself, and loved me anyway."

"No." Isabella tried a laugh, but it came off brittle, and a bit shaky. "She never *loved* you, nor you her. Not truly. Anyone could see it was based on lust."

"Lust?" he scoffed. "I would've given my life for hers." It wasn't fair to use that analogy, and James watched the colour once again flood his mother's face as she opened both mouth and hand in reflex. Two bright spots of pink rose high on her cheeks, making her look almost doll-like.

Isabella Montague obviously had an underlying fear of James' potential to suicide, to kill himself if the going got rough.

Like father, like son.

James slid the ring from his mother's suddenly unresisting finger, and wedged it onto his own pinky without ceremony.

"You… you…" Isabella took a moment to compose herself as he lowered her hand softly to the armrest. "I didn't know."

James threw one palm upward in disbelief. "How could you not?"

"You were like a couple of teenagers. Hands all over each other at the most inappropriate times." His mother wrinkled up her nose at the memory. "That kind of infatuation never lasts. Then came the arguments."

"We fought because I was never there. The business took over, and it was nothing like I'd promised. Our marriage suffered. Adele was left alone in a strange city."

"Sydney is a *beautiful* city."

"But not home to Adele."

Isabella huffed. "Near the end, she hardly spoke at all. She was cold. Unfeeling."

James rubbed a hand across his eyes, desolation setting in. "She was mourning, Mother. We lost a child."

"Not *your* child, though..." Isabella trailed off guiltily.

James' brain snapped to attention. "Yes. *My* child. *Our* child. These lies have done more damage than you can comprehend. Adele had a miscarriage, and haemorrhaged—lost a lot of blood. She nearly died."

"You never told me that!"

"No. I didn't. But you knew she was in hospital and never questioned it, never visited."

"I was told she'd had an elective abortion of another man's child."

"By Tiffany?" he barked.

"No. By... by someone else." His mother looked even more cornered, but her chin winched up a notch.

Ever the fighter. Ever the queen of dramatics. Ever protective of her youngest son.

James was going to kill his conniving brother—wring his bloody neck.

"And what do you know about Owen selling Montague tech to other companies?"

"Nothing. I don't know anything about that," his mother backtracked hastily, placing a single, perfectly manicured finger over her lips and pressing down.

"*What* do you *know*?" James finally lost control of his temper.

"Nothing!" Isabella looked genuinely frightened in that instant, and James realised he was towering over her as his father used to do. Intimidating her, albeit without intent.

He took a deliberate step backwards just as Ms Ermine cleared her throat, reminding James of her presence.

"If I find you had anything to do with liquidating Montague Holdings, or Tiffany manipulating my wife into leaving me, there'll be hell to pay," he muttered, incensed beyond belief.

"Of course I didn't! Why would I? I had everything to lose!"

"Then you won't have any trouble writing a letter to go with this ring," James suggested, waggling his pinky in her direction. "Explaining how you came by it, and apologising for any wrongdoing on your part."

"Well, of course." Isabella hesitated, before looking to Ms Ermine as if to drum up support. "Though I don't know Adele's address."

"I'll be hand delivering it," James slid in.

"You're back with her, aren't you?" Every crumb of his mother's self-pity-show was swept away by the sudden distaste in her voice. "That's what all this is about. That's why you're moving into the New Zealand viticulture market, and why she's answering your phone."

"No, Mother. Adele has more brains than to get involved with this family again, or me," James countered bitterly. "And who could blame her, after the shit she's had to put up with? She allows me to see Saffy. That's it."

"Saffron." The tightness in his mother's face softened. "That little girl lights up a room, doesn't she? You've seen her?"

James nodded, a lump forming in his throat. He hesitated before moving to the briefcase he'd left on the coffee table. Unlocking it, he hunted for something he'd slid in that morning for his mother, but hadn't particularly wanted to give her.

No matter how he felt about the flawed and manipulative woman sitting in front of him at this precise moment, he'd made a promise to his daughter, and was going to keep it.

"Saffy wanted me to give you this." James handed his mother the page Saffy had torn from her art book in the car as they'd said their goodbyes. It was a watercolour and ink landscape of the lake, Ruby Island in the distance and a single iconic tree, stubbornly rooted in the lakebed. "She wanted you to see where she lives now."

"Oh, beautiful! Such talent." Isabella had tears in her eyes, and for once James believed them to be genuine. "Will you ever bring her back to see me, James?"

"I'm not sure," he answered honestly, staring at the watercolour and thinking about his own position in Wānaka. Against the odds, like this strange little willow with its foundation under water. "That's completely up to Adele. But since you seem to have done everything within your power to ostracise her, I wouldn't hold my breath."

"Do you really think..." Isabella hesitated, tracing her finger over Saffy's careful signature at the bottom right corner. "Was she genuine? Adele."

James sighed. "If you're meaning was the child mine? The answer is yes. Whether you knew it or not, you lost something incredibly precious that day, too."

"Oh." One tear plopped onto the page, and Isabella hastily wiped it aside with her thumb. "I'm sorry."

"Are you, though?"

"Truly. For my part. I *am* sorry. It was all so quick. You met, you married." Isabella snapped her fingers to illustrate her point. "I thought you'd be happier with someone more like yourself."

"Mother, Adele made me happier than I'd ever been."

Isabella frowned. "A whirlwind romance between polar opposites, with a generous age gap, *and* ready-made family thrown in. The two of you were destined for failure. I tried to warn her."

James clenched his jaw until his teeth ached, finally finding the calm to ask, "Did you? When was that, Mother?"

Isabella must have seen some of the fury he was so carefully holding back, because her hands shook when she adjusted the collar of her jacket.

"Before you married, of course."

"You didn't meet Adele until *one week* before we married." James ground the words out with a clear image of Adele in his head. Twenty-one and new to Australia, having just dragged her two-year-old daughter from everything she'd known, everything she'd thought of as home. His fresh-faced fiancé had been nervous, but full of hope, expectation, and effervescent positivity. How would it have felt to be accosted by Isabella Montague on arrival? The bolshy, opinionated mother-in-law, warning her off. "Did you set Owen onto her, too?" he groaned.

"What on earth do you mean by that?"

"Was Tiffany your idea?"

"I swear, I don't know what you're talking about, Aksel."

James sought for truth, and thought he found it in the confusion in his mother's eyes. But that didn't begin to alleviate the ache. He'd promised Adele a close-knit family, assuming support and acceptance would be given to her as her due, but that was nowhere near what she'd received.

"You'd like to plant the blame on me for your marriage failing," Isabella decided, her voice softening. She rose to stand, using her chair as leverage much more openly than she would've a year ago. "You believe you're still in love with her, don't you?"

Yes, he believed himself still in love, but his track record on turning that emotion into a workable relationship was shite. During his marriage to Adele he'd been arrogantly obsessed with his work, and obtuse to his wife's wider needs. None of that boded well for second-chances.

Dutifully protecting his family from the wolves since his father's death, he'd secured their financial future. But in doing so, he'd left Adele emotionally high and dry, fighting wild beasts all on her own.

"There was one other small matter," Ms Ermine politely slid in as James re-packed his briefcase and prepared to leave. "Though in light of your recent request, the directive is possibly moot." She looked from James to his mother, pointedly it seemed.

Isabella Montague cleared her throat. "I'm writing Owen back into the trust as a recipient. A beneficiary. It's not right that he—"

"Your prerogative, of course," James interrupted. "Though I'm blown away he considers himself party to what's left, when he's done bugger-all to earn it, and everything in his power to rip it out from under us." He turned to Ms Ermine's silver-eyed stare, finding some understanding there, and perhaps a touch of commiseration. "Once I'm out, Isabella's free to do as she chooses with Owen. He's family, after all. But can I give you a word of advice? Stronghold the penthouse and lock it in tight under her name, so he can't touch it. Ever. Or he *will* strip the shirt off her back."

24

PUKAPUKA - BOOK

As many diverse lessons as there are pages.

Adele breezed into the farmhouse kitchen, late for pizza making duty again.

Dumping her jacket over the back of an empty chair, she flicked the switch on the kettle before plonking herself down at the table with a deep-seated sigh.

Kana and Katie sat opposite with Ruby, pizza dough and chopped toppings on the table in front of them.

"What's up with you?" Katie opened with a hard line, and even harder stare, seeing more than Adele wanted her to, as usual.

"James is driving me crazy," she grumbled.

"Ah. Ex trouble. Nothing like a discarded man acting like a boomerang to get on your wick," Kana commiserated, but something in the twist of her lips said she wasn't quite buying it.

"Well, he's gone now. So, that's something." Adele looked down and idly picked up a tomato. Drawing a chopping board closer, she ground her teeth together before slicing the red orb neatly in half.

"He's *gone*? But the house!" This time Kana looked truly perplexed, her straight, dark brows bulldozed together.

"Gone for now. Work's continuing on the house. Saffy and I have just been down there with the interior designer."

Chop. Chop. Chop.

It felt remarkably good to hack at something.

"Ohhh." Kana drew the exclamation out, then glanced at Katie and away again before adding, "That's very, um… *involved* of you."

"Right. Hence the 'James is driving me crazy' call," Adele grouched. "I'm trying to get a bit of distance, and he's gone and left all the refit decisions in his cabin up to me."

"*Distance*?" Katie snorted. "Is that what we're calling it?"

Adele turned to glare at her sister, needing Katie's brand of snark like a smack upside the head. But it was hard to keep a serious face when Ruby was blowing raspberries from her perch on Katie's knee.

"Maybe he just trusts your taste better than his own," Kana soothed. "You've got a really good eye for colour."

"Or maybe he's trying to make me fall in love with it?" Adele muttered. She was already one foot in, and could admit to herself having a hand in the decor had been fun. Colours and tiles. Sofa covers and bedheads. Saffy had been totally in her element, visualising and dreaming, and James had been right to involve her.

The builders were ripping ahead, slapping up built-in wardrobes and a new ensuite at lightning speed, while the plasterers began on the upstairs bedrooms.

"So, when's he due back?" Kana continued, transferring a mound of grated cheese to a waiting bowl, before reaching for another hunk of edam.

"I don't know." Even to Adele's own ears, that came out sounding a bit desolate. "I told him to stop texting me, so now he's taken up radio silence."

"And therein lies the ex trouble?" Katie queried, jiggling Ruby into chortles of glee. "You're not following your heart and ignoring your common sense, are you? What if you two crash and burn like last time? What then?"

"Shut up, Kit Kat." Adele glowered at her sister. The question was on her mind, sure, but she'd had about enough from Katie on the topic.

"No. I won't. It's about time you stopped calling James your ex, when you're *clearly* still in love with him."

"I never said—!"

"Snogging him on every occasion."

"I'm *not*—!"

"Has he asked you to move in with him, yet? Into his cosy cabin by the lake?"

"Katie," Kana interjected with a remarkable show of calm, as was her usual style. "Stop winding her up."

"Yeah, stop winding me up," Adele muttered, concentrating hard on not slicing off her finger, or blurting out very honest answers to those pertinent questions. Because yes, she kept kissing James. It was a very addictive practice. And no, she hadn't been asked to move in with him. Yet.

That in no way meant she hadn't been thinking about it. Often.

The implication and temptation were certainly there, hovering like Africanised honey bees. Adele's tenancy agreement was coming up for renewal, and she'd finally begun to look at properties for herself and Saffy. Nothing as high-priced as James' cabin, of course, but somewhere she could set up her first B&B, giving herself a latent income, and more time to write.

The divorce settlement no longer felt like dirty money, guilty pay-off cash on James' part, and that changed everything.

Adele had been wading through an avalanche of ideas regarding the sum she had locked in a tiered account. Yes, she considered the money to be Saffy's inheritance, but buying property would be a win-win for her daughter, growing in value while adding to her quality of life.

A car horn honked from the direction of the driveway, breaking Adele out of her reverie.

"Is that Clem?" she asked, popping a slice of tomato into her mouth and relishing the acidic tang. She'd assumed aunt Poppy and her husband were staying in Dunedin this week.

Katie stood, her chair scraping across the wooden floor. She was frowning as she handed Ruby to Kana, blinking at the door. "Are you expecting anyone else?"

Kana made a non-committal sound and smiled at her baby girl, but something in her studied nonchalance didn't quite ring true.

Adele waited until Katie had hustled out of the room before

whispering, "I was just thinking, there's enough pizza dough here to feed an *army*. Do we know who it is?"

"Mmm-hmm." Kana smiled, all smug.

"Rue?"

"All of them. Rue and the boys, Clem and Poppy, your mum and dad. They reckon she's had long enough to stew."

"Oh, thank God for that. I love her and all, but—"

"She's been driving you bananas," Kana finished for her.

"Totally." Adele grinned.

"I blame the pregnancy hormones. Even so, it's good to see you two holding real conversations." Kana angled her a look across Ruby's head. "But now I've got you alone, what's *really* going on? Did something happen between you and James?"

Adele moaned. "Ugh! As if I wasn't confused enough, he went and painted the love-seat rainbow."

Kana paused, her brow puckered as if she was trying to figure out a tricky maths equation. "Is that code for something?"

"Yes. No. It doesn't matter. I'm just... I think I've changed my mind, but just when I need to talk things through with him, he's buggered off back to Australia."

"Changing your mind is a totally valid choice," Kana answered vaguely, still looking slightly unsure. "Why don't you call him on the phone? Or, did you mean 'talk' as in Led Zeppelin mode?"

"What?"

Kana cleared her throat. "Turn up the volume so the neighbours don't complain about the sound effects?"

Adele snorted a laugh. "Am I *that* see-through?"

Kana held Ruby up in front of her. "Ruby says 'yes,' don't you Ruby-doobs? And that's a yes from me, too."

Adele looked behind her guiltily, checking they were still alone in the kitchen. "To be honest, I'm hard pressed to get my mind off James and his bloody body." She kept her voice low, conscious they could be interrupted at any moment.

"It's more than just physical between you two, though. Isn't it?"

"Yes," she agreed on a sigh. "Though it *has* been a long dry spell..." she waved a hand to indicate what her Nana Nona used to refer to as 'womanly bits.' "I'm nervous as all hell. Do you think he'd go for it?" She worried her lower lip with her teeth.

Kana began to chuckle, and even Ruby appeared to be smirking. "Are you kidding me? The way he looks at you? How has he held off this long?"

"You'd better be right," Adele muttered. "I don't think I could handle a booty-call rejection right now."

"That's what you guys call it? A booty-call?" Kana wrinkled up her nose, and Adele answered with a shrug.

No. They'd never called sex anything that offhand when they were together, but Adele couldn't exactly call it making love now, could she?

"We're talking about *James* here, right?" Kana teased. "Not Maintenance Tony?"

Adele placed her forehead on a clear piece of table, relishing the cool steadiness. "Tony backed off a week ago, when I told him there was no way in hell," she muttered. But Kana was right, the term 'booty-call' was much more Tony's demographic.

"Right," Kana hesitated. "Does James know that?" she checked gently.

Adele lifted her head to blink across at Kana, too surprised to speak. James couldn't actually think…? Not her and *Tony*. Though she'd fanned that very assumption by staying out late on their blind date, and Tony had introduced himself as her boyfriend when the two men met.

The front door swung closed, the sound echoing from the furthest recesses of the house. Running feet and voices raised in excitement indicated that Saffy and Katie's boys had just taken over the lounge as an allied group.

Their troop of adults wouldn't be far behind.

"James would've realised there's nothing going on, there."

"Would he?"

"I mean…" Adele lowered her voice to a whisper. "I *think* so."

Kana glanced toward the door, and the growing cacophony of approaching feet, while moving a jar of capers a little further out of Ruby's reach. "I feel for James. He's Saffy's dad, but has no legal right to her. Imagine how that would feel?" She shuddered. "No. On second thoughts, *don't* imagine it."

Adele stared at Kana, taken aback. "I've been very reasonable! I've allowed—"

"I wasn't suggesting you haven't been. More than accommodating, considering he turned up out of the blue without your say so. Incredibly cheeky. He's lucky you didn't turf him straight back out on the street, and slap him with a no-trespass order. What I was meaning was I'd be nervous too, in his position. You can choose whoever you like as Saffy's new stepdad, multiple if you feel the urge, and he has absolutely no say."

The only person Adele could see as Saffy's dad, the only person she'd choose as a father to *any* of her children, present or future, was James.

Rue chose that moment to enter the kitchen, so Adele and Kana put their conversation on hold, both rising to greet Katie's grinning husband.

"Katie tells me James is back." Rue had obviously meant the comment as a soft aside for Adele's ears only, but at the mention of her ex-husband's name, all other dining conversation stopped.

Adele's collective family turned towards her, pizza scoffing temporarily forgotten.

She groaned internally.

"Is he, really?" Rosa, Adele's mother, finally ended the uncomfortable silence with a question aimed squarely at her youngest daughter.

"Yes. He's visiting." Adele met the bug-eyed faces around the table, slid over Rue's apologetic wince, and caught on her daughter's tentative smile. "Saffy," she clarified, smiling back, gratified to see her nine-year-old's mouth stretch into an easy grin. "He's visiting Saffy," she re-stated firmly.

Her family could all put that in their respective pipes, and smoke it.

"*And* buying property," Daniel added, brows thunderous.

"*And* swimming in the lake." Kana had a distinct chirp in her voice, overriding Daniel's grouchy mood by making light of the situation.

"*And* playing piano for Ruby," Obāchan slid in with a nod of approval.

"And helping me paint my room." Saffy seemed to miss the undertone of warring parties, her main focus instantly back on her gooey slice of Hawaiian.

"*And* buying *property*," Daniel re-stated, presumably crotchety at being ignored.

"So?" Adele turned to her cousin and fired an imaginary round at him across a feast of melted cheese. How dare he bring up the prospect of James' potential permanency in Wānaka with her mum and dad in the room? Not to mention Saffy, ears and emotions all flapping. "It looks like a sound investment."

"You've been up there?"

"Of course I have! If it's going to be my daughter's second home when she's visiting her dad, why wouldn't I check it out?" Adele countered Daniel's question with a perfectly valid one of her own, and watched him squirm. "He's letting Saffy help choose the decor."

"Well, I think that's lovely," Rosa fluffed, ever the peacemaker.

Amos, Adele's dad, patted his wife on the hand in a familiar gesture of marital solidarity.

Rosa took the contact as her cue to add, "How nice for Saffy, to have him here as more of a permanent fixture. Is he coming for dinner tonight, then?"

"No!" There was a loud cacophony of the single word, as four people answered at once, all with different inflections.

Adele concentrated on Saffy's answer, the somewhat dejected one.

"He'll be back soon, love," she promised softly, realising she had nothing concrete to back that up with. Other than his Monday afternoon video call, there was no timeline, no schedule, no dates in the calendar.

Adele frowned. It was so unlike meticulously organised James to leave anything up in the air, and recently *all* his plans seemed transient.

It wasn't like his ex-wife had any right to know what his day to day timetable was, but it would've been good to have a heads up. For *Saffy's* sake. How were they supposed to work out a schedule if she didn't know when he'd be around?

Adele wondered how much of James' sudden air-silence was due to her snappy text, telling him to butt out of her life.

Not the smartest move, perhaps.

"You've got tomato on your shirt," Katie informed Adele as they stood outside in the cold, waiting for Rue to bring the car around.

Highly likely, considering how distracted she'd been throughout dinner.

Adele looked down to ascertain the damage to her blouse, and Katie took the opportunity to flick her upside the nose in a childish show of one-upmanship.

"Don't take this the wrong way, but I'm sort of glad you're leaving," Adele snapped. The others had all said their goodbyes to Katie and Rue inside, and Adele began to wish she'd done the same.

Katie snorted. "Don't take this the wrong way, but I think you're kidding yourself on the James front. If you're seriously still into him, what are you waiting for? You don't have to re-marry the guy, or even move in with him to get your rocks off."

"Mind your own beeswax," Adele murmured, but there was no heat in it.

"You could just date him. Keep Saffy out of it."

Katie was right, except Saffy was already tied up in all this, and always would be.

"He's her dad. What if Mum had kept us from Pop?"

"It's not the same."

"You keep saying that, but it *is* the same. It's the same to Saffy. She has a dad who cares about her, and she cares back. End of story."

"And a mum who's desperate to climb back into bed with the guy, and get herself well and truly laid."

"Bugger *off*." Adele gave Katie a little sideways shove with her shoulder, but she was laughing.

"I'm leaving." Katie gave her a strange little smile, almost nervous in its twitchiness. "But not without a hug." She held her arms open, and Adele stepped in without hesitation.

"I'll miss you," Adele murmured into her sister's mussy hair, meaning it, even alongside the constant irritation of being told what to do.

"You always give the best hugs. And I'll miss you, too."

"Are you and Rue…?"

"Alright?" Katie finished the unanswerable question for her, then sighed. "I think so. Mum's keeping the boys for the weekend, so we've got time to talk. Something we haven't had enough of, lately."

Adele knew Rue had booked them into a fancy hotel on Lake Wakatipu. Just the two of them.

As if on cue, Rue drove up and parked a few metres away, leaving the engine running as he leaned across and swung open the passenger door.

"Can I offer you a lift, cupcake? You heading my way?" Rue's grin was infectious as he propositioned his wife with a nickname she snorted at.

Katie detangled herself from the hug and turned to leave, but just before reaching the car she twisted back to face Adele.

"Dell-Bell?"

"Mmm-hmm?"

"Don't be a stranger."

The sisters smiled at each other, melting the cool edge from the evening with the warmth travelling between them. Adele wrapped her arms around herself to keep the glow in, knowing her and her sister were going to be okay. Whatever had been damaged between them was on the mend, and it looked like the same could be true for Katie and her husband.

"I won't," she promised.

Adele felt, rather than saw Daniel come to stand beside her, and together they waved the couple off.

"I think that went okay, all things considered," Daniel mused. "They both seem keen to make it work."

Adele sighed, turning towards him in the low light spilling across the gravel from the verandah. "Before we go back in, I need to ask you a favour."

"Sure."

She took hold of his arm, grounding herself. "I need you to lay off James."

"What?" Daniel's focus was suddenly laser-intent. "The Aussie? Lay off him in what way?"

"Lay off him in every way. We've got something going on."

"Are you *nuts*?" Daniel expelled the words with some force.

Insanity was a distinct possibility. Adele's heart had won over her brain, *and* her guts. Did that make her a touch cray-cray?

No more than the next person.

"Aren't we all?" she replied, overly glib.

"You've been here before, remember?" Daniel warned in quieter tones, worry lines marring his forehead.

"I haven't forgotten anything. Quite the opposite. I'm going in with my eyes wide open." Adele spoke more calmly than she felt, though her intentions were fairly straightforward. She wanted to ease her way in, dipping one toe in at a time, and see where this could go with James.

Not that she'd disclosed any of this to the man himself.

"It's complicated, but I still have feelings for him."

She knew damn well fooling around with an ex could prove disastrous, especially with a child involved. But *not* trying because she was scared of possible outcomes? That could prove even more harmful.

"The fact he's bought property here smacks of long-term trouble." Daniel re-issued his grumble from earlier in the evening.

Long term trouble, or long-term bliss?

Adele left the thought unsaid.

"I want this for myself, D. I deserve another shot."

Fran was right. Out in the open was better than tucked under a blanket of secrecy, wasn't it? Healthier. Even if Adele was still picking and choosing which truths to share.

Daniel blew out a huff of air, slow and steady.

"Yes, you absolutely deserve to live your best life," he conceded. "But I can't help being concerned. For you. For your daughter. You asked me to step in and be a father figure to Saffy, remember? *You* asked *me*."

Adele reached out for Daniel's other arm as well, squeezing them both tight. "And you outdid yourself Dante D. That little girl thinks the sun shines out of your grumpy ass, and always will. So will I. Because I asked you for help, and you did everything in your power to make it work. But you can't choose who I fall for."

Daniel groaned. "You've fallen for this guy?"

She laughed. "Stop calling him 'this guy' or 'the bloody Aussie.' He has a name."

James.

The last name she thought of when she went to sleep at night, and the first name on her lips when she woke.

25

TEINA - YOUNGER BROTHER

Born to challenge and surprise.

Adele called James' cellphone, heart in throat as she sat on the side of her bed later that evening. Saffy was safely tucked in bed, out of earshot, and Adele's nerves built as the ringtone repeated itself three times, before sliding to answerphone.

Where was he, exactly?

Adele hung up without leaving a message.

Why had she gone ahead and demanded he stop texting her? Now he *had* stopped, and not knowing when he'd turn up next was so much worse than the constant flow of information.

She redialled, and spoke before she could change her mind. "Hi. It's me. I'm not seeing Tony, the guy you met at my place the other day. You don't have to return this call. I'm just telling you because Fran says it's best to clear the air. So, ah... now I've told you. Bye." She'd already disconnected when she realised she hadn't come close to saying everything she wanted to say.

No problem, she'd just call him right back again.

James' phone didn't even ring this time, it shot straight to answerphone. Did that mean he was screening his calls? Well, too bad.

"And another thing. Thank you for painting the love-seat for...

for Saffy. She really likes it, so, um, thanks. That was a nice surprise." She went to hang up before she could garble any more nonsense, finger hovering over the little red icon.

Was she done? Almost.

"Just in summary, I liked it too. A lot. You don't have to call me back," she reminded him before actually hanging up.

That should about cover it.

Return to normal life-after-James was abrupt and grating, not the smooth slide Adele had been expecting. Everything was back as it should be, but without James it seemed to lack a certain sparkle.

His absence was everywhere—in the books on the shelf, in the single wine glass on the table, in the empty rainbow love-seat under the willow.

It was her father's sedan that pulled up on Saturday morning to take Saffy to rugby, not James' green monstrosity of a vehicle. Adele had a sudden, rather intense headache on Saturday night when Saffy was desperate to play another game of Scrabble, and avoided the wine aisle in the supermarket when she did the weekly shop on Sunday. James was in her head for the entirety of her walk with Winger along the lakefront on Monday morning, and she kept replaying his account of Rosetta.

His loss had been as big as Adele's. How had she never seen that? Men were taught to hide their emotional state, but she knew James. She should've been able to see through his businesslike mask to his hurt.

Finding suitably flat stones, she began to stack them, one on top of the other. One for the past, one for the present, and one for the future. One for Rosetta, one for Saffy, and one for James.

Standing back to contemplate the little six tiered cairn, and its lake-misted backdrop, Adele sighed. James was scheduled to video conference Saffy this afternoon, after school, and that fact kept playing on her mind.

She was getting desperate to see him.

Realising something was tangibly absent, Adele chose a suitable seventh stone for on top, careful to weight the balance just right.

One for herself.

By the time four o'clock rolled around, Adele was a ball of nerves. Saffy sat at the kitchen bench with her homework and art supplies, as usual. But instead of Adele prepping dinner, unseen but listening in the background, she was fluffing about behind her daughter, dusting the bookshelf.

James' call came through bang-on time, but Saffy turned to eye her mother before accepting it. "It's Dad," she stated, either in warning, or dismissal.

"You can go ahead and answer it." Adele waved a hand from the top of her stepladder, like it didn't matter either way if she was in-shot.

Saffy waited a beat more, rolled her eyes, then turned back to link in with James.

"*Do parana!*"

So, the man had done his homework and figured out how to greet Saffy in Bari, the common language of South Sudan. That shouldn't affect Adele in any way, yet it pleased her no end he'd made the effort.

"*Do parana*," Saffy returned, all sweetness and sunshine. "Where are you? What's that white stuff behind you?"

The angle Adele was on meant she couldn't see James clearly. Had he had a hair cut? The style looked more businesslike.

"Tasmania, and they're screens to block the wind. The easterly gets strong here off the Tasman, and the vines need protection."

"Are you near the sea?" Saffy wondered aloud.

James turned his laptop to show Saffy the view he was looking at, and she gasped.

"Oh, *wow*."

Adele strained to see it too, but Saffy's head was in the way. She crept down her ladder and shimmied a little closer.

Tasmania. Why Tasmania?

"Are you developing something to do with the screens?" Adele slid the question in as nonchalantly as possible.

"No, not exactly." Did James' voice soften a little, when he caught sight of her? It was hard to tell; difficult to read the nuances with the slight time lag. "Though I designed the original tech to monitor the angle of the wind gusts, so the screens can move into the best protective position without human intervention."

"Oh, right." How clever. All this stuff going on behind the scenes at the cutting edge of technology. "What are you working on now, then?"

Saffy turned to stare at her mother, and the look on her face said, *get your own damn video call*.

"We're trialling a program, testing the salinity levels in the irrigation system. These guys are close to the sea, so if the bores get low, salt levels can become problematic."

"Oh. Interesting."

Saffy folded her arms and sat further back on her stool, tight-lipped and resigned.

Adele cleared her throat. "Ah, just one more thing, then I'll let you two get back to it. Are you, um… Are you able to pick up messages on your phone over there?"

"My cell? Should be. Sometimes the international ones are a bit delayed. I haven't checked it today. Were you trying to get hold of me?" James' tone wasn't hopeful, merely curious.

"Who, me? No." Adele laughed, but it didn't come out sounding particularly sincere. She touched Saffy on the shoulder in apology before slipping past into the kitchen.

Snuggled up on the sofa later that evening, wrapped in her patchwork quilt to watch the late news, James' image slunk back into Adele's mind, and stayed there. She was no longer able to tell herself she didn't care, because she actually cared an awful lot. No matter how adamant she'd been that she never would again.

The problem was, she wasn't just interested in a quick roll in the hay for old time's sake.

Adele wanted Scrabble by the fire, and company at Saffy's parent-teacher interview. She wanted a neck massage after work and someone to remember to pick up a bottle of milk on the way home. She wanted someone to call *her* if they were away for work, and tell her all about their day.

Not just any old someone. James.

She wanted it all, despite knowing from experience the grass only *appeared* to be a lush, glossy green over that side of the fence. Her ex-husband would no doubt eventually get sucked back into his work, and all the details surrounding it. He'd be frowning into his laptop all hours of the day and night, ironing out kinks, re-writing codes, answering calls, and travelling at the drop of a hat, sometimes for weeks on end.

But with five years under Adele's belt, and an independent life of her own in Wānaka, James' obsession with his work no longer seemed so disagreeable. In fact, interconnected independence had a nice ring to it.

She gave herself a mental shake. Was she actually *considering* this? Considering James for the long term?

It would be smarter to categorically reject what they'd had and quash the want for anything more permanent, because it hadn't worked the first time. But that's not what her physical body was leaning towards, and not what her heart wanted.

Adele's copy of Pride and Prejudice arrived on Tuesday by courier. Alongside it in the package was a koala-handled toothbrush in what Saffy gleefully referred to as 'sick teal,' and a jar of very expensive-looking bush-honey hand cream.

Adele assumed the hand cream was for herself, though there was no message or letter accompanying it. Trust James to bypass her 'no gifts' directive by being ambiguous about who it was for.

If she complained, he'd merely say he'd intended it for Saffy.

She slid it into her handbag, slightly sheepish about keeping it to herself, but loving the rich, soothing texture too much to veto it.

What she needed was relief on the James front, a remedy to magically appear and cure her of all symptoms and carry-over desires. What she *needed* was to stop daydreaming about how it would feel to have him back in her life, back in her bed, and actually come up with a viable plan.

Why did history repeat? Because humankind refused to learn from their mistakes the first time around.

On Tuesday evening, when the house was dark and quiet, Adele climbed into her nightie and dove under her patchwork quilt before opening one of her all time favourite books. It'd been calling to her all day from her bedside table.

"It is a truth universally acknowledged…"

She allowed the familiarity of Jane Austen to soothe her angst. Skipping large chunks of text, and seeking her favourite passages and conversations, she chuckled over the protagonist's wit and censure.

The tiny bookmark almost bypassed Adele's notice, fluttering down to hide in the bedsheets when she turned the page. She ran her palm over the fitted sheet, fingers searching until they came up with the smudged receipt.

Not in English, and not in dollars. Chinese renminbi?

Did that mean this particular copy of Pride and Prejudice had actually travelled to China?

When Adele reached Darcy's fabulously flawed marriage proposal mid-book, the dialogue between characters took on extra significance due to what she'd begun to refer to in her head as The James Situation.

In fact, chapter thirty-four had a very viable, very usable format.

Adele mulled on that. She could always pull a Darcy and lay it all out like a contract, an agreement. Nothing misconstrued, nothing hidden away. James would understand, it was very much his style, and how he'd proposed to her originally. She could address it the very next time she saw him, she just needed to figure out the best way to explain her needs.

Adele's head was full of large, complicated Regency words to describe a very simple, age-old problem.

She wanted him.

A straight proposition. 'You have a body, and I want it.' Or, 'I don't rate your family, but think you're rather special.' Those were infinitely better than, 'I'm starting to realise I might still be in love with you,' which was attached to a whole landslide of additional problems.

Text message, or a phone call?

As it turned out, James didn't answer his phone, so Adele left him another jerky voicemail.

"Hi, it's me again. Adele. So, I just wanted to let you know… To *tell* you that, um… Your package arrived. You don't have to call me back. I just thought you'd like to know it arrived safe. So, bye, I guess."

Adele put her head in her hand after disconnecting, branding herself a complete dipstick.

Face to face would be easier, and she fell asleep deciding next time she saw James, she'd lay it on the line. Probably not the *in-love-with-you* bit. More than likely the *sex-with-you* part.

James wrapped up his business in Tasmania on Tuesday, leaving himself enough time to fly back to Sydney and attend his meeting with his mother's solicitor, Ms Ermine, on Wednesday afternoon.

He'd been busy, packing a lot of work and research into a few days, but his heart lifted each time he saw Adele had left him another strange little message. Her tone seemed unsure, almost frustrated, and her recordings were interspersed with a few missed calls and hang ups. To all intents and purposes they were back in touch, though she kept telling him not to call back.

So he didn't.

No need to rock an already precariously balanced boat.

But his silence didn't stop him wondering why Adele was so keen for him to know she wasn't with Tony, or if she understood the rainbow love-seat had been painted in the form of an apology, or if the hand cream was helping her tortured skin.

James wasn't surprised to see Owen waiting outside the Montague Family Trust meeting, but he was shocked by his brother's outward appearance. Owen's exuberance seemed to have sunk along with his cheeks in the six-months since they'd last seen each other, and there was a world-weary haggardness around his eyes.

"Owen." James acknowledged his brother's presence with a nod in his direction, and would've left it at that if Owen hadn't bounded up to grip him with both hands.

"Aksel. Good to see you. Good to see you." Owen dug his fingers into James' shoulders, almost to the point of pain.

Was it really so good? James studied Owen's face and tried to get a take on his almost desperate welcome, wildly at odds with the disjointed way things had been left between them.

Isabella was running later than her two sons, leaving them alone in the cloistered atmosphere of the solicitors' waiting room.

"You're back in Sydney, then."

"California didn't work out." Owen grimaced, finally letting

James go. "Mother says you're looking into the New Zealand viticulture market?" There was a false brightness to his tone.

"Uh-huh." Better to leave it at that.

They both sat, facing each other over a low table.

"Father always said you had a farming head."

James narrowed his eyes. "Father also said running a farm would be the making of you." And look how that had turned out.

Owen looked away. "I fucked up."

No shit.

James left the unhelpful thought unsaid, running a hand over his jaw. Perhaps he and his brother were more alike than he'd like to admit. They both took risks, and gambled with outcomes, sometimes to the detriment of those around them.

"We've all fucked up in the past. It's how we go forward that matters. Mother's going to rely on you more from here on in. I hope you can live up to that."

Owen was studying James intently. "Are you back with your wife?"

"Ex-wife," James corrected his brother almost automatically. "No."

"Oh." Owen's almost hopeful expression faded. "I heard you'd been in New Zealand, and thought maybe you two had patched things up. She was nice, Adele. I liked her."

"Did you?" The surprise in James' voice was genuine.

"Yeah. She was cool, you know? Got you out of your head and loosened you up some. You were more like your old self around her. Relaxed. Occasionally even fun." The little jibe was much more in keeping with Owen's usual style of communication, but his smile was fleeting. "You two were good together, in the beginning."

"So, I'm figuring you didn't have anything to do with Tiffany telling lies about having an affair with me, then?"

"No." Owen really did look confused, his forehead puckered. "You mean you weren't?"

"With Tiffany? No, I wasn't."

"Can't claim the same, I'm afraid."

"I figured."

Owen sighed. "To be fair, she was only ever using me to try to get to you. She was pretty adamant the two of you were soulmates."

James barked a laugh. "Fuck off."

"No, seriously. That's what Tiffany said when she broke things off with me. She'd wanted to make you jealous."

"Jealous?"

"Yeah." Owen looked pretty cut up about it, actually. He was gazing down at his clasped hands, nodding. "Didn't put me in the best frame of mind about you, to be honest. I really cared about her, and she…" He shrugged.

"Screwed you over?"

"She did, yeah."

A missing piece of the puzzle slowly slid into place for James. "Is that why you tried to royally screw *me* over?" He posed the question in a mild tone, but Owen's head snapped up as if the words had been shouted.

"I guess so." Owen cleared his throat. "Part of the reason. It seems pretty sour looking back on it now, but you had the wife and kid, and it looked very much like you had my girlfriend on the side, too. You had the company, and the swanky city house, and all I had was a handful of dirt. I didn't think you'd miss the tech. I wasn't expecting the whole thing to blow up like that…" he trailed off. "It was never my intention—"

Isabella Montague chose that moment to swan out of the lift, all cream silk, and floral perfume.

"Ah! My two handsome boys," she intoned, chin tilted in pride, and a faint hint of Europe still discernible in her accent. "Nice to see you out of rehab, Owen. Come and kiss your mother hello."

26

RETA - LETTER

Correspondence, once sent, cannot be taken back.

"Sorry, I'm a little late," Adele flustered, accidentally slamming Fran's office door closed behind her on Thursday evening. "I was held up with... *James!*"

She was so surprised to see her ex-husband, sitting in exactly the same spot on the sofa as he had the last two Thursdays, his name came out in an undignified squeak.

All the oxygen was sucked out of the counsellor's office for a few milliseconds as Adele just stood and stared.

Of course—he'd told Fran he'd be here, and here he was. Right on time, and just as stunning as ever.

The beard was gone, replaced by a smooth shave, and James looked incredibly formal. He'd gotten up politely when Adele entered in her customary chaotic, whirlwind state, but didn't attempt to touch her or kiss her cheeks.

She self-consciously dropped the hand that'd naturally reached out to grasp his arm in welcome.

He'd definitely had a haircut. It appeared darker with all the natural highlights lopped off.

"Adele. You're looking well."

"Ah, thank you." She smoothed a hand over her business skirt, skittering a look towards Fran for some kind of guidance through the strained atmosphere. "And thank you for returning my book. You didn't have to—I mean the hand cream was lovely—but you know you don't have to buy me gifts."

That hadn't stopped Adele from using it though, and she'd felt so decadent each time she'd lathed it on to the scent of summer memories.

"It was the least I could do."

James' face was unreadable, but his voice seemed to hold a cool indifference. Something Adele hadn't been expecting.

Back to square one. Him in his corner, she in hers.

In all her recent plans of propositioning him, Adele had never imagined James actually *aloof*, and it put her on the back foot.

"I'm happy to leave," James continued woodenly. "If you'd prefer a private session, though I think we have some things to discuss, and it seems to help involving a third party.

"What, um… What *kind* of things to discuss?" Adele could see her best laid plans getting shot-to-hell by this stilted atmosphere. What had happened in Australia to quash the growing closeness between them?

James eyed her as she sat down on her end of the sofa, knees pressed tightly together to stop them from jiggling.

"My mother."

Adele looked down at her hands in her lap, and willed them *not* to find their way into her mouth. She didn't want to be caught gnawing on her nails by her suddenly poised, untouchable ex.

James picked up a crisp envelope that had been resting next to him on the wide arm of the sofa. "I have a formal apology from my mother, that I hope you'll accept." He handed over the pale blue rectangle and Adele automatically reached out to take it, charm bracelet jangling as her fingers brushed his.

"Your mother sent me an *apology*?" She drew back from the electricity James' touch evoked, taking the envelope with her.

Adele had gotten used to him looking a little rough around the edges, and the clean shave and business shirt were throwing her off. She hadn't seen him for a week, and all she wanted to do was snuggle her forehead into his neck, surround herself in his scent, and rest quietly for a moment.

Conversely, she kind of missed his gingerbread beard.

"She did, yes." James' jaw tightened, and Adele noted that his hands were tense too as he sat back down on his end of the sofa.

"Off her own bat?" she asked, fully suspicious now.

James had the grace to smile. It was a mere twitch of the lips, but he carried a touch of humour in his eyes. "Not entirely. Under duress is perhaps a more fitting description."

"I see." Adele placed the envelope on her knees. "Thank you."

"Read it," James growled.

"What, now?" She looked from James to Fran, disoriented by the request.

"*Now.*"

Fran nodded her agreement, so rather than stand against them both, Adele shrugged and slid a finger under the envelope flap to open it. She unfolded a single sheet of expensive linen paper, and began to read.

"Aloud," James intoned.

"It might be private!" she huffed, pissed off with his holier-than-thou attitude this evening. He was all uptight and concrete in his suit, reminding her of how it'd been in the last months of their marriage.

See? *Not* such green grass over there, she reminded herself.

Where did James get off? Disappearing without letting her know where he was, or when he'd be back, then turning up again when he was least expected? Okay, so she'd *told* him not to tell her, but still.

James just stared her down, one eyebrow raised.

Show off.

Adele cleared her throat and cast her eyes back to the top of the page.

"Dearest Adele—"

She had a bit of a cough after the first line. She'd never been the least bit dear to Isabella Montague, not for one moment.

"It is with deep remorse that I pen this letter. In speaking to James this week, I have been made aware of some things I was not clear on for the duration of your marriage, and I apologise if I in any way hindered the smooth running of your connection with my son."

Adele snorted, and sped-read silently through the paragraph again to make sure she'd gotten the gist right.

"Carry on," James prompted, his impatience riling her.

"Do *you* want to read it?" She flicked the page in his direction, and he narrowed his eyes.

"No."

"Then back off, and let me do it my way. Where was I?"

"*Your connection with my son,*" Fran input helpfully.

"Right." Adele ran a finger down the page, more to piss James off than to actually find her place. It wasn't a long letter. "*You and your daughter should have felt welcome within our family, and it is my understanding that you did not.*" She laughed aloud at this point. "Jesus, James. What did you do, hold a gun to her head?"

She'd meant it as a joke, but cursed her mouth when she saw James flinch.

God. How could she be so insensitive? His father…

"Sorry," she jumped in quickly. "Poor choice of words."

James waved one hand in a brush-off gesture, like it didn't matter one iota, but the muscle in his jaw was working overtime.

Adele dropped her eyes back to the letter, suitably contrite.

"*On a more legal note, I am obligated to take full responsibility for the theft of your personal items. If you wish to press charges, you are within your rights to do so, and James will do everything in his power to facilitate the legalities. With my deepest regrets, and respect, Isabella Montague.*"

Adele looked up, confused. "What does she mean, press charges?"

James stood to remove a small box from his suit-pants pocket, and Adele was again struck by the formality of his actions when he carefully placed it on the seat between them.

"This belongs to you." James' lips were pressed in a hard line, and his nostrils had a faint flare. He was clearly furious about something.

Tentatively reaching out, Adele opened the ring box with a gnawing suspicion she wasn't going to like what she'd find.

It was a platinum wedding band, studded with dainty diamonds.

Hers?

She removed it from the box and turned it over, intrigued to find herself squinting at the very familiar inscription on the interior circlet.

Forever yours, A.J.

"She *stole* it?"

What the actual hell?

"Although it doesn't entirely vindicate her actions," James began, re-adjusting himself on the sofa cushions. His body-language was as stiff as Isabella's letter. "My mother is a kleptomaniac, Adele. She takes things. Things that don't belong to her."

"It's an obsessive compulsive disorder," Fran clarified. "Terribly upsetting for all involved."

"Terribly upsetting," Adele shadowed the words in a hollow voice, trying to get her head around this bizarre and unexpected piece of information.

"I gather it's the reason we kept moving when I was a child," James offered as an aside. "The alps to the city. Switzerland to Canada. Canada to Australia. It can come across as a very, ah… Let's say *antisocial* behaviour."

Adele replaced the sparkling circle of stones carefully, resetting it into the plush white satin.

"But where did she find my wedding ring?"

James cleared his throat, and if possible straightened his back still further. "It was in your jewellery box, as you'd taken to not wearing it."

It took Adele a moment to fully fathom his meaning, but when she did, her eyes widened.

"She took the whole box?" It was too outlandish. There must be some mistake. "*She* took it? Your mother, Isabella." The woman was a well-to-do socialite, with more money than you could shake a stick at. "Why, on earth…? She was the one who insisted I must've pawned it!"

James flinched again. "Not her finest hour, I'm afraid." He rubbed a hand across his eyes, and Adele could suddenly see how dog-tired he was.

"Did you fly in today?"

He nodded. "Christchurch."

"Into *Christchurch*? But that's a seven hour drive from here!"

"It's the only direct flight from Sydney to the South Island on a Thursday," James stated calmly, as if explaining to a child that one plus one always equaled two.

"Right." And he'd felt he needed to be here on Thursday for this bloody counselling session?

"So, would you like to press charges?"

Adele began to laugh, realising belatedly James was actually serious. "Ah, no. Thank you. The less I have to do with your mother the better. In fact…" She lifted the tiny box again and inspected her wedding ring one last time before handing it back to James. "I think you should give this back to her."

James didn't move to accept the ring, he merely stared at the monogrammed jeweller's box in her palm.

"Go ahead, really," she prompted. "I appreciate you bringing it to me, but she can have it."

"If you insist." James took the box, and Adele could tell she'd offended him by the tight little brackets beside his mouth.

"It's not that I didn't love it. I did. But that's over now, right? I'm trying to move on." Adele looked down at her charm bracelet, full of naïve wishes, and her slowly recovering nails curled in her palms. "From a lot of things."

"Of course." But rather than slipping the ring back into his pocket as she'd expected, James took it out of the satin and worked it over the knuckle of his right pinky finger, expression unreadable.

Adele experienced an acute shot of sadness.

Gone. Finished. Done.

Except it wasn't, was it?

"Whatever we build from here on in has to be on new ground, James," Adele whispered, her throat spasming once from the held back emotion. "New territory. New rules. Agreed?"

James met her eyes across the sofa, and there was a gut-wrenching level of relief in them.

"Agreed," he murmured.

"The thing is, I don't entirely trust myself around you," she blurted. "You screw with my anatomy."

"Your *anatomy*?" James blinked at her, before glancing at Fran, then back.

"I listened to my heart when I dropped everything and followed you to Australia. And I was totally caught up in my head when I left. My gut told me there was something very off, but I wasn't listening. I was in full flight-mode. So I no longer trust my heart, *or* my head. And to be honest, my gut's had its moments recently, too."

"I find in times of stress, it's best to go with the lungs."

"What?" Adele turned to Fran, surprised by the odd aside.

"When all else fails, go with your lungs. They're the more immediate part of you; the *now* if you like, and they'll remind you how to breathe in and out, and live for the moment you're in." Fran smiled. "Some would disagree with the notion, but I believe the past is merely a series of stepping stones to where you are right now. What you do right *now* is what matters most. Breathe in, breathe out. Repeat. You've got this, Adele."

James had to get away from Adele, the need to pull her in close was growing so strong. The look of her, the smell of her, that sad little smile playing on her lips, and the fact she'd said his presence screwed with her anatomy.

Her presence totally screwed with *his* anatomy, and always had, a shit-ton more than just his head, heart, and gut.

He held the door for her at the front of the office building as they left Dr Fran's, then moved to step away.

"I see you've put an ensuite and walk-in wardrobe in the master bedroom." Adele stopped him in his tracks with a hand on his upper arm, her bracelet giving a familiar jingle as old charms bumped up against new ones. "At *your* place," she reiterated, the stressed word making it clear it had nothing to do with her. "Simone said she has a range of wardrobe fittings for you to choose from."

"Simone?" James turned slowly back towards Adele, not recognising the name.

"Your interior designer."

"Right." He ran a hand over his jaw, then looked out towards the lake. "Right," he repeated, more under his breath. "Thanks for reminding me. I'll catch up with her while I'm here."

"Why *are* you here, James?"

"It's Thursday."

"So you *did* fly back for this?" Adele waved her free hand

towards the sign that touted Dr Fran Hoani's counselling services. The other one was still gripping his arm.

A passer by stopped in front of them, clearly trying to get into the building, so they jostled sideways to make room, bumping up against each other with muttered apologies.

"It's important." James frowned down at her, close enough to hear her indrawn hiss of breath as her arm inadvertently tangled with his against his stomach, and one of the sharper charms dug into him.

It was with mixed emotion he'd recognised the familiar piece of jewellery on Adele's wrist in the counsellor's office. An old favourite, reminding him of the years they'd spent together, and those they'd lived apart.

"Not *that* important!" Adele flustered.

"Maybe not to you." James' cocked his head slightly to one side as he considered her, not taking the step back he really should've for her comfort level, and wondering at the faint shadows under her eyes. Adele looked like she'd slept similarly poorly to himself the past few days.

Adele wrenched her eyes away. "You can't fly back and forth over the Tasman like a bloody yo-yo once a week. It's not sustainable," she grumbled, leaning her back against the brick facade of the office block.

"Who said I'm not here to stay?"

"*Are* you?"

"No." Not while the Tasmania deal was still in progress, and not until he was fully out of the Montague trust. "You said pie-in-the-sky wasn't an option. I'm trying to make sure the cabin's a rock solid option for Saffy, but it will take some time."

"As a holiday house, or home?" Adele's voice had become even more strained, and her fingers pinched tight in the crook of his elbow before dropping away altogether.

His arm felt bereft without the pressure.

He'd intended to live in it, his two story log cabin in the woods, but that was all dependent on what Adele decided. The house, with its views of the lake and workshop attached to the garage, had been intended as a home. A retreat. A new beginning.

A spur-of-the-moment pipe dream from the very start, empty as all hell without Adele and Saffy in it.

"Either could work. I could rent it out…" That would definitely help offset some of the costs associated with the refurb. "But I'd planned to live in it most of the time."

Adele visibly relaxed, even smiled.

"I was wondering if you'd come to a firm decision on visitation arrangements with Saffy, once things settle down a bit? You mentioned Mondays next term. Drop her to school, and pick her up for a sleepover, maybe?"

"So, you're still planning once a week?" Adele frowned.

"If that works for you. I realise it was much more frequent, initially, and that wasn't fair. I don't want to keep treading on your toes. Once a week would be amazing."

Adele raised her eyebrows, and James cleared his throat—caught under the gaze of glittering topaz, with a touch of blue fire.

"Once a fortnight, if you'd prefer? There's a winery contract I'm tied into. I'll be coming back and forth across the Tasman from Hobart. More than just coming up with systems this time, I'm being paid in shares. Investing capital, in a roundabout way." How much did she want to know? James was clutching at straws, trying to figure out why Adele was looking so petrified.

Contracts were on the table, he just had to come up with more funds for the cabin refit. Hence the opt-out of all things Montague. Ever since he'd been shown through the Lake Taimana operation, his brain had been running overtime with possibilities

"Mr Kaihanga, and co?" Adele nibbled at her lower lip.

"Yes." James fisted his hand in his pocket and watched those pearly whites worry diligently at plump, pink flesh. "I'd be more than happy to help you with childcare during the weekend if you need it, though. You've been very tolerant of me—"

Adele snorted, but he ignored her interruption.

"I could have Saffy some weekends, if that works better with your schedule, and gives you more free time? I could come to this counselling session with you, or not if you'd prefer. You and I wouldn't have to have any direct contact, if that's the way you'd like it."

Adele became very still, watching him with a flush creeping up her cheeks, and James knew a moment of pure panic.

Why on earth had he offered her that? Seperate lives was the opposite of what he wanted. What if Adele's plans had changed, and she wanted to cut ties altogether?

All for naught. Too little too late.

"You have no grounds to claim time with Saffy." Adele spoke quietly, but the words shook him.

James finally took a step back, creating space between them. He looked back out towards the lake, seeking the calming view and swallowing the emotion that threatened to underpin his voice.

"No, I know. You're totally within your rights to refuse me access."

"Yes. I am," Adele stated decisively, and when he turned back to her it was to see her nodding with a wry twist to her mouth.

His stomach dropped. Was that her verdict? A definite no?

"I realise I haven't proven to be the best role model, and my family—"

"I don't think further separation from her father would be in Saffy's best interests, do you?" Adele interrupted.

"No. I don't." James jumped at the lifeline.

"Why is this so important to you, James?" Adele's voice was little more than a whisper.

"You have to ask?" He leaned in. "I love her, Dell. She's fantastical." He used the word Saffy had coined at three years old, when she'd seen a peacock with its tail up.

They stared at each other.

James loved Adele, too. Now more than ever before. Her tenacity and fiery get-up-and-go, the light in her eyes when she was on a rampage, the strength and resilience of her, and the way she'd rebuilt herself in the face of upheaval. Her soft, pale skin, and pretty freckles. But he couldn't tell her any of that now, could he? He had no claim to Adele. Even less right than he had to claim Saffy.

Adele was the first to look away, pulling her phone out of her handbag and checking the time.

"I really have to go. I'm late." She drew away from the wall to slip sideways, leaving before he'd had time to wrap his head around the separation.

"Late for what?" None of his business, but he asked anyway.

Inspecting her nails, as if warring with herself about how much she wanted to divulge, Adele finally sighed.

"I'm looking at a property, with investment in mind. Either to live in, or as a short-term rental. My lease is up at the end of next month and I'm considering my options."

"Oh." That was *extremely* interesting, and James barely managed to keep his tone neutral. "Would you like company to check the place over?"

"No. Knowing your history with Iris, you'd likely buy it out from under me, then I'd have to hate you all over again." Tucking her phone back into her handbag, Adele slipped between parked cars and looked both ways for traffic. "But you can pick Saffy up for school tomorrow at eight-fifteen, if you want." The invitation was thrown over her shoulder as she trotted across the road.

"Tomorrow's Friday," James reminded her.

"Will you be there, or not?"

"I'll be there," James called back, not bothering to keep the flash of elation out of his voice.

27

PIANA - PIANO

An orchestra of feeling, born from a single instrument.

The secondhand piano had come with a bonus stash of sheet music under the false-topped stool, and James pounded out Beethoven's fifth as the upright's initiation piece, complete with multiple misplays and do-overs.

There was no one in the cabin to hear him butcher the crescendo, and the lack of audience was highly freeing.

James moved on to The Deer Hunter, which had always been Adele's favourite, before Vivaldi's Four Seasons. The latter was more to his mother's taste, though she wouldn't have appreciated the way her son thundered it out today, in no mood to give it the more sensitive timing it deserved.

Mother.

James should've told Adele about Isabella's condition on his arrival in New Zealand, he knew that... But he hadn't been able to bring himself to. Not when in the depths of his heart, he'd been harbouring a faint glimmer of hope Adele may still feel something for him.

There'd been so many mixed emotions tied up in that first day, on returning the jewellery box to its rightful owner. When it came to the crunch, he hadn't had it in him to come clean about where

Adele's belongings had been found.

For the longest time, James had known there was something different about his mother. Even as a very small child, he'd been surreptitiously returning small items she'd stolen, all too aware they'd been taken without leave.

A dainty china cup, or silver teaspoon, slipped into her handbag at high tea. Or a brand new lipstick, held tightly in her palm until they were out of the store. A Lego Chewbacca, snatched from one of his classmate's Christmas dioramas and pilfered away in her pocket. A mandarin from the grocery store, a small potted succulent from the doctor's surgery, a silver pen from the mayor's office, and a gold nugget from a neighbour's prized collection...

Not to mention a Meiji jewellery box belonging to James' wife, right out from under his nose.

There was no rhyme or reason. It happened in Switzerland, Canada, and Australia. It happened when the family was on the breadline, barely making enough to get by, and it happened when Isabella had been a wealthy woman with no need.

It *still* happened.

Money had in no way curbed Isabella's burning compulsion to take that which wasn't hers. In fact, in many ways it seemed to have made her condition worse.

Adele's jewellery box had been discovered during a spring clean by the housekeeper, gathering dust under Isabella Montague's four poster bed. Even when James confronted her with the evidence, his mother had denied all knowledge, angrily refuting any wrongdoing.

He was due to call her this afternoon and check in on the latest solicitor's appointments and rigmarole, hating that it felt imperative he return to Sydney, just when things seemed to be smoothing themselves out in Wānaka.

Adele was willing to let him into her schedule, and into Saffy's world. Willing to talk, leave messages on his personal line, and converse via video call. She even appeared comfortable sharing her counselling sessions.

All these concessions would've seemed unfathomable three weeks ago.

Adele was looking for a new home for herself and Saffy. The serendipity of the timing had threatened to derail James when she'd mentioned it this evening, but although his mouth had opened to urge her to consider moving in with him up at the cabin, he'd managed to stop himself just in time.

He had to keep a cool head, not push Adele too hard or too fast, or he was likely to lose her all over again.

"Good morning, Adele."

James' greeting was too polite. Adele preferred his shocking arrival on her doorstep three weeks earlier, when he'd at least looked enthused to see her.

He was once again parked in her driveway, and knocking on her door. But just like at last night's counselling session, there was a coolness to his tone—to his whole atmosphere.

The cheeky grin from the man who'd stolen hot cookies, fresh from the oven, was missing.

"Hi," she breathed the single word out, shaken by her desperate need to see him this morning, her scramble to answer the door. She stared for a moment, taken aback by the return of the business shirt. "Are you working today?"

"Meetings," James stated, looking beyond her down the empty hallway as he rummaged Winger's ruff, and attempted to calm the excited dog. "Lake Taimana vineyard. The Kaihanga's," he reiterated.

"Saffy's running a bit late," Adele informed James, following his gaze.

Saffy ran late almost every day of the week. They both did.

"Any day now, Saffy! Your dad's waiting!" Adele upped her volume to call down the hallway.

Zero response.

Glancing down, she noticed the receipt she'd left for James on the hall table, and handed it over.

"I was reading Pride and Prejudice, and I came across this. I'm assuming you were using it as a bookmark. Is it important?"

"Oh, right." James took the slip of paper and studied it. "No. I think it's just the receipt for your rainbow charm." He scrunched it, then shoved it down into his pants pocket.

Adele froze, midway through running her fingers through her tangled curls. "*You* bought the rainbow charm?"

"Of course." James' eyes gazed steadily into hers. Grassy green, and incredibly inviting. "Did you think it was from my mother?"

Adele snorted. "No. I thought…" What exactly *had* she thought? "The unicorn and the mermaid? The dragon and the little cloud, too?"

James nodded, just once. Almost imperceptibly.

"Why did you buy me charms when we weren't together anymore, James?" she whispered the question, almost too scared to hear his answer.

"It was our tradition, wasn't it? A charm on your birthday. Another hard habit to break, I guess."

"Oh." She moved a half-step closer to him, and what she was thinking fell out of her mouth in an embarrassing tumble. "Maybe you wouldn't mind kissing me hello, when we see each other?"

The heat of Adele's blush crept upward as James hesitated.

Of all the things for her to've said, when he was clearly doing his best to keep his distance.

"I mean you don't have to, of course. But if you *wanted* to, I'm okay with it." She was babbling as her insecurities rose.

Adele held her breath as James dutifully stepped forward to do the two-cheeked kiss thing, and her whole body flushed. It was all very French, but not in the way Adele would *like* to French kiss him. She closed her eyes and curled her toes.

Old cravings were a bitch when your ex-husband smelt divine and you found yourself imagining him with his shirt off every time he was within cooee.

James shoved his hands deep in his pockets when he stepped back, and there was a definite twitchiness about him.

What was taking Saffy so long?

"So," Adele started in a conversational tone. "Kleptomania. I didn't see that coming."

James seemed to relax a little at her attempted humour, shrugging. "I should've told you."

"You *think*?"

"Turns out sorting through family loyalties isn't my strong suit." The firmness of James' mouth overruled his jesting tone. "It'd been undiscussed for so long, I never thought to bring you into the loop. We were lucky to get out of Switzerland, as it happens. One particular theft was very high profile. A politician with a lot of clout." He shook his head slowly. "An engraved hip-flask, from memory. It was returned, and the charges eventually dropped, but the family reputation was pretty much toast. I thought of it as her story to tell, I guess. I figured as you two got closer…" he trailed off, not needing to finish the thought aloud.

Isabella and Adele had never gotten closer. They'd started off estranged, and drifted apart like icebergs.

"What *do* you consider your strong suit, then?" Adele wondered aloud, trailing a single finger down the door frame in a bid to keep her hands off him.

"Sofas… Or so I've been told." The glint was back in James' eye.

Adele laughed. "Damn straight."

"And showers," James slid in quietly, striking her dumb.

She blinked at him for a few seconds, remembering a conversation they'd had long ago, when she'd admitted that what they got up to in the shower was her favourite form of sex. All clean and slick, with the sensual slide of soap on skin.

Any form of making love with James had been good, but the clincher of the shower was the all-in nature of the aftermath, when she'd give herself up for her husband to diligently wash and condition her hair and body like he was worshiping his goddess at an ancient shrine.

Adele shivered as a delicious fissure of desire coursed through her at the memory.

"I still fantasise about that," she admitted, a husky rasp to her voice. "Of you, washing me."

"Christ, do you?" James closed the gap once more, stepping into her, his minted breath on her face as he tilted her chin a little further upward to look her straight in the eye. There was a burning intensity in that look, and it melted her to the core. "So do I."

Could it be that they were finally back on the same page?

Adele popped up on tiptoe, intending to kiss James within an inch of his life, but their lips never touched. It took her a moment to realise that rather than pulling her in, his hands had come up to ease her down and away. He was looking over her shoulder and smiling, but the tightness was back around his mouth.

"Hey, Saffy."

"Hey, Dad. What are you doing?" There was a world of hurt in that question. Confusion and censorship.

Adele swung around to face her daughter. "James was just—"

"Just saying, hello," James interrupted.

Saffy screwed up her face. "*Eww*, well don't."

"Don't say hello?"

"Don't *kiss*." There was a mulish line to Saffy's mouth as she stared first at one parent, then the other. "You'll just muck this up." The final statement was drilled home by a finger pointed directly at her mother.

"I beg your pardon?" Adele huffed, surprise lending her voice a royal quality.

"Do *not* go kissing Dad!" Saffy stormed, hurling her school bag over one shoulder and swinging past.

"Saffron Katherine Fergus! Get back here!" But her daughter was long gone, out the door and down the steps, all puffed-up and pissy. "Little minx," Adele muttered, as incensed with her own conduct as she was with Saffy's clear show of distaste.

What the hell had she been thinking, trying to get frisky with James when Saffy was within their direct vicinity?

"I'll talk to her," James promised, but his eyes were shadowed as he gave Adele's upper arms a final squeeze, then turned to leave.

The statement did little to settle Adele's disquiet. Talk to their daughter and say what, exactly?

Sometimes divorced people kiss. Your mother's got the serious hots for me. When you're at school, we kiss all the time.

If Saffy was all heated up about them almost locking lips, there was a lot more to worry about than Adele had originally factored in.

When James climbed into the ute, Saffy was already belted in and staring fixedly out the passenger window.

"I'm going to be gone for a few days, and I don't want you to worry if you can't get hold of me," James ignored the obvious tension and acted like nothing had happened.

"Sydney again?" Though Saffy wouldn't look at him, she was at least engaged.

"Ah, no. I'm due back there midweek though, so this will be a bit of a flying visit, I'm afraid."

While James backed out of the driveway, Saffy poked around in the loose gear at her feet, picking up the billy-can he'd bought the night before and holding it aloft.

"Hiking?" she guessed.

"Something like that."

"Can I come?" Gone was the mulish almost-tween, and in her place the excitable-child, honing in on a potential adventure.

"Not this time, Saff. Not till I know this bush." It didn't feel good to turn her down a second time, and James resolved to organise another trip later in the year. Maybe in the spring. "I'm going with a guide though, so I don't want you to worry."

"*I* know this bush. *I* could be your guide."

James could feel Saffy's eyes on him now, boring in. He glanced her way, then back to the road. "Not like this. We'll be camping in rough terrain."

"When will you be back?"

He shrugged. "Sunday evening?"

"All weekend?"

"Yes, sorry about that, but I'll try and bring you back something."

"There aren't any shops in the bush, Dad." Saffy actually laughed, and the tension James had been holding in his jaw began to ease.

"Then I'll have to find something else, won't I?" He grinned.

"Why were you and Mum kissing?"

Just when he'd thought he was out of the woods.

"Sorry you had to see that, it was probably a bit of a shock." He avoided the 'why' question and went straight for the apology.

"Are you getting married, again?"

"No." That was by far the simplest answer. Adele would never consider a second marriage to him. James knew that deep in his bones.

"But you like her."

"I do, yes." More than.

"Look, don't get your hopes up," Saffy advised. "I don't think she likes you back."

"Ouch." Direct hit. "Thanks for the heads-up," he muttered.

"I'm not joking." Saffy picked up a teacher-like tone, as if she was trying to drum information into a particularly obtuse child. "She'll stop me from seeing you again, and it will all go back to how it was before."

"No. It won't. You'll have to trust me on that." James thought of all the things Adele and himself had worked through already; all the misconceptions and misdemeanours they'd aired and closed the lid on, and knew that was the honest truth. It would never go back to the frigid Cold War again, neither of them would allow it to.

"It will. You guys will go back to hating each other, and you'll move back to Australia."

"I've never hated Adele."

"She hated *you*."

"Again, ouch." But James smiled as he spoke, navigating the give-way. "What is this, pick on Dad day?"

"Just promise me you won't go kissing her again."

James mulled on that for a moment, the not-quite-kiss that had left both parties hanging.

"I can't promise you that," he negated gently. "But I'm away hiking this weekend, so you're fairly safe for two days."

"It's totally gross," Saffy muttered, folding her arms tightly across her chest and pointedly looking out the window again.

James laughed. "I'm actually glad you think so. You had me worried with this Zane guy."

Saffy whipped around to stare at him, slapping his thigh with the back of her hand for good measure.

"*Eww*, Dad! I'm not going to kiss *Zane*!"

"I can't tell you how happy I am we're on the same page, there." He grinned as he backed into a vacant parking space.

Adele called James, ostensibly to see if he wanted to come with her and Saffy to family pizza night. Their meet-up in her hall this morning could only be described as awkward, and the man had flown across the Tasman, then driven all the way down from Christchurch to see them, after all.

Kana said she was happy having him up at the farm, and Daniel could just suck it up.

The recorded message on James' phone had changed. His twangy drawl now stated, "You've reached James Montague. I'll be off-grid for a couple of days, so leave a message, and I'll get back to you when I can."

Off *grid*? James the city-boy workaholic? Something didn't quite add up.

"Saffy!" Adele called down the hall. "Can you come in here for a second, please?" James and Saffy were thick as gorse. If anyone knew where Adele's ex-husband was, it'd be their daughter.

The nearly-ten-year-old stomped in, clearly grumpy at having been disturbed midway through a pastel drawing, and still gritty about the almost-kissing incident. She had soft crayon in a myriad of colours all over her fingers, and more smeared down the front of her art smock.

"Do you know where James is?"

"Yes." Saffy sniffed, and stared up at the portrait of Adele tacked to the wall.

"Spill." Adele didn't usually have to use a commanding voice to assert her authority, but her daughter had been annoyed with her all day. Even now, Saffy's chest puffed up in a minute show of defiance before she spoke, and that was telling.

"He said he wouldn't be back til Sunday evening, because he's going hiking."

"Hiking?"

Saffy nodded mulishly.

"For two nights?" Adele checked, both disgruntled and confused. Why hadn't he given her the same information?

"Yes. With someone."

"Someone?"

"I wanted to go, but he said no."

"Three's a crowd," Adele muttered.

"What?"

"Nothing." She tried to push all thoughts of her ex-husband to the back of her mind, furious with herself for getting her hopes up. "We'd better get ready if we're going to get up to the farm on time. Go wash your hands." She took another look at her daughter's multicoloured digits. "With the Wonder Soap and nail brush."

Saffy rolled her eyes. "We're *never* on time, Mum!"

They were only twenty minutes late, but no one was in a hurry up at the farmhouse. Adele got the distinct impression there'd been more talk than pizza making, due to Poppy and Clem being back from Dunedin.

Poppy seemed overly perky when she commented in passing, "Clem tells me James won't be able to make it tonight."

"No." Adele eyed her suspiciously. "He's away hiking."

Poppy and Clem shared a look, which shot Adele with another dose of mistrust.

"I invited him to come fishing this weekend, since he was in town, but he's trying his hand at hunting, instead," Clem dropped the news with all the delicacy of a Clydesdale.

"*Hunting*? No, no, no. Not James." Adele's laugh came off as a little unhinged.

James and guns were an unlikely mix. He hated being around them, and since his Father's death had become an advocate for gun-free homes.

"Yes, James. All kitted out and raring to go," Clem confirmed confidently, earning himself a dig in the ribs from Poppy.

"Shit." Adele stared at Clem, panic beginning to set in. It was freezing at night, and James had no idea what he was doing. What if he hurt himself? What if he never came back? They'd joked about hunting, hadn't they? That first pizza night.

"Is this because I laughed at him? Told him there wouldn't be a dry-cleaner?" Adele stressed at her hair with her fingers, checking behind herself to make sure Saffy was still out of range, in the lounge with her nose in a book.

"No. I don't think so. He's reasonably experienced, due to growing up on a working farm, and had his heart set on some bush-pork to fill your freezer. Nothing to worry about, he's gone with a guide," Clem soothed.

"A guide? Who?"

"Mullet." Clem gave the name a little reluctantly, and Adele sucked in her breath at the familiar handle for one of the mechanics down on Main Street. He was well-liked, though not often sober.

"Mullet! He wouldn't know one end of a rifle from the other."

"Don't go getting your knickers all in a twist. Mullet knows his way around, and the usual crew weren't available." Clem glanced across to where Daniel sat at the kitchen table, listening.

Adele turned on her cousin. "He asked you?"

"No. He didn't." Daniel muttered, staring at his own hands on the pine, fingers widespread like a whauwhaupaku leaf. "But to be fair, I'd already told him to fuck off, so he wouldn't, would he?"

"You told him to *what*?" Adele's back stiffened, and she flicked another look behind her, once again checking on Saffy's whereabouts.

Her daughter was nowhere to be seen.

"I told him you and Saffy deserved better."

"Oh, *Daniel*," Poppy murmured, placing a hand on her eldest son's shoulder and digging her pincers in like a small, fierce crab.

Adele pushed back on her chair and it scraped noisily across the wooden floor as she stood, fuming.

"I told you to butt out! *You* don't get to decide! You're as bad as his bloody mother, sticking your nose in where it's not wanted and driving wedges between us. I asked you to lay off him!"

"This conversation was ages ago," Daniel muttered, and there was more than a trace of apology in his eyes when he looked up. "When he came up here that first night. It's not like he took any notice of what I had to say, anyway. From where I was standing, it looked like the guy manipulated you into an unhappy marriage, used you till he was done, and left you with nothing." Daniel's face had hardened, as had his words. "Then he turns up here, trying to get to you through Saffy. I don't see why you're so hell-bent on giving him a second chance."

"The *guy* as you insist on calling him, left me and Saffy with three million."

Silence reigned in the kitchen, the only sound coming from the piwakawaka chattering outside the patio door as they fed off the midges in the low evening light.

"*Dollars?*" Clem clarified, his voice a little pitchy.

Daniel looked bewildered. "He did what?"

"Is that why he came over, to give you the money?" Poppy wanted to know.

"No," Obāchan stated quietly, and all eyes turned to the cool, calm, and collected eighty-year-old, who'd padded up behind Kana from the direction of the lounge. "James came to New Zealand when the terms of his Farmtech contract expired, and he was finally free to leave Australia."

"The terms of his what?" Adele's head was beginning to throb, and she circled her fingers around on her temples in an attempt to calm the pounding down.

"He had a contract with the Chinese company that took over Montague Holdings. They were very insistent. Four years setting up their A.I. design team and customer base, or no deal. Montague Holdings were in the… How do you say it? The poo? They were in the poo, financially, so it was the only way. He was paid half at the beginning, so he could meet your divorce settlement, and half at the end."

That gave Adele pause, and she blinked at Obāchan, trying to gather what the hell the older woman was meaning.

"He had to work for the takeover company?" Why had she heard nothing of this? "For four years?" He'd been doing a lot of internal travel within Australia, she knew that from his video chats with Saffy, but she'd assumed it was due to Montague Holdings expanding.

"Now he's finally been paid, he was able to afford the cabin." Obāchan's smile was a little woeful.

"Give me Mullet's number." Adele turned back to Clem, grinding the words out.

Clem fumbled with his phone, handing it over quick-smart once he'd found the contact he was after.

Mullet answered after four rings with just his name, in that slow, drawn-out drawl of his. "M*uuuu*llet."

"Are you with James?"

"Ah… you might have the wrong number here, missy. This is Murray Tankar, from the mechanics down on Main Street."

"I know who you are, Mullet," Adele snapped, patience at an

end. "This is Adele Fergus, and I want to speak to James. Your greenhorn hunter."

"Aksel? Well now, he's not what I'd call a greenhorn. And he's still bush. Out of cell range, I'd wager." Mullet chuckled, as if that were funny.

"You left him there?" Adele fumed. "Alone?"

"We hadn't shot anything by the time the weather packed in, and Aksel was keen to bag himself a bit of bush tucker for some sheila. But I've left him my dogs, and a vehicle."

"Oh. My. God!" Adele slapped the palm of her hand to her forehead three times, punctuating each word with sheer frustration at the man's obtuseness. "What the hell is *wrong* with you people! *Anything* could happen to him out there on his own!"

Turning away from her family, who were all listening avidly, she strode to the patio door to give herself at least some semblance of privacy.

"Now, don't go getting all in a tizzy." Finally picking up on the damning nature of her tone, Mullet took on a defensive one. "I know where he is, roundabouts anyways, and if he's not out in a couple of days, I'm to sound the alarm."

"A couple of *days*?"

"Monday."

"Jesus, Mary, and Joseph!" Adele hung up on Mullet after blasting him with the trio of saintly names, then turned on her family.

Singling out Daniel and Clem she pointed at one, then the other, her finger shaking with fury. "If any harm comes to him—*one hair on his head*—I'm holding you both personally accountable, and will skin your hides myself."

28

AHI - FIRE

Not all flames are extinguishable.

When James drove out of the bush on Monday morning he was totally exhausted, and eaten alive by midges

On the plus side, he had a good sized doe wrapped in a tarp in the back of the 4x4. On the minus side, he was functioning on approximately three hours sleep from the last forty-eight, and still had to skin and quarter the animal when he got home.

As soon as he had cell coverage, he made two phone calls. One to Mullet, to check the man's AWOL dogs had turned up some time on Sunday, and one to Clem.

Clementine was an old hand, wiry and strong, and in very little time they had the deer worked, cut, and strung up in one of the cabin's outbuildings.

"It's a fine specimen," Clem commented as he cleaned his knife-set down, carefully oiling the blades.

"Venison, not pork, though." James caught Clem's surprised look. "Saffy put in an order, but without the dogs I had to hike to higher country, and switch game."

"You can do a swap with another hunter, it's all good," the older man assured him.

"I hadn't thought of that."

"Mullet will set you up. He knows who hunts what, and I wouldn't mind a bit of venison myself, if you like salmon?"

"Who doesn't like salmon?" James grinned.

"S'pose we've lost you to the hunting bug, then." Clem gave an exaggerated sigh. "Won't see hide-nor-hair of you on the weekends."

"No. I don't think so. Once was enough."

Something in James' tone must have tipped the old man off, because Clem eyed him shrewdly. "Bit too close for comfort?"

It was the doe's eyes that had done it. Pure innocence and surprise, wide and staring. The complete opposite to Luka Montague, who'd been left with few recognisable features.

James had held his palms over the doe's eyes, and bawled like a baby into her still warm flank.

"You could say that." At least it'd been a clean shot to the neck, and she hadn't suffered unduly. Knowing deer were an introduced pest in New Zealand and incredibly damaging to the native bush hadn't been enough to counter the distress of ending one's life.

Clem perked up. "Salmon fishing, next time? Or Trout."

"Count me in." James smiled, realising he'd stumbled across a like-minded soul in Clem.

They washed the last traces of muck off their hands, side-by-side at the dual outdoor tub, James savouring the sun on his shoulders and the cool rush of fresh water on his skin, flushing everything away.

It was blissful. One of Dr. Fran's 'lung' moments, the here-and-now suddenly clearly defined, and worth relishing.

At the sound of a car approaching, James turned to see Adele's work vehicle arrive, spitting up gravel as she slammed to a halt beside Clem's beaten-up farm truck.

Dulled from lack of sleep, James couldn't fathom why Adele would be here, catapulting out of the driver's door and leaving it swinging as she strode towards him. Hellfire and brimstone was written all over her face, and to his chagrin, James found himself unconsciously taking a step backwards, coming up short against the old concrete sink.

"You selfish bastard." Adele shot the words across at him in lieu of a greeting.

"What?" He turned to Clem in surprise, then back to Adele.

"You're off galavanting in the bush and don't think to *tell* me?"

"How is that selfish?" His ire rose. "I shot a bloody deer for your freezer and carried the damn thing out on my back."

"I never asked for a bloody deer, and we didn't know where the hell you were!" Adele raised both palms to the heavens, fury etched into every tense line of her body. "Mullet's dogs turned up *hours ago*!"

"You haven't given a shit where I was for the past five years," James growled, his own anger taking off at full speed. "And if that's changed, you should've sent me a memo."

"Here's your goddamn memo."

Adele stepped right up into his personal space, eyes blazing like a Celtic warrioress and curly tresses every-which-way. Then she sank her fingers into the hair on the back of his head and dragged him down to plant a kiss on his lips that knocked his socks off.

Clem made a choking sound—half shock, half chuckle—then removed himself, quick-smart.

James was filthy. He hadn't had a proper wash for three days and wasn't fit for present company, least of all up close and personal.

He could smell the blood from the deer, the tang of his own hard-earned sweat, and the unbelievably sweet, luscious scent of Adele's peachy skin.

When Adele flicked her tongue between lips, running it along the line of his teeth, James lost all thoughts of restraint and dove in as well. She was anything and everything he wanted, this woman. As immovable as bedrock, and pliable as liquid.

Hot liquid.

James grunted when Adele finally pulled back. Disoriented, he snapped his head around to take in his 4x4, and the pile of wet hiking gear next to it on the shingle.

There was no sign of Clem, or the older man's truck.

"Ah... Thanks?" James ran a hand up the back of his hair and settled his gaze back on his ex-wife.

Where the hell had that come from?

Adele was breathing fast, and there was a visible pulse fluttering at the base of her neck. It killed him when her eyes did that, the pupils so wide there was just a tiny strip of lapis lazuli left surrounding them. You could fall right in.

"I changed my mind," Adele whispered.

"About what?"

"About kissing."

"Right." He attempted a laugh. "I got that message." Loud and clear.

"I think you should take a shower."

James grimaced and took a half step sideways, eyes latching on a large section of carcass strung up in the shed to his left. "Yeah, sorry about that, I'm—"

"I want to kiss more than your lips."

He would've answered with an incredulous retort if he hadn't just swallowed his tongue. Adele appeared to be dead serious, and they blinked at each other for what felt like a full minute.

"What the hell is that supposed to mean?" he eventually rasped out.

"You know *exactly* what I mean. I'll be back here in half an hour. if you don't want what I'm asking for, then make yourself scarce." Adele quirked her head to one side. "But if you're interested in initiating this place..." She left the notion hanging.

"Take a shower?"

"Precisely." Adele gave him a strange sort of half-smile before turning on her heel and striding back towards her work vehicle. She wore loose fitting jeans and a sweatshirt that'd seen better days, and swaggered as she walked.

James had never seen anyone look so sexy.

Adele turned, hesitating before stipulating quietly, "Just sex. That's all I'm ready for, right now." Then she slid into the driver's side and slammed the door shut, sitting for a moment after she'd gotten the engine running, facing straight ahead.

James couldn't make out her expression from the angle he was on. Was she regretting the directive? Having second thoughts?

He took a step towards the car, lungs tight under his ribcage as Adele wound down the window.

"One more thing." She leaned one elbow on the door frame and turned to face him—mouth smiling, but eyes serious. "Leave the beard." Then she was gone, with a spurt of gravel and a single honk at the gate.

James allowed some of the pent up air to hiss out from between his lips. Raising a hand to rasp over his jaw, he tested the stubble of his four-day-growth in a contemplative pinch between thumb and forefinger.

Leave the beard.

He couldn't quite believe what had just happened, and rewound the last few minutes in his head to replay it over, even as he gathered his gear and locked up the garage.

I've changed my mind… I want to kiss more than your lips… just sex.

Adele's fingers shook, so she gripped the steering wheel a little tighter and eased off the gas as she turned back into James' driveway, forty minutes later.

She'd raced home to have a shower and change out of her work jeans and into a dress. She'd also second-guessed herself every inch of the way. More than aware rash choices could get her into a whole heap of trouble, she was also pinging. Her body was fairly singing in anticipation.

James' 4x4 was still parked exactly where it had been, and Adele huffed out the breath she hadn't realised she'd been holding.

He'd stayed. Given the choice, James had stayed.

Adele wasn't so sure about that after she'd knocked on his front door for the second time without answer, her heart winding a slow pathway down to her guts.

Nope. He'd gone. Taken a walk. Decided this kind of complication was not for him, and his ex-wife deserved a taste of her own medicine.

It was James' prerogative to say no if he wanted to. She'd given him that option on purpose. But she'd thought…

She'd *assumed.*

Adele smoothed her hands down over her ridiculously summery dress and turned to make her way back down the verandah steps, blinking rapidly.

Of all the silly, self-destructive, *undignified* things to do. She'd propositioned James for sex. *Her* James. Like she couldn't find it elsewhere. Like it was no skin off her nose if he said no.

Well, her nose was well and truly skinned now.

"Dell." James' voice was soft behind her, and stopped her in her tracks. She slowly turned to face him, eyes roving from his naked chest, down to the towel slung hastily around his waist, and back again. "Leaving so soon?"

He was barefoot with his hair wet, and the warmth of the raw wooden door-frame almost matched his skin in colour. There were red welts along his arms and around his neck.

Insect bites?

They somehow made him seem more approachable; warm blooded, and inherently human.

"James…" Nothing else came out of Adele's mouth, she just stared at him, wordlessly trying to convey some kind of message.

Was this a good idea? She was scared shitless. Should never have come, should never have proposed this.

"You look good with your hair out like that." James stepped to one side, leaving both the doorway and the invitation wide open, though the strain was clear in his voice. "Pretty."

Priddy.

The accented word brought with it a multitude of memories.

Adele squeezed her eyes closed for a moment, before taking the steps necessary to get her through the door.

So surprised on entering the large living room, she just stopped and stared. There was an upright piano against one wall, a built-in bookcase against another, and her old lounge suite snuggled close to the fireplace wearing a loose cover in the green fabric she'd chosen only last week. Almost unrecognisable, but for the width of the rolled arms.

The house was mid-facelift, but still had an eerie echo when she finally stepped forward.

"The sofa covers arrived already?"

James nodded.

"You like the colour?" A moot question under the circumstances, but she was nervous, and had just realised something else while perusing the fresh cabinets in the open-plan kitchen.

The plumbing had all been switched around to her exact specifications.

A property of this magnitude would earn top dollar primped and dressed to within an inch of its life, and let out as a short-term stay. Especially in the Lakes District, with this kick-ass view. She could help James out there, for a fee. Manage the property for him if he decided to head back to Australia in the long term.

Adele's heart jolted at the realisation James' return to Oz was a distinct possibility if she screwed this up. The thought shouldn't deter her, she was supposed to be on a clear mission, but it did. It deterred her in every way.

She had no intention of making the move into property rental if it gave her grief in her personal life, and that's exactly how the past week without James had felt.

Hollow, bordering on wretched.

More than a rental, this particular cabin had real heart, and the makings of a great family home once it'd been given the right kind of love and attention.

"I really like this place," she concluded aloud. "Good bones."

Again, James merely nodded, his eyes watchful.

Looking almost shy, he held out his hand in invitation, Adele's wedding ring glinting on his pinky finger, mocking her. Instead of looking feminine, it managed to make his hand look more masculine in comparison.

The view of James with his shirt off had been drizzling kerosene on the fire Adele had been tending since he'd turned up three weeks ago. She wasn't capable of turning around and leaving now, not even if her life depended on it.

Sliding her fingers into James' palm, she let him lead her along the hall while she checked out all the moving muscles, lines, and ridges on his back. He was blessed with broad shoulders and a tapered waist, and a small ragged-edged birthmark that peeped out of the towel on his right hip.

That little birthmark had always reminded her of a single cloud on a clear, clear day.

A shiver of anticipation snuck its way up Adele's spine, and perhaps feeling her body judder, James gave her hand a brief squeeze. He flicked his chin towards the new bed in the centre of the master bedroom, where it formed a large, welcoming square.

James stopped when he felt Adele hesitate, and watched her take in the state of the place. Work was coming along insofar as the layout changes had been implemented, the en-suite plumbing was semi-complete, and the walls and ceiling had been rendered and painted a fresh dove grey. But the carpet had been stripped and used as a weed-mat around the newly planted native trees, and hadn't been replaced yet. Also absent were any soft furnishings or furniture—bar the bed. The old curtains had been donated to the last-chance dump shop, and James was still waiting on the window treatments and furniture from Christchurch.

He hadn't let go of Adele's hand, and raised it slowly to press his lips to her pale skin.

Adele was with him. He could see it in the come-get-me heat on her cheeks, the lowering of her lashes, and the quick flurry of breaths. She wanted him, too. That was something.

The fact he wanted so much more from her than just sexual release was unspoken, but understood. He may not ever get another chance at that, but he had this.

James drew Adele to the king bed, and she sank to it with a sigh, kicking her shoes off and wiggling backwards. The hem of her yellow dress rode up her thighs, showing off the creamy silk of her skin. Immediately, he was on his knees beside her. On his knees in every way.

He cupped Dell's face in his hands and brought his lips to hers as they slid back into the softness of the duvet, her tongue dancing across his.

It was like coming home.

Groaning at the thought, James closed his eyes as Adele's hands cruised over his skin and deftly tugged the towel from his hips. As one of her hands reached around his already straining cock, the other teased his nipple with minute pinches.

Adele's mouth never left his, but both of them were gasping now, panting for what was to come.

Rearing back on his heels and straining to control his breathing, James took a moment to look down and watch Adele's cunning, well-versed hands on him. She knew all his preferences intimately, as he knew hers, and each movement had him sinking a little further under her spell. Slow, slow… then fast. Using the bead of pre-come from the head to slick over his sensitive tip, she roved up and down the shaft with sure movements.

Holy hell.

Not nearly as in control as he liked to think he was.

James was naked now to her fully-clothed, or so he thought until he leaned forward to slide the hem of her dress a little higher. The tips of his fingers feathered over her skin until her dress was bunched up to her waist.

No knickers.

James groaned again, his body shuddering in anticipation at the sight of the tight little curls nestled between Adele's thighs. No doubt knowing where his eyes were honed, she eased her knees apart just a smidgen more, giving him a clearer view. He pulled back to grasp one, then the other of her busy hands, stilling both.

29

POKOREHU - ASHES

After a fire, one must deal with the ashes.

James' eyes were hooded, and he was gripping Adele's fingers tightly, his tension clearly mounting. She could see he was close to break-point.

Sliding her wet fingers from his cock, James placed them carefully on her navel, then waited.

"What...?" Adele breathed the words hesitantly before comprehending, recognising the hungry glint in James' eye as he moved off the bed and stood between her knees. He urged her further back onto the duvet, nudging her thighs further apart. "Oh, I get it." She chuckled, knowing from experience exactly what he'd be craving. She murmured the next words in a sexy purr. "You want to watch, James?"

The sound James made was something between a growl and a moan, and he nodded, his eyes never leaving hers.

A surge of empowerment hit Adele.

James had her in the palm of his hand, his to do whatever he wanted with, and boy, she could see he wanted. But rather than take her any which way, he'd just put her in charge, reducing himself to spectator.

For now.

Emboldened by James' ragged breathing, Adele settled her feet wide. Coaxed by his fingertips tracing up her inner thighs, she made space for him to kneel, splaying herself open before him.

Trailing her fingers south over her own belly, Adele took it teasingly slow.

Bending to press a kiss on one inner knee, then the other, James murmured something unintelligible. His eyes were now glued to her meandering fingers as they slid down her body and over cropped pubic hair. When she parted her own folds and immediately slid one finger deep, hips lifting of their own accord to meet the slick intrusion, he swore softly.

With James' grip now encircling each of Adele's ankles, she luxuriated in the knowledge she knew how turn this man on. There would be no awkward moments where she wondered if he enjoyed this, or preferred that. And there would be no disappointment on her part, because James could play her body like a concert pianist. Even without the minute changes in pressure on her skin, she knew by the irregularity of his breathing he wouldn't be able to hold off much longer.

"Dell." James groaned her name as she rolled her fingers in a circular motion over her swollen clit, and his hands moved up to her shins.

Adele moaned as she writhed, revelling in the warmth oozing through her veins and building in her core and basking in James' heated gaze. His grip had moved to her knees, fingers pulsing in time with her panting as she built to climax.

"James," she crooned. "I want you, now."

In answer, his hands slid under her butt, raising her hips to position her for a better view.

"*A.J.*," she pleaded, urgent now.

Another muttered curse from James, and Adele smiled to herself as she was roughly repositioned.

It wasn't until James' mouth came down on her that she figured precisely which way his appetite was roving, but she didn't much care. She wanted him any-way, and any-how.

She came with his fingers deep inside her and his tongue laving a hot trail over her core. Her thighs clamped around his head and her fingers wound into his hair, as every fibre of her being exploded into stars.

It took some time to rouse herself afterward.

Adele lay on her back, spread-eagled and languid in the afterglow, her dress bunched up around her midriff. When she finally found the energy to raise her head, James was kneeling on the floor, leaning on his elbows between her legs, watching her. His grin stretched from ear to ear.

Adele chuckled, flopping her head back down on the bed. "Quite proud of yourself, aren't you?"

"Mm-hmm." James' hum was close enough for her to feel the soft vibration on her inner thigh.

"Credit where credit's due. *I* did most of the work there."

"Exceptional work." James readjusted his position to all-fours, and pressed an open mouthed kiss to the sensitive skin just below her navel, making her jump. "Diligent," he purred, dipping his tongue into her belly-button and investigating her piercing, before cruising further up her torso over the buttons of her dress. His touch was familiar, but the rasp and tickle of his whiskers was something new, adding another dimension. "In fact, you really deserve to be presented with an award."

Adele began to laugh. "Oh, right." James was hovering over her, his mouth millimetres from one of her very receptive nipples, which puckered and budded in response under the light fabric. His fingers were working on the tiny row of buttons, exacting a slow and steady exposure. "I get it. An *award*." Reaching down between them, her fingers once again closed around his straining hard-on.

Satin on steel.

James muttered something that sounded a lot like a threat, and nuzzled into the valley between her breasts. But as she slid her palm forward and back, his breath became choppier, and he quit all verbal dialogue.

Buttons finally dealt with, James drew the cotton of her dress aside as he raised his head, and paused.

"What?" Adele looked down to see her own nipples, straining against the translucent lace of her bra.

"I was half expecting piercings here, too." James took one darkened bud in his mouth to feast on it through the flimsy fabric, and Adele's back shuddered into an arch in response, nipples incredibly sensitive due to the fact she'd already come.

"No," she muttered. "Too chicken-shit."

"Is it wrong to say I'm glad? I love your breasts, just the way they are." Between tonguing her nipples to screaming point, James was muttering in sexy growls. "So soft. So sweet. But right now I'd love to present you with—"

Adele slung her legs up around James' hips, bringing her slick wet heat right against him. She guided his swollen head deep into herself with one hand, and a well aimed thrust.

She grinned when James' head shot up, and startled eyes met hers. "I'm not—"

Writhing her hips a little made James sink the final inch into her as his hips naturally rammed forward, pushing her back down into the soft mattress.

"Wearing a condom," he finished, his eyebrows locked together in seriousness.

A condom.

How stupid of her. Who in their right mind had any sort of sexual encounter without protection, these days? It was just, she never had with James. Not before. It'd always been skin on skin.

They'd been married, after all, with plans to add to their family.

"Right." Adele attempted to lessen the deafening silence with the inane word, inadequacy filling her lungs. The need for condoms hadn't even crossed her mind.

She'd never had any doubts about having children with James, never had any qualms. He was the only man who'd ever instilled that confidence, and if she was being honest with herself, the only one who ever would.

Even now, her mind was racing ahead with 'what if…?'

"There's one beside the pillow." James flicked a nod towards the foil wrapper.

The upshot of sleeping with Mr Organised.

Angling up on her elbows, Adele brushed her lips across James' in a featherlight kiss, feeling the strain he was putting himself under by attempting to stay still within her. The muscles in his arms began to twitch, and his breath came in uneven lengths.

"Just one?" she teased.

"That's all I had, given the short notice."

She laughed, unlocking her ankles from the small of his back, and allowing him to pull out. He leaned across her to grab the wrapper, happening to position one of his nipples in the perfect spot. Adele arced up to nuzzle, then graze the hardening disc with her teeth, more than happy to interfere with the serious concentration James was applying to getting the condom on.

"Cut it out, you wee vixen."

The protection made a lot of sense now. Of course it did. No need to feel any sense of loss.

When she lay back, James' expression hadn't changed from dead serious, and there was an ominous darkness in his gaze.

"Adele, I—"

"Shut up," she whispered, suddenly afraid of what James was going to say, terrified he would bring back something black and malignant from their past into this devil-may-care moment and break the spell.

Bringing her lips back to his, Adele kissed James harder, grinding her hips upward again in blatant invitation until he was moaning, his sheathed cock nudging at her entrance.

Imploring. Insistent. Imminent.

"And *give* me my award," she murmured against his lips.

It was like it had always been between them. The outer world and everything in it ceased to exist, ceased to matter, and it was just Adele. Glorious in her strength, and murderous in her tenacity.

She made James' soul sing with her high and low notes.

Adele had always taken a little more of him every time. A little more in love with her, a little further under her spell. He was hopeless for anyone else, because this was the only duet he craved. Given the choice, he'd turn up the volume until his ears bled.

With her dress open down to her waist and the fabric pushed aside, he had the perfect view of Adele's breasts encased in pale lace, complimenting the delicacy of her freckled, ivory skin.

Every well-schooled, carefully-scheduled, polite-society thought exited his head, and he was merely Adele's.

Adele's James.

With her fierce wants and confident demands, Adele told him exactly what she wanted. Sometimes with ragged whispers, but oftentimes with minute changes in her breathing little moans and whimpers that drew him onward and drove him wild. Her body was fine tuned, and by far his favourite instrument. Every note, every pitch change, every breath and lead.

When he could hold off no longer, James gripped Adele's hips and came into her, feeling like part of his soul ripped at the climax.

The need to lose himself in her was so strong.

As his breathing re-set to regular, James realised he had too much weight on Adele's ribcage, and moved off to one side. Keeping her tucked close, with one leg still heavy across her thighs, he buried his face in the scent of her wild mane and tried to gauge her reaction to what they'd just done by her breathing.

"Your body is my ambrosia," he murmured near her ear. Devoid of jewellery today, it was settled like a shell in a sea of spun gold.

"Don't sugar me up, now," Adele muttered. "It's not necessary."

"We just made love." After six long years. "I think I'm allowed to wax a bit lyrical." Giving into temptation, James leaned forward and took her soft lobe between his teeth.

Adele squeaked a giggle and shoved at him—ticklish there, he knew. "We just had sex," she corrected him. "And it makes me feel strange. So don't."

She could call it what she liked, it didn't change a damn thing.

"Alright." He rumbled the words close enough to Adele's ear to make her shiver, but didn't touch her with his mouth again. "But you know I'm *thinking* it," he whispered. "When I touch you, I'm thinking you're pure honey. When I'm inside you, I'm thinking there's no place I'd rather be. I'm also thinking I'd like to christen every room in this house with your sweet curves."

Adele shuffled further away from him, then turned to level him a look.

"You'll definitely need to stock up on condoms, then," she shot.

"More condoms." He nodded in agreement. "Latex free."

Adele stopped all movement.

Surprised he'd remembered?

"Not in Wānaka, though. People know who you are by now. Buy them somewhere else."

Not surprised he'd remembered her mild irritation to latex, then. Just unwilling to go public about sleeping with her ex.

"Should I drive to Christchurch?" he teased.

Adele's light frown morphed into a true scowl. "I think Queenstown will do fine."

"You're right, of course. Fourteen hours, round-trip. It's a long time to wait for round two."

Adele thumped him.

"Your eyes are like topaz on fire right now," he chuckled.

Although she was clearly trying to look stern, Adele couldn't maintain it, and ended up cracking up along with him. "Give it a rest, James."

"I'll give it exactly ten minutes," he growled in the form of a threat. "Then I'm thinking the upstairs shower could benefit from your particular form of blessing."

Adele snorted another laugh, but she didn't say no.

Following James' bare ass, her hand in his, Adele tried to concentrate on placing one foot in front of the other as they made their way up the staircase.

It was a very fine ass, and she'd tripped once already, ogling it instead of minding her feet.

The family-sized bathroom had a half-finished feel, the walls in lime-green plasterboard, still awaiting tiles. Eventually it would all be gloss white, in herringbone formation, with brushed steel tapware.

Adele knew all the details, because she'd been the one to sign it all off. With James absent this weekend, the interior designer had been running any random queries Adele's way, as if James and herself were a package deal.

She found that strangely comforting.

The shower cubicle had condensation on it from James' earlier shower, and Adele dragged all her focus towards the droplets of water before she could panic.

Here and now. She reminded herself. *No thinking about what all this could mean tomorrow.*

Listening to her lungs, and lungs only, she took a deep, calming breath before leaning in to set the water temperature to her liking.

When she turned back to James, mouth open to comment on his choice of girly shampoo, the words that jumped out of her mouth instead were, "How are you *hard* already?"

James stood proudly starkers and offered her a slow grin, countering with, "Why aren't you *naked*, already?"

But his cocky smile dropped, and gaze intensified, as Adele's fingers skipped along the hem of her dress, then lifted the fine cotton up and over her head. When her bra followed in quick succession, she was guided in and under the flow water with very little ceremony by her eager partner-in-crime.

James was nuzzling into her neck from behind, his hard-on snuggled between her butt-cheeks. "Shall I wash you?" he murmured into her ear as she giggled, squirming with the delicious tickle of bristles on the sensitive skin of her neck.

"I think you'd better. You wouldn't believe how grubby I'm feeling right about now." She pushed back against him and all but purred.

Their bodies knew each other, recognising the pull of positive to negative, and remembering the depth of connection that went back aeons. It made it easy to forget everything but the moment, and Adele sighed as she gave up the last of her inhibitions and relaxed under James' familiar, soapy hands.

When James had finished washing and rinsing off her body, he began on her hair. Massaging the shampoo into her scalp, he held one hand over her eyes while he directed the water-flow through her curls, and murmured while he worked.

His little observations and reflections proved every part of her was seen, and appreciated. Infinitesimal things. Monumental things. All crooned to the tune of falling water.

"This little toe has the cutest nail, like a little half-moon… Your skin is like silk, isn't it? Fine, fine silk… Oh, sorry. You've got a bruise there, on your hip. Did that hurt? No? Sorry… It kills me, how your curls want to hold onto my fingers. So tenacious… Don't give me those come-get-me eyes yet, I'm not done getting you clean... I haven't got any of your favourite conditioner, so this one will have to do..."

Adele anchored herself on James as he wrangled and manoeuvred her. Hands on his hips, or shoulders. Head resting on his chest. Always aware of his arousal, but leaving him be. She had her forehead to his neck and was leaning against him, chest to chest, when he finally finished finger combing the conditioner through her tangles and held her to him.

"This is my favourite part," James whispered, his lips brushing her forehead as warm water ran over them both. "Just you, on me."

Adele slid one hand from round his waist, working it between them until she had his hard-on fully in hand. The indrawn suck of air through James' lips was gratifying, but so was his laughter.

"Okay, maybe you're right." Even as his penis pulsed rigid, Adele could hear the humour in his voice. "Maybe *this* is my favourite part. Just you, on me, like *this*."

Pulling back to look into the unbelievable green of his eyes, water like diamond droplets in his eyelashes and brows, Adele's heart got caught up in her throat. "I love all of it," she admitted hoarsely. "Absolutely all of it."

Then James was kissing her, the wet movement of his mouth and tongue mimicking the wet movement of her palm on his hard-on, as she stroked him to completion.

"Christ, the water's getting cold," James complained, bumping the thermostat up to hot, and getting a piss-poor response from the water cylinder.

"We must've been in here for a good forty minutes," Adele mused, stepping out onto the hand-towel James had recommissioned as a bath-mat, her skin glistening. "I'm starving. What've you got to eat?"

Adele was always hungry after making love, and usually James would've stocked up to cater for her. But today, the only two options he had to offer were chocolate-chip ice cream, or Coco Pops and milk.

The love of his life chose dessert over breakfast, leaning against the kitchen bench with her wet curls leaving dark patches on her dress.

"Is this seriously all you've got in your fridge-freezer?"

James smiled. "Soon there'll be venison, and if Clem comes through, salmon and wild pork."

"Perhaps a vegetable or two wouldn't go amiss?"

"That's a line Saffy's been pushing." James leaned his shoulder against the wall, content to watch Adele savour her ice cream.

"She cares about you. Bitching at people is how the Fergus women show love. Surely you've figured that out by now?" Adele was joking and waving her spoon at him, but something in her voice asked him to look into the words, and find a deeper meaning.

She still had feelings for him, was that what she was trying to say?

The warmth in her expression said yes, leaving James with an unfamiliar sense of peace, radiating outward from his ribcage. "I'm just beginning to," he answered, a slow smile creeping in.

Adele smiled back, all rosy and satisfied. "I should go. Thanks for the ice cream, and the orgasm. I really enjoyed both."

Her candour, and the overt wiggle of her eyebrows made him laugh out loud, even as she dumped her bowl in the sink and made to leave.

"Anytime. And I mean that in every way."

It would be too easy to get comfortable with this arrangement, Adele realised.

Sex and shared laughter in the afternoon was all very well and good, but she had to switch back to being a responsible mother now, and get to the cottage before Saffy arrived home from school.

"Give these to Saffy for me, will you?" James pushed a repurposed peanut-butter jar full of wildflowers towards her on the stainless-steel bench.

Adele contemplated them, reaching one hand out to stroke the purple bell of a lupin. "No. I don't think I will. She'll know I've seen you, and to be honest, she's still a bit antsy about the almost-kiss thing."

"The almost-kiss thing?"

"That's what I'm calling it."

"Alright." James hesitated. "It just so happens I got you something, too." He looked almost reluctant, reaching for the logoed bag on top of the refrigerator, and handing it over. "It's not wrapped," he muttered.

And that would go against the grain for James, the serial gift-giver.

Adele was beginning to figure out things she'd never understood about her husband when they were married. Gifts weren't James' way of splashing money around, they were actually part of his love language. And more often than not, his choices showed just how much notice he took of the people he cared about.

Adele pulled out a T-shirt nightie, letting the paper bag fall to the floor. It had a cartoon image of the Beehive on the front, the most distinctive government building in the capital, along with the cheesy slogan, *'I found my *heart* in Wellington.'*

A lump the size of Tasmania was forming in Adele's throat, because Wellington was where James had met her, eight years ago.

"I saw it in the airport on the way out." James sounded hesitant, until she looked up and held his gaze. His brow cleared, and he began to smile. "You like it?"

She nodded, tears clouding her vision.

"Good." James wrapped an arm around her shoulder and she curled into him, resting her forehead on his neck and matching the rise and fall of his chest with her own.

Breathing in and out.

"I don't have to ask you to be mine again, Dell, for you to know I'm yours. Everything about me is yours, if you want."

30

RĒWERA - DEVIL

Is it really better the devil you know?

James didn't know what to expect when he received Adele's text the next day at noon, asking if he was home. Though his libido ran ahead of itself, making definitive plans, James had no firm lock on what his ex-wife had in mind. Regardless, he texted back in the affirmative, inviting her over for her lunch-break.

"I come bearing condoms." Adele broke the tension with the practicality, stepping onto his verandah holding the prized box aloft. "Latex free, and ribbed, no less."

"You've been to Queenstown?" James closed his laptop and slid it to the floor next to the armchair he'd been working from, a certain part of his anatomy ecstatic to hear Adele's announcement.

"No. They were a gift, actually." She gave a nervy little laugh. "I mentioned my predicament to Maddie, and these turned up before I could say, 'Oh, shit, I just asked my daughter's babysitter for condoms.'"

"More expedient than driving an hour each way." James decided not to tell his ex-wife that was the exact trip he'd made at eight o'clock this morning, just in case.

"I thought so, considering I only have a forty-five minute break."

"Want to get started, then?" His voice may've come out calm, but his pulse had been doing a strange two-step since Adele's car pulled up.

"Absolutely. Let's christen my old sofa." Adele grabbed his hand and dragged him out of the armchair, her grin wide and wicked.

"I think you should know," James teased as he followed Adele's swaying hips into the lounge, and across the echoing floor. "I have it on clear authority I'm very good at sofas."

"Oh, I know." Adele pushed him backwards till his calves hit the sofa-edge, and he sat without ceremony. Then she sank to her knees and began pulling at his belt, stealing all the breath from his lungs. "But so am I. Now, take off your jeans and show me that cute little cloud birthmark I've been fantasising about all morning. It's high time we got reacquainted."

In a haze of post-coital contentment, Adele trailed her fingers over the planes of James' chest as they lay smushed together on her old sofa, plush in its new green upholstery. "Tell me something. Did our divorce put an end to Montague Holdings?" she murmured.

"No. Merely sped up the process." James' voice was dopey, too. "We were already in negotiations with China."

"And you never considered coming after us, rather than working for them?" There was something profoundly sad about that.

"Adele," James all but sighed her name. "You asked me for a divorce, citing irreconcilable differences. You rebuffed any attempt at conversation, and withheld contact from Saffy if I tried to negotiate outside those terms. You shut me out. If you didn't want me, there was no point forcing your hand."

"It's not that I didn't *want* you."

"Then you had a very strange way of showing it."

Though the words were spoken quietly, Adele could hear James' underlying frustration.

"I thought you'd cheated!"

"And I thought you'd come to me if you ever had questions of that nature."

"Don't get all pompous on me!"

"Pompous? You walked out, Dell. You left. Dumped me without a backward glance."

No. Not frustration. Something much worse.

"I hurt you," she whispered, sorrier than she could ever hope to express. She'd cut and run from this man, when he'd had no one else to turn to.

"You killed me. My world was imploding and you were so far out of reach, you may as well've been off planet."

"If you really felt like that, then why did you come here?"

"Your jewellery box, then your bank statement. They gave me hope, but also worried me. How were you two getting by? How were you solvent?"

"I'm quite capable of supporting both Saffy and myself." Adele went to get up, but James clamped one hand firmly around her waist.

"Of course you are. You're the most resourceful person I know."

"I *am* resourceful."

"And proud."

"That's a bit rich, coming from you," she huffed.

"Why haven't you used it?"

"The divorce settlement?" Adele shifted in discomfort, too hot all of a sudden, skin pressed up against the baking heat of his. He always ran a degree or two hotter, a trait which would be infinitely more useful in Wānaka's winter months than it had ever been in Sydney. "One, it was yours, and I didn't want to touch it on principle. And two, buying property when I was that tender was a horrible idea. Wānaka's good for us. Saffy's settled, we've got family support, and the lake gives me the kind of peace I haven't found anywhere else. But I haven't come across anything I want enough. Though I've started looking, nothing's really grabbed me."

"What is it you're looking for, exactly?"

"Home and income. The house I went to look at on Thursday had a fully lined sleep-out with running water, and it wouldn't take much to convert it into a bed-and-breakfast situation. It wasn't quite right, but it was worth a look."

"You want to run a bed and breakfast?" James didn't bother masking his incredulity.

"I don't want to clean and manage someone else's properties forever, and it's an easy step sideways for me while I write."

"Your short stories?"

"Yes." James had read her initial forays into the writing world. "Among other things."

Novels.

She wanted to see if she had it in her to write a full-length manuscript. That's why she'd attended a writer's conference last year, to study up and build confidence.

"Um, I don't know how much of an 'easy step' the hospitality side of it will be when half the description is 'breakfast,' and you're not exactly a box of birds in the morning."

Adele reached out to pinch James' nipple in reprimand, but he read the move and brought his hand up in fend-mode.

"I can manage cereal and yogurt, and scratch together a smile for a paying customer."

"So *that's* what a person needs to do to get service in the a.m.," James teased.

He got another scowl for his trouble.

"You're quite capable of getting your own breakfast," she muttered.

In Australia, James used to be their morning guru. Easing fractious moods by planting an espresso on Adele's bedside table, first thing, and jollying Saffy into her morning routine with fresh fruit and pikelets.

"You could employ me as your breakfast chef," James mused, and it was difficult to tell if he was joking or not.

Adele buried her face in her ex's neck, hiding her involuntary smile. The idea of having James around every morning wasn't a lousy one.

"Sounds like you might be too busy with Mr Kaihanga. What are you two scheming up together?" She changed the subject pointedly.

"You don't want me in your kitchen?" When she didn't immediately answer, James raised up on one elbow, shaking her off just far enough to get a better gauge on her expression. "Adele?"

"Just answer my question." She concentrated on playing with his collarbone, running her fingers down the straight line of it and avoiding his heavy gaze.

"Taimana Wineries has a lot of potential. More than I've seen before in an already functioning outfit. He's on the ball with testing. Everything's tested within an inch of its life, but nothing's automated. I've starting developing software that'll fully computerise the watering systems, infusing natural pesticides depending on the data gathered. It takes into account the rainfall, and minimises the risk of disease and pests by a whopping percentage. It's a balancing act."

"And the investment you talked about?"

"Rather than contract work, I've negotiated getting paid in shares. It benefits both of us. Kaihanga's offered me hands-on tuition to learn viticulture and winemaking from the ground up, and I've offered him a cheap mode of gaining the latest tech. The more I know, the more I can help modify and streamline, and the more interesting it becomes."

"You're excited about it." She could see it in his face, the barely controlled enthusiasm.

"I am." James nodded. "The whole process is fascinating. They're maintaining their fully organic status, and keeping all the staff they have at present, but re-training to maximise flexibility. Add solar power into the mix, and the vineyard's looking at zero carbon emissions. The wine's award-winning. If they're certified carbon neutral as well, the advertising pays for itself."

Adele snorted. "The *price tag* pays for itself." Manoeuvring up to sitting position, she scoped the room, trying to spot where she'd flung individual bits of clothing.

James chuckled. "People are willing to pay for the best."

"You would know," she mused, brushing a few escaped curls out of her mouth. Though James looked less like a yuppie right now, and more like a rumpled mountain man, lying on the sofa with his insect bites and wind-burnt cheeks. "Taimana is a fitting name for that price bracket."

"Diamond Lake Wineries," James murmured, glancing at her bare hand, then away.

It was a fleeting look, but Adele caught it, and for a moment could almost feel the weight of her long-absent rings.

"Why aren't you building from your old systems?" Again she changed the subject to a less confrontational one, sliding her arms into her bra and turning so James could do up the hooks and eyes for her. "Is the organic side really that different?

James hesitated behind her. "I don't own the old software, so I've built this new range from the ground up."

"You don't *own* it? But you developed it!" She plucked her knickers off the arm of the sofa and stood to climb into them.

"Montague Holdings developed it. Farmtech bought my existing designs, along with everything else."

"Oh."

Well, shit.

"I can access it, of course. Anyone can…" James' mouth twisted in a fleeting grimace. "At a cost."

"Ah, I see. That *would* run against the grain."

James' nostrils flared at the taunt. "Yes, it does, as a matter of fact."

Adele laughed. "Hence the move sideways into viticulture."

"That was one of my motivations." James had the grace to smile.

Pride could well be his Achilles heel, but it was also one of the reasons he was so successful at what he did.

"Are you lying on my jeans?"

James felt around under himself and came up with a handful of denim, which he dutifully passed over.

"What were your other motivations?"

"Wine making's always interested me, and I was approached by an organic vineyard in Tasmania." James caught her eye, then looked away a trifle sheepishly, stroking absently at the side of his nose. "One turned into a chain, and the rest is history."

Oh, you *liar*.

"Is it though?" Adele stepped closer to lay a finger on James' jaw, turning his head so he was again looking directly up at her. "What are you hiding from me?"

"Ah," James cleared his throat. "Well, I knew the Kaihangas had links to Wānaka before I signed on with them for the Tasmania deal."

"You were stalking me."

Adele shimmied into her jeans as James grimaced.

"I'm not sure I'd use the term *stalking*—"

"Very industrious of you, snagging two diamonds with one cast."

James' eyes shot to hers. "Wait a minute, are you telling me I've re-snagged this particular gem?"

"Too early to tell, Mr Montague. Who knows? Reel it in and see." Afraid she'd said too much, Adele moved away to pluck her work T-shirt up off the floor, shaking it out before yanking it on.

James swung his legs off the sofa and sat upright, suddenly fully alert. "I would *love* to reel it in."

Adele finger combed her hair, ignoring his outstretched hand.

"I've got to get going, or I'll be late for my second shift." She moved a smidgen forward to poke at her wedding ring, looking so at home on James' pinky finger.

Close enough to touch, but not near enough for him to grab hold, and pull her in.

"On second thought, don't give this back to your mother. It looks good on you. Better than it ever did on me."

"We're going to have to agree to disagree on that one." James gave her a soft little half-smile, and a sudden memory of her wedding day wriggled inside her chest.

Her husband, sliding that very ring on her finger, and promising to love her forever.

Turning to leave, Adele noticed the bookcase had been partially filled since her last visit. Her feet naturally drifted off target, drawing her away from the front door and over to the built-in.

Wait a damn minute.

"Are these *mine*?" She swung back to James, bewildered to find what appeared to be her old Australian romance collection, proudly displayed.

"Yes. They've been in storage, but I had them sent over. Thought you might like them back. Cleaning, or the management office this afternoon?"

It took Adele a moment to change gears in her head and answer the question. "Management. Bookings and deposits."

"Right. And tomorrow?" James leaned back, sliding both hands behind his head on the sofa cushioning where he now sat, relaxed in his nakedness and already hard again. Adele was viscerally reminded how it'd felt to have him inside her, only ten minutes ago, folded over the back of the sofa and moaning with every deep thrust.

She cleared her throat. "Cleaning. Both shifts."

"It's hard on your hands."

"I know, but the gloves are worse. This is not the only place that reacts badly to latex." She swirled a hand in the general direction of her vagina, still buzzed from James' ministrations.

"Any plans for tomorrow's lunch break that I could help you out with?" James slid the query in silkily, making Adele laugh out loud.

It became a game of secrets, Adele turning up for clandestine interludes during her midday breaks, and James religiously keeping the cabin free from contractors until later in the afternoon. That left him with mornings for appointments, phone calls, research, and steamy daydreams about what his ex-wife would have in mind when she next strode in and commenced to strip him of his clothing.

It was getting harder and harder to talk himself into leaving New Zealand. He kept putting off his next Australian trip, moving flights backwards until he could no longer justify the delay.

From experience, James knew gifts didn't often go down well with Adele, but surprises usually did. He left a box of latex-free gloves on the front seat of her work vehicle under her Spic'n'Span sweatshirt, and added bottles of her favourite shampoo and conditioner to his upstairs shower. He stocked the fridge with cheese, apples, berries, salmon, and Lake Taimana chardonnay, and placed sandalwood scented candles and bright flowers on the bedside table.

Romancing his ex-wife, one quickie at a time, became James' new purpose in life. His secondary purpose was keeping the whole affair from his bubbly, gregarious, and highly suspicious daughter.

According to Adele, she was finding that part difficult, too.

"Saffy knows about us. About this." She waved her hand between them over James' secondhand dining table on Monday, a week after his hunting trip. They sat in their underwear while sharing an impromptu cheeseboard for lunch, having just sated their carnal appetites on the new lounge carpet. "You know what I mean. About me coming to see you everyday."

"You told her we're seeing each other?"

"No, I didn't. She knew." Adele went to chew on her nail, then clearly thought better of it, popping an olive into her mouth instead. "She says I *smell* of you."

James began to laugh. "God, you can't slip anything past that child."

"No. I know." Adele rolled her eyes, and the likeness between mother and daughter was suddenly unmissable.

"So what's the verdict?"

"Apparently, the jury's out. I don't know if she actually knows what that *means*, but that's what she said to me."

James chuckled. "She knows what it means."

"Right."

"Give her time." James was all for giving Adele time too, not wanting to put pressure on her to name what it was they were actually doing here, day after day. But the wait was agonising, not knowing if she actually saw a future with him, or was just fulfilling a physical need.

There had been hints of much more, but Adele always left him with a less than concrete idea of how she felt about him. She seemed to need their connection to be discussed as hypothetical, right now.

"Obāchan says you've partially re-mortgaged this place." Adele cut in with a clear dismissal of topic, a sure sign it was a touchy subject.

"Is there no privacy within your extended family?" James wondered aloud.

"None whatsoever." Adele laughed. "What do you need the money for? The improvements?"

"Yes, and no. I'm investing deeper into Lake Taimana."

Adele nodded, chewing on her bottom lip. "I want the cabin."

"What?" That was the last thing he'd been expecting her to say.

"Sell me this house, or two thirds of it."

"Are you serious?"

"Yes. We'd each get a bedroom."

James mulled on that. It implied she saw the three of them living together as a simple step, and it had 'future' written all over it.

"Fifty percent of it, then we're both paying for Saffy's third," he counter-offered.

"Done." Adele mimed spitting in her palm, then held it out across the table. "But just so you're aware, I plan to convert the barn into holiday accommodation, and put in a spa. Maybe even a swimming pool, at a later date."

"Okaaaay." Heart pounding, James drew out the word before miming spitting in his own palm and placing it carefully in hers. "But just so you're aware, I'm aiming to have you share the master bedroom with me."

Adele didn't hesitate. "*Okaaaay*," she mimicked him. "But the third bedroom is still mine, as my office."

"Office for what?"

"Writing, and keeping tabs on my wildly successful holiday rental business."

"Hmm." He pretended to mull it over. "As long as you don't put 'grease' in the title."

Adele's chin rose. "I'll call it whatever I like."

James laughed as he squeezed her hand across the table. She *had* changed, grown stronger, with more belief in herself and her own ideas.

"Half the office," he resolved. "I need a home office, too. But my burning question is whether we'll have room for a sofa up there, in this office."

"Why, because you're good at sofas?"

"I have it from the highest authority I'm *great* at sofas."

"Then, yes." Adele beamed at him, all sunshine and rainbows. "I give you leave to buy me a sofa, as long as it's bright."

"Come over here," James invited, tugging on her hand.

Adele rose and walked around the table, swinging one leg over his to sit astride him and his dining chair, and bringing her forehead down to meet his.

"Does this mean we're together?" he whispered, sliding his hands around the cool smoothness of her waist, needing to hear her say the words. "Openly?"

"Yes."

Her single word answer was perfect, delivered with a broad smile.

"Would you ever consider marrying me again, Dell?"

Adele pulled back, blinking, her eyes startlingly blue. "I don't think so. But, thanks for asking." A light frown marred the skin between her brows. "I'd prefer to keep moving forward, rather than backwards. Is that okay?"

James nodded, and Adele's expression cleared.

"Can we have a housewarming party, though? A *home*warming party. Invite everyone. My family, Fran, the Kaihangas... You know, everyone."

Very openly, then.

James brought a hand up to smooth the stray curls off Adele's face, and left it there cradling her jaw.

"Yeah, let's do that," he murmured.

"But before Saffy and I move in with you, boots and all, I need to know the answer to a very important question."

"Shoot."

"Did you used to cheat when we played poker?"

James' laugh came out a little wheezy, due to the fact Adele's hands were on his torso when she asked the out-of-context question, her fingers gripping his pecs.

"What are you on about? I always *lost* at poker."

"Let me amend that question." Adele pulled back to look down at him, gauging his expression with that little frown back between her brows. Her thumbs had begun stroking his nipples, messing with his focus. "You used to lose at poker on purpose, didn't you? So you could take strategic bits of your own clothing off, and get me all hot and bothered."

The tactic had never occurred to him.

"God, no. I wasn't strategising beyond winning points to get *your* clothes off." In fact, right now his brain was strategising how to unhook and remove Adele's bra with one hand.

"Huh. Well, I guess it worked, either way. Though you really do suck at cards."

"It's all luck."

Adele rolled her eyes at him again. "That's what *all* card-playing losers say."

James didn't feel like a loser right now, he felt like a winner—king of the lake, top of the mountain, Jack of hearts. And when

Adele kissed him, all sweet, sensual, and sexy like that, it added to the illusion he could never come down.

"Do that thing…" Adele whispered against his lips, dragging his hand down between them, under the waistband on her knickers.

Which thing?

"This thing?" James slid two fingers into the wetness of her, arcing them up until they were parallel with his thumb, already busy on the explosive nerve endings of her clit. He caught her answering moan with is mouth.

Yep. *That* thing.

"I have to leave for Australia again," James blurted, staring up at the ceiling. They'd made it back to the bed this time, but only after the kitchen chair had proved its weight in gold as a prop. "Not for long, just for a short business trip. I need to tie things off with Montague Holdings, then check in on a couple of jobs."

Adele gave an exaggerated sigh, though she must've known this was coming.

"When?" Her voice came out muffled, face pressed against his torso.

"This afternoon."

She jerked, her body reacting with what appeared to be an involuntary twitch. In answer, James ran a soothing hand across her shoulders.

"In a couple of hours," he reiterated, aiming for a reasonable tone.

"Sydney?"

"Yes. Then Tasmania."

"I see. And how long—?

"A week, probably."

"So, you'll definitely be back for Saffy's birthday?"

"I promise."

Another twitch from Adele, possibly denoting he'd gone for the wrong choice of words. Promises could be broken, and they were still rebuilding trust.

"Why don't you move into the cabin while I'm gone?"

There was another moment's silence from Adele. "Because, it's not mine, yet."

"You want to make it official?" That again sounded like a marriage proposal, but James didn't fret it, because his earlier one hadn't seemed to faze Adele.

"In every way, bar the ring on my finger." Adele laughed.

James was in the bathroom cleaning himself up when Adele got a phone call from an unknown number.

Fully aware she was already overdue at work, she finished tying her shoelace and answered, thinking it'd be her duty manager.

It wasn't.

"You received my letter?" James' mother asked archly after her self-introduction.

Alone in the room, Adele rolled her eyes for her own benefit. "In which you briefly outlined your theft? I did, yes." There was an extended silence on the other end of the line. "May I ask how you got this number?"

"It was the first number on Aksel's phone. In his list of contacts."

"I see." So Isabella had taken it without asking. "And is this a social call, or should I be short-handing a memo for your son?"

"You stopped wearing James' rings. I thought that signified you were done, so forgive me if I have trouble understanding why you'd attempt to pick up with him again."

"I stopped wearing James' rings because we were going through a rough patch, and I felt anything but part of a pair. Is that why you thought you had the right to take them?"

"I merely put them in safe keeping," Isabella huffed.

"Along with my other personal items. None of which were anything to do with you."

"The rings—"

"Were mine, and mine alone. Gifted to me, and taken from me."

"Yes," Isabella finally conceded. "My apologies. I felt… I felt…"

"Isabella, I understand your sickness; your compulsion. James explained."

The older woman cleared her throat. "There are things that should remain within family."

Adele shook her head, knowing full well Isabella couldn't see the action. "Again, you're trying to cut me out. James did nothing wrong by telling me the truth. I deserved to hear it."

"Sometimes the truth is so much worse than you expect, though." Something in Isabella's voice sent off a warning shiver, and the fine hairs on Adele's forearms prickled.

Like Luka's death?

"Your husband?" she ventured.

"What has James told you?"

"The truth, I think. Luka took his own life."

"There's an uncomfortable truth about the truth, and that is every person has a different version."

A bit cryptic, even for Isabella Montague.

"What are you trying to say?"

"You should ask James why his brother and himself are so very far apart. As boys, they were inseparable."

A sinking feeling, not unlike vertigo, flipped Adele's insides. She'd just agreed to move in with this man and make a home together with their daughter. Did she really want to hear this?

"What happened?"

"James merely followed his father's wishes," Isabella confided ominously. "But Owen has never forgiven him for it."

"He… He…" Adele couldn't put the image in her head into words. Had James assisted his father's suicide in some way?

Isabella's voice seemed to come from a long way off. "We never speak of it. We don't discuss personal things."

Adele's mouth dropped open.

Personal things? *Monumental* things, like your father taking his own life.

Adele drew the phone close to her mouth again. "You can blame me all you like for your disconnect with your son, Isabella, but it's not my fault. Your relationship with James is totally of your own construct. Not talking about issues merely makes them larger. It's damaging."

"Don't lecture me about damage. You won't ever fully commit to him, will you?"

The passive-aggressive veneer was gone, and clear superiority tainted Isabella's words, making it easy for Adele to drop all semblance of her own politeness.

"Commitment obviously means something different on your home planet. The only reservation I have about my connection to James is the fact it ties me to *you*." She paused to breathe, calming herself. "You chewed me up and spat me out. You belittled me. Stole from me. Watched on as Tiffany humiliated me with bogus sexcapades, and tried to reduce the loss of mine and James' child to a wilful act on my part."

"You maintain the baby was Aksel's?"

"*Fucks*-sake! I don't have to listen to your cynical—"

"Wait! Don't hang up. Saffy told me the baby was someone else's."

"*What*? Why would you even—"

"She was only little, but so talkative. I should've known not to take her word as gospel, but she was adamant you were having another baby, just like her. With the same mummy and daddy. She said it was a secret from James, but an African man had come—"

"Jesus, Isabella. She was barely out of nappies!"

"Then you changed your mind, and decided you only wanted *one* princess."

"Saffy used to swear there were unicorns in the backyard, and mermaids singing to her from the bottom of the swimming pool!" Adele interrupted, venting her frustration. "Are you suggesting *that* was all factual, too?" For the second time in her life, she hung up on her ex-mother-in-law, and found herself shaking with barely controlled rage. She threw her phone across the room where it bounced off the rumpled duvet and onto James' plush new carpet.

Aksel James *bloody* Montague walked in as if butter wouldn't melt in his mouth, wearing only jeans, and drying his hands on the fresh hand-towel he'd just removed from the bathroom. Replacing towels and sheets with fresh ones ridiculously often was one of his more irritating habits, a quirk Adele had forgotten until right this moment.

It resulted in a shit-ton of unnecessary washing.

"You'd better not be aiming to put that in the washing basket," she growled.

"What? No, I was just... Are you okay? I heard—"

"Super dandy. Just on my way out."

"You're leaving?" All movement stopped, and James stared at her. Hard.

"I just remembered something I had to do."

"What?" The single word was loaded with suspicion.

"Stay away from you, and your fucked up family." Even as Adele spoke, her phone was ringing again. She had the urge to stride over and stomp on it, but instead hightailed it out of James' master bedroom, and down the hall.

31

WĀ MUTUNGA - FULL TIME

*Not actually the end,
but the beginning of what is to come.*

Adele made it to the driveway under a cloud of hot steaming fury before she realised she was running away again.

Leaving without an explanation, exiting the house she was beginning to think of as her forever home, without a decent conversation with the man she was beginning to realise was her forever guy.

Adele turned tail and barged right back around the side of the cabin, over the verandah and into the lounge the way she'd left, intent on finishing where she'd left off.

"I'm not doing all your extra washing, either. When I move in, you're in charge of the towels, and sheets. And another thing…" she broke off her tirade as she strode back into the master bedroom.

James sat on the edge of the bed, his head rising slowly from his hands, with Adele's phone on the floor in front of him.

His eyes were as defeated as she'd ever seen them, and he looked so very, very tired.

"James?"

"I thought you'd left."

"I did leave. Then I came back. We didn't do a sum up."

He gave her the merest hint of a smile. "I'm in charge of towels and sheets from now on. Got it. What was the other thing?"

"I want to know if you had something to do with your father's death."

There was total stillness from her ex on the bed, a moment frozen as they stared at each other across the thick carpet.

James' unwillingness to speak ate up all the peace in the room, until there was nothing but screaming silence left.

"No. Not exactly," he finally murmured.

"I need more than that, James. I need to understand why your brother blames you, and why you blame yourself."

"I wasn't there, that's a valid reason. I could've been there for my father, but I was out at a party, wasting my time." There was some self-recrimination when the statement finally came, disdain for his younger, more carefree self. "Because he didn't leave a note, there was some question as to whether Father could've been cleaning his gun—an accident, not knowing it was loaded."

"But you never believed that." Also a statement, not a question. The coroner had ruled the Montague patriarch's death a clear suicide.

"No, I didn't. Because I'd bought the ammunition for him myself, just that morning."

"Oh." Adele swallowed, reaching a hand out to grasp James' shoulder.

He'd never told her that part before.

"He may've shot himself, but I provided the means. The pain must've been driving him insane, though none of us knew that at the time. No conversation. No treatment. No hospital follow-ups. Just a really shitty diagnosis. He asked me to pick up some shells for the shotgun, and I didn't think twice about it. Owen's never forgiven me. To him, I facilitated Father's death, and everything that followed."

Adele sat down onto the bed next to him. "A.J.—"

He cleared his throat, perhaps not ready for platitudes. "The thing is, if Father had been straight-up with me, I don't know if I would've withheld them. He'd effectively been given a life sentence. Why not by his own hand?"

"But a *shotgun*..."

James' body reacted to the word with a faint shudder, probably a gut reaction to the memory.

"My mother was in treatment. She was going through a bad patch, and rumours had begun circulating…" His voice thinned, and petered out.

The desolation of that final sentence had Adele crawling onto James' lap, and holding him tight.

How had he turned out so level-headed, when as a kid, his world kept getting thrown off its axis? Was his even-keeled, managerial persona a direct result of all the things that had been so far out of his control in the past? All the code, all the systems he developed, could be James trying to make true sense of a world where routine and pattern were hard to find.

"Will you call me from Australia?" Adele finally asked.

Would James remain open about all the things haunting him, or clam up again, holding it all too close to his chest?

"You want me to? You always tell me not to call back."

"No, I say you don't *have* to call back. As in, if you don't *want* to. I thought you were good at details?" She managed a small, tentative smile. "In summary, I want you to call me, okay? If you don't call, I'll worry."

"In that case, I'll call."

"Every day?"

"Every day," James agreed, and Adele could hear the relief in his voice as he curled over the back of her neck in big-spoon mode, taking a long, deep sniff.

She snuggled deeper into his warmth, knowing without a doubt she was going to be in a heap of trouble for ditching her afternoon shift.

"I can't get hold of Dad." Saffy burst into Adele's room after school.

"Sorry, love. He had to go back to Sydney to see his mother. He's going to try and video-call from the airport at four, but he might be delayed. Just keep the connection open, and he'll jump on when he can."

"Is Nana Isabella okay?"

"Yes, I'm sure she's fine. It's more to do with Montague finances, I gather."

"Finances?"

"Money."

Saffy sat down on Adele's bed with a bump, looking limp all of a sudden; clearly unhappy with James' sudden departure.

"I never get to see her," she stated gloomily.

"Who, Isabella?"

Saffy nodded.

"Ah… Did you want to?" Adele studied her daughter again, unsure. "Is she important to you?" she asked more gently, mindful of Saffy's very real potential to hurt; to feel like an outsider.

Saffy shrugged. "She's important to Dad."

"Right." Adele tried to smile, but the expression felt a bit twitchy on her face. "We'll see what we can do." She hadn't factored Isabella into the mix this time around, but hell, she was a grown-assed woman who was confident in her agenda. Surely she could figure this out? "When we initially met, Isabella and I didn't exactly see eye to eye," she mused, feeling her way around her own reactionary recoil. "But people change. I've changed." Surely even the most difficult of leopards could change their spots, if the stakes were high enough?

Saffy eyed her suspiciously, Kookie the kookaburra squeezed tightly against her chest. If it were a real bird, its eyes would've popped out of its head long before now.

"Dad says when he first met you, he thought you were an angel with curly-wurly hair."

"Ha. That's a good one. When we first met, he thought I was a lightweight law-dropout, in need of a protector," Adele grumbled.

"That's not how he tells it." Saffy turned away, presenting Adele with her back as she focussed on the new pastel portrait on the wall. It was a likeness of James. She'd drawn it as a pair to Adele's, insisting it had to go on her mother's bedroom wall. "Don't send him away again, he loves it here," she added in a croaky little aside.

"I'm *not*… I didn't *send him away*."

"Good, because Maddie says he'd get snapped up real quick."

"I'll just bet she did," Adele muttered under her breath. "Look, there's something I need to tell you."

A thousand things shot through her head; reasons, confessions, mistakes made, and trepidations... But she decided to go with something simple, and positive. This should be Saffy's choice, too.

"James has asked us to move in with him."

James called Adele every afternoon at four o'clock on her cell phone. He got passed off to Saffy first if she was home, so she could tell him all about her day, before being handed back to Adele.

On Thursday, Adele arranged for him to call later, and when she switched him to video call, he realised she was sitting out under the willow tree on her rainbow love-seat.

With her hair down, she looked relaxed and comfortable, a cup of coffee and a quiet smile completing the picture.

God, it was good to see her face.

"Saffy's up at the farm," he surmised.

Thursday was Bento Night.

"Yes. I think I'm getting pork dumplings tonight. *Gyoza*."

"I just grabbed a drive-through burger," James lamented, having eaten the piss-poor substitute in his rental car, alone. "How did it go with Dr Fran tonight?"

"Good. Pretty good. We talked about depression, and the warning signs."

James remained silent, thinking of all the warning signs he had to have missed in his young wife, and how long she'd gone on, unsupported. The regret threatened to rise up and choke him.

"I haven't felt that way for a long time," Adele assured him, "but it's best to be prepared, and have a plan in place if I ever feel myself sliding again."

James swallowed. "What's the plan?"

"I go to a trusted family member, and tell them what's going on."

"Your mother?"

"Or Katie, or Dad, or Daniel, or Kana," Adele listed off her nearest and dearest. "Or you," she added more quietly.

James hesitated, his heart giving a little skip on hearing himself mentioned.

"When we lost Rosetta, you went to a very dark place. I couldn't reach you down there, Dell."

"No. I know. I can't promise I'll never go back. But if I ever get that low again, you know I can make it back out. We both know. It was the scariest thing at the time, not knowing if the bleak-black was finite, or infinite."

"I never stopped loving you. Even in the infinite bleak-black."

James' choice of words had seemed fine in his head. Honest, if a little dark. He hadn't expected them to have such a volatile effect on Adele.

She burst into tears, turning the lens away from herself abruptly so James got a jostled view of the back sliding door of the cottage.

"Hey, *hey*. Don't cry, darl. Don't cry," James crooned, on the wrong side of the Tasman to do anything about the fact he'd just upset her.

Winger trotted outside and over towards her owner, either to investigate the noise, or because she'd sensing Adele's unhappiness.

"Good girl, Winger," he muttered. It was a mild relief to know Adele had the dog there, comforting her.

"I'm okay," Adele assured James, and probably the border collie as well, through hitched breaths and strangled little sobs. "I'm okay, now. Thank you. Thank you for saying that."

A few deep sniffs, then silence.

"Dell?"

"I'm still here."

"Show me."

Adele actually smiled as she turned the camera back on herself, the dog practically up in her lap and all licky. It was a tumultuous smile, but a smile all the same.

"I used to think it would fade, your affection. You were so sure, so confident about it so quickly. I didn't entirely trust it." She swiped at her cheeks. "It hit me hard when I thought you'd cheated, because I thought I'd been proved right in a very obnoxious way. It was the most offensive surprise ever."

"Even worse than an uninvited ex on your doorstep?"

Adele laughed. "*Much* worse. If you've seen me at my lowest, and are still willing to make a go of this, I have to trust you know what you want."

"I don't just want this, it's everything to me."

Adele blew him a kiss, and he pretended to search for it up in the sky above the Tasman, before catching it in his fist and thumping it to his chest.

"Aww... You're *too* cute," Adele complained plaintively, but James could tell by the sparkle in her eyes she'd actually enjoyed 'cute'—had perhaps even needed it. "I got some good news this afternoon." Sniffing again, she touched her sleeve to her nose. "You know the short story competition Ā-tuhi Magazine runs?"

"Yes, you've entered that one before, right?" James couldn't remember if it was a two-thousand word limit, or longer. "They weren't looking for romance."

"Well, now they are. They've accepted one of my short stories."

"Fantastic!"

Adele seemed pleased, too. The publication had Oceania-wide distribution, and could well lead to other things.

"Which one?" There had been quite a few short stories in Adele's arsenal. Some funny, some sad. All of them quirky, with Adele's animated spirit pouring through.

"Heads or Tails. You haven't read it." She cleared her throat, perhaps a little sheepishly. "It's a second-chance love story."

He laughed. "My new favourite."

It was a new experience to pick James up at the airport. Adele and Saffy were bundled up against the rain, their faces pressed to the arrival lounge window as the plane from Auckland disembarked.

"There he is!" Saffy ran to the gate, excitement personified.

Adele waited a few paces behind with a bit more outward dignity, but no less inward anticipation.

Yes, there James Montague was again, larger than life and looking like some Nordic god as he stepped through the arrivals gate, sweeping Saffy up into a hug.

Adele scoured his face for details, hungry for his features after too long apart. He looked good. Tired, and once again in need of a shave, but unbelievably good. And to his credit, he'd made it home three days in advance of Saffy's birthday.

When it was Adele's turn to greet him, she took the initiative and kissed him soundly before squeezing him tight, in front of Saffy and the world.

"Missed you," she murmured against his neck.

Saffy didn't openly complain, but she did screw up her face.

"Saffy and I have come to an agreement," Adele informed James, keeping her arms locked around him when he might've moved away for their daughter's comfort. "She gets her choice of the upstairs bedrooms when we move into the cabin, and she doesn't complain about any outward affection shown between us."

When Adele pulled back, James was grinning, eyes all sparkly with mischief.

"Well, in that case…" His arms came around her too, and he dipped her before smacking her lips with another resounding kiss.

Adele emerged quite flustered.

"It's still gross," Saffy muttered, loud enough for them both to hear, and making James laugh.

"Sure, but you're welcome to look elsewhere," Adele informed her airily. Catching herself staring at James' lips again, she wrenched her eyes upward to the warmth of his eyes instead, and smiled.

"So, you've told her about the move?" he whispered.

Adele nodded.

"How did it go?"

"Honestly?" Adele laughed. "You'd think the whole thing was her idea."

"The counselling session is off for today," Adele informed James as he kissed her hello outside Fran's on Thursday evening.

James looked flummoxed. "Really?" Then his features softened as he relaxed a little. "I could take you for a coffee to talk if you like? Just the two of us?"

With their duplicate order of short black, with hot water on the side, they made a highly caffeinated duo. But another stimulant was the last thing she needed right now.

"Thank you, but, no. I'm nervy enough, already." Adele had

arranged something else. Something a little off-piste. "I've gone ahead and made other plans." As soon as she said it, James' expression flickered with uncertainty.

"Of course. Well then..."

"I'm not blowing you off." She hastened to inform him. "It's the opposite of that."

"The opposite of blowing me off?" James glanced at her mouth in an almost imperceptible movement, then away again just as quickly with one eyebrow raised.

They'd spent Adele's lunch break up at the cabin, christening the office with their combined oral skills.

"Get your mind out of the gutter." She snorted, placing a firm hand on James' arm. "Stop. Listen. I've made an appointment..." she trailed off as James turned slowly back towards her, a faint question still present in his eyes. "You don't have to take part, but I'd really like you to be there in support."

"Sure."

"Do you love me, A.J.?" she whispered. It seemed like a good idea to double-check before she went ahead with this evening's plans.

"You know I do, Dell." His voice was as soft as a caress. "I never stopped."

She cleared her throat with a nervy little *ahem*.

"Then I'm... Ah. Thank you."

"Anytime." Sardonic, with a smidgen of query left lingering in his voice.

"Me too." She licked her lips. "What I mean is, I want to *show* you how I feel. That I won't be giving up on what we have. Not ever again. I know when I walked out of the cabin the other day, you thought... You thought I might..." She couldn't quite finish James' expectation aloud.

He'd thought she would walk out and leave him again, without so much as a goodbye. Just like his father had.

The desolation behind James' eyes had been heartbreaking.

"You're a permanent fixture for me," she summed up, moving to swipe a rogue curl off her face and lock it behind her ear. But James bet her to it, his fingertips lingering on her jawline afterwards.

"You've already shown me."

She smiled. "So, you trust me, then?"

"You usually smile, and ask me that right before you do something totally whack," James informed her with an overly dramatic sigh. "Kookie should be *your* name, not the bird's. But yes. I trust you. Unless there's a snake involved. You lose all sensibility when snakes are involved."

"No snakes." She grinned. "Noted. Want to do something totally whack, James? I've been dying to, but I'm too chicken-shit to go on my own, and need you to hold my hand."

It was Saffy who had decided her and Daniel's combined birthday should be a pool party. Though it was definitely autumn, and the summer heat had faded, the weather played ball.

Adele was grateful the skies remained clear and blue, even if the pool wasn't that appealing.

Zane was the only child Saffy had requested to attend from school. Her babysitter, Maddie, was asked too, but the rest of the guests were family. That in no way meant it was a small celebration, as people had come from far and wide.

Cousins, grandparents, aunties, uncles, and plus-ones.

Adele was talking to Daniel poolside, marvelling at the sheer volume of guests bearing food, when he grabbed her arm.

"What the hell is *that*?"

Adele's charm bracelet jingled as Daniel held her arm aloft, giving the pale inner skin on her wrist closer inspection.

"It's a tattoo, Daniel. People get them on their bodies." She sighed. It was the first day she'd had it uncovered, and her cousin hadn't been the first to notice it. "You're acting like a Grandad, again." He'd had an identical reaction when she'd pierced her nose. "No one else gives a shit about it." She waved in the general direction of her parents, over from Dunedin for the weekend, reclining on the new poolside chairs with an evidently harmonious Rue and Katie. "Why should you?"

"Diamonds?" Daniel frowned at the dainty outlined design. "What do they even mean?"

"That's for me to know. Not you."

"Is this the bloody Aussie's influence?" Daniel growled, letting her arm go.

"No. I think you'll find I'm the one who's a bad influence on him." She turned towards the pool, where Saffy, Zane, and James were the only three thick-skinned enough to brave the 'lovely' water.

James and Adele certainly *did* influence each other, but she refused to see any of that as bad. Their differences complimented each other.

"Kanako's working on a new clay bust," Daniel informed Adele suddenly, his tone as dry as sawdust. "It's a private commission from your dogmatic daughter to go with the pair I already have of you and herself."

Adele did a double take. "Saffy's commissioned a *bust*? As in, a full sized one?"

Daniel cleared his throat. "A 3D portrait of the bloody Aussie," he divulged, not sounding particularly happy about it. "She said her dad should be standing behind you."

Adele began to laugh.

"Oh, my God. So, you'll be expected to display a likeness of James in your living room?" The thought was just too funny, and it took her a while to get her snorts and giggles under control. "Since I'm planning to spend the rest of my natural life with this particular Aussie, my totally unbiased advice would be to suddenly decide he's not too bad. Think of him as French, if it makes it any easier."

Daniel issued another faint growl, making Adele smirk again. The national rugby team held fierce rivalry with both Australia *and* France.

James stood thigh deep in the pool, his back to Adele and Daniel as he watched Saffy and Zane play. A beautiful back it was, too.

His small tattoo was barely visible, peeping out from the top of his swimming trunks. The cloud birthmark had been carefully outlined and shaded, with a multicoloured rainbow bursting from behind it.

Quirky and whimsical, with an optimistic twist.

Adele glanced around the pool, then over the fencing to the patio, where her extended family milled and gathered, laughing, talking, and eating.

With hugs, awkward back slaps, and handshakes, her parents and other family members had shown Adele if she wanted her ex back in her life, they were willing to give him a second chance. Sure, there'd been some questioning looks, and a touch of dubiousness, but the only person openly wary of James was Daniel.

"I guess he's beginning to grow on me." Daniel smiled, and it was like the sun coming out on a rainy day. Her cousin could be gruff, but he had a heart of pure gold. "I notice you've stopped chewing your nails," he admitted.

Adele held up one hand and inspected her fingertips. "Yeah. That's true. Must be less stressed. I wonder why?" She pointed at James, very deliberately, then turned that same finger on Daniel. "Make it work, okay?"

"I'll try." Daniel folded his arms across his chest.

"Excellent! Because you're helping me and Saffy move in with him next weekend."

"I'm *what*?"

"Make. It. Work," she repeated, poking a finger into his bicep for emphasis, before sauntering away in a bid to get closer to James.

Kicking off her shoes and hitching up her dress, she stood on the first step and tested the water on her shins. It wasn't as cold as it had been last week, so the solar heating must be doing something. Shimmying her hem a little higher, she braved the second step, water lapping at the back of her knees.

Saffy and Zane were frolicking like it was midsummer in the deep end, racing each other across the width of the pool.

"Hey, rainbow guy."

James yanked his swimmers up a bit higher, effectively hiding the top of the small tattoo as he turned towards her, perhaps still a touch self-conscious of his first ink.

"Hey, diamond girl." He welcomed her with a grin. "You're not coming in?"

"Not this time, no. I was planning to have fewer spectators for my initial lesson."

James had promised to teach her to swim, and weirdly, Adele was actually looking forward to it. She sent him what she hoped was a sizzling come-get-me look, crooking her finger to motion him over to the shallow end. He backed up towards her, focus still on Saffy and Zane.

Adele threaded her arms either side of James' neck and pulled him back against herself.

He smelt better than good. He smelt like hers. Just the right height one step below her, she was able to whisper directly into his ear.

"You know, he's not going to pounce on her. You can relax your vigil for one minute. With you and Daniel both scowling at him, it's a wonder the poor boy hasn't apparated."

James laughed, as he turned towards her. "I've just realised it could be quite handy having an ex-rugby player as Saffy's bodyguard as she gets older."

"Hands down the best defence. Only the most tenacious contenders get through, present company included."

Adele watched a latecomer arrive. Using an ebony walking stick and supported on the other side by Poppy, the woman still managed to make a grand entrance in what was undoubtedly an unforgivably expensive frock.

Isabella was looking quite a lot older. Even a bit frail.

Adele nipped James' neck for her own gratification, just to see if he tasted as good as he smelled, before murmuring, "Now, I don't want you to freak out, but your mother's just showed up."

"My *what*?" Janes tensed up, head flicking towards the group on the other side of the pool fencing.

"It's alright, she's not gate-crashing. I invited her. Saffy really wanted to see her Nana Isabella, and I decided I could be the bigger person, here."

James groaned. "She's not staying with you, is she? Or *me*?"

Adele laughed at the level of foreboding in his voice. "No. Neither. She's staying at a five-star resort on my recommendation, and only for three days."

"God help their collectables," James muttered.

"Actually, I don't think that'll be a problem." Adele took James' shoulders in her hands, and turned him until he was fully facing her. "Isabella and I have made a verbal contract." It had been a very strange phone conversation, to say the least. "She was so desperate to see Saffy, she would've just about agreed to anything, I think."

James brought a hand up to rub at his stubbled jaw. "But your family—"

"All know about her kleptomania," Adele interrupted to assure him. "It was part of the deal. Full disclosure."

"Nana Isa-*bell*-la! Nana Isa-*bell*-la!" Saffy had spotted James' mother, and was thrashing about in the pool in a very unladylike manner, waving both arms in the air to get the fastidious old biddy's attention. "I'm so glad you came!"

Saffron-all-things-Fergus, just being her joyful self.

James rested his forehead on Adele's shoulder for a moment. "Dell, this is totally whack."

"No, *I'm* totally whack. About you, as it happens," she whispered in his ear. "Or I wouldn't be feeling this relaxed about my dragon of an ex-mother-in-law coming to visit."

James lifted his head to stare at her, his eyes so green they sparkled. Evergreen, like the grass you'd expect to find in a well tended unicorn paddock.

"I very much like the look of the lawn you're offering on your side of the fence." Adele went to straighten her opal pendant the same time James did, and their fingers tangled together over the fiery stone.

He looked a tad confused—eyebrows drawn together.

"What I'm trying to say is, I'm not scared anymore, James. I trust you. I trust this. Official or not, my family's agreed to help Saffy and me move into the cabin with you next weekend, if that suits you."

James' brow cleared, and his grin built gradually, until it seemed to take over his whole bearing.

"That suits me just fine. Because it just so happens I'm totally whack about you, too, Adele Fergus. As they say in Romancelandia, LAFS."

"What's LAFS?"

"You don't know that acronym?"

She shook her head. She'd learned a few so far in her studies, but not that one.

"Love at first sight."

"Aww…" Her heart melted a little bit, so maybe the concept wasn't so ridiculous after all. "You're just a sucker for curly-wurly hair," she teased. "And damsels who you seem to think are in need of supervision."

"Just the *one* damsel, and I'm definitely observing, not supervising. This particular curly-wurly-haired angel has it all sorted."

"And you do *so* enjoy watching," she mused.

Sliding his hand around until he was cradling the back of Adele's neck, James' fingers tangled in the hair at her nape, just the way she liked it.

Then his lips claimed hers in a smiling kiss, just the way she loved it.

THE END

WANT MORE?

Thank you for reading LAKE TAIMANA. I hope you enjoyed Adele and James' story as much as I did! Read about Cam and Shal's journey in MAKO BAY, and Daniel and Kana's in RUBY ISLAND—book one and two in the Otago Waters series.

Love Otago Waters? ADD A SPLASH OF LOVE is the connecting anthology of short stories, with sweet, funny (and occasionally steamy) peeks into surrounding characters lives. TANIWHA CREEK, a novella in the VALENTINES IN THE VINES anthology, will take you on Maddie and Todd's journey, and TINSEL RIVER, Pieta's story, will be available December 2023.

For information about new books, sign up for my newsletter at www.stephanie-ruth.com, and you'll be sent a short-story prequel to the Otago Waters series, Scent, Not Sensibility.

I hugely appreciate your help in spreading the word about my books, including telling your friends. Reviews help readers find books, too. Please review Lake Taimana on your favourite site.

Turn the page for an excerpt from TANIWHA CREEK

TANIWHA CREEK
— Mad-One and the Toddinator —

Chapter 1

With a single shot of Windolene on a soft cloth, every smudge of evidence disappeared.

Sticky fingerprints and smeary nose circles from smaller customers, their faces pressed against the cabinet to view the foodie delights up close, all gone.

If only all Maddison Stalwart-Jones' problems were so easily eliminated.

Maddie absorbed the quiet spell.

Wanderer's Café had just entered the coveted after-and-before stage, an interval not to be taken for granted.

After the clockwork morning take-outs, breakfast sit-ins, and preschooler fluffies. After the ravenous muffin-in-a-bag crowd, and bleary-eyed, caffeine deprived double espressos, came this gift from the fairy-godmother of baristas.

The before-lunch-lull.

Indoor tables were being set to rights by the other staff member on shift, and the two lingering outdoor customers had already been served.

Maddie slipped back behind the counter to put away her cleaning paraphernalia, casting an eye over her workspace. She shuffled the EFTPOS machine two centimetres to the left, and the basket of hand-painted table-numbers a smidgen to the right, eyeing the result critically before humming in satisfaction.

She'd taken a psychology paper a couple of years ago, *Common Mechanisms to Combat Stressors*, and ever since then had blamed her tendency to micro-manage space on her mother's distinct lack of comprehension in that area.

"Everything in its place," Todd teased her on his way back from clearing tables, coffee cups stacked up his corded arms like wonky towers of Pisa.

The newly appointed manager never used a tray, though the café had multiple. It was maddening.

Todd Kaihanga had been on Maddie's radar since primary school, and he'd always done things his own way. Two years older, he'd actually been her brother's best friend from Sailing Club.

Not the fancy type of sailing, the optimist dinghy kind.

That's how Maddie had got the café job over nineteen other hopeful applicants, some with a lot more experience. Todd liked to imply it was on account of her Shirley Temple dimples and customer service skills, but she knew it was also due to his father feeling he owed her something.

Every upright citizen of Wānaka felt they owed Maddie and her mother something, because—Mitchell.

Two years after her brother's accident, the tasteless pasta meals and red-eyed sympathy on the front doorstep had long-since petered out, but the ongoing attentiveness of her small-town neighbours still felt relentless at times.

Survivors' guilt—human nature at its finest. When your own family was intact, tucked up safely in bed at night, guilt came hand in hand with the relief all that shit had happened to someone else.

Maddie wasn't particularly comfortable with everyone knowing her business, and up until the secondary barista position had come up at Wanderer's Café, she'd been trying to stay off centre stage.

She needed this job, though. It more than covered her rent and expenses, and together with her regular childcare gigs, was going to be her ticket out.

One day she might even own her own little sweet-treat eatery in Dunedin, or Christchurch, where nobody knew her. She'd rather do it on her own, though, not by hitting up her mother for a slice of her dad's life-insurance pay-out.

There couldn't be much left of that, at any rate.

When Todd came back out to the front servery from the kitchen, Maddie turned to him. "Does the P stand for Pessimist?"

"What?" Todd had dark hair from his father's side, wavy and incredibly thick. Right now it was getting in his eyes and he swiped it sideways, blinking.

"The P-club down at the yacht club. P is the next step up from the Optimist, right?"

Todd stood with his head to one side, eyeing Maddie as if she were a tricky coffee machine to be figured out. Then his mouth began to quirk up into a grin.

He was generally okay looking, in a guy-next-door kind of sense, but when he smiled it became trickier to see him as merely that, eyes all crinkled up and laughter lines bracketing his generous mouth.

Maddie had never fished that river, too close to home, but that didn't mean she hadn't *considered* it.

"You're legit asking me if there's an optimist class, and a *pessimist* class?" Todd mused, standing at the coffee machine with busy hands.

Maddie didn't think to quiz his actions until he passed her a frothy cappuccino, still smirking.

Heat crept up her cheeks.

"Don't laugh at me. It was a genuine question." She'd inadvertently opened herself to the dumb-blonde stigma again, and hated it.

Not finishing her final year at university had less to do with lack of brain matter, and more to do with her big brother dying mid-semester.

Mitchell, who'd been the glue to everything.

Guiltily, Maddie looked behind herself before taking the offered coffee, but no customers had entered in the meantime.

"Um, thanks," she muttered.

"For your information, Goldilocks, the P stands for primary trainers."

The cappuccino slid down like a dream, eliciting a groan of pure pleasure from deep within Maddie as it warmed and soothed her from the inside-out. The last molecule of her morning tension lifted, like mist off the lake.

"Unfair," she decided aloud. "Pessimism deserves a boat, too."

"Oh, it's got a waka already." Todd leaned forward to tap lightly on her temple. "It floats around up here. All day, every day."

True.

"Sod off," Maddie grumbled, but had the grace to smile rather than truly bite back at Todd's jibe. After all, the guy had just made her coffee-to-die-for without even being asked.

Todd was a master barista, her trainer, and had fashioned

Maddie a perfect heart in creamy white foam—though she knew he meant nothing by it. He was the one who'd taught her how to implement the simple design when she'd started working at the café last year.

Wanderer's Café staff decorated all cappuccinos with hearts. Lattes got ferns-fronds, and alternate milks were graced with a koru. It was easier for the servers to deliver their orders correctly if everyone stuck to the same rules.

As Maddie opened her mouth to ask more about primary trainers, the trickier of the two boats to navigate, a pīwakawaka flitted in through the open door.

"Oh!" She grasped Todd's arm with her free hand and they both froze, watching in wonder as the little fantail dipped and dived, completing a full circuit of the seating area.

It stopped to hover in front of the pair of them, white tail-feathers flashing in unintelligible Morse code, before escaping the way it had entered.

"Pīwakawaka in the whare—a message from whānau," Todd murmured, sounding ominously like a soothsayer.

Mitchell.

Had to be. Who else would have anything to say, after all this time?

"I thought it signified death?" She glanced up at him, seeking confirmation, but he never took his eyes off the bird.

"Sometimes. Every iwi seems to have a slightly different interpretation."

Maddie let out the breath she'd been holding, but it wasn't so easy to shake off the faint sense of foreboding.

"What message, then?"

Todd looked down at her, eyes dark and questioning. "I don't know. You tell me."

Though the café was warm with late morning sun streaming through the west-facing wall of windows, Maddie shivered.

Mum?

Maddie pounded on the front door, but when she got no answer, braved the waist deep grass to get around to the back—treading gingerly to avoid semi-hidden obstacles.

She barked her shin on the handlebar of an old bike, discarded in what used to be the veggie garden, but arrived otherwise unscathed.

"Mum! It's me. Open up!"

Ever since Mitchell's death, Sian's tendency to collect had shifted into something much more obsessive. She'd given up bothering to hide the evidence behind the house's peeling weatherboards, and her 'goldmine finds' were now spilling into the yard, stacked on the porch, and piling up outside the garage.

The place was eerily quiet, and Maddie was about to wade through to the front again when the door opened a crack.

"Maddison?"

"Yes. You okay?" Maddie didn't bother hiding the relief in her voice.

Her mother hadn't been answering her phone.

"Of course!" Sian opened the door just wide enough to slip out, but Maddie caught a glimpse of what lay behind her in the laundry. Piles upon piles of clothing atop the tub and washer, and banana-boxes filled with heaven-only-knew, stacked almost to the ceiling.

"I called you."

"My phone is, ah… It's gone flat."

Not a very convincing lie. Sian had clearly lost her phone again—the second one this year. It would've slipped down behind a pile of something, never to be seen again. Maddie sighed, knowing a brand-new phone would already be winging its way to Sian as they spoke, purchased and paid for online by the shopaholic standing right in front of her.

Bizarrely, Sian was never too badly turned out. Today she wore jeans, and a masculine dark-green shirt, knotted at the waist. Her hair had been tamed into two neat braids, and she even appeared to be wearing a lick of mascara.

But she'd lost more weight. When they hugged, Maddie could feel each and every bone in her mother's spine.

Was the woman even eating?

Self-reproach kicked in. She shouldn't be turning up empty

handed. Next time she'd bring a filled roll from work, or a muffin. Savoury had always been Sian's favourite.

"I got this from the mailbox." Maddie flapped another council court-order in her mother's direction, but Sian pointedly refused to look at it.

"Busybodies. Why do they even care?"

"They're not *busybodies*, Mum. They're doing their job. You can't keep living like this." Maddie squinted skyward, the duck-egg blue of midsummer vaguely calming. "And even if they didn't care... *I* do," she admitted with a touch less aggression.

The latest council demand was that Sian's street-view be up to 'inspection standard' by February 14th, and that was as much Maddie's responsibility as her mother's. She'd moved out years ago to attend university in Dunedin, stepping sideways rather than addressing the burgeoning issue.

"Let me help."

"I don't need any help." Sian looked genuinely surprised.

Maddie scoped the backyard, and grimaced. It looked like a scene out of a post-apocalyptic movie, with Mother Nature reclaiming every man-made structure.

"Just the front yard. Just to keep the neighbours happy," she cajoled, wondering how the hell you went about cutting grass-turned-to-jungle when it was peppered with rusting appliances and old vehicles.

"A weed-whacker." Todd offered the name of the tool Maddie needed the next morning in the café kitchen, before they opened. "Whaea Tania has one for the grass around the waterhole. I'll bring it over on Sunday. I can probably borrow the vineyard trailer, too."

"You can't *come*," Maddie squeaked, the panic born yesterday rearing its ugly head again.

She was loath to let anyone else see the level of neglect up close, let alone Todd Kaihanga.

"Mum doesn't have people around, nowadays."

Just the courier, postal delivery officers, and council 'busybodies' wielding court-orders.

"She knows me," Todd reasoned.

Todd had been Mitchell's right-hand man since preschool, in and out of each other's lives like yo-yos, so he wasn't wrong.

But, still…

"She's gotten a lot more, um, *shy* over the past couple of years." Introverted. Aggressive. Withdrawn from society and all its petty little rules and regulations, like mowing your lawn.

Todd shrugged. "We've kept in touch."

Maddie pulled back a smidgen, blinking. "You have?"

"She comes to all the Yacht Club meetings."

"Oh. I didn't know that."

"And sometimes, Dad takes her out on the lake."

"Really?" Maddie hadn't known that either, but it was weirdly comforting, knowing Sian had social interaction above and beyond online retail personnel.

Maddie had no idea how her mother would react, having Mitchell's best mate strolling around on her home turf, so it was prudent to have forewarned Todd. Sian would be well within her rights to tell him to bugger off and mind his own business.

Maddie and Todd moved through to the servery, both actioning their respective set-up jobs on autopilot. Switching on the coffee machine to pre-heat, stacking fresh cups atop, and re-stocking all the ceramic sugar sachet holders and cutlery boxes before placing them out on tables.

Maddie stood on a chair to chalk *Pumpkin Soup* as the daily special, taking the time to draw a bright orange jack-o-lantern for fun, though they were at the wrong end of the year for Halloween.

Feeling eyes on her, she glanced down to catch Todd staring.

At her butt? Thighs?

Hard to tell, as he looked away so abruptly.

"What?"

"You've got some chalk on your jeans." Todd waved a hand in the general direction of her backside.

"Oh, right. Thanks." She brushed at the slim-fit denim as she climbed back down. "All gone?" But Todd was already moving through to the kitchen, and didn't answer.

Maddie unlocked the main door right on seven o'clock, smiling her best welcome to the first batch of morning regulars from the health services over the road.

"Mōrena! Beautiful day!"

It was a steady flow from there on in, Maddie stationed front-of-house, dealing with the till and customer service, and Todd on coffee orders.

"I'll keep to the yard, help with the heavy lifting. Sian won't mind." Todd re-opened the discussion as he slid Maddie two short blacks to go with the orange and date muffins she'd just plated, his mouth set in a stubborn line.

"She 'minds' about all of it. The whole idea. She doesn't want anything to change," Maddie muttered, jigsawing everything onto her tray and slipping out of the servery.

"So we'll take it gently," Todd called after her.

The queue was reforming when Maddie returned, and they did a run of take-out lattes and melting moments to go.

"I can't pay you," Maddie worried aloud.

"Low blow, Mad-one." Todd scowled, calling her by the old pet-name that took her straight back to the boys' tree-hut when they were kids, with secret handshakes, and ever-changing passwords to enter.

Mad-one, the Toddinator, and Mitchell Moose.

"Like I'm looking for money. I've got a job, haven't I?" He rapped his knuckles on the reflective front panel of the coffee machine. More than a job, Todd part-owned the business now, and was slowly paying his father out. "How many times has your mum fed me dinner, driven me home, or band-aided my scrapes?"

"Okay. But if she freaks out at the sight of you, you have to leave. Clear?"

"Crystal."

Todd's hand on Maddie's shoulder felt solid and dependable, making her wonder if it wouldn't be such a bad idea to share the load a little.

Continue reading TANIWHA CREEK

TE REO MĀORI - MĀORI LANGUAGE
GLOSSARY

Ā-tuhi – written, in writing
Ahi – fire
Aotearoa – New Zealand
E noho – sit down
Hāneanea – sofa
Haere mai – come here
Hāngī – cooked in the earth
Hoani – John, Johns
Kahukura – rainbow
Kai – food
Kani kani – dance
Ka pai – good, well done
Karāhe – mirror
Kawakawa – native shrub, pepper-tree
Kei te pai ahau – I'm good, I'm well
Kei te pehea kōrua – how are you both?
Kia ora – hello, good wishes, thank you
Kiwi – native flightless bird, New Zealander
Kōrero – spoken word, conversation, story, narrative
Kōrua – both
Koru – coil, curled shoot
Kuia – grandmother, old woman, female elder
Māori – indigenous people of New Zealand

Mānuka – native shrub, small white flowers
Marae – courtyard in front of the meeting house
Matariki – Māori New Year, star constellation
Moko – traditional tattoo
Mōrena – good morning (loan from English)
Nau Mai – welcome
Ngaio – large native shrub/tree, pink berries
Papangarua – quilt
Piana – piano (loan from English)
Pihikete – cookie, biscuit (loan from English)
Piwakawaka – native bird, fantail
Pokorehu – ashes
Pōuri – regret
Pukapuka – book
Putiputi – flower
Rēwera – devil
Reta – letter (loan from English)
Rua – two
Tahetoka – amber
Taimana – diamond
Teina – younger brother
Te Reo – the language
Tātoru – threefold
Tika – truth
Tino pai – very good, excellent
Tōurangi – rain
Wā kāinga – true home
Wā mutunga – full time
Wānaka/Wanaka – town and lake in Central Otago
Waiata aroha – song of love
Whānau – family
Whaea – mother, aunt, respected older woman
Whakaohomauri – surprise
Whakatuma – challenge
Whangaono – dice
Whare – house
Whauwhaupaku – large native shrub, five fingered leaves

*For an extensive dictionary,
and to hear Te Reo spoken aloud,
go to Te Aka at maoridictionary.co.nz.*

NIHONGO - JAPANESE LANGUAGE
GLOSSARY

Bento – *packed lunch*
Daikon – *white radish*
Gyoza – *Chinese dumplings*
Ko – *girl, female*
Niwatori – *hen*
Obāchan – *grandmother*
Oni – devil

ACKNOWLEDGMENTS

Firstly, to the romance readers and writers, who really know how to self-soothe, escaping into a world of luscious make-believe when the going gets tough. Tino pai! I applaud you. Communicating with you has been one of the highlights of this journey.

To my fellow RWNZ members, who try (and sometimes even succeed) to organise and attend conferences, writer's retreats, and competitions in the face of a global pandemic—managing to smile and support each other through it all. Kia ora! Thank you!

Aotearoa is a stunning backdrop, and I'm proud to call it home. However, the cultures here are as diverse as the people, and I can't claim them all as my own. Ranui and Fiona, I can't begin to tell you how much I appreciate your time, enthusiasm, and invaluable suggestions in Te Reo Māori. This taimana wouldn't be anywhere near as shiny without your help, neither would the pihikete smell as sweet!

To Aaron, who cooked many meals and vacuumed many floors throughout, and knows what compromise and communication looks like. As always, you're my rock.

Carmen and Lyssa, I'm so very grateful for your editing skills and support, and Mel, for seeing my white flag waving, and wading in multiple times to pull me out of the deepest publishing potholes.

To my betas and ARC readers, your continued appreciation for everything I throw at you makes me confident enough to climb that next peak.

And last, but definitely not least, the friends and whānau who walked me through their kōrero of miscarriage—a sadness that befalls so many, but is talked about so rarely in our society. Aroha nui to you all.

A great many people have helped steer my waka as I wrote Adele and James' story, but any errors remaining are mine, and mine alone.

ABOUT THE AUTHOR

An award winning contemporary romance novelist and short story writer, Stephanie Ruth lives in the South Island of Aotearoa, Te Waipounamu, with her husband, three children, and an ever-expanding array of animals. If it doesn't have a happy ending in some form, Stephanie's not writing it. Lake Taimana is her third novel, and the third book in the Otago Waters Series.

You can find her on Facebook @stephanieruth.nz, Twitter @ruth_writes_nz, Instagram @ruth_writes_nz, and TikTok @_ruth_writes_nz

Sign up to her newsletter and receive exclusive access to short stories, prologues, epilogues, and cut scenes on her website www.stephanie-ruth.com

ALSO BY STEPHANIE RUTH

Otago Waters Series

Mako Bay

Ruby Island

Lake Taimana

Taniwha Creek

-Otago Waters novella-

Valentines in the Vines Anthology

Tinsel River

-Otago Waters novella-

Kiwi Christmas Anthology

Add a Splash of Love

- Otago Waters' Short Story Anthology-

Independent Short Stories

Hair and Now

-Rising Heat Anthology-

Between Friends

-One Kiss is Never Enough Anthology-

Printed in Poland
by Amazon Fulfillment
Poland Sp. z o.o., Wrocław